The King of Erotica 4

The Dethronement of the King

THIS

is a different introduction from the *Official Book 4* being released in July. Only YOU special folks get this special letter directly from me. This is raw and unedited. This is on my heart to write so bare with me. Hello, you all. How are you doing? Me? I just put a load of laundry in the washer, sweating like a pig. Today is June 7, 2009 and I've been thinking a lot about the course of my life and why God chose me to be a writer. I worked *hard* for this. This was not an easy road. I built my empire from the ground up with a family who always tried to control me, manipulate me or bash me. From homeless man to trauma to dilemmas to success; from being an ex-con to being a respectable, respected and respectful Negro with goals, ambitions and a knack for shunning public opinion for the greater good of mankind. From bitterness, anger and maliciousness to a handsome brothah with a future brighter than the sun; from being a jobless, broke Niggah who worked under the table to becoming a Supervisor at Dolphin Stadium (The Boston Culinary Group) in my first two months of employment, then becoming a successful author who had all three of his the King of Erotica books in the Barnes and noble.com Top 100 Bestselling Books at the same time on February 20, 2009. I shared that list with President Obama, Steve Harvey, the Twilight series and John Grisham.

Has that gone to my head? No.

Yea, I live in the 'hood and half the time I'm walking around Naranja, Goulds or North Miami and books are the last things on my mind. I'm always jamming with my iPod on at the bus stop, listening to Janet. When I hang with family and friends and associates I don't talk about the King of Erotica or books. I am Larry. I talk about guy things. ESPN, sports, dancing, Janet Jackson (my favorite entertainer for 27 years) or helping others write, edit or better themselves. A few people always try to dictate what I can and can't do. Oh, you're a successful author. Why are you hanging out in the 'Hood? Um, because I grew up in the very same 'hood for over 20 years and that's where I'm the most comfortable.

People either stare at me with amazement that I'm an author who is so grounded and humble that it's surreal. I catch the public bus like everyone else. I eat at McDonald's. I LOVE the Dollar Menu and my McChicken sandwiches. OMG. I'm occasionally asked, "Larry. You have been through so much in your life. Raped as a kid, stripper, confused teenager…you hated yourself, you went to jail…you just found out you're HIV positive…how do you keep moving forward with jubilancy and happiness?"

The answer is simple. When you give it to God, God takes it away. But before he does you will be tried and tested for purity. I was tested, and I nearly failed.

But I never gave up on God and I never tried to be some sanctified, holier-than-thou person. When I talk to God I talk to him ALONE. I don't need to fellowship to prove to God I am loyal. God already knows my heart and my true intentions. I am a sinner, and I sin every day. I can admit that. And that's why God looks out for me. Because I keep it 100% real, no matter how it makes me look.

When I go to the store, people in certain positions always thank God for me when I turn down their discounts, phone numbers, sexual advances and freebees. I'm no better than nobody else. I am human and imperfect.

Eleven years ago I went to prison for helping police find my best friend's killer. I was 19 at the time, labeled as a snitch, marked for death by the Blood gang and when that didn't scare me a few people from that camp accused me of hurting a child. I was then sent to prison and labeled a sex offender for something I never did and would NEVER do.

Did I give up? No.

Did I just lay down and cry? No. I manned up, kept my head high and went through one of the most embarrassing moments of my life. That's what I got for cooperating with the police. And guess what? I'm GLAD I did. That was four years and nine months of hell, but I endured. Even from prison I was writing and setting them on their asses with my books.

I remember when I first walked into a prison cell. I was 21 years old, confused and very angry. The cell was damn near shoulder length, with a rusty toilet and angry souls crying out every night for freedom and relief and never getting it. I never cried. I never cried out. I prayed a lot. Not only did I have to cope with my best friend of 15 years being gunned down in his car in Portland, Oregon…but I was put in the same prison with the individuals who murdered my best friend and helped concoct that bogus charge on me. So I had to see them every day face to face and all they did was laugh in my face and tell me that's what snitches get…death or the death of their reputations.

It took hell and high water for me to forgive them. It took hell and earth for me to give it to God because I wanted to kill them the way they killed my best friend and my reputation.

But hurting them wouldn't bring him back. That's the bitter truth.

Going to prison changed the course of my wild, young life and I became a writer and never looked back. When weapons are formed against you GOD dismantles those weapons. I needed prison. *Not* because of what I went through, not for what I lost…but for what I was BEFORE I was incarcerated. I was too wild. I was drinking alcohol too much. I was smoking weed too much. I was a stripper and didn't tell a soul and I was a security guard as a cover. Life was a party and everyday was an event. I didn't pray to God. I didn't acknowledge his existence. I put friends before myself and family. I was very disrespectful. I was fucking 'em and leavin' 'em without remorse. And God knocked me on my ass and woke me up.

The year 2009, eleven years later, GOD is having his say with the success of my books. I love my flaws and my progress. I love who I am and my struggle. I climbed my way back to the top. Believe me I didn't always feel this confident. When I was 14 I poured bleach on my body in the bathtub and used a butter knife to try to scrape the black off. Trust me, when I do decide to write my autobiography it will sit the world on its ass. But I'm not ready for that yet. But one day its coming. Hans Bidon, shut up LOL!

My nieces, Aliyaih and Sunjaraih, are out in the pool with their father and his new chick right now and through the window I can hear their laughter (which melts my heart) and the splash of water. It's relaxing me. Mom is talking about whatever with her favorite brother out in the living room. It's hot as hell outside and I have an entire future to think about and decisions to make.

I recently been offered to speak to at risk teenagers and I will take on the challenge. It's about saving the youth. It's not about what you been through in your life, it's not about being awarded for endeavors. Life is about choices and saving lives. Through my life, what I've seen and my struggles I will speak to as many young adults and adults that I can, hoping something I say will either change their life, help them re-adjust their lives or cause them to take their lives more seriously. If you are reading this page then you should be one of the winners of the Face Book contest. This is a special edition. The stories within are the same as the ones in the Original version, dropping July 24,

2009. But this volume has an erotic back cover. If you haven't read The King of Erotica Book 1, the THRONE, Book 2, The CROWN and Book 3 VIP then you should. Book 4 concludes everything in a nutshell. All the sex, lies, devastation and mishaps summed into a massive overload of entities I am proud of.

The King of Erotica is a book empire, it's not me or all I'm about. I'm Larry writing as Dapharoah69. The King of Erotica has been a persona of mine that got me in a world of trouble when I was younger, when I was young, dumb and full of bullshit, come and lies. I was a different man then. In fact I wasn't a man. I was a teenager nursing four years of devastating abuse I suffered as a child. I didn't know if I was coming or going. I didn't have anyone to talk to. I shielded myself from hurt and I hurt people in the process. I didn't trust blacks. I didn't trust me. I felt my father abandoned me and left me to fend for myself. I had a lot of hate. I hated women. I hated animals. I hated life. When I did pray I used to ask God to give me a way to channel all that hate and anger into something quiet, loving and sincere. He answered my prayer the day I started writing the King of Erotica Book 1. And finished it in 5 days.

I decided to create a contest last minute. It just hit me. I wanted to show my gratitude and appreciation for all the people who have supported me. The King of Erotica has become successful. Not monetary wise, because every penny I make I put back into my product, but because of the lives it has touched.

I appreciate those who allow me to be frank, blunt and real. I write to express myself, and that's the first and LAST impression I'll ever make. I don't seek acceptance or praise for my writing. I don't care if you like it, love it or hate it. As long as you GET SOMETHING from it then my job is done. You can't please everyone so I don't try. Sex is a way of life and we're all born into sin. I have always been a raw individual and I will always be blood raw. Life is vicious. It has its moments of prosperity, endurance and perseverance. But even during my birth life was painful and vicious and I came out bloody and ignorant to a world sick with racism.

I thank GOD for all the blessings. Without God I would have never defeated homelessness, suicide attempts (yea, I really tried to snub myself because of people who let me down). Because of self-love and learning to love myself I defeated the enemy. I learned one valuable lesson. Love YOU more than you love ANYBODY. Love GOD first and the love for self will befall others in a natural way that heals, ignites and inspires. When I found out I was HIV positive I went through a metamorphosis. I was devastated. Instead of finger pointing and blaming others I embraced myself in a way I never had and I moved forward and decided to give it to God and save some lives in the process. I have since become a spokesperson, the Modern day Magic Johnson, for HIV. In the coming months you will see images of myself advertising HIV Awareness and I will use my pull, heart and celebrity to educate all who are willing to learn.

My books are filled with sex, yes I know. But there are morals to the stories. It explains why they have the type of sex they desire. It digs into the characters' emotional state of mind. It talks about taboo subjects others are afraid to touch. I feel God allowed me to walk that dark path to gain knowledge, wisdom and experience so now I am QUALIFIED to write such stories with aplomb.

Concluding this letter to you, my friends and fans, I want you to live life to the fullest. Be who you are, keep GOD first in all you do. If it doesn't feel right run like hell and don't look back. If it feels good make sure it's right. Get tested for HIV and other STD's. And love you more than you love anybody.

I love you all.
Dapharoah69
The KING of Erotica.

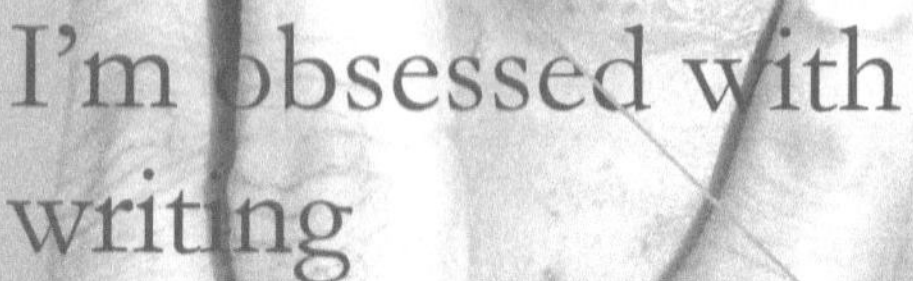

I'm obsessed with writing

My mother birthed an intelligent Nassau, Bahamian WARRIOR! Look into my eyes. I am everything my parents could never be: LARRY. Why should I stop when a single word, phrase or story changes a life? I was born to birth words. Why does it bother you that I don't care what you say? The more people hate me the more abundantly God's blessings will continue to shape my life. There is a reason these books exist. If you can't look past the sex then get out the bedroom. And close this book.

£aℝℝ¥

2008-2009

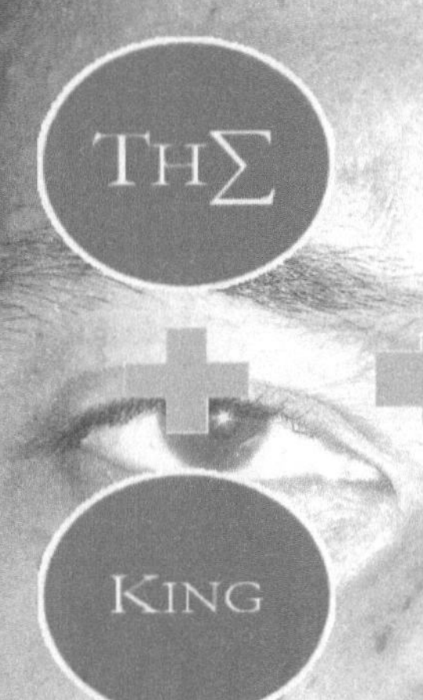

K.Φ.C. Publications
BARNES AND NOBLE.COM— AMAZON.COM

Books by Dapharoah69

THE KING OF EROTICA EMPIRE:

The King of Erotica 1: The Throne
The King of Erotica 1: The Throne Special Edition
The King of Erotica 2: The Crown
The King of Erotica 2 Special Crown Edition
The King of Erotica 3: V.I.P. Edition
Some Men Wear Panties

Phaze Publishing

The Diary and the Strap

Anthologies
Voices From Within
WSN Network
Mocha Chocolate

All praise and thanks to Dapharoah69
Should go to the Creator.
GOD.

Heavenly Father
Why do I write what I do?
Who will these stories help?
Some lash out at me because
They say I'm sexual, sensual and lustful
But I know why they hate
They hate because they didn't think of
These stories first.
God.
There is a reason these stories exist.
God.
I don't apologize for being frank and blunt.
You can't reach the darkness of an abysmal cave
By whispering
You have to scream, make your point
And plug in a lamp
To see what radiates.
My Lord I love you.
I'm not perfect and I don't try to be.
Thank you for my voice.
Thank you for my life.
Thank you for the opportunity to create,
To write, to inspire.
Thank you for these books.

D.Phar.69

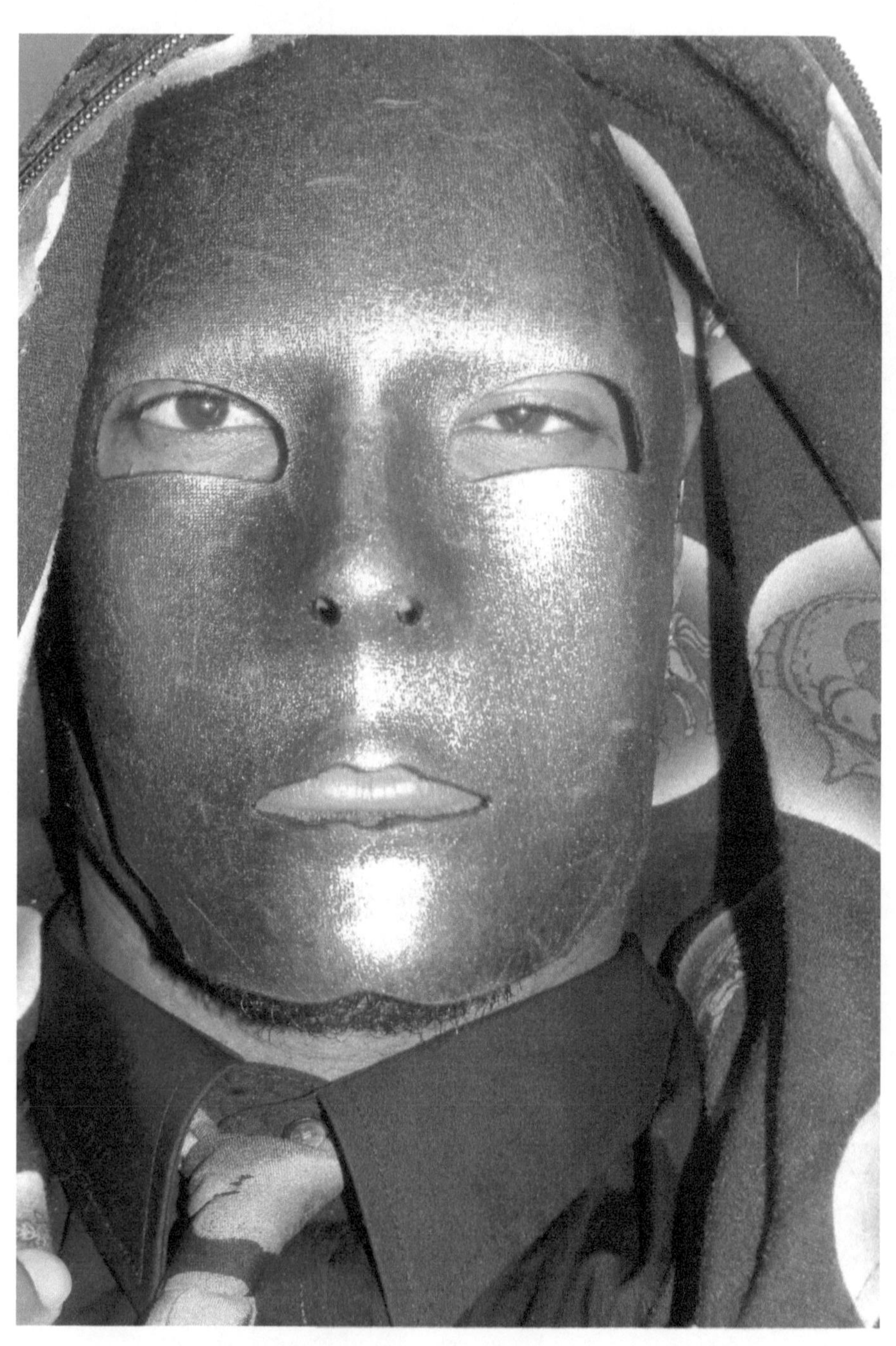

I AM

THE KING OF EROTICA

£a®~®¥

╬.Ҟ.Φ.Є. Publications
PUBLISHED BY LARRY WILSON, JR.
GOULDS, FLORIDA
ISBN# 978-0-615-23681-0
COPYRIGHT © BY TYRONE PAYNE, ALIYAIH HERNANDEZ WILSON
SUNJARAIH DENIESE WILSON, AMARAIH HERNANDEZ AND
LARRY C. WILSON, JR.

FRONT AND BACK COVER BY THE WONDERFUL
STEVVE SHIRES, FT. LAUDERDALE
ALL OTHER PHOTOS BY LARRY WILSON, JR:
LIBRARY OF CONGRESS CATALOGING-IN-PUBLICATION DATA HAS
BEEN APPLIED FOR.
PUBLISHER'S NOTE:
POETRY BY KELVIN LEE BROWN, MY BROTHER.

The Meal Table

The Dethronement Begins:
THE SHORT STORIES

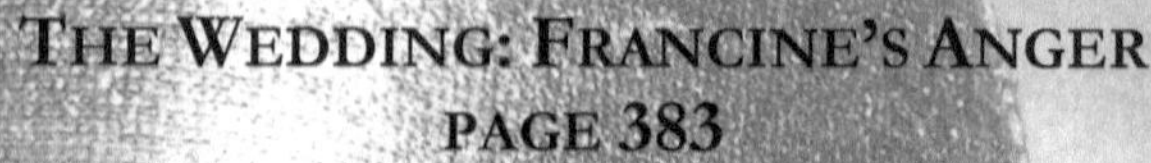

FŘƩAЖ
O
F

ThΣ: Oath

Remember *The Oath of the Freak* in the King of Erotica 1: The Throne? Well, if you read all the books leading up to *this* one then you are **The Freak of the Oath**. If you cheated and read Book 2 or this one before reading them in order than you *aren't* a Freak of the

Oath. You are lost until you read Book 1 and Book 2. If I had you from day one then you realize with a jolt that as the King of Erotica I don't give a shit about feelings and emotions. The King slays, he doesn't edit a goddamn thing and he doesn't give a fuck about what YOU gotta say about him. The more you talk the more I'm gonna *make* your ass talk. So get over it. As Dapharoah69 I don't care about Larry or the King of Erotica. He edits, so get over it. As Larry I am a humble sonofabitch. I give my last and don't expect it back. These books should challenge the alter ego in you. We all have many different sides. Some of you are too scared to be free. So you bash those who *are* free to build yourselves up. As I requested in BOOK 1, you have pledged The Oath of the Freak with yourself or a friend. You have read these books in private, in public and before bed at night. You have cried, laughed and gotten angry with me. You have taken cold showers, had hot flashes, jacked your dick, played with your dry-ass pussy and looked at your goddamn door knob differently. You have shaken your head and told yourself, "Oh no he didn't write that!" That's the Freak of the Oath. But don't claim the title as of yet. Just because you lick ass and listen to the rapper Plies doesn't make you a damn freak. You don't have to have sex to be a freak. A freak is simple. They talk about it, they *be* about it and they be *safe* about it. Freaks are erroneous fucks. If you're still hiding in the closet looking for her husband, if you still can't read "dick" or "pussy" without cringing then you are still holding on to your inhibitions and what the public thinks dictate your life and your decisions. If you're still having unprotected sex then you aren't the Freak of the Oath. You're playing with fire. If you're a married man fucking men behind your wife's back then you aren't a Freak of the Oath. If you're a married woman licking pussy behind your husband's back, then you aren't the Freak of the Oath. If you don't know your HIV/STD status you aren't the Freak of the Oath—1 in 4 people don't know they are infected with an STD. I don't give a damn about you rolling your eyes. Save a life. If you're purposely infecting people with STDs stop now and save a life. God is a God of understanding and forgiveness. If we were made in God's image then be as forgiven as God. Do *You* then do *your* part. If you cherish your lover without cheating you are the Freak of the Oath. If you love, nurture and have compassion for your wife I applaud you. Keep those whores from your home. They will wreck it. Keep your friends outta your private affairs. They will *run* it. Everyone has a goddamn past. Embrace your flaws and live for your inner beauty. Only then will you be the Freak of the Oath.

I'm the King of Erotica
And I approved this message.

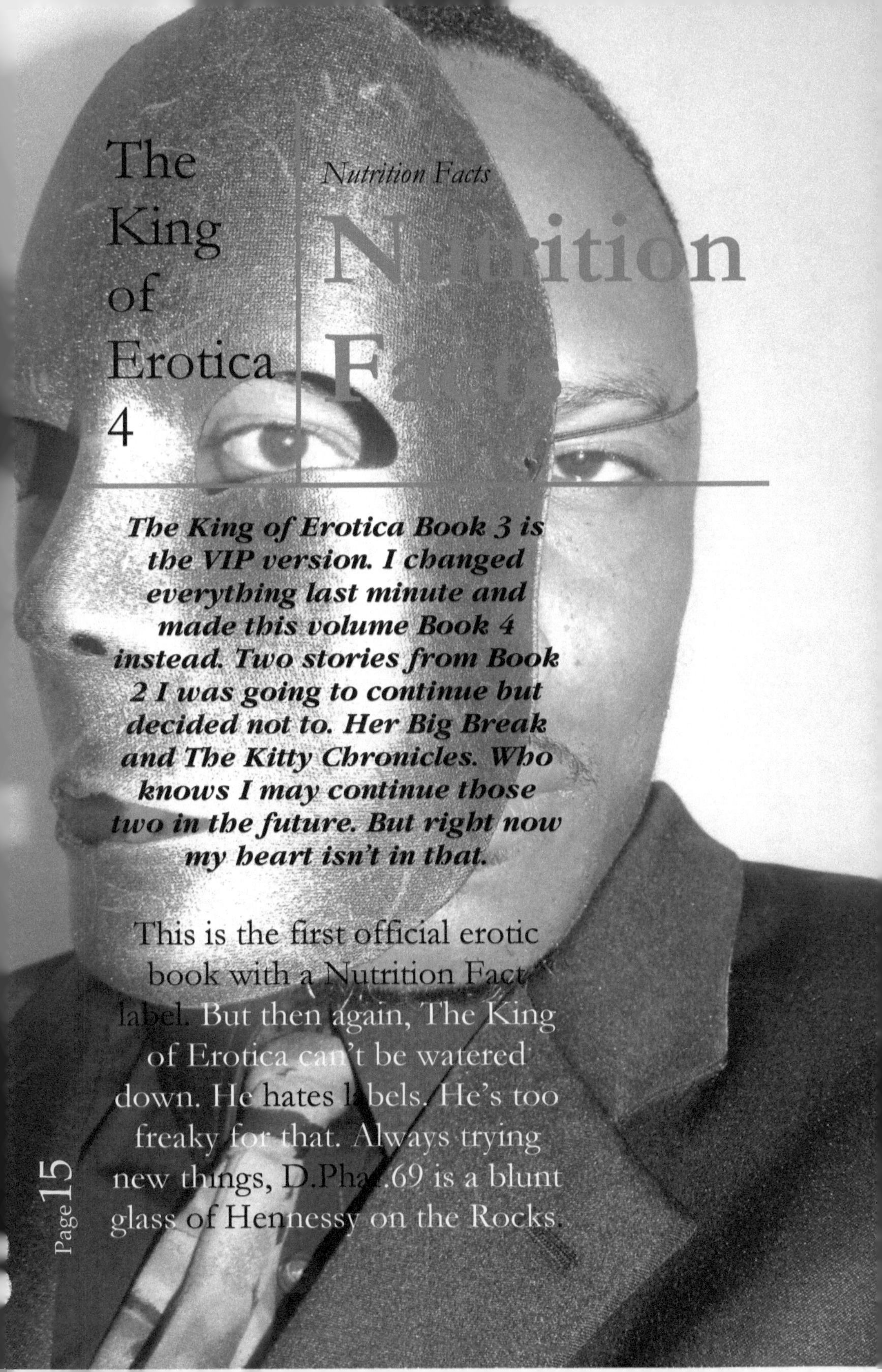

The King of Erotica 4

Nutrition Facts

Nutrition Facts

The King of Erotica Book 3 is the VIP version. I changed everything last minute and made this volume Book 4 instead. Two stories from Book 2 I was going to continue but decided not to. Her Big Break and The Kitty Chronicles. Who knows I may continue those two in the future. But right now my heart isn't in that.

This is the first official erotic book with a Nutrition Fact label. But then again, The King of Erotica can't be watered down. He hates labels. He's too freaky for that. Always trying new things, D.Phat.69 is a blunt glass of Hennessy on the Rocks.

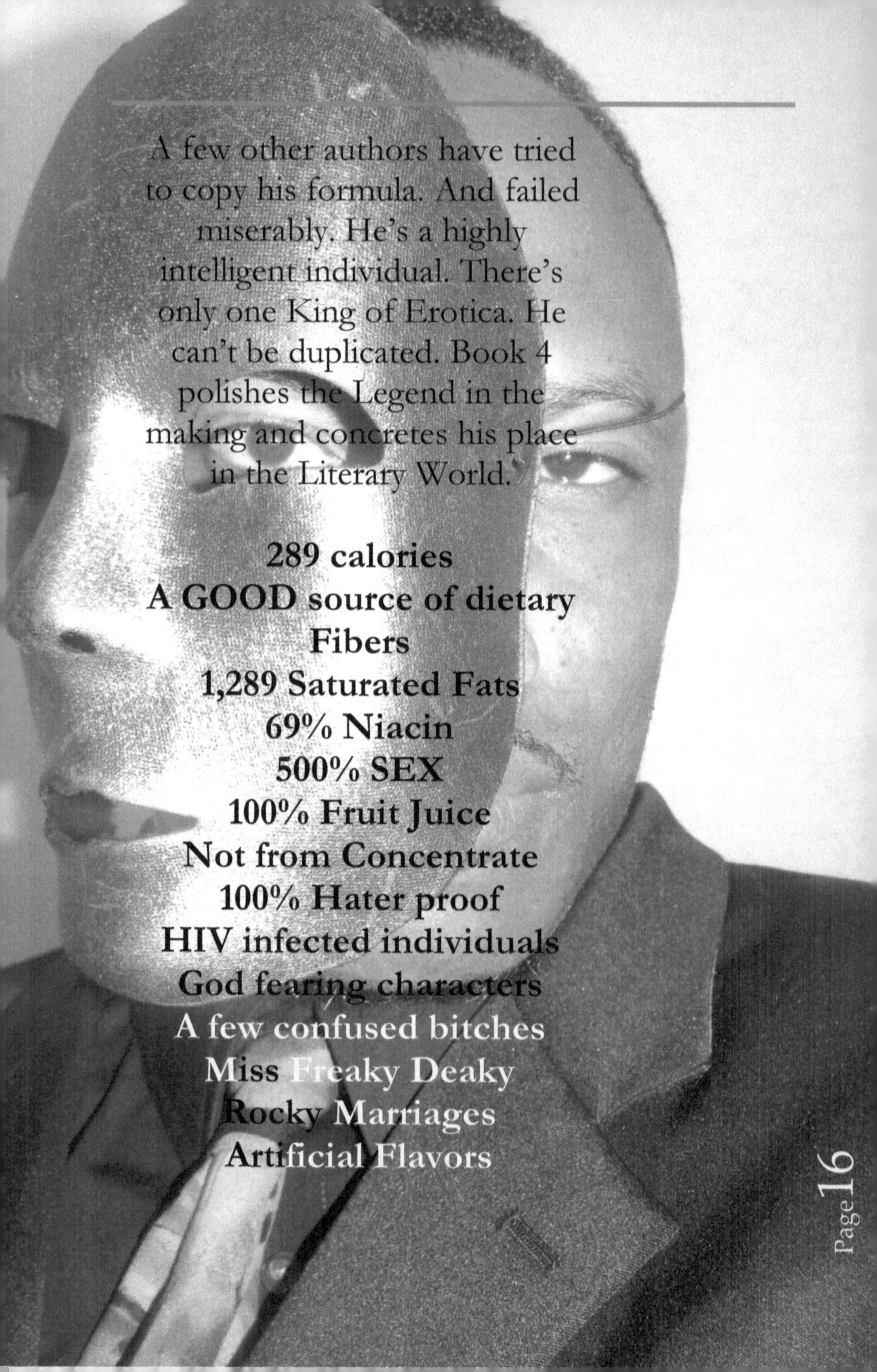

A few other authors have tried
to copy his formula. And failed
miserably. He's a highly
intelligent individual. There's
only one King of Erotica. He
can't be duplicated. Book 4
polishes the Legend in the
making and concretes his place
in the Literary World.

289 calories
A GOOD source of dietary
Fibers
1,289 Saturated Fats
69% Niacin
500% SEX
100% Fruit Juice
Not from Concentrate
100% Hater proof
HIV infected individuals
God fearing characters
A few confused bitches
Miss Freaky Deaky
Rocky Marriages
Artificial Flavors

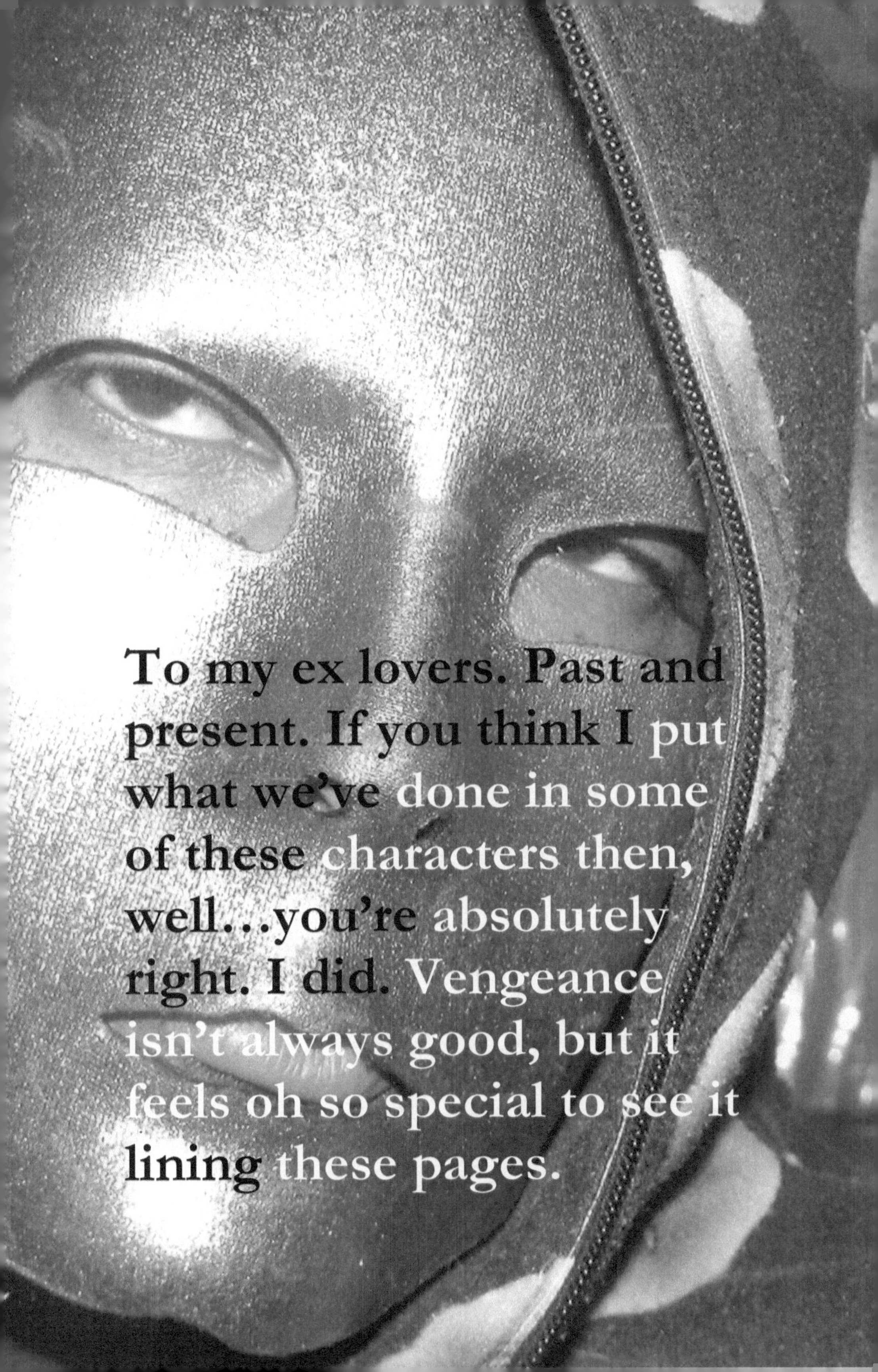

To my ex lovers. Past and present. If you think I put what we've done in some of these characters then, well...you're absolutely right. I did. Vengeance isn't always good, but it feels oh so special to see it lining these pages.

Letter to Larry Wilson, Jr.

My big brother

The KING of Erotica

Wuz up big brother from another mother! Ever since I met you my life has changed. That fortunate day I asked to use your phone 5 years ago has turned into a thing of beauty that could only be a gift from Heaven, one I don't think I'm deserving of. Remember that 20 minute conversation we had when I gave you the phone back? I do. I will never forget it. My life at that point was amounting to nothing. I had goals and dreams but they seemed out of reach. Yet there you were telling me to believe in my dreams with my heart, keep God first and then reach for them and it worked. You added the extra fun to my life, the financial part was added and it's cool because whenever I asked for something you made your little bruh work for it, you didn't just give it to me. That taught me that something worth gaining is worth working for. That brotherly love was added. You taught me how to truly interact with others without being phony. So all my thanks to you big brother. You took a gigantic weight off my shoulders, being that I am the oldest of nine kids and all the weight was on me. You showed me that other opportunities are available if I wanted them. You told me to use the way I raised my siblings as a means to one day raise my own family if I choose to have one. You called it "manhood training 101." When I needed some good advice, I could call you morning, noon and night. I saw you at your highest and your lowest and you always remained strong. You taught me that it's all right to cry without your manhood being compromised. You are a blessing sent from above. And believe it or not I thank God every single day for bringing you into my life. Everybody meets for a reason and your reason has turned into Big Brother and Little Brother forever. When I needed help with my college decisions you were there to guide me through your faults and failures. You encouraged me to leave Miami to further my education and I have and it worked and I am excelling, having made the President's List for my good grades. When I couldn't find a big brother anywhere else I found him in you. Man you are the best thing God has ever given me. I give you much respect and love as a man now and I stand behind *every* decision you make. So this is your little bruh Tyrone and you go get 'em with your books and show the world you can't be imitated or duplicated.

Love you for life
Tyrone Payne

Dedicated *to:*
Jimmy Grant and Kelvin L. Brown
my brother

Jimmy Grant.
Thanks for helping me let go of the past. I love you always.

Kelvin Brown. My little brother. I am very proud of you. You are going on your final year in college and you are doing your thing. I never dreamed that you would be going to Fayetteville University. Knowledge is power and you mastered it with skill and grace. Mama did something right when she gave birth to someone as beautiful as you. I can still remember changing your diapers and taking you all over the projects when you were little, when we lived in HUD housing (christened Hollywood Squares) by Miami Southridge Senior High School (Class of '95 Go Spartans!). I taught you your ABC's and 123's before you started Pre-K and it paid off. I learned a lot from you. No matter how tough life and school gets…never give up hope. Always live your dreams and if you need me I am always there. I will die for you. This section will feature your poetry. You have the gift of words and I am so very proud that I am NOT the only writer in the family. From your Facebook page to your big brother's book I present to you and the world your OWN creative poetry. I love you.

ROZELLA ROLLE: THE BACKBONE OF A BROKEN FAMILY
by Kelvin L. Brown

This poem will do my crying
Sad, confused and hurt when you were dying
A great woman you were
wish you still were here
family divided you kept us together like glue
Now we're apart and alone feeling so blue
I still hear you talking to me when I went into your
house and didn't see you there
Now I miss you everyday man life isn't fair
You raised my mom, brothers and sister
like we were you own
Tell stories about me storing my food in my mouth
even when I was grown
I never got to say goodbye
But I never let my memory of you die
You told the story of me getting the name chipmunk
I never forget…it always sunk
A woman that couldn't see

You always believed in my family and me
I remember always going to your house
those were the happiest times
When the family never cared
about nickels and dimes
I never got to go to the funeral to say my goodbyes
I always remember you never told us any lies
When we talk about you there's always
smiles on our faces
Family was the shoes and you were the laces
I know you're watching, smiling down on us
Never once will we frown
Your memory lives in us
Even if we're out of town or on a bus
Your house was a welcoming door mat to all
Like students walking down a hall.
Things change when God come
no pain or hurt when you left and now you're home
I don't know what life have to offer
or what it has in store
But when we hear your name we don't hurt no more
When I go to heaven I hope you open the door
So my heart will not be cracked like a broken floor
I woke up one day crying
Because I finally let go of you dying

Your Love is like Water

Every time I take a sip it taste so good
It always put me in a good mood
It has to be a part of me everyday
I thank God that I don't have to pay
The body needs it to go on in life
Sometimes it keeps me in strife
But I'm glad it's something that I will never sacrifice.
No roll of the dice.
In a river or a bottle…it's always there
Something that you can't get rid of
Because it's always there.
Hot or cold it's always good for you.
Without it I feel dehydrated.
With it my mind, body and soul is inflated.
It's the key essential in all of our lives.
Everyday I want to take a dive.
Your love is like water.
It's there for me like no other.
I have to soak every bit of it like a mop.
Because it's good to the last drop.

Different Breed

Life is like a bike with different gears
a person like me is wise beyond my years
Days of picking on me are over
Because of things I like to do here and there
But I like it because people know I'm here
a beautiful soul like me is hard to find
I write words of encouragement
For people who have no hope but to be on the grind
either drugs or in the books
Society will always gives us these looks
I say that it's cool just to be yourself
the same people that judge
Will never know your wealth
I walk on campus to see if people are the same
the things you like to do or say
Don't make you lame
doing what everybody else is doing
Makes you a follower
People that tell you to sit, stand or holler
Are miserable beings
they look at me weird
And don't like the things I do
They are just readers
Get up from the book and be leaders
I'm going to tell everyone
Doing the things you want to do
Isn't as hard as it seems
Wake up from the bed and follow your dreams
if you do the same things as your friends
They'll see it as dope
we all have different paths

and a person like me will offer hope
2pac said it best. He will be the spark in the brain that
pierces the heart of the person that changes the world.
I make these words I write my girl
She knows me in and out
My wife besides my family will know what I'm about
One day I'm going to speak
These same words to my seed
To go chase your dreams
and the world because you're a different breed

I Am…

The King of Erotica! I'm the leader of your most intimate desires. I love to create imbalance in your way of thinking and get you hot and horny then destroy your lustful tirades with characters doing unexplainable things. I will get the dick hard and the pussy wet. Sometimes I creep into your eyes and redirect your retinas so by the time you lay down to rest at night you will remember my name and face while you stroke your pussy, jack your dick and pull on a cigarette or a blunt. I manipulate the keyboard and recreate your irises to the point of torture. I love sex and I *do* it responsibly. Don't misconstrue Larry Wilson with DaPharoah69 or The King of Erotica. Larry is a God-fearing, soft-hearted push over who edits his words to keep *you* happy. DaPharoah69 is an abundance of intelligence and keeps it grown and sexy. The KING of Erotica doesn't give a shit! One can't exist without the other. If I don't get it hard or get it wet then teach you something you didn't know before you opened the book then I have wasted my time. Either way, when you close this book you will never be the same.

THE KING OF EROTICA 3.
CLOSED CAPTIONED
FOR THE HEARING IMPAIRED!

NC-17

Nobody under 17 is admitted.

The Kg of Er 4.©

100% ALL NATURAL EROTICA

DO NOT PURCHASE UNLESS YOU ARE FREE OF INHIBITIONS AND JUDGMENT

No Preservatives
No Artificial Flavors
No Artificial Colors
Erotica + this book = Smashing the competition

Ingredients: a mixture of erotic thoughts, experiences, fabrications and embellishments. A lot of imagination, redundancy and originality. Twelve ounces of a man like me not having sex in about four months. A quarter ounce of people can't act right to get my time. Twelve fluid ounces of Dapharoah69 not having any head in a very long time. A pinch of heart, a dash of class, an ounce of morals and a piece of realism. Poetic words are derived from the berries of Dapharoah69's heart. I shook this book to knock all the chapters in place. Sometimes you gotta slap your woman's butt to get it to jiggle right. Characters are figments of my imagination. Stories are filtered through the King of Erotica's mind and produced in the factory of his finger to keyboard interaction in a matter of minutes. Panties, boxers and birthday suits swirl the pages.

Shake Well

Refrigerate your body after opening. Because your
body may suffer heat flashes, sweat, unwarranted
wetness in women and hard wood inside the male
briefs.

The inside of this book is all Erotica. The outside is,
well a front and back book cover with my picture on it
in a purple mask.

367 FL. OZ.

E:4 ©

Erotica/berries: (E+Sex)

How do you like this Vitamin water type intro? Hot, huh? I tell you. I'm always doing something new. Things you haven't seen before in a book. Did you check out the Nutrition Facts label above? There's 400% worth of sex in this book. Heck yea. *Whoop, whoop!* Who *knew?* Books, well mine, since this is the first official Erotic book with its own Nutrition Facts label, should be like Diaries or avenues to explore experiments and ideas. Books should be vessels for your heart's content. If you feel it then you should write it. Forget about those who don't like it. I never paid attention to lame or phony people, and never gave the prudes the time of day. I don't entertain negative people because they always have other people's business on their tongues and if a penis were words they'd always have it in their mouths.

God gave a selected few the ability to write a complete sentence. He gave others the ability to write more than one. A handful of people can write a complete story. Others can't make it past Writer's

Block. I've never experienced Writer's Block. I don't sit on a keyboard for hours and write. I'll write for an hour. Stop. Go do some jumping jacks, have sex, get some head. Play some music and dance to some Janet Jackson *Discipline*, because I'm feeling her album. I go to work. I argue with Mama over hotdogs. Take my nieces to the movies. Die inside from them chanting UNCLE LARRY UNCLE LARRY UNCLE LARRY fifty million times a day. Sleep. Shower. Eat. Come back to the computer. Refreshed. And write. Works like a charm. With movies like Silence of the Lambs and Seven, anything is possible in the world of literature. Who dictates what literature is and what it's not. The white man? Please.

They can't hide things in books anymore. I got black people reading, baby. How do you like that Jim Crow? I never liked Huckleberry Fin and I heard Shakespeare stole his plays. So how's that for authentication? Books shouldn't be a bunch of edited bull crap from editors who think the book belongs to them instead of the author. I've come across some editors who told me to take my pictures out. Sike. Why should I do that when they prove to be good marketing tools? I stand behind this Erotica book. The pictures seal the deal. Plus I'm cute (I'm blushing) in my early thirties and giving the twenty year old's hell.

While editors separate their butts from a socket in the wall, I am kicking some realism in these books. Some editors tell me to stop being raunchy. OK. *Not.* Next. The world is built on sex, drugs and rock and roll and I'm not a willing participant of the "drugs" part, thank you very much. But sex, hmm. I'll be quiet about that one. And I love Aerosmith, System of a

Down and Disturbed's rock music. I can get a little Snoop Dogg and Lil' Wayne on your hind parts, too. Don't trip. I don't deal with close-minded people. Frankly, they have their heads so far up their booty holes they dress as ostriches for Halloween.

One editor, a friend of mine, who was very educated and certified claimed he couldn't edit my book because he didn't support anything bisexual or gay, yet I saw him in a gay club a few weeks later hopping all over a tall basketball-type with pants on so tight his nuts were bunched in the front like a mass of fat. When he saw me he covered his face in shame, ducked, and made his way to the bathroom. You know me. I'm remained cool, so I glided across the floor, to the bathroom and stood behind him while he faked like he was urinating.

I like suspense so I tapped his shoulder and was like, "Yet you wouldn't edit my book because…"

He shook his head and said, turning to face me, "I'm sorry. I shouldn't have…"

I covered his lips with my hand. Don't want to hear it if it's a lie. I shook my head with a smile and danced off. The entire book isn't about bisexuals. Don't put orientation on my stuff.

The stories inside are about ALL people, all walks of life. I love all people equally.

After I badgered Mr. Editor, making his basketball-type friend laugh, I called it a night and came home, turned on the laptop and got to work piecing this together.

To put it bluntly, many authors have tested me. Others have provoked me. A few authors come to me in private and ask me to write some things for them.

They want their names on it, mine in the grave and a paycheck in my bank account.

I don't think so.

I don't do the ghostwriting thing.

I never say anything. I pick up the ink pen and I write silently. I type silently. I plot these stories silently. Each story takes no time to create. I think things up fluidly.

Imagine having an imagination as sexually witty as mine. Imagine being much more than Erotica. Imagine changing lives and schooling people in the process. Imagine reading this book and getting from it something besides sex. Imagine changing one's perspective about why people have the type of sex the way they do. If I gotta piss you off to get my point across then so be it. I don't care one way or the other. I have a Box for Comments and Suggestions on my testicles. Lick, I meant insert accordingly.

Imagine shining a light on why someone chooses their sexual orientation. I've accomplished that. I continuously push boundaries. I am doing what I feel no one else wants to do because they aren't strong enough to handle the outcome. I come all the time, so out with it.

If you're going to compare me to anyone compare me to myself. Everyone else has or have paved their own way; it's not fair to put me in the limelight with them. There's only room for one. And there's only ONE King of Erotica. And that's me. Book three shatters 400 pages. This edition will be possibly my LAST.

I wrote about EVERYTHING in this one. I am gritty. I am raunchy. I am unpredictable. I am sexual. I am real. I am raw. I am unedited. And of course

Dapharoah69 is uncensored. I come to one conclusion: I have a brain. I am sexy. I am intelligent. I don't need accomplished authors when I am already accomplished. I may not have sold millions, but I am well on my way. Each book takes me deeper and

further than the previous work of art I pen so eloquently.

That's what makes the Erotica Nutrition Facts in this book so refreshing. The berries are ripe and they are ready to be plucked.

Which berry will you pluck first?

Dapharoah69.

I'M FOREVER

A

MIAMI

S
O
U
T
H
R
I
D
G
E

Spartan
Class of
1995

I joined the

Future Business Leaders of America

My Junior Year at

Southridge.

I'm glad I did.

Acknowledgement

ALL PRAISE AND HONOR
GO TO GOD
MY HEAVENLY FATHER
WHO LOVES ME FOR ME

Hello, Everyone
Welcome to the Larry Wilson, Jr.
Show!
This is the KING of EROTICA speaking.
Presenting my fifth book.
THE DETHRONMENT OF A KING!
They said I couldn't do it.
Family doubted me, bashed me, and talked
about me.
Friends turned on me.
GOD NEVER LEFT MY SIDE!
I was homeless.
I was in jail 11 years ago.
I'm from GOULDS, Florida

I tested positive for HIV.
I'm an advocate for HIV awareness
It's all about saving lives.
They say Goulds have no talent
They say Dade County Public Schools
Produce lackluster students…
This is what happens
When you believe in yourself
And pray to God,
Then do it on your own

The

L
E
G
A
C
Y

Walk down the KING hallway with me.

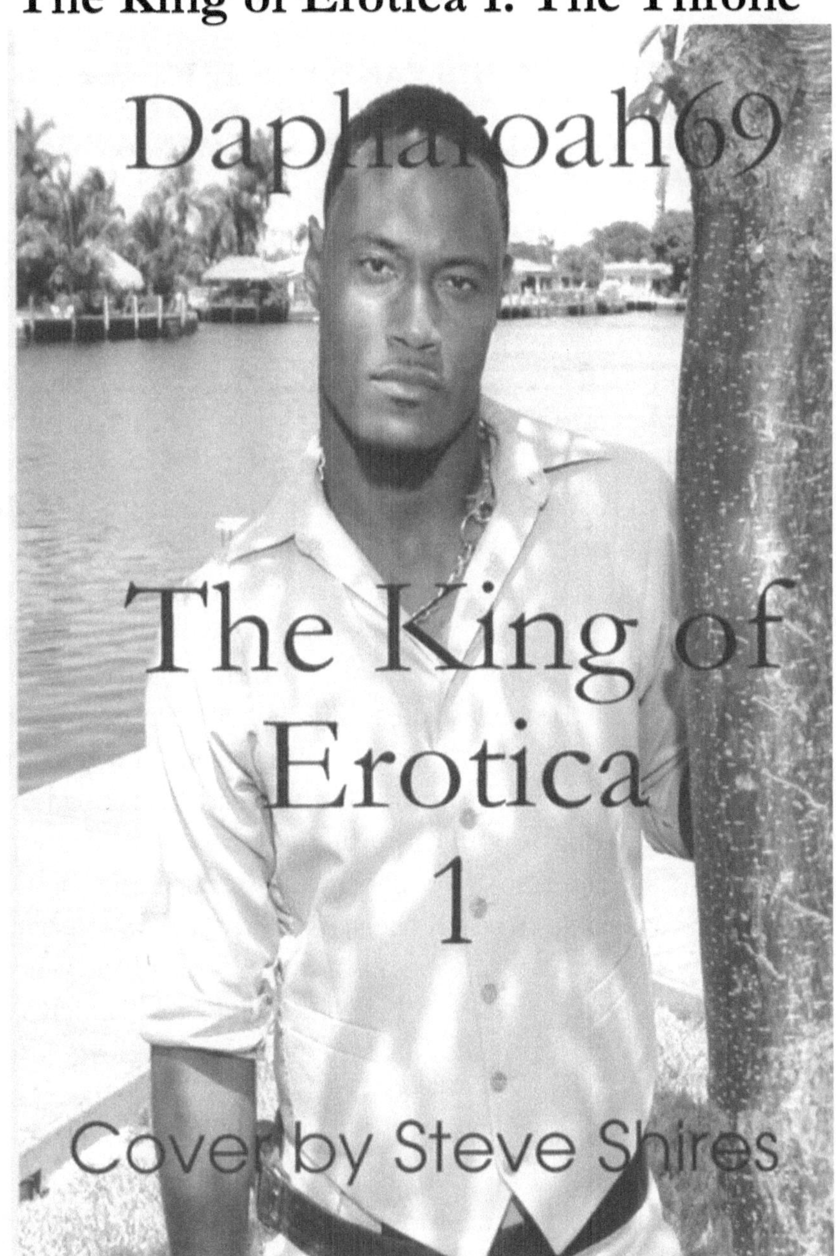

Dapharoah69
The King of Erotica 1
Cover by Steve Shires

THE LETTER TO HIS FAMILY IS EPIC. THE LETTER TO HIS FATHER LARRY C. WILSON, JR SPEAKS FOR ALL YOUNG BLACK MEN WHO GREW UP WITHOUT FATHERS

From: Miss_Afrikkans

It was hard for me to read this haunting book. It is haunting on many levels. Never have I read a book that grabbed me just from reading the credit page. I read everything, examined every photograph of him. THE LETTER TO HIS OLDER COUSINS is epic in itself. He disclosed years of silence, years of his older cousins, who were supposed to be setting examples for him, turning their backs on him when he was being raped. He also expressed his anger towards his family not sticking together and only coming together when someone in the family dies. The letter opened me up a great deal and I examined my own family. I admire this author for being blunt and diving head first into his book. Reading it you know he took his time creating it. He defied the odds. I appreciate his candidness and his openness to share with the world himself, his vision and why he wrote the book before getting into the actual fictional stories. THE LETTER TO LARRY WILSON, SR. put tears in my eyes. I shared the letter with a few male friends who grew up with fathers. They were all in tears and very quiet and emotional while reading it. He expressed hate, anger and then love, self-confidence and he ended the letter by saying, "Mama did her part. Now come do yours." I was literally crying like my dog died. THE KING OF EROTICA should be a book given to all young black men 18 and over. It's multi-faceted. Young black men need to know what's truly going on in the world. Maybe they experienced the same things but the harshness of society pushes them to be silent and to be quiet. Dapharoah69 takes it on full throttle. Dapharoah69's name in itself is art. In an interview he said the "DA" is slang for "THE" Ebonics. PHAROAH (purposely misspelled, to remind him of a time in the first grade a white teacher told him he was learning disabled...when he was making better grades than everyone in the room) A title given to the King of Egypt. And "69." It isn't the sexual position. No. It's the Sign of the Cancer. 6 on top and 9 on bottom. And this allows, in my opinion, the author to be sensitive in his characters and the characters in this book are mind-blowing, real, hardcore and don't sugarcoat. Marvelous first book.

This Book is the Real Raw Unedited Deal

Real. Raw. Unedited. Powerful. Innovative. Sinister. Compelling. Enduring. Blunt and Trendsetter. Dapharoah69 is a rule maker and breaker. His enterprise is astounding. He has changed what one should expect from an author. A lot of authors present books that read more like extended versions of school reports. Someone else on the cover. The material. And something on the back covers. But Dapharoah69 single-handedly changed the rules. He OWNS his images and work and he provides a service by writing such good work. The Golden Masks. He deserves an award for this story. An award for Awareness. An

Award for teaching and educating. The passion in On the Low Low. You FEEL what these two men feel before they kiss. The Hotel, the Elevator will have your mouth open. They way he pays attention to detail are amazing. Incredible book!!!

50 (5) Star Reviews Barnes and Noble.com
A Barnes and Noble.com Top 100 Bestseller
Featured in National Bestselling Author
E. Lynn Harris' Literary Café, Sizzle 2009
Subject of over 205 Book Clubs Nationwide
Subject of 56 Church Book Clubs
(THE GOLDEN MASKS)
Subject of 130 Gay and Lesbian Book Clubs
Subject of 19 Transgender Book Clubs
Featured in the Express Gay News
Playa4Playa.com's Book of the Month
For half a year
Featured on Nubian101.com
Available on over 300 online retailers
Worldwide, including Japan, China, the
Untied Kingdom, Germany and Canada.

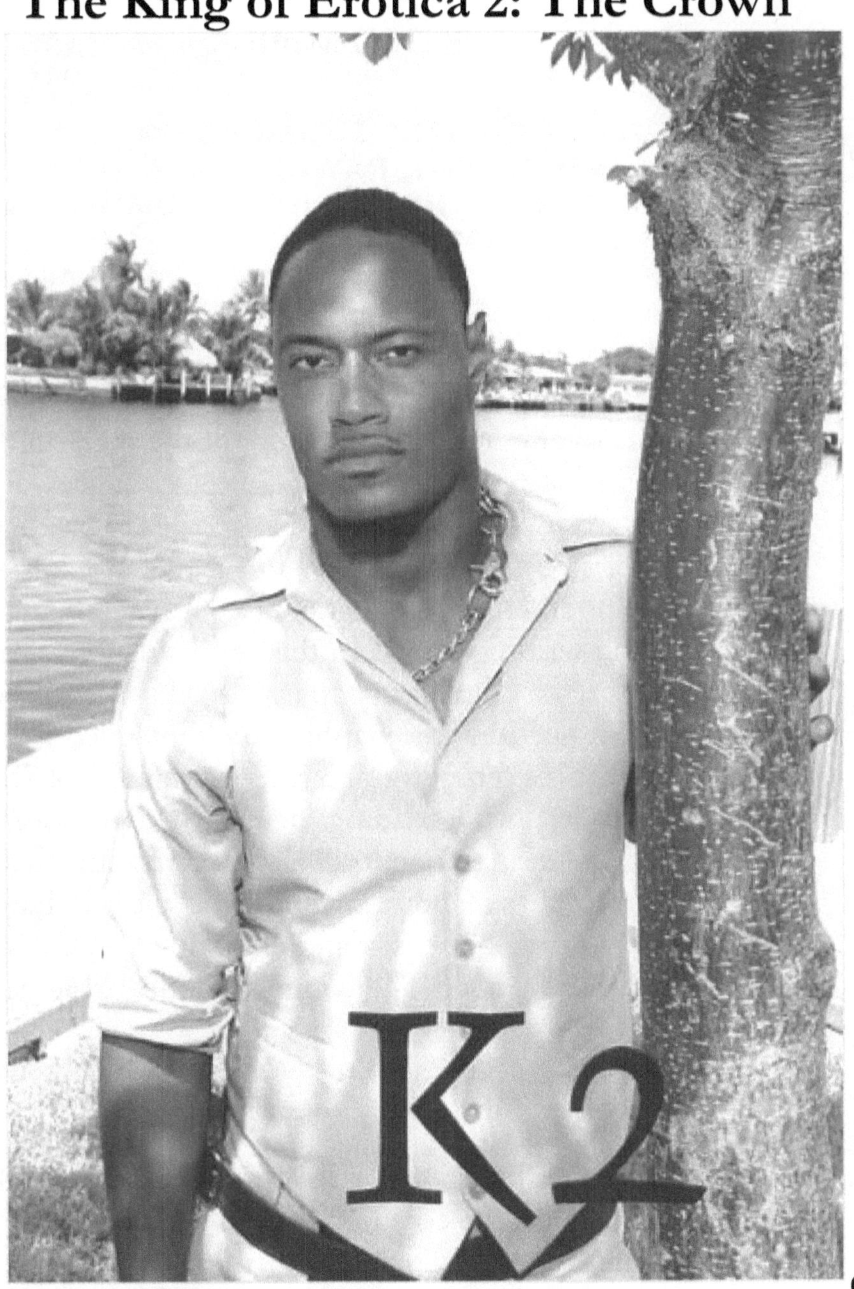

THE KING OF EROTICA 2 THE CROWN SHOWCASES TALENT, RAWNESS AND THE EMERGEANCE OF THE AUTHOR BECOMING AN INSTANT SEX SYMBOL.

When you buy a book what do you do? Why did you pick it up? What grabbed you? Did a friend call you and tell you to check it out? Did the cover grab you? Well, the cover grabbed me. I thought the man on the front was a model. No. It's the actual author and he stands in front of his work and in the back. This man is a master story teller. And let's not forget awesome, awesome poet. His poetry is the best. A black man writing and writing poetry. In this book what grabbed me the most was the essay paper an FIU student wrote on The King of Erotica. Dapharoah69 included it in the book for his fans. And it is very revealing. I could not stop crying. After reading the essay paper I closed the book and didn't open it till almost a month later. Dapharoah69 has testimonies and he is like a walking Bible. Full of life, hope, sex and endurance. The King of Erotica 2 surpassed The King of Erotica 1 big time.

Book 1 put him on Zane's level. Book 2 left her in the dust

I was panting after book 1. I love Zane. God I do. But this sexy man on the cover and the same sexy man wrote what he would do to a woman's panties in his characters is extraordinary. The stories had me bitter, mad, upset, happy, horny, frustrated, appalled, and jubilant. It was a roller coaster and never have I read a book that affected me in those ways in a four hour period. Book 2 is more daring, more introspective and when the King writes the sex scenes he makes porn look like a walk in the park. Zane definitely has competition and in this case, he surpassed her by a landslide.

This Book was the Subject of my Book Club 2 months in a row

To fully understand this amazing author is to dissect him. What he's seen, where he's gone and the pain of his awful childhood. To understand Larry I held two book club meetings for the month of January and February. To discuss the man took a couple hours. By the time the book club ended we hadn't even discussed the book. So we did another meeting. Larry is old soul. He sees things with his eyes and expresses it with a passion unseen in erotic writing. That's because Zane is sex. Larry is deeper than sex. If Zane is two lovers getting it on, Larry is the male penis diving DEEPER into the womb and the explosion of his words waters the seeds of life. That's the King of Erotica Book 2. The characters are memorable. Princess Webster. Georgia. Melissa Jackson (is a bad bit*h!). The stories are longer and more daring.

Stand behind your work!

Steve Harvey may have the number 1 book, but Dapharoah69 has the number 1 erotic book of the moment and he didn't have a publisher to help him make it successful. I bought eleven copies of this book to give to friends in my book club. I wrote the author on MySpace and Facebook and he responded with humbleness and kindness. How many authors do you know will stop to talk to the little people with love and understanding? Look at the man on the cover. That is not a model. No. That is the actual author. You know what that picture represents? It represents tough love, perseverance and stability. He has survived being repeatedly raped as a kid, jail, suicide attempts, hating and loathing himself...and all that has transformed into a beautiful man who writes an art form, not a book. This book details a do-it-yourself attitude. Publishing houses said No and he said go to hell I'll do it my way. That's the message you get from DaPharoah69. I don't care what he writes, he will always get my last dollar because when I read his books, I don't get a book, I get pure entertainment that will make me laugh, think and blush.

84 (5) Star Reviews Barnes and Noble.com
A Barnes and Noble.com Top 100 Bestseller
Subject of 75 Book Clubs Worldwide
Subject of 36 Gay and Lesbian Book Clubs
Subject of 13 Transgender Book Clubs
Subject of 2 Book Clubs in South Africa
Subject of 24 Book Clubs Germany
CLIK Magazine's Top 25 Sexiest, Most Eligible Bachelor 2007
Available on over 300 online retailers Worldwide, including Japan, China, the Untied Kingdom, Germany and Canada.

VIP
Gould's
Finest
A TKOE Publication

KING Mail:

HE CONTINUES TO AMAZE ME/
ALL HAIL THE KING OF EROTICA:

I CAN'T BELIEVE I ACTUALLY THOUGHT THIS BOOK WOULD NEVER BE AS GOOD AS THE FIRST, BUT ONCE I BEGAN TO READ I WAS CONVINCED THAT THE KING HAD PROVEN ME WRONG, ONCE AGAIN. THIS BOOK IS AMAZING. ZANE EAT YOUR HEART OUT. I'VE OBTAINED SO MUCH MORE FROM DAPHAROAH69'S WORK THAN ANY OTHER AUTHOR OF EROTIC LITERATURE (NO DISRESPECT, JUST BEING HONEST). THE STORIES ARE SO REFRESHING AND INCOMPARABLE. THE CHARACTERS WILL LEAVE YOU BREATHLESS.

AND THE COVER PHOTO IS SO SEXY. KING, YOU'VE BECOME EVEN MORE FIERCE WITH EACH PROJECT. YOU'RE DOING YOUR THING. HANDS DOWN YOU ARE A CREATIVE GENIUS. EVERYONE, THERE'S A NEW KING IN TOWN AND HIS NAME IS DAPHAROAH69. IF YOU HAVEN'T HAD THE PLEASURE OF EXPERIENCING WHAT "REAL" EROTICA LITERATURE IS, THIS IS IT. AND DAPHAROAH69 IS THE "IT" GUY. I PLAN TO PURCHASE AT LEAST 20 MORE COPIES OF THIS MASTERPIECE FOR MY FAMILY AND FRIENDS.

THEY HAVE RAVED OVER THE KING'S WORK BEFORE WITH 2 OF HIS OTHER WELL KNOWN BOOKS: THE KING OF EROTICA 1&2

AND I KNOW THEY'LL BE LEFT IN AWE WITH THIS ONE. ALL HAIL THE KING...

OMG BOOK 3 BOOK 3 BOOK 3 TOPS THEM ALLLL!!!!!

I AM GLAD I BOUGHT ALL THREE BOOKS AS A COLLECTIVE WHOLE. SO WHEN I FINISHED ONE I DIVED INTO THE NEXT. BOOK 3 ITS OVER. OVAHHH YOU HEAR ME. GOLDDIGGER. COMPELLING. AALEXANDRIA CURSING OUT EVERY MEMBER OF HER CHURCH REMINDS ME OF JULIA ROBERTS IN "SOMETHING TO TALK ABOUT," AND HE PULLED IT OFF BETTER THAN THE MOVIE AND WITH SOME BLACK FOLKS WHO ARE PHONY IN THE ORGANIZATION. I FEEL CONNECTED TO AALEXANDRIA. "DOMESTIC VIOLENCE." OH MY GOD. THAT STORY ALONE HAD ME IN TEARS AND SHOWED THE MAN AS THE TRUE VICTIM...I'M GIVING TOO MUCH AWAY. AND HIS ABILITY TO WRITE PICTURES IN YOUR HEAD AND NOT JUST WORDS IN YOUR EYES SHATTERS HIS COMPETITION. DAPHAROAH69 IS ON THE SCENE AND THE BOY IS RELEASING FOUR BOOKS THIS YEAR TO SOLIDIFY THAT HE ISN'T PLAYING WITH YOU PEOPLE! GO GET 'EM PHAROAH. THAT'S WHAT A KING DOES. DIVIDE AND CONQUER. BUT YOU CONQUER MINDS.

This book is the BUSINESS!

DaPharoah69. OMG. I have a new favorite author. This isn't a page turner. It's a page flipper. When I tell you that every story in this book is better than the previous I am telling you this man this man this man right here is the shit! He does what Zane never could. He has more talent in his pinky finger than she has in her whole Sex Chronicles. I mean just looking at his book cover I applaud him for pulling those DL men's antics out of the closet and SCHOOLING a sister. I love that picture. He stands behind his sh8t! He does the writing game his way and he doesn't care who don't like it. The man is bad and to say that he is Zane's competition is a massacre because he shatters anything she has every written. His short stories alone shatter After burn and leave it to catch its breath on her nightstand. Me and my girlfriends bought this book and had a book club meeting. He doesn't just know a woman's thoughts...he crushes them with his unpredictable endings.

**27 (5) Star Reviews Barnes and Noble.com
A Barnes and Noble.com Top 71 Bestseller
Subject of 125 Book Clubs Worldwide
Subject of 96 Book Clubs Nationwide
Subject of 12 Book Clubs in South Africa
Subject of 10 Book Clubs in Germany
Subject of 7 Book Clubs in Japan
Available on over 300 online retailers
Worldwide, including Japan, China, the
Untied Kingdom, Germany and Canada.**

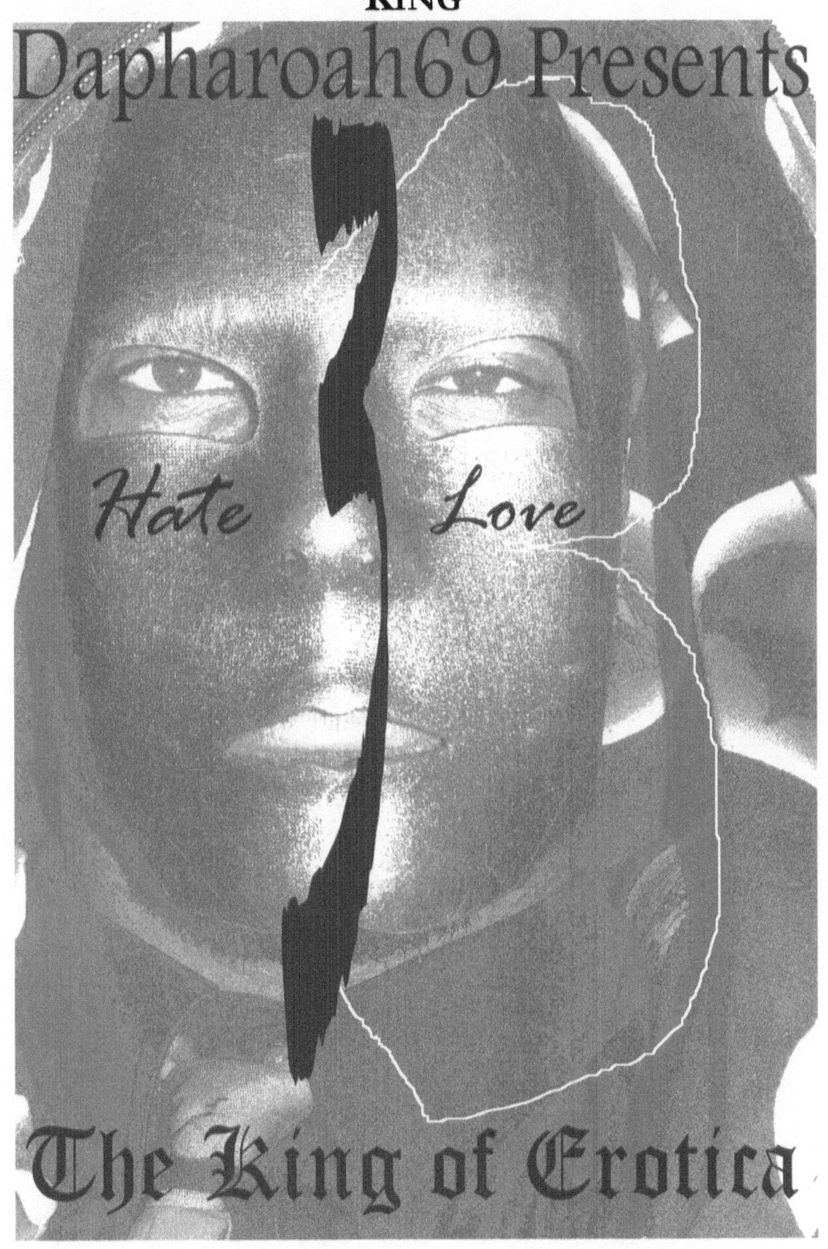
Dapharoah69 Presents
Hate
Love
The King of Erotica

**780 PRE-ORDERS
BEFORE ITS RELEASE
JULY 24, 2009**

**OVER 290 BOOK CLUBS
REQUESTS (AND COUNTING)**

YOU'RE READING BOOK 4 NOW.

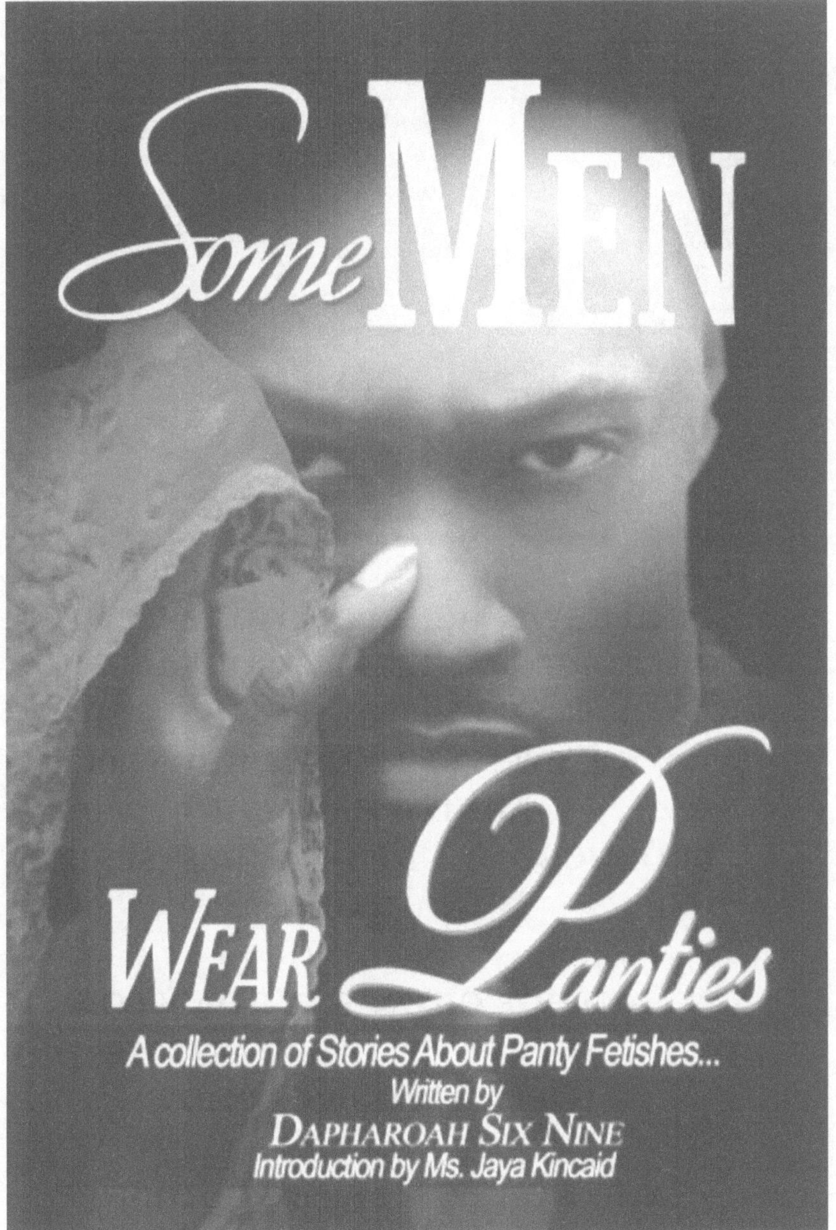
Some MEN
WEAR Panties
A collection of Stories About Panty Fetishes...
Written by
DAPHAROAH SIX NINE
Introduction by Ms. Jaya Kincaid

JL KING, LARRY WILSON (KING OF EROTICA)
AND KEVIN MCNEIR, SOME MEN WEAR
PANTIES EDITOR

WRITTEN BY LARRY WILSON, JR.
AKA DAPHAROAH69
PRODUCED BY NATIONAL BESTSELLING
AUTHOR
JL KING
AUTHOR OF ON THE DOWN LOW
(HE WAS FEATURED ON THE
OPRAH WINFREY SHOW)

AND NOW BOTH KINGS COMBINED
PRODUCED

SOME MEN WEAR PANTIES

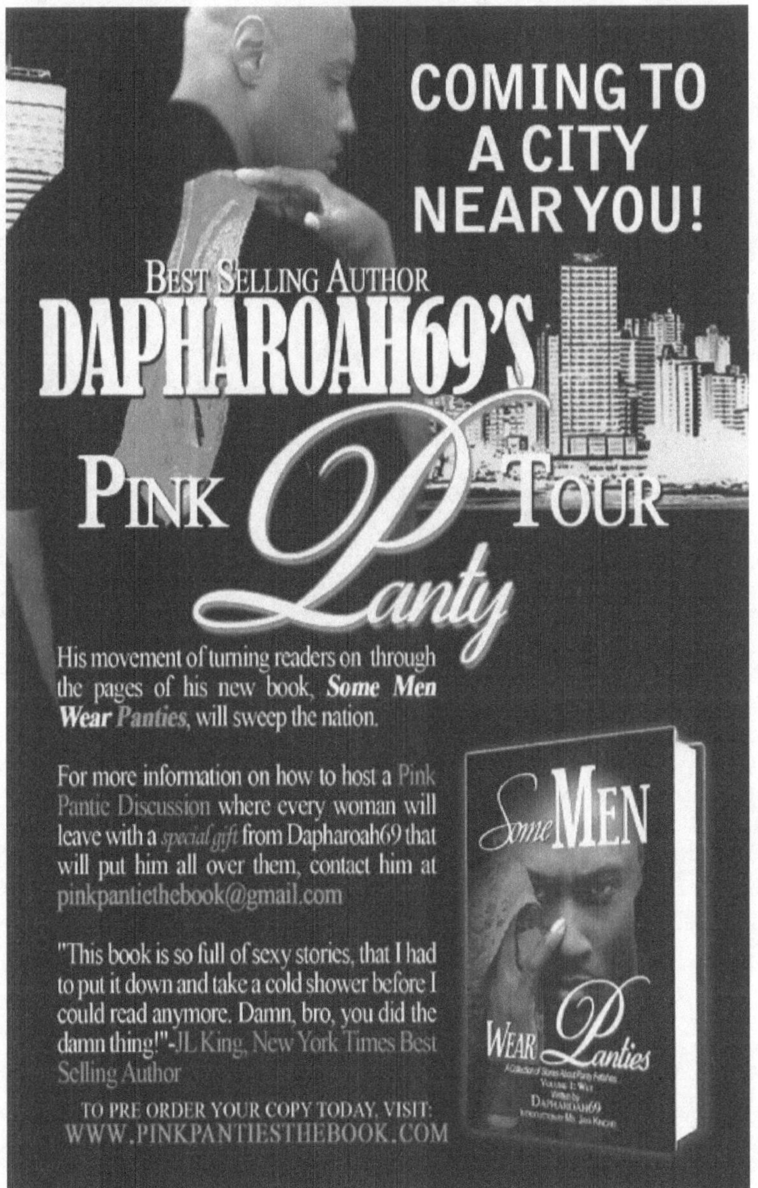
COMING TO A CITY NEAR YOU!

BEST SELLING AUTHOR
DAPHAROAH69'S

PINK PANTY TOUR

His movement of turning readers on through the pages of his new book, Some Men Wear Panties, will sweep the nation.

For more information on how to host a Pink Pantie Discussion where every woman will leave with a special gift from Dapharoah69 that will put him all over them, contact him at pinkpantiethebook@gmail.com

"This book is so full of sexy stories, that I had to put it down and take a cold shower before I could read anymore. Damn, bro, you did the damn thing!"-JL King, New York Times Best Selling Author

TO PRE ORDER YOUR COPY TODAY, VISIT:
WWW.PINKPANTIESTHEBOOK.COM

Some MEN WEAR Panties
A Collection of Stories About Panty Fetishes
VOLUME 1: WET
Written by DAPHAROAH69

2489 Cheshire Bridge Road, Ste 229D / Atlanta, Georgia 30324
Toll-Free Office: 1-800-631-5685

OFFICIAL FACES
Chapter One
Spring Quarter

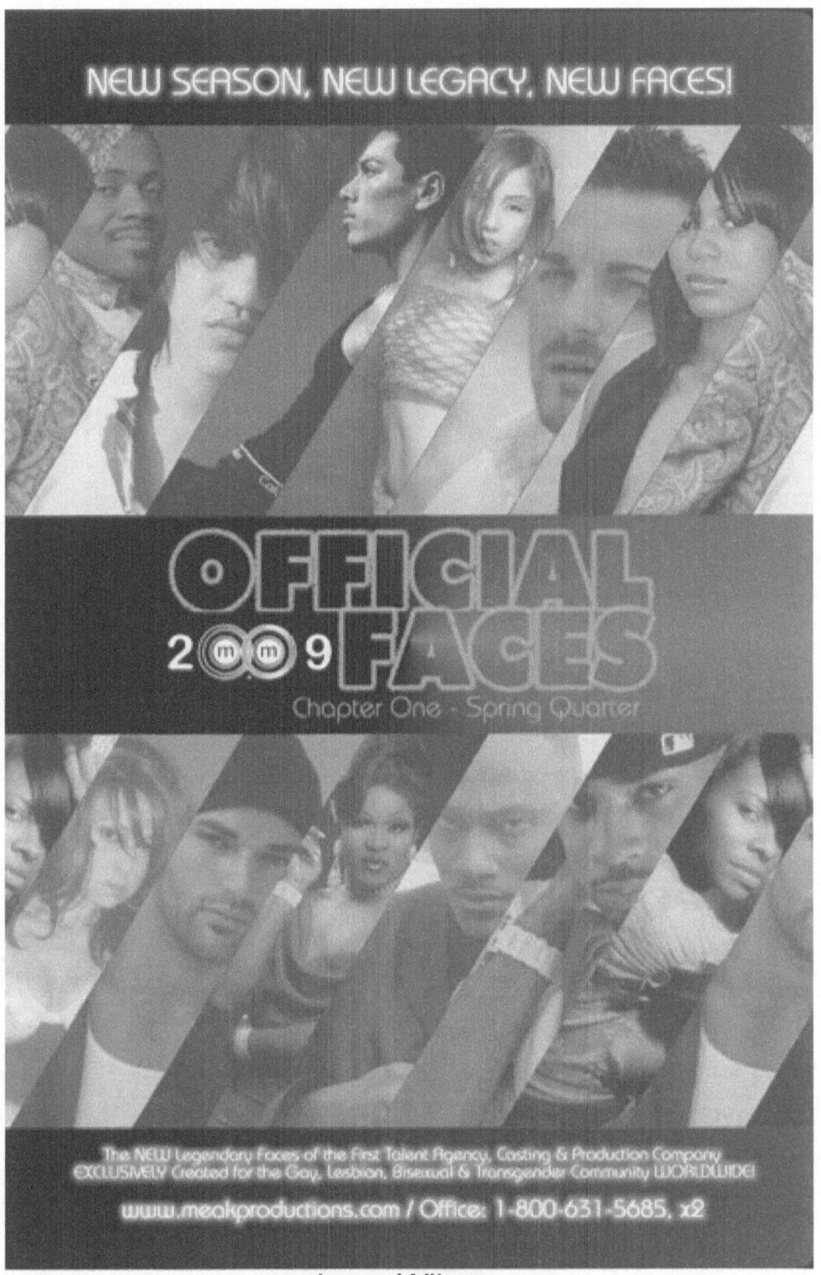

Larry Wilson

PROFESSIONAL AUTHOR, DANCER AND ENTREPRENEUR

LARRY WILSON, JR.
DAPHAROAH69
THE KING OF EROTICA

DaPharoah69
The King of Erotica

TKOE PUBLICATIONS
THE KING OF EROTICA PUBLICATIONS
LARRY WILSON, JR, LLC.
SELF-MADE BUSINESS MAN
❖ CEO/OWNER
❖ ACCOUNTANT

- ❖ DANCER
- ❖ PHOTOGRAPHER
- ❖ EDITOR/COPY EDITOR
- ❖ HYPE MAN
- ❖ FORMATTOR
- ❖ TYPIST
- ❖ MODEL
- ❖ MAKE UP ARTIST
- ❖ STYLIST
- ❖ SEX SYMBOL
- ❖ ADVERTISING GURU
- ❖ MARKETING DIRECTOR
- ❖ OUTREACH COORDINATOR
- ❖ HIV AWARENESS INSTRUCTOR
- ❖ **PUBLIC SPEAKER**
- ❖ SOUTHRIDGE SPARTAN

EDUCATED BY THE MIAMI-DADE COUNTY PUBLIC SCHOOL SYSTEM.

SUCCESS!

THAT'S HOW YOU DO IT ON YOUR OWN
WHEN YOU GIVE IT TO GOD
AND SACRIFICE FOR IT!

GOULDS STAND UP!

Steve Shires
Photography

The Museum
Of the
KING
Of Erotica

You believed in me
when no one else did.
you had faith in me
when the world turned its back on me
you where there during the storms
you were there when I was down and out
you were there when I needed a friend

you were there when I gave up
you told me nothing comes to you easy
you told me I was the king of erotica
you told me no one has done what I'm doing
you shared with me the pain
of losing your mother
I thank you for the images
I thank you for capturing everything i was,
am, and will be
you immortalized my legacy
and for you this is my thank you
love you always, Steve
Larry

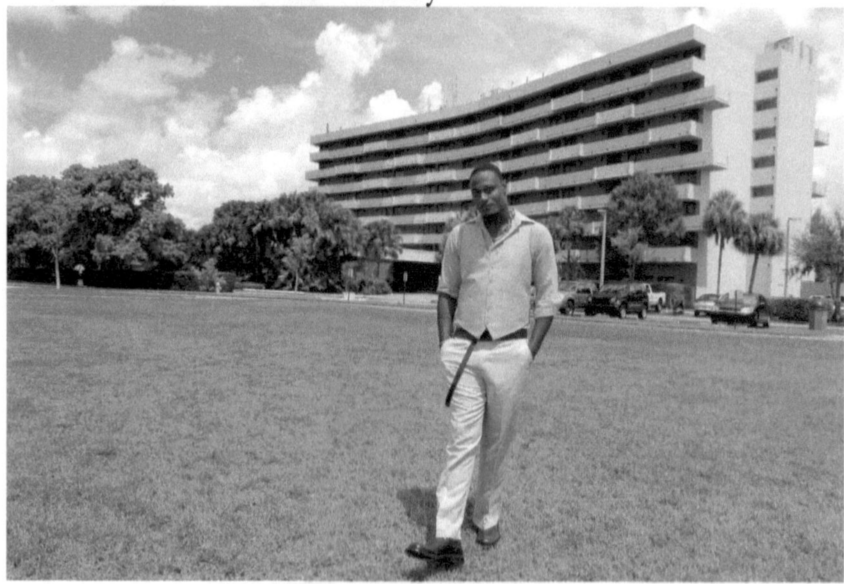

THE INVERRARY HOTEL
FT. LAUDERDALE, FLORIDA
17 YEARS AGO, I WAS 14
STAYING IN THIS HOTEL AFTER
HURRICANE ANDREW DESTROYED MIAMI
17 YEARS LATER, I RETURNED AS A PUBLISHED AUTHOR
TO DO A PHOTO SHOOT.

ThΣ DΣthronΣmΣnt BΣgins:

Flip the Page like its good pussy.

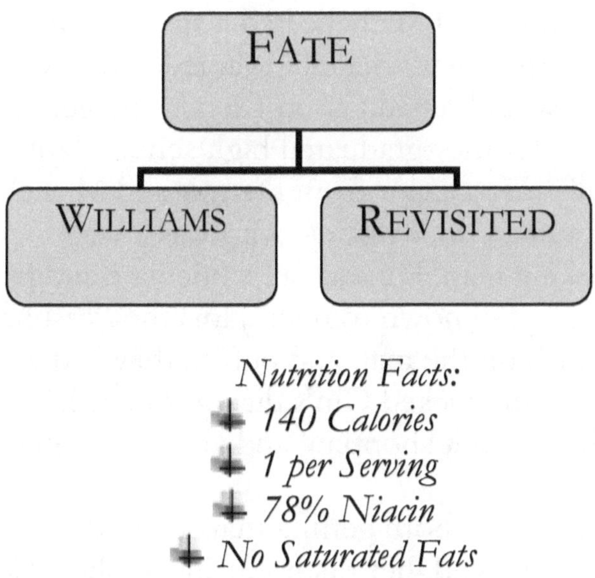

J anis the Pearl loved Michelle Lakes-Williams. She was an upstanding citizen who paid her taxes on time, loved making people smile and had a fantastic career with the federal government. And let's not think about that gorgeous $450,000 home she owned. Michelle has certainly done well for herself. From poor, nappy-headed black girl to a career-driven woman with power and control left one to be desired. It was because of Michelle that Janis the Pearl decided to go back to school, after twenty years of doing nothing but mixing drinks at parties, and get her G.E.D. She could remember when she met Michelle. They were in junior high school. They liked and fought over the same boy. They both screwed the same boy. The boy played games. Janis the Pearl got tired of *sharing* the boy. So she quit the boy and befriended Michelle. Even in junior high school Michelle had a strong, intimidating presence. She knew what she wanted and how to get it.

They would remain good friends and get married together after they graduated high school. Janis eventually met a sailor from Detroit and Michelle met a man named Gin Williams, who was a very hardworking man. He was tall, chocolate and had the dreamiest eyes known to man. Janis the Pearl had a secret crush on the man and before they had a double wedding, Janis sucked Gin's dick in Michelle's bed while she was out shopping and gave him some good pussy.

"Since we're both getting married to different people," Janis said, her tits bouncing as she rode Gin's thick dick, "We might as well fuck. Kiss the single life good bye."

Gin, such the eager, whorish lover, didn't really love Michelle. He wanted a wife who would stay at home and cook and clean and do what he needed to run a successful household. He wouldn't trade in the women, he wouldn't trade in men sucking his dick on the down low and he wouldn't give a bitch his heart.

When they tied the knot, Janis to Earl and Michelle to Gin, they lived happily ever after.

Not so.

Michelle moved away and started her life with her husband, cutting Janis off completely. Janis gave birth to a beautiful baby girl. She would love and nurture her daughter more than her husband. Janis hated the fact that Michelle moved away from her. She hated the fact that the man she really did want was married to Michelle and the thought of Michelle enjoying that big dick depressed her.

She started losing weight and neglecting her nutrition. A wonderful wife in the beginning, she started slacking off. Her husband was never happy with her.

She constantly complained about every little thing. She prided herself in her daughter. She gave her the nickname *Autumn's Rose*, because she was born at the start of Fall. She was a very gorgeous young woman. She had her father's cheeks, eyes and nose.

Whatever her daughter wanted she gave her without question. Earl didn't like his daughter being spoiled. And to make matters worse, Earl's mother, Josephine, didn't like Janis, didn't attend the wedding and swore to everyone that Autumn's Rose wasn't her grandchild. This angered Earl and the rest of the family.

They lashed out at Josephine, telling her to stop being incredulous and, feeling betrayed, Josephine moved out of town, met a decent man, married him and never contacted her children again.

After Autumn's Rose got in the seventh grade, Earl decided that he'd had enough of the marriage. Rumor had it that Michelle moved back to Miami-Dade County but no one knew her whereabouts.

Between teaching Autumn's Rose about her developing body and her acquisitions about boys, she started the transition back to the single life while sitting back watching her soon-to-be-ex-husband frolic with a much younger woman, named Jonnie Bullard, who was about 20 years old and already knocked up with a baby. This angered Autumn's Rose. She felt betrayed. How could her parents divorce? Was it her fault? Was it something she did wrong?

"Mama, why did you just give up on Daddy?"

Janis was lying in her bed, with the covers over her naked body. She had been crying into the night and endless coffee cups. She needed nicotine and caffeine.

"He left me, Baby. He's divorcing me for that young girl."

"Who is she?" Autumn's Rose asked, vowing to find out.

"Her name is Jonnie Bullard. Her people are from the Bahamas. She lives not too far from here. As a matter of fact she attends our church."

Autumn's Rose closed her eyes.

Before Janis knew it her daughter was in high school and doing very well for herself. She fell in love with a boy and Janis loved him very much. He was kind and decent and sweet. She hated Jonnie with a passion and when Autumn's parents were officially divorced she was suicidal. But that quickly blew over.

Before her daughter fell in deeper with her love for the young man, she lost a lot of sleep, wondering would she ever find her friend Michelle Lakes-Williams.

She missed her very much.

But she missed her husband Gin even more.

J anis got a rude awakening one day in church. Jonnie had come late and when she showed up, clad in the most gorgeous dress she'd ever seen and her hair done up in Shirley Temple curls, she had her new husband on her arm. Earl.

Earl and Jonnie didn't acknowledge Janis when they walked by. Janis didn't even look at them. She tugged on her flowing skirt and ran her shaking hands through her hair. Church members gossiped and whispered their disapprovals. But Janis didn't care. Life went on.

Autumn glared at Jonnie. She sat on the back pew, fanning herself with a hand-held paper fan. In her heart was blackness. She wanted Jonnie to pay for destroying her family.

Did she really destroy them? Or were my parents on the verge of breaking up before Jonnie came along? Either way Daddy should have never divorced mom. For better or for worse. 'Til death do you part. What happened to those vows?

Jonnie stood up from the pew and whispered something to Earl. Earl smiled, kissed the rock on her ring finger and Jonnie disappeared to the restroom.

Autumn looked at her mom across the room. Janis was talking with one of the men. She looked sad. She wiped a few tears away.

Autumn stood up and went to the back of the church.

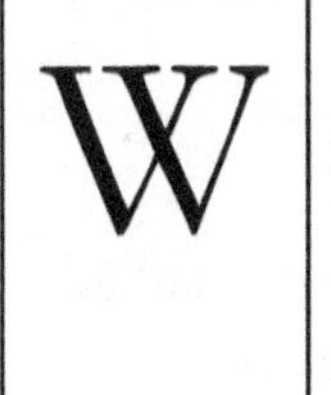

hen she entered the restroom she bumped into Jonnie. "Excuse me, ma'am. I didn't mean to bump into you," said Jonnie, extending her hand. "I'm Jonnie."

"I'm…Pleasure," said Autumn, summing her up. *Whore. Slut. Home wrecker.*

"Nice to meet you." Jonnie turned to face herself in the mirror. "It's hot in here. Don't you agree?" Jonnie asked rhetorically, patting her curls and tilting her head like Ginger Rogers. "My dress is starting to stick to my skin. I feel rather…itchy. I shouldn't have worn cotton in the heat."

Attracted to her, Autumn's eyes danced all over her gorgeous body. Nice butt. Huge breasts. Heart-shaped lips. Gorgeous face. *Oh my God! Why am I looking at this woman like this?*

"Nice to meet you, too. And it's always hot in this stupid church! So are you *new* here?"

"No. I have been attending for some months now. I moved down here from good ole Savannah, Georgia!"

"I never *noticed* you," said Autumn. "Probably because I stay to myself. Are you married?"

Jonnie's eyes lit up. "Yes. To a man named Earl."

"Earl?" Autumn was shaking her head. "I don't know him. Does he have any children?"

Jonnie looked Autumn deep in the eyes from the reflection in the mirror and said, "No. He said he doesn't have any kids. And quite honestly I don't want to give him any."

The tears fell from Autumn's eyes.

He disowned me.

Jonnie turned to face Autumn. "I should…get back to the service."

Autumn's lips were inches from Jonnie's. The chemistry built from their toes and mounted all over their breasts. Jonnie couldn't breath and Autumn wanted to know what she tasted like.

If Daddy can have her then so can I. I got a plan. I hope it worked.

Jonnie reached up and touched Autumn's lips. They started to kiss, pouring into each other like the sunlight through the worn curtains. Like poetry they crafted prose and words and similes on their lips and passion dancing in their juices spilling into their panties.

Autumn told Jonnie to sit on the toilet. She pushed Jonnie's legs back and put her nose down between her legs, smelling her pussy. It smelled of perfume and some type of expensive lotion. She knew the fragrance was expensive because the smell lingered like butterflies in the sunlight.

Jonnie couldn't breathe. She wanted Autumn and had wanted her ever since the first day he saw her in this church. She used to dream about her and desire her and need her when she played with her pussy, bringing herself to earth shattering heights. When Earl made love to her she thought of Autumn.

Autumn took off Jonnie's panties and tossed them on the floor. Jonnie held her legs back and let Autumn get a visual of her pretty pussy. Autumn dove into her, tasting her sweaty flesh, making her moan obscenities.

Jonnie's legs trembled. Autumn was glorious. She knew just how to touch her. Earl ate her pussy like she was a piece of T-bone steak. He was good but he was too aggressive. Too strong. Too demanding.

But with Autumn it was different.

"Do you love Earl?" Autumn asked, playing with her pussy. Her hand on her soul revived her, and she almost forgot her plan.

"No."

"Then why are you with him?"

"I needed a roof over my head…Damn, baby. You eat some good pussy."

"Leave…"

"What the fuck is going on in here!" came the boom from a familiar male voice. Autumn paused, and didn't dare get scared. Jonnie, on the other hand, was shaking out of her mind.

She tried to stand up but she fell back on the toilet. She bent over and took up her panties, putting them on.

Autumn stood up and turned to face the man who denied her.

"*Hi*, Earl."

J onnie was confused. "Do you know him?" she asked Autumn. "I need to know. Because the way you looked at him when you stood up and said his name is a bit unusual for two people who never met."

"Yes. I know him quite well."

Earl was so upset he couldn't breathe. He pushed past Autumn and took Jonnie by the neck and he squeezed as hard as he could.

"We just got married and you're cheating on me already?"

Autumn took him by the arm. "No, Earl. Don't hurt her. You could go to jail."

The thought of jail scared him, so he released her and took a few steps back. He was deeply heart broken and devastated.

Jonnie regained her composure, swallowing hard.

"Earl. I can explain."

"How do you explain this?"

"I was just…" Jonnie looked at Autumn with contempt in her eyes. "You lied. You *do* know Earl. How do you know him? Is he your ex boyfriend?"

"No," said Autumn with a smile. "I'm his daughter. The one he hid from you."

Jonnie started vomiting all over the floor.

Mission Accomplished, Autumn thought, walking out of the bathroom.

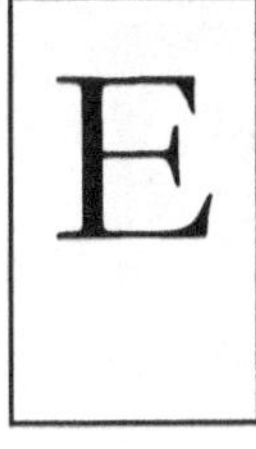

Earl filed for an annulment. He kicked Jonnie out of the house and Autumn never told her mother what happened in the bathroom at church. All Janis knew was that Earl's marriage blew up in his face in a matter of days.

Janis was pleased.

When Autumn's Rose graduated, she moved away from her mother. She wanted to branch out and do her own thing without Mommy holding her hand. No matter how Pearl protested, Autumn wasn't hearing it. She wanted to discover America. She went to college and focused on getting an education, amongst other things.

After four years she graduated with honors and felt good about her future. She had no desire to contact Earl. She didn't care to share with him anything she had going on in her life.

Harboring the death of a very special person, she dedicated her life to getting over her loss, and getting through her pain.

She vowed it on her life.

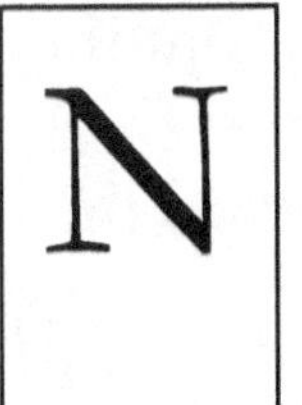

Now Janis sat in the Main Lobby at Miami Jackson Memorial Hospital, with tears in her eyes. She cried so hard her throat was sore. Michelle. Her good friend. Was dead. After all those years of looking for her and wanting to know if she was ok, Michelle had found her. Janis was mixing drinks at a friend's party that Michelle happened to be attending a few months ago. They ran into each other and they embraced and sobbed and ignored other party goers and they talked and talked and talked and got caught up in what one or the other was doing.

"Where's Gin?" asked Janis, her heart racing. *I can't wait to see him.*

Michelle said, sadly, "Gin died so long ago."

"Oh, Michelle," said Janis, hugging her.

Good dick gone to waste.

Now Janis mourned the loss of her friend. There was so much she wanted to tell Michelle but she felt the time wasn't right. She didn't know how to bring herself to tell her.

We were just at a party together. We were having a good time.

I met Fate Williams, her daughter. She was a gorgeous girl.

I wished I knew where my daughter was and what she was doing. But she cut all ties with me and said she wanted to live her life and not worry about me.

She wrote me a letter and told me I was a pretty, smart woman and that I would survive without her.

Oh, Michelle. Now I don't have anybody.

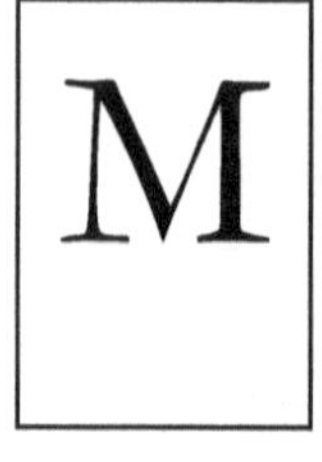

Michelle Williams lay on a medical gurney. Her body was being examined. When she dropped unconscious at her party the paramedics thought she was dead. But they felt a weak pulse. On the way to the hospital, while she was on a gurney in the back of the ambulance, she flat lined. A short, gracious-looking fellow initiated shock treatment. Each time the two pads touched Michelle her body jumped.

But nothing happened.

"She's dead," was all he said.

*P*oisoning *Mama was the best thing I could have done to her.* "Fate Williams" was on my I.D. from my job. I should have taken my credentials off while I was parking my car but I didn't have the energy. I worked too much. Then I had two sons who drove me absolutely nuts. Between keeping up with their grades and making sure they weren't into too much MySpace or Black Planet, supervising them to ensure they weren't trying experimental drugs and booze, monitoring what they watched on TV and put in their bellies, I didn't have much time for myself.

I entered the hospital. My tired eyes red, I decided to come see about my dead Mama alone. This was my cross to bear. Not Red's. Bad enough that one day God was going to judge me for killing the whorish bitch.

All the years of abuse, all the taunting, all the lies and the pain she inflicted on me has gone to the grave with you, Bitch!

I told my girlfriend Red to stay home and watch the boys.

Good. After all these months of being together I haven't met any of Red's family. Was she ashamed of me? Was she trying to hide me like I was a four leaf clover amongst the well-cut green grass? I asked about her parents and a glow befell her face. She said her Mom's in a nursing home up in Toronto. And her father was a senile cop trying to hold onto his badge. She said she had two sisters and one brother. Yet she didn't have any photos of them. She claimed she lost all her photos in Hurricane Andrew back in 1992. I understood that. Because I lost a lot of things I could never get back in that storm as well.

Slowly realizing that some folks in the Lobby had bigger problems than I faced, I hesitantly went to the front desk and told them my mother was rushed there. I wanted to run. Why did I come here anyway?

"Her name?" asked the gorgeous RN.

"Michelle Williams."

The fat woman's eyes lowered to the desk.

"What's wrong?" I asked.

"Come this way. You can speak to the doctor."

"I already know she's dead."

A few days later, Red was in a myriad of thoughts. She was working at the CVS store on South Beach. She was a Pharmaceutical Technician. Tears falling down her face, she took a break and walked out into the drizzling rain, heading for her car. Her cell phone rang. She looked at the caller I.D. flashing in her face.

My baby. Fate Williams.

Inhaling deeply, Red answered. "What's up, Baby."

"What's up, Baby? You say that like we don't have problems."

"I *know* we do, Fate. We have talked about this twenty-eight times today and you're still not satisfied."

"I wouldn't care if it was ninety four times to the square root of your asshole. You lied to me. Yes, I came back to you. Yes, I want our sons united. They do share the same Daddy; the man you stole from me back when we were in high school…Dunn McKinney was the love of my life!"

Dunn McKinney…Dunn…Oh, God! Even the mention of your name pricks the love for you out of my heart and presents to my soul your passion we once shared. How I miss you, baby. I will never get over your death. I will always love you.

Red placed her arms on the top of her car, leaning against it. She looked at the S Metro Bus slowly parading up 5th Street, past the Walgreen's.

"Get over it. That was over ten years ago, Gurl."

"When my clit extended an inch I wasn't a girl anymore. I became a woman."

"OK. I don't need Anatomy as given by Fate 101. And you're being a whiny brat."

"Well shut the fuck up 202 and tell me why did you lie?"

"You know why. And your Mom has died, Fate. We should talk about…"

"Like hell!"

"Baby, we should *talk* about it."

"Talk about *what*, Lolita Harvey? How she has hurt me?"

"She's dead, Fate. Damn. It's in God's hands now. And call me *Red*, Fate. Please."

"Oh. I'm sorry. Did I hit a nerve that happens to be in your skull and not your sweet tasting pussy? I'm *sorry*, Lianna Gregory. That is your *real* name."

Angrily, Red gripped the phone.

Why does she say my fake name like that? I know why? When we started dating I told her my name was Lolita Harvey, when in fact my birth name is Lianna Gregory. I had fake I.D.'s made, fake certificates and all. I like Lolita better. I didn't want to be the girl I used to be in high school. That cookie cutter bitch that was too afraid to stand for anything.

Good thing I went to court and legally got my name changed, so there wasn't a need for the fake paperwork anymore. The courts authenticated it all. Why can't Fate understand that after my Baby Daddy was brutally shot to death, a huge part of me died with him? Why can't she understand that me and her both had his sons the same year, and that I wanted my son to know his brother?

I had to some kind of way worm my way into her life to make that happen and now that it has I can't change the outcome.

"You know…"

"I know what, Red?"

"Your Mama…"

"My Mama *what?*"

Red unlocked her car and got inside, sticking the key in the ignition. She turned it on and turned on the AC, so she didn't sweat to death. The bass kicked in so hard it felt like her seat punched her in the back so she turned the tunes off.

"I know you miss her."

"I don't, Red."

Red watched a few fine black men walk by.

Damn, they are fine as hell. If only I didn't enjoy eating pussy. I haven't had any dick in years. Not since my child's Daddy died.

"So you aren't going to plan the funeral?"

"No. I mean, Yea. I don't know, Red. Mama has hurt me so much in my lifetime."

"She's dead, baby."

"*So!*"

"Baby, it's not good to hold onto your anger."

"Listen to Martha Stewart Living."

"Martha Stewart Living can go to hell. And I resent that shit."

"I resent your lies."

"Oh, *Boy*! Will you let me live that down?"

"I don't know. You came into my life under false pretenses. You had me thinking you were one person and you turned out to be someone else. I found out my ex boyfriend, my child's Dad, also fathered your son. They are brothers. You knew all along and I didn't have a clue. You then told me Mama shot and killed my Baby Daddy when she didn't have enough to buy his drugs. So yea I'm still pissed."

"Well, I guess this isn't a good time to tell you that I got a tattoo today."

"You *what*?"

"It's a really small one. I got a name."

Fate tried to laugh. "Does it say Fate Williams?"

"No, Fate. But it says something."

"Like what?"

"Let it go. I'll show you later."

"Tell me now!"

"No!"

"Fuck it then. I am not begging you."

"You need to let the past go, Gurl. Yea, I fucked up. But you said you forgave me."

"*Ha*!"

"I thought that when you moved back in with me you let all that go."

"You thought wrong. And just because you sucked on my pussy doesn't mean I'm over it."

Red shook her head, looking herself over in the rear-view mirror.

"Fate. Why do you argue and fight with me? What happened to that fun, loving Jamaican woman I fell in love with?"

"She's still here. She just doesn't trust you like she used to."

"Then why are we together?"

"Because, good or bad, this pussy belongs to you. Hell I tattooed *Red* above my clit. Yet you couldn't get my name tattooed on you. I still want to know what kind of new tat you have."

Oh, no she didn't! "Is that all I own? Your *pussy?* What about your heart?"

"My heart is incarcerated at the moment. And if my soul had daytime minutes I'd have to buy some more because right now I'm just too upset with you."

Red closed her eyes when Fate's mournful voice drifted through the phone.

Baby. Please don't cry. I know we won't get over our problems over night. I know I lied and deceived you. I know what your Mama has done to you. Abusing you. Emotionally destroying you. Even after she died your Mom has a hold on you, Baby. But you have to let it go or it will destroy you.

"Red. I don't mean to take it out on you." Red pushed in the car lighter and whipped out a half-smoked joint. "…It's just a lot to deal with. I never expected her to die any time soon. I remember when I was a little girl. I used to beg God to kill the sadistic whore but he never did. And now she drops dead?"

The lighter popped out. Red took it by the black handle and pressed the glowing tip up to the joint. "God heard your plea." She pulled on it, holding the smoke in her lungs.

"God is *love*. I don't think it was him that killed Mama."

I need a fifth of Hennessy. "You're right. It was her time to go. Rumor has it that someone poisoned her…"

With rat poison and weed killer, Fate thought bitterly. "I heard that, too. I don't know who could have done such a thing. The cops are investigating everybody who was at the party. *Anyways.* I have to meet with Paul's Funeral Home tomorrow. I have to go over the arrangements."

Red's brows rose. "Can I be present?"

"No. I got it."

Red started to cough, beating her chest, her eyes watering. "What do you mean? I have a right to be included. We're in a committed relationship."

"Well this ship has sailed, Popeye. And I need to do this alone."

"Like hell. And what about the boys? They should be included as well."

"Goddamn, Red. Fine."

She is really pissed off at me. Maybe I should eat her pussy from the back tonight and slide her favorite toy deep in her tight asshole the way she loved.

"Do you hate me?"

"*No.* I love you."

"Then include your family in the funeral arrangements."

"Ok. But I might wait until Wednesday."

What? Hell, No, Fate! "That's in two days. We already made plans. We're taking the boys to Haulover Beach and we're barbequing, Baby."

"Oh, Well. We have to cancel."

Red looked at her watch, running a hand over her low-hair cut. *My break is almost over.* "That's a negative, Houston. We are not canceling our plans because you want to plan your abusive mother's funeral."

"Says who?"

"Says *me*! I'm the Aggressor. I'm your Man."

"You're a woman with a fat pussy who happens to dress and act like a man. Big difference."

"Fate. *Please.*"

"Red, drop it. You can't always get what you want."

"You're a spoiled little bitch!"

"Tell it to my clit, bitch!"

"And you're sleeping on the couch."

"Bitch, it's a pullout bed and I'll be just fine sleeping on it."

Red's blood boiled.

There's no way you're canceling our date with the boys over your goddamn Mama!

"And you're telling the boys you canceled our big day."

"YOU TELL THEM."

"Tell it to my clit, bitch!"

Red hung up.

athering her wits, and stubbing out the rest of the joint, Red squeezed anti bacterial gel in her hands and rubbed them together. Reaching into her back pocket, she pulled out a folded note. She kissed it and attempted to open it but she didn't.

Why doesn't Fate want to include me in the funeral arrangements? Aren't we a couple? Doesn't she love me and the boys? Am I truly enough for her?

What if I'm not?

Red slowly opened the letter.

t Jackson Memorial Hospital, Michelle's body was being prepared for autopsy. Doctor James was talking to one of the nurses. They were holding a series of folders and having the police combing their asses.

They wanted to know how Michelle Lakes-Williams died. The Feds also wanted to know. They vowed to get to the bottom of it.

Would they?

 *love Fate more than I have ever loved anyone. I hated to admit it, but I loved her more than my child's Daddy, Dunn, also. I feel so connected to her. I can't live without her.*
She makes me happy, mad and sad in ways no one ever has.

No one has ever captured my heart the way she had. Our love making is always an event.

She makes me come in ways I never knew existed. Without her in my life how will I go on? She's the reason why I am so happy! She's my sunshine and my joy.

So why are we arguing and fighting all the time?

Red carefully read over the letter.

Red,

What's up! I want to be in your world because I really feel God put us together.

[Well Fate, if you felt that way then why are you trying to push me away?]

I'm writing in text form, the way I do when we text with cell phones, because it's easier to say what I have to say and it's quicker to write.

[I wish you would have verbally told me this. It means more when you say it, instead of being impersonal and writing it.]

I have tried nothing like this before but I want to be happy so I'm willing to do this for the first time in my life to be in a relationship with someone I care about, which is YOU.

[Ha! You want me? Are you sure? The way you talked down to me on the phone when I was at work? Commitment means thinking outside of the box and being faithful in thought, in your heart and soul. Yet you said your pussy belongs to me, and not your entire body. That doesn't sit well with me.]

I want us to just accept each other for who we are. We are soul mates. We will last and finally get it right because we want to and because we are ready to start over fresh with no judgments of any kind, please.

[No *judgments*, Fate? You didn't mean a word of this letter when you wrote it. When you moved back in with me you gave me this letter and you said you wanted to move on, yet when we spoke on the phone you keep throwing my mistakes in my face.]

When I come to you I will trust you and I do trust you. I have and will make sure I put all my baggage behind me.

[You didn't put the baggage behind you. I take it you didn't get a clue from Erykah Badu. Bag Lady. You g'on hurt your back. Carrying all those bags like that. Well, bitch. You're about to crowd my space. You're pushing me away. So you better pack light.]

Thanks for going to therapy with me, to help me deal with my past. This truly allowed me to open up about my life and work on myself, and that made me a better person. A better mother. And a better lover.

[Bullshit, Fate. Therapy helped temporarily. Now you slipped back to the state of mind you were in before therapy. A better lover? *Please.*]

I don't know how much more of this I can take.

[Honestly I don't know how much I can take, either. Maybe we've said and done too much. Let's call it a quits.]

Deeply upset, Red crumpled the letter in her hand.
     And tossed it out the window.

I was writing some thoughts down. How could I not? I had a lot on my mind. Maybe I was wasting my time. All this goddamn writing served what purpose, exactly? I didn't want to be an idiot. But they say writing could be therapeutic.
     Yea, right.

I inhale convulsions
igniting in Rome explosions
on my face I lay in ruins
reminiscent of elegant intrusions
Mama pushed me out her womb
and threw me out a few months after June
Why does Satan try to attack my stellar vessels
Boxed with chocolates: bite into my cerebrum

Many want my taut body
they want to taste the result of my mind's gate
open them to find my rates
too high for the Dow Jones
up three points
down the slope of my pussy by six
go to bed by nine
setting clocks
I can't tell time
Booker T Washington on my mind
sleeping on both sets of sheets
Hold an umbrella over my head as I teach
I inhale convulsions
On my face
lay Rome
in ruins

I loved my lifestyle, even though I didn't ask for it and if I could change it all I would because, in some unexplainable way, I *did* want a husband and a family.

But I know in my heart of hearts that will never, ever happen. Dick turned me off, quite frankly. And men were full of shit.

These days they couldn't think past their little heads and when the little head decided to go ballistic and get all hard and Gangsta, men really showed their asses. And I didn't have time to babysit a grown ass man who was supposed to be the carvers of the earth.

I didn't know what point I was trying to prove by writing that poem, but I did know I felt good when I wrote the last stroke on the "s" in "ruins."

Looking at my diamond-encrusted watch (a take-me-back-gift from Red, my Butch Bitch), I realized it was about 10:39 p.m.

I needed to check in on my son Renaldo and his brother (Red's son) Jameson (they share the same baby father, rest his soul) but I really didn't need to because I could hear them playing John Madden '08 on Playstation 3.

They loved and breathed that game console the way I used to breathe my Atari and Miss Pac Man and Pole Position back in the day.

I turned on Patti Labelle. I didn't know what song played, but I did know she was just what I needed right now.

My sons turned up the volume on the game a little louder. Oh, no!

Not over Patti!

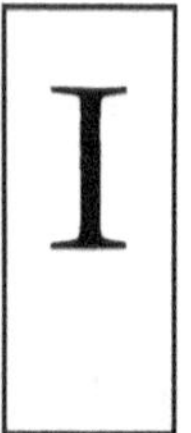

I stood up, clad in night clothes and red furry slippers (shaped like the male penis) and beat on the wall. My breasts jiggled.

"Turn that shit down!"

"SORRY MOM!" They said in unison.

But the sound didn't relent much. I waited about five minutes.

Busying myself in the process with putting a few rollers in my hair, I thought about me and Red's phone conversation.

She could be a bitch when she wanted to be. I didn't want to deal with Mama's funeral and I didn't want to talk about it. I still hated her.

The sound of my children's video game didn't decrease and my anger did. I hated when my sons didn't pay me no mind. I opened the bedroom door, stamped down the hall, with my hand on my hip and kicked their door open. They were startled, dropping the joysticks on the floor.

"*Mom.*" Renaldo turned it down. He and Jameson had on Scooby-Do pajama pants and do-rags tied over their silky wavy hair.

Jameson gave him a secret look.

I unplugged the game and slapped them both in the back of the head when they tried to get rowdy.

I stood my ground. "Don't you two have school tomorrow?"

"Yes," they said together. I thought it was cute. They always said the same things.

"Why are you still up?" I hated that 50 Cent poster on the wall. He was aiming a pistol at the camera lens.

Renaldo challenged me. "Ma. I'm not sleepy. I'm not a little kid anymore. I want more freedom!"

Jameson was his back up. "*Yea.* And I don't want to go to sleep, either."

"Word?" I said, putting my hands on my hips.

"Mama, people don't say 'word' anymore," Renaldo corrected, standing up, stretching. He wrapped his arms around me and I saw Jameson in my peripheral trying to plug up the game.

"Yea. Get with the times," said Jameson. When he picked up the plug I back kicked him in the chest and he slammed into the wall.

"*Bed time!*"

"MAMA!" shouted Jameson. He called me "Mama" and he called Red "Ma."

"NOW!" I said more sternly. I meant business.

"Come on, bruh," said Renaldo in defeat. He crawled in his bed and pulled the covers up to his chest.

"…Let's go to bed. Red isn't home and Mom has to use the toy by herself."

My mouth fell open in shock. "What did you say?"

"Come on, Mom," said Jameson, snickering at my shock. "We are teenage boys. We chase girls and we know storks don't deliver babies. We hear you through the walls."

"And can you say yuck?" said Renaldo, covering his face.

I wanted to die.

"GO TO BED!"

Embarrassed, I ran out of the room. They were laughing at me.

I didn't care what anybody said.

Knowing my sons have listened to me and Red get our groove on sickened me to my stomach. I never thought they would ever hear us through the walls.

I got to be more careful.

Sitting at my desk, a composition notebook open before me, my heart lay in ruins as if it was Rome. Mama tore down my Acropolis years ago, back when I was a little girl. She used to eat my pussy better than any man ate hers. I never understood why Mama wanted to destroy me.

I never understood why God allowed the dumb bitch to give me my first orgasm when I was seven years old. I remember the day well. I didn't understand the feeling that came over my body.

But I did know that I started to love when she ate my pussy and made me come and I didn't want it to stop. Not to mention she took my virginity with a banana when I was 13 years old.

I remember the day well.

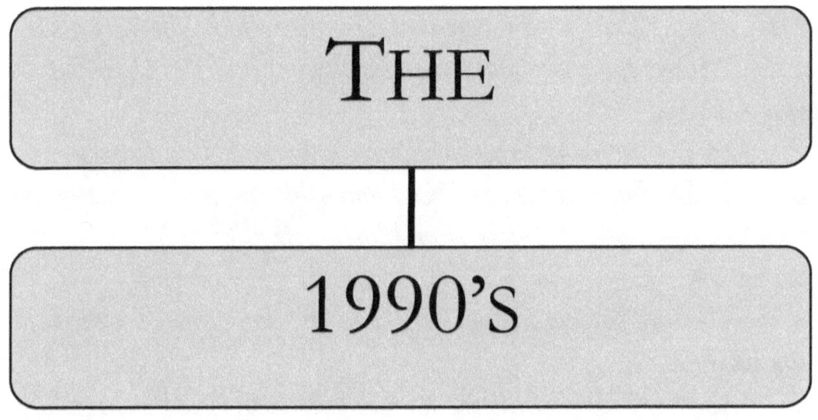

*I*t was just after Easter, and I was going over to a friend's house. Initially, Mama said I could stay over for a few days, because she was going out of town. She worked for the federal government and we hardly spent time together. I didn't like being alone in the house all the time so Mama trusted my friends and allowed for me to stay over.

But Mama had a dark side. She was starting to get jealous of me staying over. I wasn't allowed to talk to boys and when she caught them trying to tell me hello or good bye when I got out of school, she whipped my ass so badly when I got home I couldn't think straight.

And let's not talk about the men who crept in and out of my room when I was growing up. She did this behind Daddy's back. I never understood why she allowed it to happen. Maybe she hated me that much.

But after a while I stopped questioning it and I just let nature take its course.

Mama claimed I put people before her and it didn't sit well with her.

When I got to my friend's house I wasn't there for an hour and Mama knocked on the door. In fact she pounded on it. Miss Rogers, my friend Gloria's mom, answered. She was a bit upset. Mama took one look at Miss Rogers and darkness fell over her face.

Driving me home, she didn't say a word. I didn't say a word. I closed my eyes and sucked down my anger. I didn't want to go back home. The more time I spent away from Mama the better.

When we got home, Mama closed the door when I went into the kitchen.

"So that's why you want to stay over to Gloria's all the time."

I opened the refrigerator, ignoring her.

Mama poured a drink in the blender and some strawberry daiquiri. She turned it on and the whirl filled my ears.

"You don't hear me talking to you?" she asked, turning the blender off.

My heart hammering through my chest, I tried to keep myself under control.

She took out a small glass and filled it to the brim with her concoction.

"FATE!"

"Yes, Ma." I drank the milk from the carton. She snatched me by the hair and slapped me so hard the milk carton flew across the kitchen.

"You're letting that whore suck your pussy?"

I was disgusted. "No, Ma! Nothing like that is going on!"

"Did you ask could you drink my milk? Do you think I have time to keep running back and forth to the market to buy this and that?"

My throat constricted into my chest. A ball formed in my throat. "No, ma'am!"

She handed me the drink. "Drink it up."

I did. It tasted good. But I didn't know why she gave it to me.

"You're a whore! I'm glad your Daddy is dead. He wouldn't approve…"

"Approve of what, Mama? That you have destroyed me? That you have turned me into society's enemy?" I set the glass on the counter and wanted to pack my things and leave town and never talk to her again.

She sat on the table, looking me up and down, her eyes becoming the sinister creatures they were. She stared at me so lustfully I felt like I was naked.

"Get naked."

"No, Ma. I'm on my period."

"GET NAKED!"

I felt helpless and worthless. The way she talked to me reminded one of a homeless dog.

"Mama! No! I don't want you touching me anymore. I can't stand it. It grosses me out. I want a normal life. Can't you understand that? Is that too much to ask? There's a bulletin in school that says if anyone is touching me inappropriately to call the police. Maybe I should."

"Don't test me, bitch!"

"My teacher said I am a Queen. I'm not a bitch!"

"You're the Queen's feces. You know what they do with feces? They flush it, whore."

Mama, *don't* you love me?

"Why do you hate me?"

"I don't hate you. No. I hate myself."

I believe you do.

"Mama, why? I'm your daughter…"

"I should have had an abortion."

Hearing those words hurt me beyond reason.

"Why do you hurt me?"

Tears fell down my eyes. I really wanted an understanding. Why a grown woman would molest her own child.

There has to be a sick bitch living in her pussy somewhere, controlling her needs through what she thought she wanted and desired.

Mama tilted her head.

"Your tears don't move me, Chile. Do you think the white man care about a black bitch's tears? They used to rape our women back in the slave days. Hell your great grandfather is a white man who used to own a plantation."

"Who cares, Mama? Don't tell me now!"

Her eyes were glowing coals.

"LISTEN!"

"No. For years I wanted to know my grandparents and you made up stories about them. Now you want to tell me?"

"Shut up, bitch! My Mama bared nine of the white man's babies. She was raped every time. She didn't have a chance. Mama sold me to the white man but after a few weeks they gave me back to her. She didn't wanna loose her six penances or her efficiency on the white man's property. My aunt, my Mom's sister, was forced to eat my Mama's pussy in front of white plantation owners for entertainment."

I had to lean on the counter. The room was spinning at the revelation.

"…She then had to suck them all off and swallow their seeds. 'Die in the belly of the whore!' they said together, playing their music and drinking their wine. When my aunt became

pregnant, the white man cut her baby from her womb and hung her from a fucking tree. Where were your tears then, bitch? How do you think I feel knowing my father used to whip slaves, sell them as property and rape my mother for his own sick pleasures?"

Oh, God! This is the first she's spoken of this. It helps me understand her and what she is doing to me a little better.

Mama went on, wiping water from her eyes. She refused to cry. She had up reinforced steel walls. "I pay bills. Your job is to cook my food. Clean my house. Go to school and make good grades. Eat my pussy and make me come. And give me your body when I see fit. God put you here to be my sex slave, bitch!"

I decided to stand up to her. Enough was enough.

She can't make me suffer for another man's mistakes!

"Show me in the Bible where it says it's all right for a mother to abuse her child."

"Sure!" She hopped up to her feet, opened the kitchen drawer and pulled out a huge Bible. Taking a black Sharpie, she opened the good book and wrote

FATE IS MY WHORE!
SHE WAS PUT HERE AS MY SLAVE!

She held the book up so my eyes could drink her edit. With no scruples, she guardedly walked over to me, one foot carefully crossing the other one, like a tight rope walker. She looked me over the way a master looked over his property. She then hugged me close, holding the Bible.

I was getting extremely tired. My eyes were getting heavy.

"You see…in the beginning was the Word. The Word was God and the Word was with God. And so were you."

She slowly pulled away and licked the tears from my face. I wanted to puke. Her saliva on me didn't sit well. I wiped it off and she slapped my hands.

I was about to give up and give in. I couldn't fight her any longer. If I told someone, what if they didn't believe me?

"Mama. I don't have anybody. All I have is you."

"Yes. All you have is me. You don't even have God. Read your History. Even Harriet Tubman returned to her master in the beginning. Yes, Child. She tried to taste a piece of heaven from the sugar bowl and was caught. She ran when her master got the raw hide. She hid in a pig pen. But she didn't have food, nothing to drink. Night fall was on the horizon. She knew what was to come when she returned, yet she did just that: went back. And that's the point you're at in your life. If you leave this house, where will you go? What will you eat or drink? God has forsaken you. He doesn't love you, Girl!"

She was right. I had nowhere else to go. "I don't think God has forsaken me, Mama. Maybe you have but certainly not God. I love God above all else."

The words were blows to her gut. "You love God above all else?" Mama taunted me, running her hand through my unruly hair.

"Yes."

"The Bible says that?"

"Yes, Ma."

"The Bible also says you're my whore."

This crippled me to hear. My own mother treating me this way. How could a mother treat her child like she wasn't worth the very breath she breathed? "You wrote that, Mama."

"Because you saw me write it, correct?"

I whispered, "Yes."

"So you don't believe it?"

I was shaking my head feverishly. "No."

"Yet mortal man wrote the Bible, correct?"

"Yes." What was she getting at?

"Did you see mortal man write the scriptures and the verses?"

I looked deep into her evil eyes. "No, Mama."

"Yet you believe what is written? Have you contested the versus? Read them for yourself to see what they mean to you?"

"No."

"So why do you believe a man made Bible, believing in versus you never saw Paul or Matthew or John write? Yet you don't believe what I wrote, when you saw me write it?"

She had me.

"You're right, Mama. I still believe in the Bible. It's been read and studied and taught for decades."

I had a longing to sing. I heard slaves used to sing spirituals in the face of danger and it got them through. Maybe I should try it. So I opened my heart and I belted.

"… Jesus loves me, this I know…."

"For the Bible tells me so, 'ey, Fate?" Mama mocked me. "…Sing it with me. Yes, Jesus loves meee. Yes, Jesus loves me," I sung with Mama, tears dripping from my chin. "Yes. Jesus loves meee. For the Bible tells me so…"

"Fate. God doesn't love whores. God doesn't love white men who rape black women and give birth to innocent babies who grow up to be shamed. Where was God when my aunt's baby was cut from her womb? Where was He when four white men clad in fancy garments tied her to a huge tree in the back of the Big House and cut her hair from her scalp, spitting on her?"

I was horrified. The way Mama made the revelation filled my head with grotesque images. I didn't want those images, but she was planting them in my brain and they refused to leave. I shook with anger.

Mama hugged me. I cringed inside. My arms remained at my sides. They were unmoving. She then kissed my ear lobe. She started to sensually whisper, rubbing her body against mine.

"I can tell you what kind of blade they used. It was a bayonet used in the Danish Army many rains ago, Child. The blade was 137 mm…"

Mama was tracing my arms with her fingertips, withdrawn into her story.

She said, "The blade thickness was 2.8mm…I know this, because my mother told me, right after she…tried to…touch…" Mama clammed up. "Never mind, Child. That's not important."

"I can't deal with this, Ma. I'm too young for this."

"If Booker T. Washington can give hoes to children big and strong enough to carry them in the late 1800s then you surely are old enough and strong enough to handle whatever I have to give you. They say God don't put on you more than you can handle."

"I'm not Booker T. And you don't believe in God."

"No. You're not Booker T. Listen…what do you want to be when you grow up?"

Was she serious? "A sniper. To assassinate whoever hurts me."

Mama rolled her eyes. "Funny. You know, to be a sniper takes skill. Determination." Mama was slowly walking around me, looking me up and down. "You have to dress like the white man, eat the white man's food, talk like the white man and believe in the white man's religion. Without those four things you will forever be labeled a nigger in this country."

"Ma…"

"Kiss me, Fate?"

"No…no, Mama," I stuttered. She reached under my dress and grabbed my panties. Her breath on my face she tried to pull them down. I let her.

"You say you're on your period?"
"Yes."
She gripped the string to my tampon and pulled it out, tossing it by the trash. "I love you."
"I doubt that you do…I will stop this…"
Mama took a few steps back and opened the fridge. She pulled out a banana and started to suck on it, as if it was a penis.
"I want fried chicken for dinner. Cook it naked, bitch. I don't want any garments touching your body. I might get jealous."
"No, Mama. I will not do this. I am not your slave. I've been that long enough."
Nothing I said registered in her brain.
I was shaking my head. Saying "no" was like telling her "yes."
"I want you humping my tongue while you cook the mashed potatoes. You got that? "
I got to put a stop to this!
"I am telling the police!"
Threatened, Mama ran up to me and backhanded me.
I slammed into the fridge.

T*hat hurt. I fell to my knees. She pushed me on the floor, my head slamming on the tile. She got on top of me. She was trying to frisk me. Her breathing increased.*
"You are mine. You won't tell anybody anything or I will kill them and kill you, you little cunt!" Her hands were on my pussy. She tried to feel the warmth and I squeezed my legs closed, being defiant. Once I did I remained still, too afraid to breathe or move. I feared her with everything in me.

"Disobedient children won't see the kingdom of heaven."

"And sick mother's will die and see eternal flames!"

Mama was brutally punching me in the gut. Holding my stomach, I have never felt so much pain in my life. She stood up and started kicking me.

Why did she hate me so much? What had she gone through in her life? She was taking out her anger on me and it wasn't fair! I didn't ask to be here! Hadn't she done enough to me?

Crawling in the fetal position, my head was spinning. I was moaning piteously. What was happening to me? Mama nearly looked like a ghost. I felt my legs opening. I saw her sucking the banana.

"Don't worry, baby. This will be quick and pleasurable. The drink I concocted seems to be working. Life is full of shit. I should know. My Mama taught me that. When she, well, you know, took my virginity!"

Mama violated me with a banana.

Taking my virginity. Or was it truly my virginity she took? I lost that when I was a little girl.

I had a lot on my mind. A helluva lot. I didn't even know why I went to therapy a while ago. I thought it would help to talk to a complete stranger about my abuse, but it didn't do anything because I had a lot of issues pulling me in every which direction. I didn't *love* myself. I didn't *care* about myself. Now that I was in my late 20's, I wanted to control my past. I could defend myself now and protect myself.

However, every time I tried to mentally go back and stop Mama from deflowering me it didn't help. Because she didn't really take my virginity in the kitchen with the banana.

I lost that back when I was eight years old, with the men Mama and Daddy had parading through our home. What I went through was a second virginity.

Since mine was forcibly taken, I vowed in my mind that I would give myself to the person I loved when I was older and he or she would love and adore me and take his or her time with me. I did that with Dunn.

Red being there helped more than actually talking to the shrink. She would hold my hand, watch me lash out in anger and listened to me wail my scrutinized life helped me to release some of it. I couldn't forget what happened. Why should I? I was the one who went through it.

Mrs. Martinez, the therapist, with her pale, expensively perfumed skin and designer suits, told me that there were people in the world that had it much worse but I wasn't trying to hear that.

Why did people say that?

Why was I letting a Spanish woman tell me what was logical and what was surreal?

It's almost like a person was minimizing my pain and magnifying a complete stranger's personal strife.

"Think about it, Fate. There are people who are going through much worse…"

In my mind Miss Martinez said, *"Oh, yea! Forget about your mother twitching your clit because Tom in Delaware had a Daddy who beat him until he saw blood."*

OK. I didn't want to sound mean but *fuck Tom!* I didn't *know* Tom! I didn't *understand* Tom! I never *met* Tom! *I* didn't know if he had *titties* or *sideburns*. Tom didn't even *know* I was alive! So *why* should I put my pains and my struggles aside for Tom or whoever else who had it *worse?*

Looking at blotch marks didn't help. I thought I could move past it but something didn't feel right. I couldn't explain it. Mrs. Martinez told me there were no wrong answers, yet every time I looked at the blotch mark I saw one thing:

Mama abusing me.

Mrs. Martinez asked one thing that baffled me. Even Red had to hold her breath.

"When are you going to realize that the abuse you suffered wasn't your fault?"

I had looked at her. I released Red's hand.

"Mama said it was my fault." I felt like a little girl trapped in a cage.

"Fate. The day your mother abused you was the day you mentally stopped maturing. You are now an adult woman, yet you have the mind of a child."

"Bullshit, Mrs. Martinez! I'm grown!" I snapped, flipping a small table over. I sulked.

Mrs. Martinez challenged me. "You're *seven* years old. You are the little girl who had a mother who let men come into the room and deflower you over and over and over while compensating your mother. Your mother allowed these men to do the same things to *her*. Your father secretly authorized it. He was a pimp. *You* thought he was at work earning honest money yet he was accepting cash and favors in exchange for your security being broken in two and handed to you through sex, lies and orgasms too powerful for your body to handle at the time. Your mother was a part of a vicious cycle. Your great grandmother abused your mother!"

"SHUT UP!" I was starting to crack open. I stood up and rubbed my arms.

Mrs. Martinez was on a roll. "Your mother had to pay the price for those white slave owners using her for entertainment. You told me your mother once told you white men watched your grandma and other women eat each other. They suffered psychologically because of it. They never recovered."

Shut up, bitch! What do you know!

Red reached up and squeezed my leg.

Mrs. Martinez flipped her glasses into her reddish hair.

"...*Perpetrators* always say it's the victim's fault. They shouldn't have looked at me. They shouldn't have worn those get up shorts. They shouldn't have kissed my cheek. They asked for it! I'm sorry! An eight year old girl asking an adult to have sex is absurd."

Red nodded in agreement. She remained quiet and didn't say anything.

Making silent assumptions, Mrs. Martinez sipped her Evian water.

"Even if the child does ask for sex the adult has to be an adult and say 'No' and seek help for the child. Therapy, in some cases. Because the child is reenacting what they saw their parents or other adults doing and they become curious. They were probably exposed to adults having sex in porn movies and they want to know. Kids are very impressionable. *You* were a child. Your mother's flesh and blood daughter. She wanted control. She thought she could get away with it. You were a lab rat. Her abuse was a needle. Stick you and see what you do. Poke you and see what you say! She had distorted thinking. *When are you going to forgive yourself for what happened?"*

Red looked at me and I was at a loss for words.

hen I left the office with Red, I never returned again. I was too confused. I was worse off than I was when I first came. *When are you going to forgive yourself for what happened?*

Then on top of that I was in love with Red. I hid this from our sessions, since it was solely based on helping me deal with abuse. I *loved* her with everything in me. But she has lied to me. I had a big problem with that.

Despite the letter I wrote her (and I hated expressing myself) she turned out to be the girl I was in love with back in high school. I was still coping with that.

And if that wasn't enough my Mama died on me. I didn't *want* to poison her but I had no choice. She once drugged me. She blended the drug with strawberry daiquiri and gave it to me. Then she told me about what my Aunt and grandma faced in the air of oppression. I still shuddered, thinking about my aunt being tied to a huge tree at the Big House (the Master's Mansion) and those sick bitches cut her baby out of her womb.

Good riddance, Mama! Part of me mourned her. But the other part, the part she molested and shaped and molded, detested her. Rumor has it that she dropped dead at her birthday party. Janis the Pearl served drinks, and for some reason that lady spooked me. Something didn't sit right with her. When I told her I was Michelle's daughter her eyes lit up and her attention span was directly placed on me.

God, please forgive me for killing Mama. I had to, Lord. You know what that woman put me through. I had to protect myself. I had to protect my son.

I was standing up, about to go shower when Red walked in the room. She didn't look at me and I didn't look at her. *Well, fuck you too, bitch!* Taking off her white lab coat, she hung it up in the well-organized closet, with her well-structured ass, and took off her dress pants. She hung those up, too. She was humming a Sam Cooke cut.

Infuriated, I walked into the bathroom and turned on the shower. If she wasn't talking to me I wasn't talking to her.

That simple.

I turned on the hot and cold water and took off my sleeping clothes. I looked my body over in the mirror. Why did women love looking at their bodies in the mirror? What did the glass possess that the male eye didn't quite capture?

I put my hand under the water and made sure it wasn't too hot or too cold.

It was just right.

B efore I could get in the tub Red hugged me from behind, planting her warm lips on my neck. I felt good in her arms, but she lied to me and despite what I wrote in the letter, I was thinking of taking it back.

"I love you, Fate. I will help you get through this."

"And how are you gonna do that?"

"I will show you the tattoo I got."

"Really." *It's a start. Trying to re-evaluate our trust.*

"But first…you said your pussy is my pussy, right?"

"Yes. But I have to shower…"

"Sit down on the toilet."

"Ok, Miss Thing." *Damn, she looked like Gerald Levert. Baby suck on my Private Line. You can call it any time!*

Red spread my legs apart. She was massaging my thighs, taking her time. I loved when she did this. She never rushed when she munched on my vaginal walls and made them feel like sushi.

She ran her tongue over my pussy, my clit pulsating. I was about to explode.

While she ate me out and steam formed in the bathroom, she was saying, "The tat is on my neck."

It was very small. Between focusing on my nut and enjoying her tongue lashing, I read it.

What the hell does "Autumn Rose" mean?

The next day I was dressed in a nice pants suit Red bought me. Renaldo wore a shorts set that matched Jameson's. They looked very handsome with their neatly cut hair. They were putting coolers in the truck and Red was grabbing the beer and putting it in the truck as well. She never let me lift heavy stuff or open doors. She wanted to be the Man and I let her because that's what I loved.

Jameson came into the house and called my name. I was in the kitchen, putting the finishing touches on the sandwiches. I cooked the chicken and marinated the ribs over night. So when we got to the beach Red could man the grill and I could look cute in my bathing suit and look forward to buying Janet Jackson's new line of lingerie coming out Early 2010 called "Pleasure Principle."

"Ma!"

"*Yes*, Jameson."

Red kissed my cheek, looking at her son with a huge smile. She rubbed his head.

"There's a woman here to speak to you."

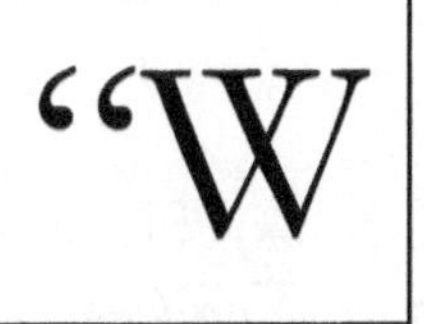

ho?" asked Red, her guard going up. Red didn't trust strangers showing up at the door unannounced.

"She said she is a friend of your mother's."

Oh. OK. "Invite her in. Bring her to the kitchen." Red busied herself.

"OK, Mom. I'll go get her."

"What lady is here?" asked Red.

"Baby, I don't have a clue. Mom had a lot of friends. She did work for the government. I may be getting a lot of visitor's between now and the funeral."

"You better get ready for it."

he short, stocky woman followed Jameson through the living room. She clutched her purse. "What a lovely home," she said, looking over the boy.

He is so handsome.

She paused when she saw a few photos

hanging on the walls. The two women looked so gorgeous.

They were very photogenic. Her heart leapt with joy. She loved photographs, she always has.

Jameson studied her briefly.

"Ma'am, the kitchen is this way," said Jameson, taking her hand. "Are you ok?"

It took her a moment to get her thoughts together.

"No. Michelle was a very dear friend. I can't believe she's gone."

"She's in a better place. At least that's what Mom tells me."

"And she's right."

Jameson pulled her into the kitchen.

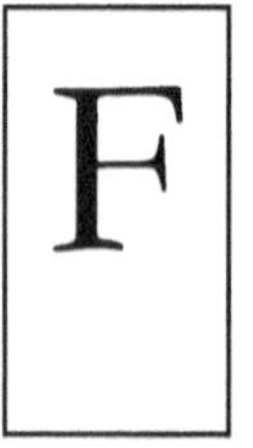

ate Williams recognized her. "Oh, *hey*! How are you?" She hugged the woman. *You look just like your mother and father!* "I could be doing better. I am so overwhelmed. I came here intending on giving my get wells and my condolences and I was thrown into the shock of my life."

"Why, Janis the Pearl? That is your name, right?"

"Yes. That is my name. I'm glad that you remember."

"So what truly brings you by?"

Janis paced the kitchen. She was deep in thought. "Something troubles me, Girl."

"Ok. What?"

"Family. Ever since your Mom died I've been thinking about family. What it means to have them. Why family hurt each other before their friends do."

"Tell me about it." Fate sat at the table, thinking about her horrible past. "My parents let me down."

"In a way I let my daughter down, too. We haven't spoken in years. She graduated high school and wanted to do things on her own. She didn't want my help." Janis had huge tears in her glassy eyes, but they didn't fall.

"Have you tried to get in touch with her?"

"No. I don't even know where to begin."

"Try your heart."

Janis sat at the table with Fate. She took her hands. "I don't even know where to begin. My heart is in disarray. I made a lot of mistakes. Granted, I never hurt my daughter. Never. Not once in her life."

"Then why doesn't she call you?"

"She is upset that I focused on her father, my husband at the time, more than her. But she never went without anything. I fed her, bathed her and bought her what she wanted. I even helped with her schooling and taught her things a woman should know." Janis set her purse on the table.

"My Mama never taught me womanly things." Fate's face grew dark and Janis shuddered.

What are you trying to tell me? Janis thought silently.

Janis stood up from the table and walked over to the counter. She saw a few sandwiches that needed to be finished. She turned on the tap water and rinsed her hands. She took a paper napkin and dried them. She picked up the Mayo and a butter knife.

"Maybe it wasn't meant for my daughter to always be in my life, Fate. Obviously you weren't made to always be in your Mom's life. She died at her birthday party."

Fate appreciated her finishing the sandwiches. She really didn't feel like making anymore. She wanted to go to the beach with her family and enjoy the rest of the day while she prepped her mother's funeral.

Fate stood up, the chair sliding back audibly. Stretching, she walked over to Janis, her heels clicking against the checkered marble floor.

"*Fate*. You and Red look so happy together. I envy that. I haven't had a man in my bed in years. When my husband died I couldn't bring myself to remarry, date or give away his body. It's so hard!"

"I understand that. You truly loved him…

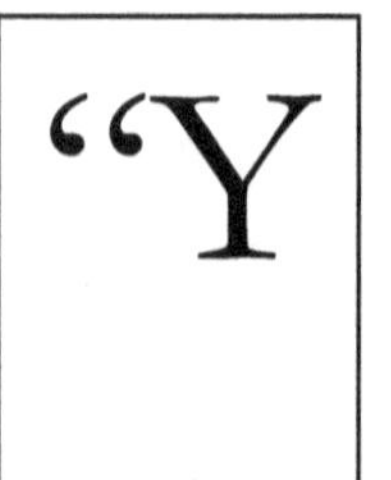

es, I did. My second husband, I should say. I loved him more than my first husband Earl."

"How so?" Fate asked.

"Earl left me for another woman. Her name was Jonnie. I never forgave him for abandoning me and leaving me with a daughter. My child blamed me for the split."

"Divorce is hard on children. They feel it's their fault," Fate said knowingly.

"That is true. But it's not their fault that adults can't get it right," Janis said.

"I agree, Janis."

"I hope you and Red get it right," Janis said. "I don't support gay marriage, but one look at the boy who led me to the kitchen showed me that he is truly happy. Who am I to judge? I wish you and Red all the luck in the world!"

"Thanks. Red and I are happy. We have our problems."

She looked over her shoulder and made sure Red was still out back, loading the truck. Red hated Fate telling her business to anyone. She felt very strongly about that. "I don't really trust her like I used to.'

"Why?" Janis put a piece of bread on top of the ham and she grabbed a sandwich bag, putting the sandwich inside. She set it off to the side by the nine other ones.

"She lied about who she was. In the beginning I thought her name was Lolita Harvey. It turns out her name is Lianna Gregory. We went to school together. Why would she do that? Yes, we talked about it and I understand her reasoning, but when you lie about something as small as your name, I have to wonder what else she lied about."

Janis touched her shoulder. "Get over that, Child. Life is too short. OK, she lied about her name. But look around. You two share a home. Those two boys are gorgeous!"

Fate beamed. "Thank you, Janis."

Janis asked, "Have you met her family?"

Fate said, "No."

Janis thought about it for a moment. "You *should*. If she loves you she will share you in every aspect of her life. I'm not trying to pry. But if she's hiding you and your son then something is seriously wrong."

Fate was shaking her head. "I don't think she's hiding me…"

"What do you call it? I know if my daughter Autumn's Rose hid me I would be greatly saddened."

"As you should be. I know with…" Fate's eyes widened.

Autumn's Rose?

Where have I heard that name before?

Red opened the backdoor and peaked in. Janis was making another sandwich.

"I'm sorry for interrupting."

"No problem, Baby," said Fate, hoping Red didn't hear any of their conversation.

"Hi, ma'am," Red said.

Janis looked over her shoulder. "How are you?"

"Thanks for helping Fate make the sandwiches."

Janis turned back to the jar of Mayo.

"The pleasure is all mine."

She smiled.

Fate waited until Red walked back to the truck. She saw the boys running behind her, trying to tackle her. They loved Red. It melted her heart to see her family bonding.

"Fate. I think you should inquire about meeting Red's parents. Does she have any brothers and sisters? What is her father's name?"

"You're right. I will ask to meet her family."

Where have I heard Autumn's Rose? I heard that name before. It's right on the tip of my tongue.

Where have I heard that name before?

Red came into the kitchen again, closing the back door. Beads of sweat were on her face. She smiled, watching Fate walk up to her. She looked so elegant, so sensual.

They embraced. "You feel good in my arms," said Red, her heart fluttering.

"And you feel good in mine."

"I want to marry you."

"Really?"

"Yes. I know we can survive, baby. I love you and I will bend over backwards taking care of you and our sons."

Janis opened a huge bag of chips, trying to be quiet, and filled a few sandwich bags.

Fate looked at the back of Janis's head. Janis looked over her shoulder and nodded. Red's back was to Janis.

Fate shook her head "No."

Janis turned around, crossing her arms, leaning against the counter. She picked up a marker and a notebook. She flipped it open and scribbled something.

"Fate. Will you marry me?" Red asked, kissing her neck. Fate melted from her touch, like a hot poker through butter. Fate kissed Red's neck, running her tongue across her new tattoo.

Fate then bit the bottom of Red's earlobe, her pussy getting wetter by the second.

Fate slowly pulled away, her eyes landing on the tattoo.

The breath caught in her throat, but she played it off and pretended that she had to sneeze.

The tattoo.

Autumn's Rose.

Oh, God! Janis the Pearl is Red's mother!

Janis held up the notebook when Fate looked at her. Fate was shaking her head, stuck in the middle of a game. Red wasn't to be trusted. Everything she has ever told her was turning out to be well contrived lies. Why would Red do such a thing to a woman she claimed she was in love with? It made absolutely no sense to her and her heart was turning black because of it.

Now we can't be together. I don't want to be in this house. I don't want her touching me. Janis said her daughter's name was "Autumn's Rose." Coincidence? Or sick, twisted game Red was playing, using human lives and human emotions to her sick advantage?

Fate read the note Janis scribbled.

Ask to meet her family, Fate.
She's hiding you and your son.

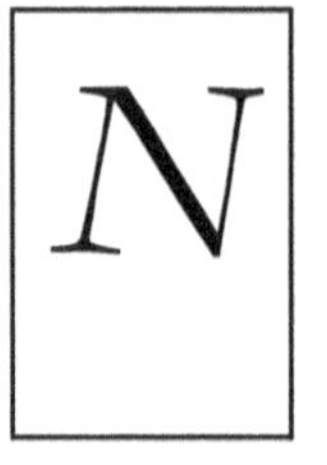

No, she's not hiding me. What does she know? But she is my elder and elders know the drill. They been there and done that. What if Janis is right? What if Red is ashamed of being a lesbian and don't want her family to meet me? After all, Red met my Mama. Mama didn't like her but they still laid eyes on each other. They at least tried to be civil with each other. Red met my son. My son loves her. I really don't know anything about Red. Except that we share the same Baby Daddy.

Janis closed the notebook.

Fate had an idea.

"**B**aby. If we get married I want your parents to come," Fate said lovingly, her heart torn.

"You know they can't come."

"*Sure* they can, Baby. I got a confession to make. I did something behind your back that might upset you."

Red pulled away from her. "What did you do?"

"I called Orlando. I checked into that nursing home your Mama is in…"

"OK…" Red was getting scared.

"They said Sasha Lloyd isn't registered there. I also called California, to check on your Daddy. They said he's doing well."

Red smiled. *My Dad is dead.* "Is that right?"

"Yes," said Fate. "I bought a plane ticket for Orlando. I'm going to find your mother. I want to meet her. Then I am flying to Cali to meet your handsome Daddy…"

"I won't let you."

"I'm grown."

"I don't want you meeting them."

"But I want to. And I'm taking my son."

Red slapped Fate so hard she held her face. Janis looked up from the sandwich, but didn't turn around.

Red sunk to her knees, holding Fate's legs.

"You struck me for the last time."

"Fate, please."

"You know I was abused greatly in my life. And you do this to me?"

"Baby."

"When you hit the one you love it's automatically over. My Mama is dead. She hit me enough."

Red broke open. "Please…"

"When I get back from meeting your Mama and senile policeman Daddy I will pack my things and leave."

"Fate."

"My plane leaves today. I bought the tickets while you were packing the truck."

"But what about our picnic?"

"Stand up, Red. Please. Company is here."

"Can you please leave and go home," Red told Janis.

Fate said, "She can stay. I don't want her to leave. She is my mother's friend…She will always be welcome in this home. She didn't do anything to you."

Defeated, Red stood up. She tried to hug Fate.

"I will marry you under one condition."

"Name it."

"I want to meet your parents."

"Baby…"

"Why are you hiding me? Are you ashamed of being with me?"

"Baby, that's not it."

"We've been together for a long time and not once have I met any of your family. Do you have cousins?"

"Yes."

"Where do they live?"

"They live in Wisconsin."

Fate laughed, walking past her. She stood beside Janis.

Red eyed her evilly, shaking her head. *Send her home. I don't like discussing my business with strangers present. You know I hate that shit, Fate. She won't leave me. I'll suck the lining outta that pussy.*

She won't go anywhere. I'll beat that pussy with my tongue and dildo 'til she rolls over and go to sleep.

Then I'll fuck her in the ass the way she liked. She loves dildos in that asshole.

And I love fucking her in it.

I love bouncing in that pussy.

Making her skeet in my mouth.

Making her take this tongue.

"They don't live in Wisconsin, Red."

"They do."

"What does Autumn's Rose mean?" Fate asked and Janis stopped breathing. "The tattoo on your neck. *Who* gave you the name?"

"My great grandma. She loved me so much. She said I reminded her of a Rose in Autumn."

Janis chocked.

 ate said, "Do you want something to drink, my friend?"

Janis looked at her. "No."

The look in Fate's eyes told Janis that she knew Red was her daughter.

Fate knows!

 anis silently walked over to her purse.

"Red. If I don't meet your folks we are not getting married."

"OK. We will meet them."

"Really? Where is your Mom institutionalized?"

"In Orlando."

"Liar."

"She is."

"Try Ontario. Isn't *that* where you told me she was institutionalized?"

Red's heart stopped. *She's catching me in all of my lies. Why didn't I realize it? Orlando?*

Orlando should have been my first clue.

Janis was pulling out her wallet. She quietly looked it over, tears falling down her face.

Fate asked, "Why is your Mom in a nursing home? Why didn't you bring her here to live? You are in good health. She birthed you and raised you and I'm sure she did everything for you."

"She…"

"The truth, Red!"

"OK. I hated my mother. She loved my Daddy, Earl, more than she loved me."

No, baby. No. I didn't love him more than you. I just wanted to be there for my husband the way a wife should. I didn't love him though. I loved Gin, Michelle's husband.

"Are you sure?"

"Yes." Red walked up to Fate, taking her hands. Tears spilt from her eyes.

She's trembling, thought Fate. *She's telling the truth. Finally. She trembles when she tells the truth about emotional things.*

"When my Dad divorced Mom I blamed her. Maybe she didn't love him enough. Maybe she could have done something better, whatever that something was. He started dating a much younger woman. Her name was Jonnie. I *hated* her. She went to our church. Dad eventually married her. I used to watch Mom in church, amongst gossip, trying to pretend like it didn't bother her and it did."

Fate shook curls from her face.

Janis opened her wallet.

"No one knows why Daddy left Jonnie. But I know."

Janis paused, holding her breath.

"Why did your Daddy leave?" asked Fate, looking past Red at Janis. Janis turned and stood behind Red, her daughter, the missing link in her life has been found.

"I had sex with Jonnie."

Fate's and Janis's mouth fell open.

"I didn't want Dad with her. I thought that if I broke them up Dad would go back to Mom and rebuild the family. I ate her pussy in the church bathroom, on the toilet. Daddy walked in and caught us. He had lied to her and told Jonnie he didn't have any children…"

Janis held her neck. *Why would he say that? Why would he deny Lianna Gregory?*

"So where is your Mom, truly? And where is your Dad?"

"Earl is dead. He's been dead for years. And my Mom…I don't know where she is. After I graduated high school I hit the road and never looked back."

Renaldo and Jameson silently came through the back door. They sat at the table, and didn't say a word. Something wasn't right with their Moms and they wanted to know.

"So your Mom never met your son?"

"Yes. She met Jameson. I had him the year I graduated. But once I left, I cut all ties. She hasn't seen him since."

Fate looked at her boys. Janis was looking at Jameson, her grandson. She was overwhelmed with joy. She always wondered how he was doing and what he looked like. Now she knew. Jameson was uncomfortable. *Why is that old lady looking at me crazy?* He wondered. But he decided to let it go. Didn't really concern him.

Renaldo said, "Are we leaving anytime soon, Mama? I waited all week to go to Haulover Beach with the family."

"Trip is off," Fate said and Jameson and Renaldo started getting upset. They silently fumed.

Red said, "OK. I told you everything. Can we please leave?"

"Red. Turn around and face your truth."

Red was confused.

"What?"

"The truth is behind you. You always tell me to look forward, never look back. Well, sometimes you have to look back to see your future. Look back. It'll make sense."

Red turned around and saw her boys. She smiled. "I love my sons."

Janis said, "I love Jameson."

Red said, "You don't even know my son."

"But I know you…"

"Woman you don't fucking know me!"

Fate said, "Don't curse Janis!"

"She doesn't know me. Who is this woman? I never saw her before in my life!"

"Think long and hard about it. Don't deny me three times, Girl. When you do you will suffer the wrath of God."

"This Looney toon bitch needs to get out of my goddamn house!"

Janis handed her a photo. It was folded and turned backward.

"Jameson looks just like Dunn," Janis said.

Red said, "How do you know Dunn?"

"Open the picture."

Red opened the picture.

She was sitting on her mother's lap. She looked up, shaking her head.

"How did you get this picture of me and my Mom? This was taken over fourteen year ago."

Fate extended her hand to Janis.

Janis shook it. Red was taken aback.

"Nice to meet you Janis Gregory. I finally meet Red's mother."

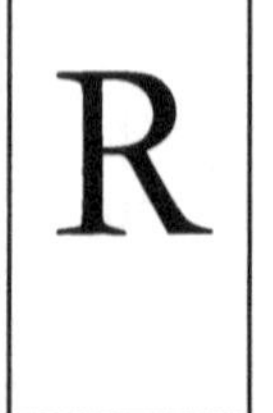ed started to take a few steps back, shaking her head in denial. "No. *Noo*. No. she's *not* my Mom."

Janis took off the wig and set it on the table.

She picked up a paper towel and wiped off some of the make up.

"*Hi*, Lianna. It's been years. I thought I would never see you or my grandson ever again."

Red covered her face.

ameson and Renaldo stared at her. Jameson said, "You're my Grandma? You mean to tell me that you aren't really in a nursing home in Ontario, like Mom always told me?"

"Yes, son. I am your grandmother and I love you very much."

Jameson hugged her. "I thought I would never meet you."

Renaldo glared at Red. "You are a liar. I don't want to talk to you ever again in my life."

Fate was in tears.

Red walked up to him and Renaldo ran behind his mother. "You keep the lying wrench away from me, Mama. I want to go. I don't wanna live here anymore."

"I love you, Renaldo, like my own son," Red pleaded desperately.

"I wanna go with Fate and Janis," said Jameson. "I don't trust you right now, mom. You whip me for lying yet you are the biggest liar I've ever seen in my life."

"I lied to protect you," said Red, ripping the picture in two. "I had to lie. I didn't want her in my life. She loved Earl more than she loved me."

Fate said, "Red. It's over. I hold no malice. I will take my things and go."

Jameson said, "I'm going, too. I'm going with Fate."

The demon came out of Red. "You're staying with me. I'm your mother."

Jameson ran at his mom, swinging fists. His hand hit her in the face and Janis grabbed him, but Jameson was a beast. "Why are you breaking up our home, Mama?" Jameson asked Red, in tears. He didn't want his family divided.

Red tried to hug Fate and Fate walked away from her. "I will never marry you. I still love you. I always will. But our relationship is a lie."

"*Fate!*"

Fate said, "Janis, watch the boys. I gotta get out of here. I can't deal with this. I still have to plan my Mom's funeral. How can I do that with all the lies being told to me by those I love the most?"

Janis said, "Take all the time you need. I've been without my grandson Jameson long enough."

"You are leaving my son here, Mama," said Red. She got in her face. "If you take my child I will call the police."

"I'm glad Fate opened her eyes about you, Lianna."

"It's *Red.*"

"It would have never worked. What's done in the dark would have come out eventually."

"You made sure it did."

"I have to tell you something. And I know it will hurt. But I have to tell you."

"What?"

Fate sat at the table, her face buried in her hands. Her soul cracked open. Renaldo was rubbing his Mom's back and Jameson was trying to kiss her forehead.

"Before Michelle married Gin, something happened."

"What, Mama? What happened?"

"You can't marry Fate if you wanted to."

"Why, Mama?"

"Earl isn't your biological father…"

Fate looked at Janis, with her mouth hanging open. "Janis. Are you sure?"

"Yes. I am. I was a different woman twenty plus years ago. I was young and naïve. When I met your Mom we fought over the same boy. We eventually became friends. But when she met Gin he was gorgeous! I wanted him to myself."

Red was shaking her head.

"I slept with him in Michelle's bed one day when she was shopping. I was already engaged to Earl and Michelle to Gin. We had a double wedding a few days later. When I learned I was pregnant with Lianna, I didn't tell Earl. Because it wasn't his. I had sex with him a few more times before I lied and said I was pregnant with his baby. Michelle and Gin left town before I could say anything. And I kept it between me and God."

"Are you saying…?" Fate stood up, walking over to Janis. "No. You're not saying…"

Red said, "She's lying, she has to be."

Janis said, "I wouldn't lie about something this deep. Fate. And Lianna. You two are biological sisters. You've been dating your own half sister."

Her world destroyed, Fate ran out the back door, jumped in the truck and sped up the block.

God! God! God! Please tell me she's lying!

She's not, a voice said in her conscious.

She's not lying at all!

er cell rang. Fate, parking at a near by Hotel, looked at the Caller I.D. It was Paul's Funeral Home. "I can't deal with that. Not today. Not ever. Red is my sister? Are you kidding me? Janis fucked my father before he married Mom? I can't believe this is happening. God why do you keep dealing me shit? Do you hate me? Or does Satan love me? Am I cursed, Lord?"

Fate turned off the truck and rests her head on the steering wheel.

"What do I do now?"

The cell rang again.

She answered. "Yes."

It was Red. "Come back. I don't care if we're sisters."

"I CARE! It's bad enough my own Mama molested me and now you're telling me to pretend like we're not blood relatives?"

"But we didn't know."

"You're right. We didn't know. But now we do. Do I look like a V.C. Andrews novel? *Petals in the Wind? Flowers in the Attic?*"

"No, but baby I love you…"

"We can't be together! God is playing a trick on us! Punishing us for the crimes committed by our parents! I don't know if I'm coming or going! This can't be happening!"

"Baby, please don't cry!"

Click.

A few hours later, Fate was back in her old apartment. Again. From another lie that was told. Why couldn't people be honest? Why did people cheat and make children and hide them? Didn't the parent realize that maybe one day the unknown siblings would meet up and might like each other? When Janis learned she was pregnant from her Mom's-then-husband she should have came clean. And because of her mistake, *life* caused Red and Fate to meet in high school. Then again in Goodfellahs. And they fell in love and fucked all over the place.

Gross! Why did God allow this to happen?

It wasn't God's fault.

Sure it was!

No, it was Gin and Janis's fault.

But God allowed it.

Satan influenced it. God just let it happen. Free Will. Every Human has the power of Free Will.

Fuck Free Will.

Every one has choices to make in life. They make them. They have to live with them. No one can escape it, no matter how hard they try. Decisions must be made!

Fate went into her bedroom and turned on the light. The stale stench was enough to make her gag. She hadn't been there in a very long time. Disoriented, she looked around the dusty room, inhaling, her heart broken in two. She saw the Bible on the dresser. She walked over to it, picking it up.

She thought of the Book of Job. She turned to it, ripping out the pages.

She put them in a neat pile on the dresser.

Going into the bathroom, she set the Bible in the tub. Taking out the alcohol, she poured the liquid all over the book. She took out a book of matches from the drawer under the sink and she struck it, the flame dancing before her eyes.

She dropped it, the Bible going up in flames. She wiped tears from her eyes.

It was done.

round nine thirty p.m., Fate was done reading about Job. He lost his land, his kids and was plagued with diseases. But he never gave up on his faith. *Then why does it feel like faith and God is slipping through my fingers?*

There was a knock on her front door. "Who is it?" Fate turned her cell phone off so she knew that deep down it could be Red, checking on her. Or maybe it was Janis.

Couldn't be Janis. Janis never has been to her apartment before.

Yawning, Fate walked to the door and answered it.

"Hi, baby. Long time no see."

Fate's face lost its color. "Oh my *God!* OH MY GOD!"

"No, it's not God. It's me, Michelle. Your mother!"

Fate closed her eyes.

This must be a trick.

A tired smile on her blotchy face, Michelle theatrically entered the apartment and closed the door. "But you died."

"Yes. I did. In the back of the ambulance I flat lined. But I was revived, Fate."

Fate was stuttering. "I *poisoned* you…I wanted you dead! I had to save you from yourself." Fate was crying. *No! She's back! She is back to destroy me, to try to rape me again. God, why are you doing this?*

"You didn't put enough poison, Child. You should have seen the doctor's face when I started breathing and the levels on the EKG machine started to beep. They called it a miracle."

Fate's lips trembled with fear. "Mama…"

Michelle was trying to hug her daughter, Fate ran over to the dining table, and picked up a knife, her hands shaking uncontrollably.

Michelle smiled deceptively. "Mama is back…Don't you miss me?"

Huge tears fell down her face. "No, Mama. I don't. Get out! Get out!"

"Sure. I'll leave. But, believe me, Fate. You will see me again."

Michelle put on a pair of rubber gloves. "I don't want my fingerprints in this apartment. I don't want the authorities knowing I'm alive quite yet."

Fate set the knife down. Michelle slowly walked up to her. "Were you going to cut me?" she asked.

"I will if I have to."

Michelle picked up the knife and studied it. It was a very small, compact knife. The blade was a little rusty and dull. She ran her tongue over it, making Fate's stomach turn.

"I don't think you want to do that. You're in enough trouble. I'll let you stay free for right now." Michelle walked behind Fate and put the knife to her neck. "You will give me some pussy when I want it. You will be my little whore. Remember, the Bible says you were put here to be my sex slave. Nothing has changed. If you don't adhere to my demands you will go to prison. I will go to every police and tell them you poisoned me. You got that, bitch?" Michelle asked, running her tongue on the back of Fate's neck.

Fate held in her grief. She refused to cry, but tell that to her pussy because it was suddenly like a leaking faucet. Michelle opened the door and left it open. Fate listened to her heels click down the hallway.

Mama is alive!

F ate covered her face, sobbing. *She's not dead! She will go to the police and report me. I will go to prison and I will never see my son! I should have known I couldn't escape her claws. What was I thinking?*

She wiped her face, getting herself

together. Her house phone rang but she chose to ignore it.

She thought about what her mother said.

Damn, what do I do now?

Red was face to face with her mother. She sent the boys over to their friend's house down the street. She didn't want them hearing what she was about to say. "You destroyed my home, bitch!"

Janis handled the words effectively, careful not to get upset. "You were the one who cut me off, moving away. You were never the same when Dunn died."

"OK, but that doesn't justify the lies you've told."

Janis laughed. "Lies? I told lies? We all lie, girl. In our own little ways we all lie to get what we want."

"If you say so. Maybe some of what you're saying is true. But you know what this is about, don't you? So *Gin* is my father and not Earl. How cold hearted can you get? You actually let me grow up thinking another man fathered me. You tricked Earl's family into thinking I was a part of their bloodline. You lied with a straight face. What kind of woman does that?"

"What kind of woman sucks pussy?"

Red swallowed hard. "I resent that, Mama," Red said, insulted. She shook her head. "You're *not* a perfect woman."

"I know I'm not. God knows I've had my share of mishaps. As far as your biological father is concerned, I had to lie. I didn't want to hurt Michelle. How could I just come out and tell you?"

"It was easy, Ma. You preach the honesty rule, yet you are anything but honest."

"I had my reasons."

Red's eyes widened. "What were they?"

"How was I supposed to know you'd turn out to be a pussy licker? I had no goddamn clue! Was I to know you and your sister would meet up?"

"Mama! I mean Janis! Listen to yourself."

"I am…"

Red grabbed her by the arms. "You destroyed my life."

"I didn't destroy your life. *You* destroyed your life."

"I can't believe you're not taking accountability for what you've done. If you would have been honest I would have known Fate was my half sister."

Janis slapped Red's hands off her arms, walking past her. "I'm going home."

Red grabbed her above the elbow and yanked her into her face. "Oh, no, bitch! You're not going anywhere. Time to face the music, bitch."

"Watch your…"

Red smacked her mother and Janis kicked at her, falling to her knees. Red was backing up into the counter, covering her face. She couldn't keep it together. "I don't understand you, bitch. You are playing games with human lives."

"And so are you! You have lied to Fate, making her think I was in a nursing home in Ontario. I could barely say the word."

"I had to lie to her. I didn't want her ever meeting you."

"Why?"

"I don't know, Ma. I just wanted to do things on my own. I wanted to live my own life."

The door bell rang.

"I thought I told my boys to go over their friend's house. I'm not in the emotional mood to deal with them right now."

The door bell sounded again.

"GO BACK TO YOUR FRIEND'S HOUSE!"

The door bell sounded four times.

"Goddamn it, I am going to break my foot off in their asses."

"You are not going to touch my grandson."

Red said, "Bitch *get* outta my house. He's my son."

"And he's my grandchild. I am already pissed that you excluded me from his life."

"Don't get used to it. I'm going to burn you out of his life next. At least I know who my child's father is."

Red stamped through the living room. Janis was on her ass, grabbing her by the arm. Red was snatching it away.

The door bell sounded yet again.

"And you have a key. Why are you ringing the door bell? I am going to beat both your asses…Stop grabbing me, Janis."

"Please don't hit them. They didn't do anything wrong."

"This is my household. I will run it how I see fit."

"The answer is not in violence."

"Whipping their motherfucking asses isn't violence…its discipline!"

"Red, please!"

Red pushed her mother on the floor. The pain shooting through Janis's knees blindsided her. She wouldn't give up on her daughter. She would weather the anger and stick it through. She refused to let the devil win over her daughter. She vowed it on her life.

"I am going to kick some ass!" She snatched open the door and the color left Red's face.

"Hi, doll. It's me, Michelle."

The room was spinning.

 Oh my God! You are supposed to be dead. I know I'm seeing a ghost."

Michelle walked into the house, closing the door behind her.

"I assure you, bitch. I am not dead."

Janis looked up in shock. "Oh my God. You're alive."

"Well don't look so excited."

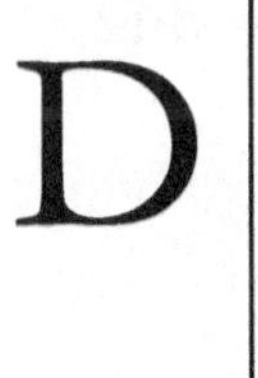arkness enveloped Red's home. Her white Dodge pick up truck sat serenely in the drive way. A few lizards crawled along the thick bark of the oak tree, a masked man leaning against the side of the house, breathing hard. He never took his eyes off Red and Michelle arguing. He saw them through the living room window.

He smiled.

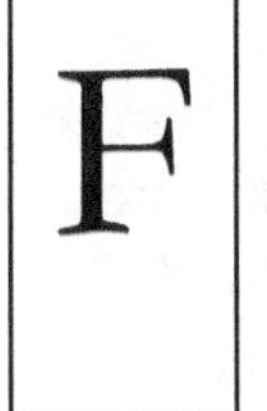ate picked up the phone and called the police. When the phone rang she quickly hung it up. "No, girl. Get it together. Don't incriminate yourself. Mama's too sophisticated to go right to the police. She would milk this situation to her advantage.

What does she want? Something had to give. Something was not right. I can't believe the nightmare isn't over. God, why am I going through this?"

She sat on the sofa, smoking cigarette after cigarette. She wolfed down some liquor, and tried turning on music. It didn't help. She tried exercising to Carmen Electra's aerobics video. In it she was in Las Vegas, performing her routine. She tried to concentrate but she couldn't. She was given two devastating blows. One, Red was her half sister.

And two, her mother wasn't dead

Red had to sit down to gather herself. Janis stood up, using the low table for balance. She was getting old. She wasn't as strong as she used to be. "You're alive…but, but you dropped dead at your party."

Michelle smiled, running her shaking hands up and over her hips.

"I dropped, yes. But I didn't die, obviously. I breathe the same air as you." Michelle looked at Red. "Hi, whore."

Red jumped up to her feet. "Get out. I don't care how you managed to survive. Get out."

"Make me."

Janis held up her hands. "Please. So much is happening. I am still trying to grasp the idea that you're alive."

Red was in Michelle's face. She took her by the arm and Michelle kicked her in the shin. "Look, bitch. I just came back from shaking Satan's hand in hell. He told me he wasn't ready for my induction. I have another purpose to fill."

"Get out," Red said, running over to the closet. Opening it, she took the Gat from the shoe box. She aimed at Michelle, meaning business. "I'm not Fate. You're not going to touch me, bitch."

Janis lowered herself to the Lazy Boy. She was getting migraines, and she had to press on her forehead.

"What are you gonna do? Soot me?"

"Yes."

"In front of your mother."

Janis looked up. "Red, *please.*"

"So does Michelle know the truth?"

Michelle looked at Janis. "Know the truth about what?"

Red said, "The truth about Earl not being my father."

"What are you talking about?"

Red said, "Gin is my father. Mama slept with him before he married you. Fate is my sister.

M ichelle said, "This has got to be a sick joke." The air seemed to leave her body.

Red still couldn't believe it. "Oh, no. Tell her, Ma! It's not a joke at all."

"It's true," Janis began. "I made some huge mistakes back then."

"I would say you did. You fucked my man at the time and smiled in my face?"

"And you molested your own daughter, bitch. I know you're not trying to preach to me."

"Yes I am! And you can't prove that I molested my daughter. It's her word against mine. If Michael

Jackson told you he loved pussy would you believe it? Just because he said its true doesn't make it true. You dumb bitch. You'd believe my pussy was flour if you fried your chicken right. You fucked Gin, now that is a fact. I trusted you."

"The same way your daughter Fate trusted you. And you violated her time and time again. I didn't even have a clue. But now I know, and I can't believe you would do this to your own child."

"Fate the *victim*. The bitch tried to poison me and all of you seem to forget that. How could you? I didn't ask to be treated that way."

"And Fate didn't ask to go through all that abuse," Red stammered, keeping her aim. Her palms were starting to sweat.

"I tell you what. Let's make a deal."

"I don't make deals with the Devil," said Red.

Janis said, "Michelle, just leave. What's done is done. Fate is a big girl. Obviously you couldn't break her. You tried to destroy her but her spirit remained intact."

"I want to make a deal. Red. Leave my daughter alone. Stay outta her life."

"And if I don't?"

"You and Fate will be going to prison for murder."

Red lowered the gun.

Outside of the house it started to rain. Water engulfed everything it touched. The branches on the oak trees shook wildly from the strong wind. Footprints were in the mud, leading to the front door. They stopped just before the truck.

The masked man was gone.

"I can't leave Fate alone. We didn't know we were sisters. And how do we know Mom was telling the truth? What if Gin really isn't my father?"

Janis said, "Gin is your father, baby. I'm sure of it. I wouldn't make something like this up."

"Yes you would! You hate the fact that I'm a lesbian," she went on, setting the Gat on the low table. "I believe you will say whatever you have to say to keep us apart. Why are you so against my lifestyle? I don't bring it around you. I don't bring it around my family."

"Yet you prance around my grandson, hugging and kissing on another woman," Michelle said, sitting on the couch, crossing her legs. "You're confusing the boys. You are letting them know that it's all right to fuck other women."

"No I'm not."

"Face it. You're a lesbian, a gay bitch."

Janis said, "You can't talk about my child."

Michelle stood up and walked over to Janis. "We have been friends for years."

Janis looked up at her. "OK."

"And you betrayed me. You are walking on thin ice."

Janis slowly stood up. "Now wait a minute. Wake up, Susie."

"Bitch my name is Michelle."

"I don't have to take your rebuttals."

"I didn't ask you to. You slept with my husband before we got married? I'm still stuck on *that* part."

Janis thought about it for a while. She hated confrontations, but she wasn't about to back down and look like a pussy in front of her daughter. "It was years ago. Just accept the fact that you weren't the queen bitch you thought you were."

"So were you jealous?" Michelle asked, fiddling with her bra.

"Of what?"

"Me? You had to be jealous. If you weren't you wouldn't have slept with my man."

"Ha. And why do you have on rubber gloves?"

"Mind your business."

"I'm not minding shit. I wanna know. Why are you wearing those gloves? You are starting to worry me. You're a sick bitch."

Michelle was getting darker by the second.

"Shut up."

"What did you go through in your life? If I would have known you were a fruit cake I wouldn't have befriended you. I don't even know what Gin saw in you."

Lightning and thunder boomed. Michelle smiled to herself, something in her soul dying.

"He saw a real woman."

"He saw himself, probably. Both of you were sick. I can't believe you would harm your daughter."

"You're talking like you're a perfect woman."

"I'm more perfect that you."

"SHUT UP!"

"Were you raped as a kid? Something made you snap and turn into the whore you are."

Michelle whipped out the rusty blade, snatched Janis by the hair and sliced her neck from ear to ear.

She dropped the knife on the floor.

Red was nailed to the floor. She couldn't move. "Oh my God! You killed my mother!" Janis lay twitching on the floor, grabbing at her neck. Blood spurted on the floor. Michelle looked at her, tilting her head. She then looked at Red, walking over to her, her heels clicking against the tile.

"I remember something, something you don't know. To reply to something your mother said, yes. I was raped as a kid. Brutally. I only passed to my child what my mother taught me."

"I can't believe…" Red was wiping tears out of her eyes. She thought she hated her mother. That was until she was cut with a blunt knife. She realized then she would die for her mother.

"You know what? I'm not gonna talk about the past. Let's talk business. That knife has Fate's prints all over it. You will stay away from her. If you go around her or even phone her I will go to the cops. I will let them know you knew she poisoned me. You aided and abetted a murderer. I will tell them she killed Janis."

"But you killed my mom. In my face. I swear to God. I will find a way out of this. And when I do I will kill you myself."

"Ah, baby. You feel passionate about that, don't you? I would advise you to stay away from my daughter. That's my pussy, you feel me? I promise to treat her the way she needs to be treated. You can't hang with the puppet master, bitch. You are a butterfly amongst killer bees. You can't compare to me. Don't try." She patted Red's shoulder. "I suggest you hop in your truck and get the fuck outta my face."

"I'm not leaving my mom…"

Michelle picked up Red's cell phone and dialed 9-1-1. When the operator answered, she said, "I would like to report a murder…"

Red snatched the phone out of her hand and hung it up, dropping it on the floor. She crushed it with her foot.

"Please, don't do this to Fate. You've hurt her enough."

"I know, sweetie. And with you outta the picture, we can begin to make memorable Kodak moments."

"Kodak moments? Why would she want a moment alone with you? Haven't you given her enough bad memories?"

"Good or bad she's still my child."

"I don't understand freaks like you…"

Michelle tilted her head back and laughed. "What is it you inept whore? Are you jealous?"

Red smirked. "Jealous. Of a woman who raped her own daughter and boasts about it? You are sick and deranged. You need to be locked up in a mental institution."

Michelle was slowly walking up to Red. "You are jealous. Jealous, jealous, jealous. Look at you. You look like a man. Fate loves pussy…yes she does. Want me to tell you how she makes Mama come all over."

"Shut up!"

"Oh, yeah." Michelle paused in her face, licking her lips. "Fate begs for it. Oh, Mama. Lick my pussy. Make me come. Make me come. She begs and begs…"

"SHUT UP!"

"And begs and begs and begs oh yea Mama slide that dildo in my tight asshole, work my walls like you're hanging Picasso, you nasty bitch!"

"SHUT UP!"

Michelle turned on her heel, her hair whipping behind her head. "No one saved me when I was being destroyed. I was somebody's daughter. I was a fucking kid. No one protected me. SO DON'T TALK TO ME ABOUT PROTECTION!" she barked viciously. "DON'T ASK ME TO GIVE A FUCK! EVERYONE TALKS ABOUT THE VICTIM, VICTIM, GODDAMN VICTIM BUT DO YOU SONSOFBITCHES STOP TO REALIZE THAT THE PERPETRATOR WAS ONCE A GODDAMN VICTIM!"

"Michelle…"

Michelle paused, raising her head, her shoulders slumping. "I never wanted to hurt my girl. But the little girl in me still lives. She cries, breathes and she is me. She doesn't love; feel emotion and she doesn't trust. She wants to be safe but doesn't know how to. My mother did so much to me I lost sanity. I was near insane when I got pregnant with Fate."

Red was staring at Michelle's backside. "Michelle, I know you've been hurt…who am I to judge you?"

"Believe me, Red, I wanted to be a good mother. Trust me, I did. I did everything I could to stay a complete woman. But men broke me and my child's father was scum and he denounced the core of my soul and somewhere in me I died. I was insolent and void. I didn't comprehend human emotion. The little girl in me wants to be free…free to grow, to prosper and to endure. But how can she?"

Michelle turned to face the barrel of Red's gun.

Red was shaking. "I sympathize. Believe me, I do. You didn't have help or therapy and you grew into a destructive system. But, you see, I *love* Fate. I will not let anyone hurt her ever again. You are still hurting and you are taking that hurt out on your child. Do you feel no shame Michelle?"

Michelle gritted her teeth. "Fate is your fucking sister."

Red spewed, "And she's your fucking daughter."

"Bite me, Bitch. Does it look like I care about what you have to say? Does this look like As the World Turns. THIS IS REAL LIFE, WHORE! Why should I listen to a woman who sucks her own sister's cunt? The shit you talk is real salty. No wonder Fate looks like she suffers from malnutrition. You are sucking the nutrients from her clit you thirty bitch! Let's clock your tea, shall we. Isn't that how you gay bitches talk?" Michelle went on, tossing her weave behind her head. Red wouldn't break away from her demanding gaze.

"What's the tea, bitch?" Michelle mocked. "Well I'm a Moet kind of bitch. I like the best. I have the goddamn best. Women like you play the Captain Save a Ho role. You throw your cash, money and dildos like goddamn confetti, trying to save whores that don't want to be saved. Does it look like I'm scared of that goddamn gun, bitch? I work for the Feds. I shoot guns all the goddamn time." Michelle licked the opening of the pistol. "Mmm…tastes like Fate's…"

Red lowered the gun to Michelle's heart.

And pulled the trigger.

Michelle, in a state of shock, was thrown into the wall, her arms and hands up and over her head. Red held her stomach, backing into the low-table, nearly falling to the floor.

Michelle was making gurgling sounds, slowly sliding to the floor, leaving behind a trail of blood on the wall.

Indecisive, Red stuffed the gun in her waist line and slowly walked over to her mother.

She dropped to her knees, taking her mom into her hands. *Oh my God, Mom! I'm so, so sorry. It wasn't supposed to be like this.*

Crushed, she rocked back and forth, her life over. She felt it. She knew it would never be the same.

How could it be?
Two murders happened in her home tonight.
"Mom…I love…"
Red swallowed the words.

Red was in her truck, punching the steering wheel. She was on the turnpike, mashing down on the gas pedal. She stopped by her friend's house and asked her would she keep the boys away from the house. She made up a lie and said that she set up roach bombs all over the place, and she didn't want them anywhere around them. Her friend said sure.

They'll be safe there.

She turned off the radio, the rain picking up harder. She didn't care. "I can't believe this. She killed my mother. How could she? I can get out of this. I know I can. I can call the police and tell them she killed my mother and I shot her in self defense. Yea. Yea, they had to believe that. They had to. I can't go to prison. And I won't!"

She opened the glove box, maneuvering around a slow-traveling SUV. She took out her other cell and called Fate.

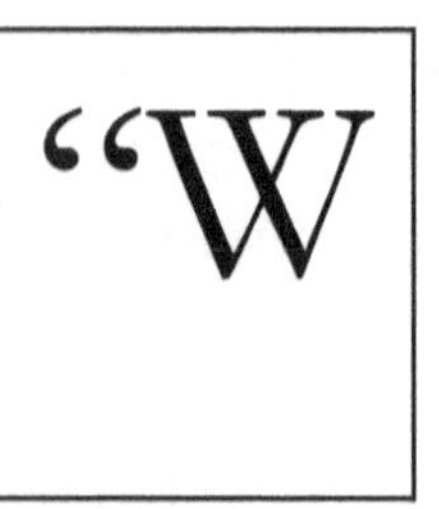

hat, bitch?"

"Baby…please. Listen to me."

"About *what?* You're my sister. We can't be together. Mother is alive. Everything is going wrong."

Red omitted the part about

Michelle killing Janis. And she didn't think about shooting Michelle. Good for nothing bitch.

"Can I see you?"

"Will you give up? Leave me alone."

"I love you."

"I don't."

"So you don't feel anything for me?"

"NO!"

"Well fuck you!"

"No, fuck you! I have too much going on. If you died tonight I wouldn't give a fuck! I can't stand you anymore. Everyone in my life lies to me! I can't deal with this."

Michelle managed to crawl over to the couch and climb on it, blood gushing all over the place. She has never experienced so much pain in her life. She prayed to God so hard in her mind she was sick to the stomach. She reached over and tried to light a cigarette. It fell from her lips, into the blood, the lighter falling on the floor.

She stared at Janis's body, pleased with her handy work. She felt nothing inside anymore. She didn't care about life, love and liberty. *Good thing I am dying.*

She thought back to her birthday party. She remembered Fate brought her a Rum and Coke, smiling in her face like everything was all right.

She tried to extract another cigarette from the pack, her hands trembling, her energy seeping rapidly from her body.

The room was getting blurry, the pain even greater. Michelle closed her eyes.

She never opened them.

ed felt betrayed. *She doesn't love me. I knew it. She is no better than her mother. She's probably mentally fucked up. Who wouldn't be? Michelle fucked the girl so much she doesn't know if she's coming or going. I wanted to love Fate. She is my world. But not anymore. God dealt a devastating blow. Fate is my sister. My mother is dead. I can't believe this. Fate doesn't want me. I didn't know we were related. Why can't we go on pretending that we aren't sisters?*

Red saw an accident approaching. She started to brake, but the brake peddle went all the way to the floor.

At 85 mph, the truck sped towards four state trooper cars.

Red screamed for dear life, covering her face.

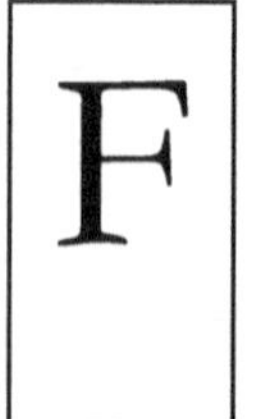

ate tried calling Red, but she didn't answer. She wanted to see the boys. Something in her heart wouldn't let her relax until she spoke to them. Fate shook her head, pacing the living room. She tried calling Red again but she didn't answer. Now she was getting fed up.

"OK, bitch. I know you're mad at me. Yes, I do love you. Yes, I wanna be with you. But I had to lie and tell you those things so you can get over me. We can never be. We are blood. We have the same father. I can't lay up with you knowing this. I would be no better than my Mom if I continue fucking you. I would be guilty of incest. I can't fuck my own sister. The forbidden fruit from the Tree of Life has been bitten. Eve has been cast from the Garden of Eden. Now we must reap the consequences."

"I love you. For some reason my heart won't let you go…"

Fate hung up the phone, turning on the TV.

Baby I love you. But it's over.

Everything has changed.

R enaldo was getting out of the shower, drying off his exhausted body. He took a moment to put on his boxer briefs and T-shirt. He smiled, thinking about his mother. He wondered what she was up to. Krishna, Red's friend, had come into the room, looking him over.

"Hey, Renaldo."

"Sup, Krishna."

"Have you seen Jameson?"

"No. I just got out of the shower."

"That's weird. One minute he was in the kitchen making a sandwich and the next minute he vanished."

"Maybe he's…"

Jameson walked into the room, slapping palms with Renaldo.

"Where were you?"

"I took a walk to clear my head. It ain't everyday you find out you had a grandma you didn't know existed."

Krishna rubbed his head. "I understand. Red told me all about it. Why don't you go take a shower and get ready for bed?"

Jameson said, "That sounds like a good idea."

F ate was channel surfing. How could she focus on TV when her life was in shambles?

Her mother was alive and was blackmailing her. Red wanted to continue a relationship that has become forbidden. She didn't know where her sons were.

Her house phone rang and she answered, just as a Breaking News Report interrupted an episode of *The Golden Girls*.

"Hello."

"Hi, Ma!"

Fate smiled. "Baby, what's up? Where are you?"

"I'm at Krishna's house."

 short, stocky man entered the local bar on Oakland Park Boulevard. He ran his hands through his unruly hair, sitting at the back table. Four huge plasma TV's blared in his face. Good. The news was on. He took out his cell phone and made a call.

"Yo…when do I get my money?"

A sexy waitress paused at his table, holding a note pad. She flashed a smile, thrusting forward her perky tits stuffed in a light blue uniform.

"Hi'ya handsome!"

Real airheaded bitch. "Hey…"

"Welcome to Jerry's. Can I get you something to drink?"

"A shot of Vodka, light ice. Straight."

"Can I see your I.D.?"

He stood up, grabbing his dick. "Access denied, bitch."

"Well you don't have to be rude about it. I'll go get your Vodka."

"Thank you…"

He waited until she stamped off. "OK, I'm back. So when do I get my money?"

"I'll get it to you tomorrow," the caller said, hanging up.

J ameson was in the shower. He lathered his body with soap, refusing to use a wash cloth. Shampoo in his head, he smiled. His cell phone rang but he ignored it. It was probably Vanessa, with her fine ass. He already got the pussy a few times. He even fucked her sister. Yea, he loved being a horny teenager. Life got no bigger than the Ho's.

Well, maybe life did get bigger. He was happy that his grandma came into his life. She was gorgeous! Her name was Janis, from what he understood. He wanted to know everything about her.

He wanted to know her favorite color and her favorite foods.

Where she was born and where she was raised. Did she have other kids?

Why didn't his mom tell him he had a grandma?

He knew his Mom was talking to her, and when tomorrow came he could go see her and talk to her and get to know her and she would tell him old stories of when she was a little girl.

Yes, that's exactly what was going to happen.

He looked out the bathroom window. It faced his mother's house.

He frowned when he noticed that her truck was gone.

Ma?

Where are you?

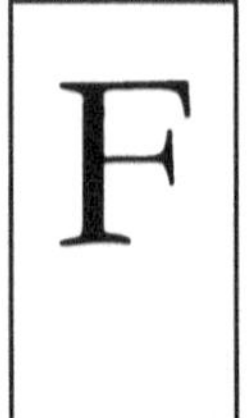ate clutched the phone. "Have you showered?"

"Yes, Ma. And I rubbed the stick deodorant under my arms, and used my hand to massage it in."

"Good. Where is Jameson?"

"In the shower."

"I still don't understand why Red took ya'll to Krishna's house."

"She didn't want us at the house with all the drama that's going on."

"So you know what's going on?"

"Not really. Jameson knows, but he won't tell me. He said he'd protect me, that it's best if I didn't know. I do know that his grandma Janis is in his life. And I think that is so cool. Finding out you have a grandma you didn't know you had. I'm jealous."

"I know."

"I miss Grandma Michelle. When's her funeral? Have you planned it yet?"

"No, Baby. Not yet."

"Why? I know it's hard, Mama. But we all gotta go."

I haven't planned it yet because the bitch is still alive.

"I know, baby."

"I don't think I wanna go. It's gonna be hard telling her good bye."

She closed her eyes. "*Look*, get some rest. I'll come get you two in the morning. I'm tired."

"OK, Ma. I love you. Good night."

She kissed through the phone.

The waitress brought the man his Vodka. He thanked her with a killer smile, slipping her a twenty with his phone number on it. "Do you want to order something to eat?"

"No. The drink will do."

She was smiling at him, her hands pressed down on the table. She licked her lips.

"Well, if you change your mind."

"I'll be sure to let my dick know."

"You're so direct. I like that!" Her nipple were erect, her pussy wet. He inhaled. He could smell it in the air. *I betcha that pussy is pinky tight!*

He focused on an old episode of *Friends*. He laughed when he saw Lisa Kudrow. *She's the entire show,* he figured.

The show was interrupted by a Breaking News report. The anchor woman looked vexed.

This just in. A speeding Dodge truck slammed into stare trooper cars, killing three armed officers before careening over a banister.

Poor officers. Awww. Poor, *poor* officers!

The truck, said to be driven by a woman, slammed into the road below, blowing up instantly.

Fucked up way to die, he thought gruesomely.

We have footage from the scene, and parents, if you have children viewer discretion is advised...
His eyes widened. "Oh my God!"
That's the truck I rigged.

Fate was about to turn off the TV when an anchor woman said:

This just in. A speeding Dodge truck slammed into state trooper cars...

She shook her head. "Thank God it isn't anyone I know..."
She stood up, heading for the bedroom. When she got inside, she picked up the remote, pointing at the TV. The same breaking news report was on. She didn't have time to mingle in other people's problems. She had to work tomorrow, and when she got off she was going to get her boys and sit them down and tell them the truth.
They deserved to know that she and Red were sisters. They would be devastated, but she wanted them to hear it from her.

We have footage from the scene, and parents, if you have children viewer discretion is advised…

Fate sat on the bed. Before she could press the "Off" button, she froze, her blood curdling. Bile rose in her throat and she jumped off the bed, in a fit of tears. Her world exploded, blinding her. All logic and reason suddenly became null and void.

"Oh my God! RED RED! NOO OH MY GOD THAT'S RED'S TRUCK!"

She grabbed her purse and keys and ran out the front door, closing it behind her.

J ameson and Renaldo were watching TV. Krishna, taking off her apron, smiled at them. They were in the Den.

"I think its bed time, you guys. You have to go to school tomorrow."

Renaldo sneered. "Man!"

Jameson patted his shoulder. "Come on, Bruh. We gotta go to bed. Wouldn't want to be late for school."

"Actually, I do wanna be late."

Krishna picked up the remote. Jameson's cell phone rang. He looked at the number and frowned.

Krishna was taking Renaldo's hand, trying to pull him into the living room.

Oh my God! Red's truck just plummeted off the Turnpike! I can't let him see that.

Renaldo was laughing. "I can walk on my own, Jeez. You're about to pull my arm out of its socket."

Krishna played it off, her heart hammering.

Jameson waited until they vanished. He answered the phone.

"Hello." His back was facing the TV.

"Yo. Those brakes I rigged for you…"

Jameson sat back on the couch, smiling. "I will pay you. I'm just glad you did it. I didn't want my Mom jumping in her truck trying to leave. She needs to talk to my grandma. Having her brakes rigged was the insurance policy. She hopped in her truck she would know the brakes were out so she would go back inside and finish talking to her mother. I want us to be a family."

"Bruh…"

"So you will get the two thousand I promised. I know where Mama keeps her stash. Plan failed anyway, her truck is gone."

"Bruh? I hate to tell you, but are you close to a television set?"

"Yea…"

"Turn it to the news…"

He turned to face the TV. "Hell, the news is already on…"

He watched quietly.

When a picture of his mother popped on TV, and then the visual switched to her burning truck he threw the phone at the TV, shouting so loud Krishna stormed into the room, Renaldo behind him.

"Bro! What's wrong?"

"Mama is dead! Oh my God! I fucked up, bruh! I just wanted her to talk to Grandma! I paid to have her brakes rigged. And now Red is dead! My Mama is dead!"

Renaldo fell to his knees, with his face in his hands.

Krishna couldn't believe her ears.

Fate arrived at Krishna's house. She had to get to her boys and tell them before they saw it on the news. She hopped out of her car, heading for the front door. She knocked on it, her skin crawling. She was shuddering, and the tears wouldn't stop falling.

My baby is dead! She died thinking that I didn't love her anymore. Oh my God! Can this situation get any worse?

When Renaldo opened the front door, he wrapped his arms around his mother.

"Mama! Something terrible has happened! Red died in a car accident!"

"I know, baby. I just heard…"

Jameson was digging up the carpet in the living room, blaming himself. Fate looked at him, pushing Renaldo to the side. "Why are you blaming yourself?"

"Mom!" He engulfed Fate, digging his claws into her blouse. "I did it! I didn't mean to! I just wanted them to talk…"

"Who, what…slow down…"

"I paid to have Red's brakes rigged. All I was doing was trying to ensure that she didn't leave the house. I wanted her to talk to Grandma. That's all. I didn't mean to kill Mama!"

Fate was stunned. Krishna remained quiet.

The man stood up, grabbing his phone. The waitress seemed to drop from the ceiling. "Where are you going?"

"Away from here."

He had never run so fast in his life.

Fuck the money! I don't wanna go to jail. Thank God this phone isn't registered in my name. I stole it from some dude at the Mall Earlier.

Nothing can be traced to me.

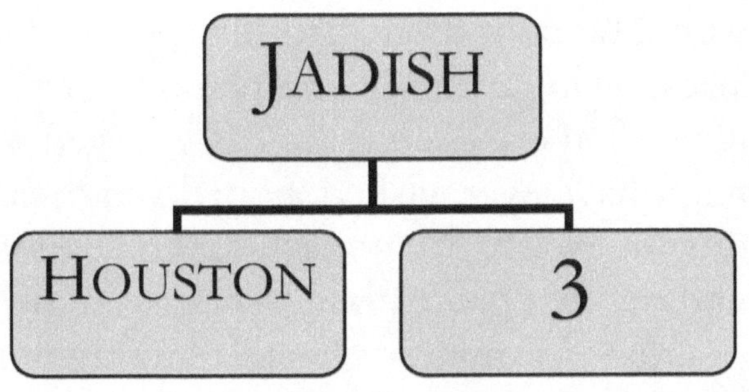

Nutrition Facts:
100% Fruit Juice.
65% Protein
100% Sex
689 calories
Do not purchase if Seal is broken
Questions? Comments? 1-800-Fuck-the-Haters

My world exploding, I hesitantly sat in my car and leaned back against the seat. I couldn't stop crying, my heart beating out of my chest. Silently, I guardedly stared at the house before me. The place owned by a man who shattered *my* glass house. The house owned by a man that destroyed every logical nerve in my being. A house owned by a man I used to love. A house owned by a man that had a few of my pictures on the walls. Now I have become a stranger in the photos on his dusty mantel. I was now the stranger in *all* the photos. I didn't know who the hell he was anymore. Had I ever known him? I loved him so much. I could recount the times, when I was a young, impressionable girl, he would wipe my tears. He helped Daddy teach me to ride a bike. Daddy was mean, always spanking me for falling and scrapping my knees. But my God Daddy would be right there, brushing off my buttocks or my knees, telling me to "Get up and try, try again." In the blink of an eye everything has changed. Everything I have ever wished, hoped and dreamed has become hogwash. My pre-school graduation picture and my first grade class picture were on his dresser. Pictures of my first cheerleading try outs were in his photo album. My lungs felt like flames and my stomach was the identical twin. I held my legs but they continued to shake. It was hot in this car but I welcomed the heat. My panties stuck to my pussy with both sweat and lust. Lust for a man who used to be my Godfather. Lust for a man I *used* to trust. Lust for a man my father once brought in our home when I was a little girl. I loved him like an Uncle. I used to tell him my most intimate thoughts and his ears became my diary. I even let him *read* my diary without shame. He told me I was beautiful. He told me to watch out for men who would promise me the world just to get a shot of coochie. He told me that men were vicious creatures. They wanted what they wanted and didn't care *who* they hurt. He also told me to never trust those closest to me. They would hurt you first. And that's exactly what he did. Hurt me first. Why didn't I listen?

Who would have known that I *should* have been watching *him*? That's what happened when you were young and naïve. When you have blinders on, you look for the good in people. You become a sitting duck. I've been wounded from the pump shot gun of Tommy's selfishness. His sickness was blinding. He taught me the ups and downs of love in ways Daddy used to hide from me. I appreciated Tommy for telling me that I shouldn't marry the first piece of dick I get. He told me to live and learn and find out what worked best for me.

Daddy wanted me to be his little girl forever. How long did he expect me to keep my legs closed? Forever? Tommy said I would grow into a beautiful woman. He watched me sprout like a rose.

Betrayed, I punched the dash board. Dried blood was on my bottom lip. Yes, the blood from Tommy's dick. I tried to *bite* it off. I should have cut it off. Goddamn it, Tommy! Why? I was thinking this entire time I was a virgin. I prided myself on being one of the *few* girls that kept the cherry bush set up in my pussy and thought I would let my George Washington chop it down or dig it up, which ever way he preferred, when I got married. It didn't quite work out that way. And what hurts the most was that I put my husband Sax through two years of emotional hell. I punished him for *Tommy's* mistake. Wait a minute. Raping me wasn't a mistake. Why was I minimizing what my God Daddy did? Was I in denial?

I put my husband through unconscionable hell. I wouldn't let him get the pussy because I was distraught over the nightmares I used to have. In it, an evil man with a big red X over his face was chasing me to the Red sea. I now knew I was the woman being deflowered in the middle of the ocean floor. Why hadn't I seen the signs before? Did I *not* remember anything about my graduation night? The night Tommy had his way with me. I hoped he enjoyed it because he would never touch me again. I hoped he died. I couldn't believe a man I trusted like an Uncle would unabashedly destroy me and rob my future husband of taking my purity.

I thought back to a conversation my husband and I had years before this grueling moment. I had begged him to tell me why he got in a fight with Tommy when he took me and my family out to eat. He told me Tommy fucked me on my graduation night and I was so taken aback I instantly shut down and started defending the man and Sax was right, right, right!

I closed my eyes and silently prayed to God.

Lord, please forgive me for punishing my husband. You sent me a very sweet man who was a virgin himself and innocent and pure and I spit him back in your face because the taste in my mouth reminded me of what I thought I had. It overshadowed every logical nerve in my body. All Sax wanted was love and acceptance and I gave him hell and it's unapologetic wrath. What kind of woman jacks her man's dick on his honeymoon and didn't make love to him? I didn't give him me, all of me. I gave him some of me. The selfish part of me. The part of me I have tried to erase for so many years and have been unsuccessful in doing so. But now I want to correct the wrongs and give myself to my husband.

If I can get past Tommy's betrayal.
In Lord Jesus name I pray.
Amen!

I have never *willingly* given myself to a man. I used to sit back in high school and watch the boys pick out vulnerable girls and fuck them and their reputations to hell. I didn't want to be one of them so I never put myself in the position to become victimized by boys with testosterone problems. My girlfriends didn't have an ounce of class. They gave away free pussy like the boys paid for it. Where was their self-esteem? Where was the self-confidence? I remember, during high school, I stayed over to Sasha's house. We were about fifteen and she told me her parents were out of town. Initially she told me it was going to be me and her chilling and eating popcorn and lusting over Denzel Washington movie posters. I especially loved *Ricochet*.

I had told my parents I would be staying the night with Sasha, since her parents grew up with my Mama. Hesitantly, Daddy told me to make sure I had the dishes washed. Tommy, who was sitting at the table drinking a cold brew, looked at me and smiled and I melted. It took a while for him to look away and I couldn't stop lusting over his gorgeous smile. Once I was done with the dishes and cleaning my room Tommy drove me over to Sasha's. When I got out of the car and grabbed my night sack I kissed Tommy's cheek and he left.

The instant I knocked on the door Sasha whipped it open and snatched me inside.

"Why are you pulling on me like that?" I asked, confused.

She closed the door, hugging me.

"I have my reasons. Glad you could make it, Girl."

I looked around. I saw her clothing thrown everywhere. Her shoes were all over the place. The TV was on an old episode of *Good Times* and the sound was muted. I smelled something cooking from the kitchen. I sniffed. Chitterlings? Maybe, but I did know that it smelled like shit.

Sasha was picking up her clothing in a hurry and stuffing them in the hall closet.

"Help, Girl."

"*Hell*, no." I looked at her like she was crazy. I still didn't know what was going on and I wasn't sure if I wanted to know. "I'm your house guest. *Not* house keeping."

Shaking my head in disgust, I tossed my bag on the couch. A roach ran from by the pillow and I jumped behind the end-table, making shrieking noises and she laughed at me.

"They probably came from outside. It rained earlier and they seek shelter in the living room."

Right, bitch. You had roaches for years. And don't blame it on the neighbors, either because you haven't had a neighbor in three years. *Why do black people blame the climate for their roach problems?*

I threw some salt in the game. "It looks dry as hell to me outside."

She kicked three pair of her shoes in the closet. Then she tried to push the door closed but she had too much stuff in there.

She was struggling. "*Help* me, Girl."

Like hell. "I'm cool. I'll *watch*."

She tried her best to get it closed. She even pressed her body against the door and she gave it all she had until *finally* it closed and she sunk to her knees, sighing with relief.

She had on her mother's dress and pumps. She overdid it with her mother's make-up. I didn't understand *why* she dressed that way, since she dressed like a bum in school. Holes in her jeans never did anything for her front crooked tooth. She had a teaspoon of nappy hair and it didn't do anything for those god-awful shoes she wore that smelled like spoiled milk. Hell, the silly bitch didn't even have enough hair to get the famous Halle Berry or Toni Braxton look.

She stood up and stretched. "Bob, Sam and Micro are coming over, Girl. We gotta get ready for them. The finest niggahs in school are coming to stay the night with us. Isn't that exciting?"

I wanted to whip her ass. What was this? A sex party? "Uh, no. I didn't come over here for that…you said it would be me and you." I glared at her.

"It is. For *now*. Plus I'm pussyphobic. I break out in hives when I'm around another woman for too long. I like dick, not fish, you feel me, Gurl? No offense."

I didn't want those boys around me. They fucked any and everything on two legs. I wouldn't be surprised if they fucked each other. Birds of a feather flocked together. Or, as my Grandma once said, *"Gays masturbate and lick it from the one eyed snake."*

"I'm not offended and I happen to like fish sandwiches. With a lot of tartar sauce."

She chocked on her saliva and she held her burning throat.

"You eat fish?" she asked, short of breath.

"*Duh*, bitch. I *love* catfish."

The color left her face. She avoided my eyes and started moving away from me, like I had a disease and that offended the hell out of me.

"Oh," she went on, chuckling. The color returned to her face. "*Fish*, fish. I got you. You eat *real* fish sandwiches."

I was even more confused. She was acting like a ditzy bitch.

"What are you on tonight because you are acting dumb as hell."

She rolled her eyes. "*Anyways*, Chile. Check this. *Hoes* are already talking about me and you. Half the school wants Bob and Micro. They are the stars of the football team. When you rush over a thousand yards you deserve to get all the pussy you want…"

I gave her a confused look. "And *why* are you telling me this?"

She was patting my shoulder and pushing me up the stairs.

"Because I heard Tonna wants to fight you. You know she likes Micro and he is going around telling everyone he wants to eat your pussy and give you some dick."

"Like hell. Not in this lifetime."

She led me into her Mom's huge room. About five or six nice dresses were on her mom's bed. I liked the green one with the green floral bust.

"*Pick* a dress. We don't have much time. Verona and Lily are coming over, too."

Now see. Now the game stopped. "I don't like Lily. I heard she fucked half the basketball team."

"So *what*. Don't hate. She is giving her pussy some experience. Men don't want inexperienced twat. They want their women skilled enough to pay the bills with the flick of the clit." We were laughing. She was so silly.

She went on, warming to her subject. "So when Lily marries Ted, when he makes it to the NBA, she'll know how to hold him down with her pussy-popping skills, Chile…He's her meal ticket. You know she put holes in the condoms so she can get pregnant and be set for life. Who wants to live in the projects forever?"

"I feel you. But I don't know about having a man's baby just to hold on to him. I don't believe in being deceitful. Eventually it blows up in your face."

I could have been talking to a pig. *Oink, oink, oink, oink.* Nothing I said registered in her brain. She picked up the red dress and held it up to my body. "That looks good on you."

I pushed it away from me. I hated the color red. Yuck. I think of my period when I see red. Plus I used to wear red pants to school when I was on my period, especially the days Mom couldn't afford maxi pads. "I like the *green* one."

She tossed the red dress on the bed like she never liked it. I took off my black skirt and red blouse and she snatched off my bra and I was startled. *But you don't do fish, 'ey?* My breasts were bare and I didn't like other women looking at my bazookas.

"Take off your panties," she said, handing me a pair of green pumps. "It's best if you stay naked underneath the dress so when the boys come they can eat your pussy without the hassles."

Oh, no. It's not going to be *that* kind of party.

"Eat my pussy? *Wait*, what kinda…"

She was determined. "Put on the fucking dress. You walk around school keeping your pussy guarded like Michael Jackson's room. Give it up. This is high school. Let's fuck now and tomorrow we can worry about everything else."

I guess you think you tell me what to do. "I don't…"

"We're young once. Do you want to turn sixty years old with a shriveled up pussy you never used?"

Ugh! "Girl. Don't say it like that."

"All right then, The Mummy. Let's get to it. Let Micro dig Nefertiti outta your asshole and slide it in your mouth to taste the tombs of the Sphinx Pyramid. I heard he has a big, juicy dick!"

She walked over to her Mom's nightstand and picked up a blue cup. She handed it to me.

"What is this?" I asked, wanting to puke. I felt my pussy shut down. I suddenly wanted to go home and crawl under my blankets and die.

"Liquor."

She picked up the other cup and wolfed it down. I didn't want to look amateurish in front of her so I wolfed it down, too. I cringed then gagged. It burned my throat. What the hell.

"Girl, that's what you call that good shit."

"It's nasty."

She was staring at me. I was confused.

"What?" I asked.

"Feel it yet?"

"Feel what?"

"That's my special blend. Grey Goose and weed."

"Weed?" I wanted to gag.

"Hell yea. Drunk and high is the way to go. Ever get fucked high on weed? That's what you call 3D dimensional dick."

She put the dress over my head and was pulling it down. It fit perfectly. I helped her situate it on my body, silently thinking about what she said. About turning 60 and never being with a man. I did want to know what sex was all about.

Daddy fucked Mama in the ass every night. He wanted the ass more than her vagina. I found that weird but every time Mama said, "Plow that ass like Frederick Douglass planting okra!" I shut right up and gave it to God. I heard them through their bedroom door all the time and they didn't try to be quiet about it either.

Sasha told me to sit down on the bed and I did, still trying to take this all in. She pulled my hair into a bun and then put her mother's long curly wig on my head. It was a little itchy. I looked in the mirror. I looked hot. Damn. Maybe I needed to let go and have fun. It didn't make sense to hold on to my virginity and not experience sex at it's greatest.

She took out her Mom's make-up bag and she artfully coated my lips with light green lipstick.

"Oh, Girl. You're hot! Watch out Iman!"

She pulled out the dark green rouge and blush. She coated my cheekbones with some glitter. I was watching her the entire time, her breath smelling like ass but who was I to rain on her parade? Might run some more roaches into her house for cover. I still couldn't believe she said that. She was so worried about my pussy and my image when she needed to focus on brushing her goddamn teeth but I didn't say anything because I didn't want to hurt her feelings. Nappy headed bitch.

She looked fabulous but her breath was like going over to Madonna's house and finding feces on the low-table next to the caviar. I chuckled at the thought.

"What's so funny?" she asked, the rush of her breath making me wince. *Goddamn, bitch! Gargle!*

"Nothing." I could barely get the word out.

"Something must be funny. You keep chuckling."

"I can't be to my thoughts?"

"You need to be thinking about how you're gonna give Bob that *ass*."

"You make it sound so gross."

"Girl, sex is a *business*. Find your pension and hope it's a hefty 401 (k) plan. Mama taught me that."

"That's why I'm going to college. To care for myself. Plus your Mama is weird. Why would she let a married man screw her and he doesn't even pay ¼ of her bills?"

She didn't like the comment. "That's her…"

"Where's *her* hefty 401 (k)?"

Sasha's eyes flashed dangerously. "*Listen* Abigail Adams. Find you a John Adams and hope he becomes the President of the United States."

"No."

She looked me over with a smile. "*Look* in the mirror. Your transformation is complete." I stood up and closed my eyes, wondering was I making a mistake. I slowly opened them and I saw a gorgeous young woman with green lips and the dress brought out the rhinestones in the pumps. I was gorgeous. Wow. *I should go lock myself in my room and fuck myself.* I couldn't stop smiling. Why was I staring at the door knob?

I hugged her. "I love it."

"Are you sure you like it? You're not just saying that?"

"I mean it." I pulled away from her, taking up my bag. I pulled out two peppermints. I popped one in my mouth.

"Give me one. I brushed my teeth earlier but this candy will keep it cool."

What did you brush your teeth with? Shitty diapers? And you need that peppermint more than I do.

Just then the doorbell rang.

I followed Sasha down stairs and when she answered the door I saw Bob and Micro. They took one look at us and fell in love. Micro and Bob grabbed my hands and Sasha tucked her chin back.

"Excuse me? All this right here and you ignore me for Jadish?"

Sam crept up behind her, pulling her into his embrace. He was sucking on her neck and she was trying her best to get the dress off. Micro closed the door and looked at Bob.

"Damn, Jadish. You are hot, Gurl."

I couldn't take my eyes off him. He looked really good. He was dressed in a black shirt and black slacks with black boots. Bob was trying to kiss me, feeling on my booty and I didn't feel good about it so I pulled away from them and Micro pulled me back and Bob got behind me, trying to take off the dress.

I felt uncomfortable. Micro pulled out my titty and was trying to suck on it and Bob pulled up the back of my dress and was breathing all over my neck. He pulled down his zipper and pulled out his dick and I turned and slapped him.

"No, man. I am going home!"

Bob snatched me by the wig and Micro ripped off my dress. Sasha was naked. Sam bent her over the low-table and sex filled the air. She loved every inch of his dick.

I couldn't go down like this. I didn't want to be a Ho. Not like this. I didn't want my first time to be with boys who took first times for granted.

Bob brutally head butted me and a rush of pain and nausea fell upon me. The force of the blow knocked me to my knees. I had never known pain like that before in my life. Micro picked me up and threw me on the chair, positioning himself between my legs.

He was a beast. "If you don't give up the pussy we'll take it."

I tried to kick at him but my head hurt so badly it felt like I was dying. Bob put his dick up to my lips and tried to force it in but I wouldn't budge and he was slapping me in the face with his dick and it hurt.

"Suck it!"

"No," I mumbled. I wouldn't let them break my spirit. *God please help me! Help me, Lord. You said you will never leave my side. What is going on? What have I ever done wrong?*

"SUCK IT!"

I turned my head away from his penis and he turned my face back to it and he pissed in my face and I was flapping my arms and trying to stand up as urine soaked in my hair and the dress.

Micro kissed all over my titties, tasting the piss. He smiled, rolling his tongue all over my nipple. And Bob pulled my legs back. I felt a cool breeze blow across my pussy and Micro looked at me evilly and said, "I'm making you a woman tonight, Ho."

"No, please, Micro. Sasha…Sasha, help me…"

She didn't hear me. Her moaning and obscenities reached peak levels and I knew then this was all planned. It was all a set-up.

Sasha wasn't really my friend and now Micro was going to rape me.

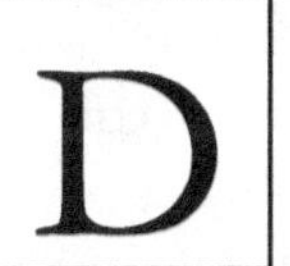

Micro wiped Bob's piss all over my pussy and he buried his face in it. Bob joined him. I couldn't move. It felt good but at the same time I didn't want this done to me. I wanted Mom! I knew then I would never spend the night outside of my home, where I felt safe.

Bob and Micro tongue kissed each other and then two tongues started slithering all over my pussy. Bob pushed my legs back and I felt weak.

Micro then tried to kiss me and I bit his lips and he raised his fist and just as it started to plummet towards my face Tommy grabbed his hand and snatched him off me.

Thank *God*.

Daddy grabbed Bob by the throat and threw him so hard he flew through the living room window. The sound of shattering glass made me scream. His body lay still by a row of cherry bushes. Sasha was in shock. While Tommy beat Micro under the low-table, blood seeping from his nose and lips, Sasha tried to flee and Daddy snatched her by the wig and it came off. She ran up the stairs and he was behind her. When she reached the top of the stairs Daddy picked her up and threw her down the stairs, her head slamming into the pedestal. Her body remained still.

I lay there, trying to take it all in. I was praying to God and wondering why the room was turning black. My breathing came in spurts and I felt vulnerable to the sudden pleasure that came over me. The darkness seemed like a nice place to lay and to sleep. Yea. I tried to keep my eyes open and Daddy was in my face. He was tapping my cheek. "Baby…Are you ok? Baby!"

His voice turned into vicious wails and screams. "BABY! WAKE UP! BABY!"

His voice seemed distant. I smiled at him and his tears fell on my face and he pulled me into his arms and I saw Tommy standing behind him, shaking his head in denial.

I felt my body immobilizing. Daddy opened the front door and rushed to his truck.

I blacked out.

I felt elatedly good. The cold air enveloped me like a second skin. I was weak. I inhaled deeply. I felt something in my nose. It was hard and uncomfortable. I opened and closed my hands. Something was in my right hand. I couldn't raise it. Something had a grip on it. OK. My left hand worked. I slowly opened my eyes and it took a minute for the room to come into focus.

Daddy was sitting in a chair, holding my hand tightly. He was snoring loudly. Mom was sleeping on the chair over by the TV, wrapped in my old Big Bird blanket. Why did that make me smile? Tommy was sprawled on the floor under another blanket.

Where was I?

"Dad…Dad…" My voice horribly cracked.

Mom opened her eyes and looked at me and when she realized I was blinking she jumped up to her feet, screaming with joy. "My *baby*!"

Daddy and Tommy were startled.

"She's awake! She's awake!"

Mama pushed Dad out of the way and she threw her frail body on mine, showering my face with tears and kisses. Tommy hugged Daddy and they pat each other's back.

"What happened to me?" I asked Mom. I could not remember anything.

She was studying me. "You were almost raped."

I was quiet. "Raped?" I grew pensive, tears forming in my eyes. "Somebody *raped* me?"

Tommy took my hand. "No. Your Dad and I got there in a knick of time."

"Daddy!" I called out for him. A few nurses rushed into the room and a doctor, holding a clip board was behind them.

Dad hugged me and I wouldn't let him go.

 police woman asked me some questions and I told her all I could remember. Not that it did much because Daddy told her, "Please let her rest."

"Its protocol," said the white cop with the prettiest hair and the bluest eyes I'd ever seen.

"I don't give a fuck about protocol. My daughter was almost raped. And if they would have succeeded I would have murdered the motherfuckers and you woulda been asking me the goddamn questions now get the fuck outta my daughter's fucking room!"

"I understand you're angry. I would be, too, if it was my child," said the cop. "But I have to do my job, Sir."

"Well hurry up. Then let her sleep."

I answered a gazillion questions. Once I was done she left. Two nurses checked the EKG machine and the third nurse flashed a little light in my eyes to see if I responded to it. She scribbled down something on her folder and the doctor told them to leave. Mama was telling me that Micro was in intensive care in the very same hospital I was in and that Bob suffered a head concussion. Before I could question her any further, the doctor asked me how did I feel and I told him I felt like Frederick Douglass planting okra and the blood left Mom's face and Tommy and Daddy chocked and I was smiling.

"I see you have your sense of humor," the doctor told me. "Whatever *that* means."

"Ask Daddy," I told him. "Mama tells him about Frederick Douglass and his okra every night through the walls."

Mama covered her face and Tommy pointed at Daddy, laughing at him.

The doctor got the hint and he quietly sped out of the room. I asked Mom how Bob suffered a concussion. Tommy looked at Daddy and Dad told me, "He tried to rape you. Micro, also. Tommy and I got there and saved you. I threw him out of the window. The glass cut up his face pretty badly."

"Is he ok?" Not that I cared.

Tommy said, "He's in a coma."

Everything was happening too fast. I was still trying to formulate in my brain exactly what happened. I remembered Sasha wanted me to stay the night. She told me that Bob, Sam and Micro were coming over. She dressed me up in a green dress and she did my make-up. I remembered Micro and Bob grabbed my hands and they tried to force me to have sex. OK. It was all coming back to me.

"What happened to Sam?" I asked Mom.

"He's ok. But as for Sasha, she was treated for minor injuries and I pressed charges against her for luring you to her home to have sex with her male friends."

I was antsy. "She's my friend. She wouldn't hurt me."

Tommy said, "She lured you there with the intention of being raped."

I tried to sit up. "How dare you!" I steamed. "She's my friend! Don't bash her in my face!"

Tommy looked hurt. "Jadish. It's true…"

Daddy put his hand on Tommy's shoulder and shook his head. Tommy nodded and moved to the back of the room.

"Baby," said Mama, trying to calm me down. I tried to attack Tommy. He was lying. He better watch his mouth!

Daddy said, "Jadish. Please. Calm down."

Hesitantly, I settled down.

Tommy said, "I hate to tell you this but Sasha dressed you up in that dress and make-up so your body could be sacrificed. She set you up to be raped by two horny school boys."

"Mom!" I called out in fear and she kissed me and held me until I fell asleep again. This was too much for me to handle.

Why would Sasha do this to me?

A few hours later the doctor discharged me. I wasn't talking much and Mom helped me wash up in the bathroom. When I put on a pair of pants and a white blouse, Mom pulled my hair into a bun. I thought about when Sasha put my hair in a bun, just before she put her Mom's wig on my head. Nausea filled my stomach. I took my hair from the bun and let it hang.

"No, Mama. I don't want my hair like that."

"Why?" she asked.

"Sasha put my hair like this before her friends came over to rape me."

She understood.

Mom and Daddy were in the back seat arguing over who was going to cook dinner and Tommy drove. I had on my seat belt, riding in silence. Tommy would occasionally look at me but I didn't recognize or acknowledge him.

"Are you still mad at me?" he asked.

I sucked my teeth.

"I'm sorry, baby girl. I don't want you to be upset with me. I was only telling you the truth about Sasha."

Mom and Dad were yelling at the top of their lungs. I could hardly hear Tommy.

In my hands were papers. The doctor wanted me to see a psychologist and I told my parents I didn't want to talk about the situation with a stranger and they said they wouldn't force me. They told me they would handle the legal part of the attempted rape and they wanted me to focus on getting well and returning to school.

"Jadish."

"What?" I whispered harshly, wiping tears from my eyes. "What do you want?"

Mom and Daddy talked over the music. They were heated with each other.

Dad said, "You are *gonna* cook. I can't cook tonight. I'm tired."

"And I'm tired too, goddamn it and you need to cook sometimes. Motherfucker I'm not a robot!"

Tommy said, "I told you the truth."

"Bashing Sasha is not the truth."

"Listen. Your Dad and I went out tonight. We stopped by the pizza parlor and we ordered a large pepperoni."

"OK."

"A few girls came in. Your Dad and I checked them out. But they were too young. One of them, I think her name is Lily…" The color left my face. "Told another girl in the group that a girl was going to be deflowered at Sasha's house. Initially *your* Dad and I didn't think nothing of it. Lily then told the other two girls 'Jadish has been a virgin long enough. Micro and Bob just arrived at Sasha's house. They are going to rape her.'"

I was so quiet I seeped with anger. I hated Lily so much. She never liked me. And to think Sasha was in on the plot. Why would she do that to me? I prided myself on keeping my virginity.

And after tonight I would keep my virginity until I got married.

Tommy grew quiet when he saw I squeezed my hands into fists.

"I'm sorry."

I didn't say anything.

L ife went on. I told my parents to keep me in the same school. Bob never recovered from intensive care and he died. Daddy was charged but in court he won his case. He protected his daughter from being raped by two men who beat her and urinated on her and humiliated her. Even Bob's parents couldn't do anything. They actually shook my father's hand after his victory, not that Daddy gloated. He loved all people and taking a life would be on his conscious forever.

Bob's parents were so in shock that their son tried to rape me (and the fact that he died) that they decided to move out of town. Micro recovered. Charges were brought against him and Sasha and he wound up getting three years in a juvenile detention center. Sasha got probation and was withdrawn from the school. Her parents stopped talking to my family and we were now bitter enemies.

Micro was kicked off the football team and slandered in school. My business traveled but I didn't care. I kept my head high and I still went to school. I didn't care what anybody had to say. Tommy helped me get through the ordeal. He was easy to talk to and he told me him and Daddy would always protect me.

I wound up going to see the shrink. It wasn't bad at all. The psychologist's name was Advance Stevens, a frail-looking white woman with huge freckles and curly red hair. Over the next few months she helped me deal with what happened through essay writing and role playing and she loved holding a mirror up in my face before and after our sessions ended.

I started to gain my self-esteem and self-confidence back. I felt like a new person. I knew in my heart I would never trust people the way I used to.

Boys tried to go with me in school. They treated me like flowers. They tried to nurture and protect me and everyday a different boy bought me chocolates or roses or brought me a teddy bear.

My sexuality kicked in, despite the attempted rape. I wanted to know what it felt like to have sex but every time I came close to doing it I chickened out. I thought something was wrong with me. I used to suck on a little dick or let the boys eat the pussy but I have never been penetrated. I didn't know that my virginity would be taken from the same man who saved me from being raped.

I was married now and I hadn't even let my husband fuck me yet and it's been over two years and I didn't know how to move beyond the apprehension. There were brief sexual encounters. We would be licking and tasting but I was too afraid to go any further.

Despite Tommy drugging me on my graduation night and fucking me all night long, to his heart's delight, he secretly prided himself on being the first to get the pussy and I didn't have any knowledge.

I should have known! I thought back to that unfortunate morning.

The day after graduation.

I had awakened with blood everywhere and my body on fire. I didn't know what to think or what to say. Where did the blood come from? I looked at my arms and legs but I didn't see a cut. After throwing up in the toilet, I called Tommy. He always came to the rescue. I told him that I didn't feel good, that I saw blood everywhere and he was like my knight in shining armor.

He showed up in his polished green Buick and he looked after me. He brought me some changing clothes and he stayed in the room until I showered and was dressed up like a doll.

I loved the way he used to look at me.

He didn't give me the I-wanna-fuck-you stare like most guys in my neighborhood. But the gleam in the corners of his hazel eyes reminded me of love.

I knew then he was in love with me but I didn't know I was face to face with the man who raped me. I felt so foolish for thinking I was still a virgin. It would take a lot to forgive myself for what happened. I blamed myself for what Tommy did. Did I lead him on? Did I give him signals? No. I *never* looked at Tommy in a sexual way.

Breaking the silence was my ringing cell phone. I was still parked in Tommy's front yard and I knew I had to go but I wanted to burn his house down. I felt so betrayed.

I answered and it was Daddy.

"Hey, pop." I faked it, trying to sound upbeat and my insides felt like tropical depressions.

"*Hi*, Baby. How is your day going?"

I turned the key in the ignition. I smiled, tears falling from my eyes.

Help me, Daddy! Your best friend raped me on my graduation night! How do I tell you? I wanna kill him! Damn it! Why do I feel so murderous?

"My day is magnificent."

"Magnificent?" he asked skeptically. I heard Al Green in the background. *Let's stay Together.* Very nice song. But right now I wasn't a nice bitch. My whole world just blew up in my face.

"Yea." I put the gear in reverse and backed into the road. "Magnificent."

"Darling, you don't use words like that. Something is wrong."

"Mr. Lenny Houston. I do feel that way."

"Baby I know you better than you know those panties you're wearing."

"That wasn't a very good summation, Daddy."

"Get over yourself. Can you take a joke? But you feel magnificent, right? Your voice betrays your feelings. What is it? Just tell me."

He intimidated me. "I'm good, Pa."

"Pa?" He was chuckling. And it wasn't pleasant. "You never call me 'Pa.' Do I look Spanish? Pa? I'm Daddy! I love being black."

"Don't we all."

I put the car in drive and sped up the block.

"Why are your tires biting into the pavement like that, Jadish? Are you ok? Where are you?"

"Dad, I'm good." The tears fell harder. I slowly braked at the approaching stop sign. I put the car in park, pressed "mute" and I threw my head on the steering wheel. I hurt so much my shoulders were shaking. The heat didn't help matters and everything I felt for Tommy was compromised.

"Why, Tommy? Why did you rape me? Why did you do this to me? I trusted you!"

"Jadish?"

I sucked in air and my nose was stopped up. I sat back against the seat and I smelled my pussy in the air. It was still in heat.

I was remembering Tommy's dick in my mouth a few minutes ago, when I was secretly picking him for information.

And to think my husband Sax knew all along what had happened on my graduation night.

He told me that but I wouldn't listen.

I guess I was in denial about it all.

But I wasn't in denial about it anymore.

Question was: what was I going to do about it?

Would I call the authorities?

Would that be beneficial?

Would I feel better?

I have already been violated by a sinister man.

Would he do another woman like that?

Had he done another woman (or women) like that? I couldn't have been the goddamn first?

I pressed "unmute."

"Daddy, where is Sax?"

"He's next to me. Are you ok?"

I smiled. Someone blew their horn at me and I put the car in "drive" and started up the block doing the 35 M.P.H. speed limit.

He put Sax on the phone.

Sax could remember the first day he saw the woman who was to be his loving wife. They were going to the University of Miami. College.

Both led an individual life that was going nowhere. He was leaving the Convocation Building and he saw her in a plaid skirt and white shirt.

Women laughed at her style of dress but she was unlike anything he'd ever seen. He was directly behind her, inhaling deeply, trying to get a whiff of her womanly scent.

What kind of perfume did she wear? It was soft and invitingly gorgeous. It made him smile. Her earrings weren't elaborate. And her shoes were simple.

She had tripped and he caught her just before her chin slammed on the concrete step. They had been inseparable ever since.

Now Sax frowned. He didn't want to talk to his wife. His loving wife. The woman who sat on her pussy like it was a bank account reserved for a rainy day.

He was happily married to the woman of his dreams. Sex came with the package. Sure, it wasn't everything but goddamn, it's been two years and she hasn't let him fuck or make love.

Why?

He knew why!

He was indirectly being punished for Tommy's betrayal. He knew Tommy fucked his girl when she graduated high school.

Giving her all those drinks.

Each laced with GHB.

He knew it.

But he couldn't prove it.

Sax glanced at Jadish's humble, broad-shouldered father. *Should I tell him that his best friend fucked his daughter and left her bleeding?*

Sax cleared his throat, taking the cell phone and putting it to his ear.

"Hey, Jadish."

"Why do you sound so down?"

Because you're my wife. And you'd rather fuck yourself with bedroom door knobs than your own husband.

"I'm good," he lied.

"I have something special planned for you."

He closed his eyes.

I heard that before.

A very tall, handsome man boarded a plane in Chicago. He carried a leather attaché case and he stayed to himself. Freshly clad in a business suit with red tie, the ladies swooned over him. He had on thick shades, making it impossible to see his eyes and his shoes gleamed just as brightly as his moderate jewelry. On his finger was a wedding ring. He found his appropriate seat and put his attaché case under it. He sat down and sighed. He hated flying. But he had business to handle in Miami, Florida.

He snapped for the stewardess, who stuck out her bubble ass and perky tits and licked her lips as she approached him.

"I'm happily married," he said and her tits and ass deflated instantly.

She then had an attitude. She didn't like being rejected.

Fag!

"Can I get a coke?"

"When the plane gets in the air…" He handed her a five dollar bill, changing her mind. "Coming right up. Try to keep it inconspicuous."

All Hoes loved money. He winked at her. He had no plans on being inconspicuous. He was a grown man. Fuck the lames. Indifferently, he pulled out his Blackberry. He called his wife. The phone rang for what seemed an eternity. *Answer the phone.* It went to voice mail. He hung up, calling the number again. This time she answered.

"Hey, baby"

She acts like we're doing ok. "Hi. How are you?"

"I'm feeding our son."

"Cool. I won't be long. I just wanted to say that whatever happens, just know that I love you."

"Whatever. Our son needs me. Bye."

She hung up.

 e then clicked a few buttons and a name popped up. He smiled when each glorious letter shined in his handsome face.

I can't wait to see you, Bruh.

Tommy was in his bathroom, crying from the pain. His dick burned. *Goddamn,* Jadish. He didn't mean to hurt you.

He picked up the phone to call the paramedics.

"What do you have planned? Another church Bake Sale?"

Jadish rolled her eyes. He was getting an attitude. He has been Attitude Country for the past few months.

"No, man. *You're* so silly."

I'm so horny but you won't fuck me.

"I'm just Sax."

"Baby I hear it in your voice. Something's wrong. What are you not telling me?"

"I'm good, Jadish. And you know we're having problems in our marriage."

Lenny's brows rose. He held his breath, listening. They couldn't be having problems because if they were she was *not* moving back into the house. Daughter or no daughter. Make your own way in the world and stay out of his way. He was fucking his wife butt booty ass naked the day she turned 18 and left and he'd be damned if she jeopardized his pussy any time soon.

"Baby, is this about sex again. Its like all you think about."

"JADISH!" he exploded, infuriated. Lenny was startled. He wondered what was going on.

"Why are you yelling at my daughter?"

Sax didn't give a shit. He felt like they were trying to double team him and he didn't like being pushed into a corner.

"Can you stay outta of me and my wife's business, Lenny? Thank you."

Lenny averted his face.

Sax had enough. "All I think about is sex? We have been married for two plus years. You haven't let me make love to you. I am a man. You haven't made me a complete man yet and there's *nothing* you or your goddamn father can say about it."

Against his better judgment, Lenny was quiet. He certainly understood. He been there done that before. When he married Jadish's mother Paulette, she was 19 years old at the time. He was gang banging. She was wishy-washy with the pussy in the beginning. But once he got it he was hooked. Lenny wondered why Jadish hadn't had sex with her husband yet. He used to talk to his wife about it all the time. No one knew. But Paulette told him and Sax, "Just don't pressure my daughter. Don't force her because the more you force it the more resistant she will be."

That was an understatement.

"Baby…Just be patient. Tonight I planned a special dinner and everything for us."

"What about my dick? It wants to eat, too. And not any head. I wanna be inside you."

Sax shook with anger and frustration. He never cheated on his wife but every day women threw good pussy at him and he turned it down because he was faithful to this stuck up bitch-of-a-wife. And what thanks did he get? Misery. This was crazy. He lived once and he did not WANT TO DIE A GODDAMN VIRGIN AND HE WOULDN'T!

Even if I gotta pay for pussy.

"I love you."

Sax was quiet, wiping his eyes. Men didn't cry.

"I love you too. I won't be home tonight. I'm staying at your parent's house."

He hung up in her face.

Completely devastated over Tommy, Jadish pulled up into her drive-way. She understood her husband was just mad and he was ego tripping.

She unlocked her door and took a quick shower, getting Tommy's blood off her. Once she was done, she dried off and put lotion on her body. She eyed the door knob, went over to it and she attempted to put her dripping pussy on it but she decided against it. Tonight, masturbation stopped. The touch of her hand would be replaced with her husband's. The veil had been lifted. The burden was gone. She could now fuck her husband for the first time.

And she couldn't wait…

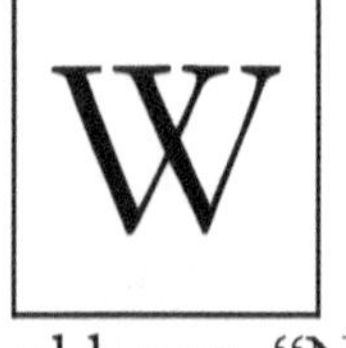hen Sax's father-in-law pulled up in his drive way Sax's eyes swooped over to the worn-down two door Mustang sitting on four cinder blocks. Sax smiled. He loved old cars. "Nice car. Every time I come over here I look at it."

Lenny worried about Sax. He knew what he was going through. Lenny cut the engine. "I wish I could fix it up, but I know nothing about it."

Sax looked at him. "I do."

Lenny was chuckling, his Adam's apple moving. Yea, right Sax. "About fixing it up?"

Sax smiled. He loved cars as much as he loved his wife. "*Hell* yea."

Lenny was skeptical. "Yea, right. Show me."

Sax felt the challenge. "Sure." He got out of the car and walked over to it, his hand on his chin. He observed it and started to walk around it, analyzing. Hmm. He pulled a small notepad from his back pocket and a pen from his work shirt. His dad-in-law stood in the background, smiling.

"Do you have the yellow pages, sir?"

"Yea, I do. Come inside. Plus your mama-in-law cooked some stewed chicken and cornbread and rice. And we know you're going to attack the pot." Lenny's big ass was rubbing his stomach, anticipating the meal. Sax followed him into the house. Thinking of leaving his wife.

For good.

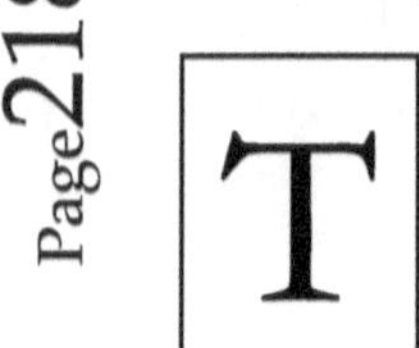ommy staggered from his home, with a towel pressed hard on his dick. He tried to

keep his pants pulled up. He debated calling the paramedics but he didn't. He didn't want to be embarrassed. Blood was dried in his hair. He remembered Jadish ferociously beating him in the head with a frying pan. He'd looked in the mirror. Wasn't too bad. Nothing iodine couldn't get rid of.

A black man carried out on stretcher with his dick half bitten off wasn't the image he wanted to project in his neighborhood. Well, not half bitten off. Just Jadish's teeth marks were in it. He felt like shit. She knew the truth and suddenly he feared his life. Jadish's father used to be a Gangsta, a feared one at that. He knew people who still owed him favors and would do *anything* for him if he decided to get back into it. What if Jadish went to him and told him what happened. He'd be a dead man. And he had his whole life to live, things he wanted to accomplish was his main goal. He couldn't let anybody stop it.

I should leave town!

He got in his car and his hands shook while putting the key in the ignition. Turning it on, he continued to put pressure on his dick until the blood clotted and he drove himself to Miami Jackson Memorial Hospital. He had a few friends who worked there. One was a doctor and the other was a RN.

His cell phone rang.

Lenny's name flashed from the screen.

J adish lit some candles. She had them strategically placed all over the house. A few in the kitchen. On the stove she warmed up the meal she had cooked for her man. Fried chicken. Cream corn. Asparagus and vegetable rice. She pulled out her good China. Smiling exotically, she thought of her husband's dreamy eyes and her pussy was wet and she was slowly rubbing her tits and her fingers suddenly gained weight and dropped to her clit and she was massaging her vaginal walls, cooing into the air. She grinded on her fingers, the wetness electrifying her thirst for her man.

I should do something different. Yea, I think I will. This is a big night for me and my husband. I am going to give him so much pussy he won't know what hit him.

Smiling, she used her pussy juices and with her index finger she wrote *Jadish* on the plate. She clipped a few roses and set them nicely on the edge of the it.

She felt so giddy. But part of her wondered about Tommy. Was he OK? What the hell! He raped you and you're having empathy flashes for him? Get a grip, Chile. *Who gives a rat's ass about Tommy*! I trusted him. But I love him. *But he violated you.* But he's a giving man. *Shut up, Conscious!*

She turned on some Mary J. Blige's "We Ride." She loved Mary. Mary spoke for all women of color, all women in the struggle. She sang for the women who have been up and down. That's what Mary J. Blige meant to her.

And she would share that with her husband.

e took off his shades when the plane was flying into Miami. He pressed some keys on his Blackberry and the name that flashed in his gorgeous face made his heart skip a beat.

Saxophone Jenkins.

J adish was washing a few dishes when the house phone rang. "Must be my baby. Seeing if I'm home. I *knew* he would come."

She dried her hands with a dish towel and turned off the water. Walking past the dining table, she picked up the remote and turned down Mary to a dangerously low level. She paused at the end table and looked at her wedding photo for a second. Sax was so fine.

And he's all mine. I'm gonna make him suck honey off my pussy while fucking me in the ass with a dildo. Hell, yea. I wanna do it all. I'ma kinky bitch and I can finally break free of those nightmares and reclaim my life.

She took up the phone. "Jadish speaking."

"Hey, Girl."

She narrowed her eyes. "*Who* is this?"

"Philippe."

"Oh my God! *Hey*, boy! How is the family?"

"We're good. Is Sax around? I need to holla at him."

"He's at my Dad's house. Call his cell phone. And call me back. I miss you, man. And did your wife like those pictures I sent her of Sax and I?"

"Girl, its all she talked about. Now she wants me to take her to Cancun, Mexico."

"You should. Give her some on the beach."

Philippe closed his eyes and thought, *Yea. Not in this lifetime.*

"Cool. We'll do that. I'll be in touch."

"Ok and you…"

He hung up in her face, leaning back on the seat.

The airplane continued to travel without any turbulence.

ommy rushed through the sliding doors in the Emergency area of the hospital. He was screaming and a few nurses rushed him.

"Sir, what is it?"

"My penis! Someone tried to bite it off."

Several patients were very upset. How did he get to go before them and they were there before he arrived?

Tommy thought about Lenny.

ax saw Miss. Paulette enter the room from the kitchen. She had on a simple black dress and an apron tied around her hip. She smiled when she saw her handsome, sexy ass son-in-law.

Jadish looks exactly like her mother.

She embraced him. "*Hey,* Son."

"Hi, Miss Paulette."

"I didn't know you were here?"

Sax frowned. "Yea. I am."

Lenny cleared his throat and Paulette brushed Sax to the side and she hugged her man. Kissing his lips, he was feeling on her booty and Sax was laughing.

"Ya'll are so nasty," he joked.

"We're in love," Lenny said. He looked into his wife's eyes. "Sax is going to fix up the Mustang."

She looked back at him. "Oh, yea? Good luck. Half of the parts are hard to find. Plus so many bushes and weeds are growing throughout it you might find a few snakes in the carburetor and under the engine. I wouldn't mess with that car if I was you, Son."

Sax opened the phone book. "Really?" he asked rhetorically.

"Yea," Lenny went on, hugging his wife. "We called all over the place for parts."

Sax found a phone number. He took out his cell and called it.

The other line beeped with *Philippe Laagers* in the screen but he didn't see it.

"B ob's Junk Yard."

"Yes, how are you, Sir?"

"Who are you talking to?" Lenny wondered.

Paulette said, "No stores have the parts, Son."

"I know," Sax said. He held up his hand at them. They tucked their chins back with a smile.

"What parts do you have for an '85 Mustang?"

"I have them all. Pricey but affordable."

"Good. How soon can I come by and check it out?"

Lenny's eyes were wide.

Paulette said, "Who *are* you talking to?"

"You can come tonight. We close at about 7 p.m. It's 6 o'clock now."

"Lenny and I will probably be by tomorrow morning." Sax put a thumb up with questionable eyes. Smiling, Lenny put two thumbs up confirming the scheduled date.

"Cool. And your name is?"

He looked into Paulette's eyes. "Sax."

T ommy was told to take off his clothes and to put on the polka dot gown. As part of an emergency measure, one of the doctors put antiseptic and a bandage around his penis. The bleeding stopped. The doctor told him the wounds weren't life threatening, and he'd live. He could still urinate, have sex and do what he do with his penis. He could breathe again. Tommy smiled, but on the inside he was a wreck.

What was I thinking? I can't believe I drugged Jadish's drink and raped her.

Was I not in control?

Should I go to Lenny myself and tell him the truth?

Should I call the police and tell them what happened?

He felt safe right now. The hospital had skin-tight security so he didn't worry about anything.

Did Jadish tell Lenny what happened? This burned him up because he just had to know.

Oh, God. The suspense is killing me. I don't wanna say too much if Jadish didn't say anything yet. If she keeps quiet I will keep quiet.

He picked up the hospital phone and called Lenny's cell.

God please don't let the shit hit the fan.

He sighed. His room door opened and two uniformed cops walked inside.

"Are you Tommy?"

The American Airlines plane landed in Miami at approximately 7:40 p.m. When he grabbed his attaché case, he put back on his glasses. He had serious jet lag.

He slid his Blackberry into his pocket and made his way towards the Budget Car rental place. With Sax on his mind.

"Hello, how are you, Sir?" the woman said, wearing a God-awful black dress. Her hair was thrown into a bun, and thick braces were on yellowing teeth.

"I'm good. I'm here to pick up a rental car."

"Have you already made a reservation?"

He pulled out his I.D. from his wallet. "Yea."

She took it and began typing his information into the computer. His Blackberry rang. He looked at the called I.D.

It was his wife.

He slid the phone back in his pocket.

ax was eating some food. He told Jadish's mother that the reason why he didn't want a lot of food was because Jadish cooked for him. And part of him wanted to go home to his own house and be with his wife.

If only she fucks me. It's going on two and a half years. How many Niggahs would have stayed with their wives if they refused to give up the panties? Not many. Hell, if any I should say.

Lenny sat in the Lazy Boy, barking at ESPN.

Sax set the plate down. "I'll be back. Gotta use the bathroom."

Lenny was so into the sports channel that he didn't hear him.

Sax thought about Jadish. He wanted to go home but his heart wasn't right.

I need a diversion. I can't go home and be with a woman who doesn't even respect me. I have been a gentleman. I never rushed her or tried to force her. But she refuses to love me. I want to have sex. I don't wanna die a lonely virgin who didn't get three minutes playing time in some pussy. Coach, put me in the game. I'm tired of giving my ass to the bench. The bench has fucked me more than I fucked my wife. I want to run out of bounds on that pussy.

Coach, give her my balls so I can give her an orgasm.

Sax opened the front door, without telling his In-laws good-bye, and the house phone rang. He noticed that his mom-in-law was in the bathroom and Lenny refused to move. So he left the door ajar, walking through the living room. He looked at the caller I.D.

It read *Miami Jackson Memorial Hospital.* He answered.

Tommy asked, "Where is Lenny," as the cops stood by the bed with note pads and smiles. *OK, they aren't here to arrest me. If they were they would be looking at me sternly.*

Sax looked at Lenny. "He's…out."

Tommy hung up.

Sax stared at the phone.

Why is Tommy calling from the hospital?

Sax left, getting in his car.

Jadish was in the bathroom. The bubbles went flat and the bath water has turned cold. She drained the tub, ran more warm water and put in some Mr. Bubbles. Sax loved bubbles crackling on his nuts.

He once told her that. It was something that followed him since childhood. She smiled, lighting more candles. The ones she lit previously have burned out. Particularly because they were too little. She should have bought the more expensive ones.

Sitting on the toilet, she glanced at the small boom box. Zhane's CD was on cue. "La La La" would be the first song she wanted him to hear. There was an envelope entitled "Mr. Jenkins" leaning against the tub.

Picking up the scented envelope, she slowly took out the letter, smelling the light perfume and pussy radiating from the page. Setting the envelope on the sink, she unfolded the note and read it over. Making sure there were no misspellings or mistakes.

Everything had to be perfect.

Hello, baby! How are you doing today? I hope this little "note" found you in the best of health and good spirits. I know you're fed up with the fact that you haven't boned your wife yet. Bitter pill to swallow, I know. But this is only temporary. I compiled a little list, which I'm typing right now. You have to do everything on the list so lie back in the tub, relax, smile and be to yourself and your thoughts. Forget about church today, even though it's Sunday. We need alone time. Please don't fight me on this. While you relax, I want you to think about your past. Do you remember how we first me? Do you remember the first words we said to each other? I can remember when you first smiled. I nearly fell down the stairs at the Convocation Building on the University of Miami College campus. Do you remember that? Do you remember our bond? Reflect. The glow and the warmth of the candles should dig silence in your head, allowing you to open-mindedly engulf everything you feel for me. The incense and the gentle smell should open the deepest part of you, a part you thought was forever sealed, and you should let what comes out walk out so you can examine it and hope it makes you a better person. It should allow you to flow with what I'm doing for you. The bubbles in the tub and the warmth of the water, mixed with some edible oil should make your skin soft and collaborate with your being able to allow yourself to let your special Day engross you. I went all out for this day, pulled out all the stops. I know you work 6 days a week and you come home drained and tired. Today is your day, baby.

Let go your inhibitions. Let go of your problems. Forget that people exist in the world. When you hear my voice let the universe cease to exist. The only two people that exist are you and I. The bathroom is the Meditation, Release Room. Utilize it. Let go of imposing bills. I'm cutting your phones off. The special request goes as listed below:

1) Open the envelope titled: Mr. Jenkins, leaning against the wall on the front of the tub. You should be facing it.

2) Secondly, listen the Zhane songs "La La La," and "Off my Mind." Listen to the words. That's how I feel about you.

3) Then listen to Mary J Blige's "Beautiful Ones." And "All I have to Say." "Beautiful Ones" embody everything I feel for you. When I hear this song I think about you.

4) Then put in the PM Dawn CD and listen to "Die Without you" from the Boomerang *soundtrack. This used to be my "cry" song. When I was depressed I'd play this to cry to.*

I know in my heart you are my soul mate. Life is too short for all the fighting and arguing and fussing and alienation.

By now you should know you have a beautiful best friend who thinks the world of you and would do anything for you.

Sincerely,

Jadish Houston. Your wife.

Yes. It was perfect.

She picked up her cell phone and called him.

Sax pulled up into Tommy's front yard and killed the engine. Getting out, he closed the door and looked over the home. Something wasn't right. He felt it. Walking up the sidewalk, he approached the front door. He knocked.

Nothing. The house was dark, the glow of the TV came from his bedroom. He tried the knob. The door opened. His phone rang and he answered it.

"Hey, Sax. Where are you?"

"I had to make a stop. I'm coming." *Wish I was coming in your pussy, you selfish bitch!* "Just keep the food warm. I'll be there."

"OK. I love you. Tonight changes everything, Sax."

Surely does. Because I'm leaving you.
Right after I eat dinner.

Tommy was looking at the cops. "What brings you by?"

"One of the doctors said that someone tried to bite your penis off."

The short, blonde-haired cop asked, "Who was she? What exactly happened?"

So Jadish didn't squeal.
Good.

Sax went inside, closing and locking the door. *Why did Tommy call from a hospital?* The question has burned through his mind. He turned on the living room lamp. The place was a mess. Empty beer cans here and there. Overflowing ash trays. *Ugh! A grown man shouldn't be living this filthy!*

He looked in the dining room and an open bottle of lotion lay on the floor. One of the dining room chairs was angled about four feet away from the table.

He went into Tommy's room, snooping. The room hadn't been cleaned. Tommy was a slob.

He opened the nightstand and looked through open condom wrappers and other bullshit. He opened the bottom cabinet and saw photo albums.

He took one of them out and opened it.

He frowned at the red X's crossed over the faces.

"Oh my *God!* Jadish dreamed of a man with a big red X over his face chasing her."

It now made sense.

J adish looked at her watch. It was going on 8 p.m. Where were you, Sax? She could only warm up the food so many times. She was starting to get the point. Sax wasn't coming home. Her heart burned. She hoped she didn't prepare all that food for nothing. Get a clue, Jadish. The man wants to fuck his wife, not eat any food.

What if he's with another woman?

Nah. He's with my Daddy. She picked up the phone and called her father. He didn't answer. She called again. Her Mom answered.

"Hey, Baby."

"Hi, Mom. Is Sax there?"

"Yes. He's eating. I'll go get him. Hold on."

I knew I could trust him. He's a very sweet man. And I have been unfair to him. He has a right to make love to his wife. I've been so plagued with nightmares that it didn't make sense. Now it's over. Tommy will pay for what he did to me.

She sat on the couch and turned on the TV. Deciding to watch an episode of *Extreme Makeover. Damn, Ma. What's taking you so long?*

"Baby, I'm back…Sax is gone."

Tears filling her eyes, she hung up the phone.

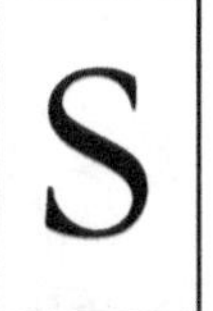

S ax closed the photo album, setting it on the bed. He grabbed his keys and went back out into the living room. Just as he walked past the low table something caught his eye. He walked over to the lotion bottle and got on one knee, looking it over.

He tried to ignore the uneaten KFC on the table, and three ashtrays overflowing with more cigarette butts.

He blinked a few times. A frying pan with dried blood on it was on the floor next to an empty Coke bottle.

Tommy hates Coke. He never drinks Coke.
Jadish lives for Coca-Cola products…
Why is blood on the floor, chair, frying pan and the bottle?
And why was one of Jadish's earrings glittering under the chair?

S ax called the hospital from his cell phone. He went through a series of automated prompts, which got on his nerves. He pressed "0" for Operator.

"I wish to speak with a Tommy Bullard."

"Is he an employee or patient?"

"A patient."

"Hold, please…"

"OK." Why was Tommy admitted into the hospital? Did Lenny know?

What was going on? He knew the frying pan, Coke bottle and his wife's earring told a story.

What was it? He would get to the bottom of it.

"Yes. He's a patient here…"

Sax held his chest. "What room number is he in?"

"Room 567."

"Thank you."

He hung up, running out of the house.

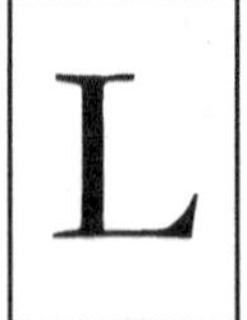enny turned off the TV, standing up. He felt a weird sensation in his gut but before he could give it much thought it dissipated into nothingness.

"Why would Sax leave without telling us good bye?"

"He probably went home to his wife."

"Yea, I suppose. But that's not like him to just up and leave. Especially after we spent the day together fishing and shit."

"What did you catch?"

"Some panties, high heels and fledgling clits," he joked and she didn't find it funny.

"Watch it, Lenny."

He hugged her. "Ah, Baby. I'm just playing. You know this is your dick."

"Whatever."

Lenny kissed her lips and squeezed her ass. She melted from his touch. She gave him some tongue.

"I'm about to shower," she said. "Wanna join me?"

"Yea. Get the water started."

She kissed his cheek, walking towards the bathroom. The phone rang. Why did Miami Jackson Memorial Hospital come up on the Caller I.D. screen? He picked up the phone.

"Hello."

"Hey, Lenny."

"Tommy?"

"Yea, Man. What's up with you?"

"I'm about to go hop in the shower with my wife. Why are you…?"

"Well, go handle your business. I'm at a party, having a good time. Brandisha's here."

Lenny narrowed his eyes. "Really?"

Tommy laughed nervously. "Yea. She says *hi.*"

"Let me talk to her feisty ass."

"She just walked off. But I just called to see how you are doing."

"Cool." Lenny hung up. He sat on the chair, thinking to himself. Why did Tommy call him from a hospital? Easy. He said he was at a party. At a hospital? Yes. OK, if that were true, then why did he say Brandisha said "Hi?" Maybe she did. Well, she must be a ghost because Brandisha died two years ago from breast cancer.

So how in the hell did she say "Hi?"

Tommy, what's going on?

S ax called Lenny. It took him a moment to answer.

"Hey, Son."

"Have you heard about Tommy being admitted into the hospital?"

Lenny jumped up from the chair. "My boy is in the hospital?"

"Yes. Room 567."

"Thanks for letting me know."

Lenny hung up, and went into the bathroom with his wife.

J adish was in the shower, soap all over her body. She was so distraught, she failed to think logically. She didn't want to lose her sexy husband, but in her heart she knew it was already too late. Too much has been done. It was beyond repair. She threw away the food and she trashed the candles. She ripped up the note.

He doesn't love my anymore. And it's all my fault.

She was scrubbing the perfume and expensive lotion from her body. She felt like a fool.

I started this mess. He's a good man.

I should have known he wouldn't wait forever!

L enny entered his bathroom, enveloped in warm, moist steam. He pulled back the shower curtain, looking over his wife. She had soapy bath foam trailing her curvaceous body. He took a moment to look her over.

"Are you getting inside?" she asked, licking her lips. She faced him, her tits perky and ready for the taking.

"I gotta step out for a minute. I want some…ice cream."

She frowned at him. "Ice cream?" She narrowed her eyes. "This time of night?"

"Yes, Baby."

"Ok, Joseph Jackson. Who is she?"

"No, Baby. It's not a she. I want some ice cream."

She slapped him with the soapy rag. "There's ice cream in the freezer, jack ass."

"I don't want nuts in my ice cream."

She chocked, smiling. "OK, boo. But hurry back."

"I'll hurry back, Baby. I promise."

She wrapped her arms around him, sucking on his neck. He pushed back a tad. "You're getting my clothes wet."

"I'm putting hickies all over your neck so a bitch knows you're taken…"

His eyes rolled to the back of his head.

Thirty-eight minutes later, Sax pressed the elevator button. Once it opened, he boarded it and pressed "5". He hated elevators. His heart pounding, he closed his eyes. Something wasn't right in his soul. Why was Jadish's earring under Tommy's chair?

Why?

Two cops were leaving as Sax walked into Tommy's room. When Tommy saw Sax he grew wearily quiet.

"Hey, Tommy." Sax threw a teddy bear at him.

Tommy caught it.

"I guess I should say thanks."

"Nah, you don't have to. Nice wrap on your head. Somebody hit you with a frying pan?"

Tommy was quiet, looking over the bear. "I always liked Curious George."

"That's why I bought the Curious George teddy. Figured you were…curious."

"Why are you here?"

"Talk to me, Tommy," Sax said, sitting down in the chair. He turned off the TV.

"About?"

"Um, life. Let's connect as boys. In the beginning we got off to a slow start."

"Yea. Until you blamed me for the cob webs and tumble weeds in your bedroom."

"I didn't blame you."

"Sure you did. You think me and Jadish got something going on."

"Do you? Is there something I should know?"

"You can't handle a woman of Jadish's caliber."

"Oh, yea?"

"A woman like that you have to fuck daily, to keep her tamed."

"And how do you know?"

"I don't, shit. I would like to know."

Sax was brooding. "I'm not gonna let you get to me."

"Well, the door knob gets to your wife. Tell me something, Sax."

"Shoot."

"Something is wrong when your wife will fuck a door knob and not her husband."

"It's deeper than that."

"Really."

"Yes. It's like those huge red X's on the faces in your picture book."

Tommy grew pensive then. "How do you know?"

"I just left your house."

"You went through my shit?"

"*Yea.* Figured you needed a house keeper. I mean, my wife's earring was under your dining room chair. And an open lotion bottle was on the floor."

"Stay outta my crib."

"Why was her earring…?"

"Like I said, a woman like that needs to be fucked daily…"

"And you say that because…"

"Let's just say Jadish has been watching High School Musical."

"Meaning…"

"She keeps her…head in the game. Ask her. She sucked my dick today, and man let me tell you, Sax was the last thing on her mind…"

A trail of cool air blew over Sax's neck. But he didn't think about it because, angrily, he stood up. About to bash Tommy's head in.

"Why are you trying me, Tommy? Should I go get the cops? Bring them back in here? So we can all talk?"

Tommy was suddenly guarded. "Why should I do that?"

"Because you drugged my wife on her graduation night. You fucked her senseless, Tommy. Come on, Man. Let's not play around anymore."

Tommy cringed inside.

Damn it! He does know! I gotta do damage control.
I can't afford for this to get out.

"I didn't do no such thing, Sax."

Sax sat on the edge of the bed, smiling down at him. "Oh, yea? Why did she wake up with blood all over her? Why was she having those nightmares, of the man with a big red X over his face chasing her through open fields and her high school before he raped her in the middle of the ocean floor after the Red Sea split?"

"Sax, you're accusing me of something unconscionable."

Sax played around with the strap on Tommy's medical gown. "You're right. It was unconscionable what you did. She trusted you. You've been in love with her for years, haven't you? How have you groomed her?"

"Groomed her?"

"Yea. How did you groom her?" Sax stood up, toying with his cell phone.

"I don't know what you're talking about."

"Let me use words from the NiggahCology Dictionary. How did you fatten the Hen before you slaughtered her for Thanksgiving?"

"Sax you're starting to piss me off."

"I know how, Tommy. You were there for her. You offered her your shoulder to cry on. You granted her things her Daddy disapproved of. You read her diary and supported her decisions. You told her she was beautiful and she could do anything."

Tommy was weakening. He wanted to bash Sax's head in. He was in the danger zone and he better trek cautiously.

"Shut up, Sax!"

"Am I right? You warned her of the big bad men in the world. If they promised her the stars grip her panties and run like hell. But what you didn't tell her was that you would be the one to destroy her. You selfishly fucked my wife all night long while she was unconscious, and you should pay."

"It's your word against mine."

"I'm going to tell her."

"She won't believe you…"

"Why shouldn't she?"

"You're just mad because I fucked her and you haven't. Dumb Niggah. You been married to her for over two years and all you did was scratch and sniff the pussy. You virginal asshole."

"You're pissing me off, Rapist."

"So how do you explain Jadish's earring on my dining room floor? She sucked my dick. She knew to bring the pussy to Daddy. Poor, poor Sax. She made me come so fast she swallowed my shit, moaning my name. Begging me to fuck her from the back. But I thought about you and told her I couldn't… You'll die a lonely virgin. How pathetic! You're a bitch ass Niggah. As Puff Daddy says, I don't have time for your Bitchassness, Dawg. I should make you suck my dick, Punk!"

Sax was so upset he walked over to the EKG machine and snatched the cords from the wall. Tommy tried to lash out at him, but Sax punched him in the rib cage, jumping in the bed. They were wallowing, both falling on the floor.

The cool trail of air stopped flowing on Sax's neck.

Two nurses ran into the room, both males, and one grabbed Sax and the other grabbed Tommy. "Call Security on his ass," Tommy shouted. "Putting your hands on me."

"No, call the police," said Sax, trying to push the nurse off him. "He raped my fucking wife, you sack of shit!"

"You two need to calm down," said the thick, stocky nurse. "Larry" was on his name tag. He pushed Sax to one side of the room. The other nurse, "James," pushed Tommy to the other side of the room.

Tommy said, "I am going to shoot your ass, Niggah!"

"Oh, yea? I should shoot your rapist ass, you sick bitch. Why did you rape my wife motherfucker?"

James said, "Calm down you two. I'm not getting in the middle of this, but I will call security on you man if you jump on the patient again."

Sax said, "No need. I'm going to talk to the police."

Sax walked out of the room, burning with rage.

So, Jadish…you sucked Tommy's dick?

Jadish was on the sofa, Maxwell singing into her ears. But she didn't know it because she was sound asleep, the candles on the end table slowly burning out.

And the TV flashing in her face.

Sax was burning rubber in his car. When he turned onto the 836—West Expressway, he whipped out his cell phone. Tears were in his eyes but he refused to cry. The nerve of Tommy! He had to be lying on his wife. Jadish would never give him head. She wouldn't touch him with a ten foot pole. Or would she? You couldn't put anything past a bitch these days. If it quacked the pussy would duck it.

He attempted to call his wife but he hung up, putting the phone on the seat. He didn't know how he felt. Tommy's words replayed in his head.

You virginal asshole.

So how do you explain Jadish's earring on my dining room floor?

She sucked my dick. She knew to bring the pussy to Daddy.

Poor, poor Sax. She made me come so fast she swallowed my shit, moaning my name. Begging me to fuck her from the back. But I thought about you and told her I couldn't…

You'll die a lonely virgin.

How pathetic!

You're a bitch ass Niggah. As Puff Daddy says, I don't have time for your Bitchassness, Dawg.

I should make you suck my dick, Punk!

"Jadish, I hope to God he's lying. Because if he isn't, then I am leaving you forever."

Just then the phone rang.

He answered it with an attitude.

"WHAT?"

"Damn, Homie. It's *Philippe.*"

Sax was ecstatic. He slowly put on the brakes, changing lanes. "Oh my God! Is that my Dawg? My Niggah? My Homie from college?"

"Yea, Man. It's me. Long time."

Sax was about to burst with joy. "Hell, yea! It's been a long time. Where are you?"

"I'm in the Marriot Hotel by the Dadeland Mall."

"You're in town? And you didn't call me?"

"I called your wife, but she said you were out," he said.

"Man I'm coming to see you right now!"

"Where are you?"

"I'll see you in about twenty minutes. What room are you in?"

"Call me when you arrive. I'm at the bar. Let's have some drinks and get caught up on everything."

"I'm on my way, Niggah. Goddamn! My motherfucking Homie is in town."

Sax hung up.

Smiling.

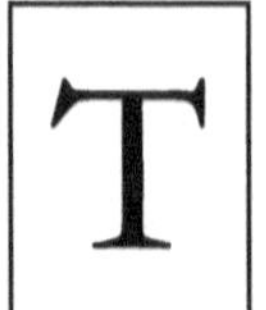T
ommy was being checked by Dr. Williams, an old, black man from South Carolina.

"Well, you're in good health, Tommy."

"Thanks."

"I would advise you to take it easy. Your head is fine. We ran a CAT scan. Everything looks normal. As for your penis. There wasn't any damage. May I make a suggestion?"

"Yes, Doctor."

"Treat the ladies with respect. If you don't…you may not get teeth next time."

They chuckled. Lenny walked into the room, with a small purple, suede bag in his hand. A bottle of E&J protruded from it.

Lenny shook Tommy's hand. "Sup, Niggah."

The Dr. said, "If you will excuse me…" and he left the room.

S
ax pulled up into the Marriot Hotel and a valet parked his car. Graciously he thanked the man and made his way to the front lobby. A very gorgeous black woman greeted him. "Where's your bar?"

She smiled. "Donna, can you watch the front desk." She shook Sax's hand. "Follow me. I'll show you where it is."

Sax looked at her ass the entire time.

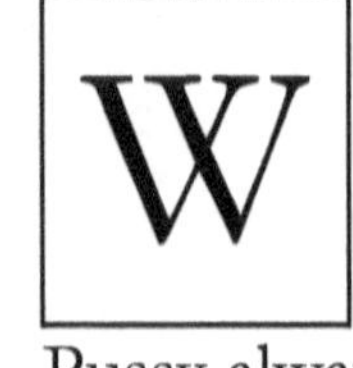W
hen they got there, Sax's mouth fell open. What a bar. It was very clean and classy and he especially drooled over that because a clean bar was like a clean pussy. Pussy always came to clean bars and he had a clean bar

to stick in pussy and that pussy could come, come, come all over the bar, the floors of the nuts and drip down his asshole to keep it consoled, soothed and satisfied.

Suffice it to say, this bar was a little dark, but the dimming of the lights made it look mysterious.

Loving her perfume, Sax shook her hand. It was soft. "Thanks."

"No problem," she said, tugging on her skirt. She looked at him a little too long. Smiling again, Sax pivoted on his heel, walking over to the bartender. The last thing she saw was the gleam from his wedding ring.

Damn! He's married!

Sax sat on a stool, looking around. There were about twenty or so people present, and most of them had on suits and classy dresses. Very adult. Sax liked it. He looked over his shoulder and saw an empty table, towards the back.

Maybe he went to the bathroom.

Sax stood up, walking over to the table. He thought about his life and his wife. He loved Jadish so much. But she had to learn that when you found love you nurtured it, you didn't become a selfish bitch. He waited two plus years to make love to his wife. Not his girlfriend. Not his fiancé. But his wife! And he couldn't wait any longer.

He sat down at the table and folded his hands, lowering his head. He bit back tears, a fire erupting in the pit of his stomach. His skin was hypersensitive. Everybody and everything was turning him on. Temptation called his name everywhere he went.

I don't know how much more of this shit I can take.

Checking his watch, he was startled when he saw Philippe sitting in front of him, smiling.

"Is that my boy Sax?"

Sax gushed with excitement. "Oh my God!" They slapped palms, jumped up to their feet and embraced, patting each other's back. *In five seconds Philippe has shown me more love and affection than my wife has in two plus years, Lord.*

"It's been years, bruh!" Philippe loved his cologne. *What kind of fragrance are you wearing, Sax?*

Don't let me go, Philippe. "I haven't seen you since we graduated college."

Reluctantly, they pulled away, looking each other over. They could not break the gaze. Philippe had arrestingly gorgeous eyes. Pupils that ignited his irises and made for good *aqueous* humor.

"Well damn, bruh," said Philippe, his eyes sparkling. "You put on a few pounds."

"Well, you know," Sax joked, chuckling. "I'm a man now." *And you look good yourself.*

Philippe let the words settle in his ears. "Yes you are. At least it's not fat."

"I know, right! I acquired muscle, and I do watch what I eat." *Except when I'm eating pussy, but my wife is acting stank with that as well.*

"I do that sometimes myself, even though my wife love piling on the food."

"You don't look a day over 20, bruh."

"Well, I'm reaching the thirty mark in a couple years. A Niggah isn't looking forward to pushing up daisies anytime soon."

"Don't even mention daisies. You remind me that I'm right behind you pushing up roses."

Philippe shook his hand. "Ha, ha…how about a drink. My treat."

They tightened their grip, not letting each other's hand go. "Ok. Because I need one." Sax's voice lost its luster and Philippe noticed.

Philippe searched Sax's face. "Are you ok, bruh?"

Sax averted his face. *Can't give anything away. He's in town for a few days. I can't burden him with my problems. Why should I?* "Yea, I'm good. So how's your wife."

Philippe lowered his head and faked a smile. *What do I say?* "She's ok."

"Go order the drinks and we'll get caught up," Sax said, sitting down.

"All right. What do you want?" Philippe asked, pulling out his wallet loaded with plastic Visa cards.

"Buy the whole bottle of Grey Goose."

"Got'cha."

Philippe made his way to the bar and Sax lowered his head.

I stood up my wife. What kind of husband was I? I'm in pain. She stood me up for years. Making me think we were going to make love and she chickens out because of those nightmares. But now that the secret is out, now that she knows that Tommy slipped drugs in her drink and raped her, maybe we can get back on track. Nah. Psychologically my wife is probably fucked up and we need to seek professional help.

But she won't do it.

And Philippe. He looks as good as ever. That's my best friend right there. I love the hell out of him. We met in college, when he was going through a divorce at 19 years old. He was married to an older woman who treated him more like her son than her husband. He had a good job and she was on public assistance with four grown children older than Philippe. She only married him for his money. I was passing by the little park by the University Metro Rail Station when I saw him. The University of Miami loomed behind me. He was sitting on a bench with his head hanging low. What gravitated me towards him was the sadness on his face.

Why was the brothah so sad?

"Are you ok, bruh?" I asked, sitting by him.

His eyes were red. He had Grey Goose in a McDonald's cup, and from the looks of it he was intoxicated.

"No. I'm not, man. And who are you?" he asked, glaring at me.

I extended my hand. "I'm Sax. I go to school here."

"So do I," he said, reluctantly shaking my hand. "I would suggest you leave."

"Why?"

"I'm not in the best of moods, bruh. I'm getting divorced."

"You are?"

He turned away from me. "Yea."

"How old are you?"

"Nineteen," he answered, sighing.

"Damn. And you're married already?"

"It's complicated."

"I would imagine."

"Have you ever been in love?" he asked with an attitude, glaring at me maliciously.

"I can't say that I have. Women are weird asses and I can't figure them out."

He chuckled. "Isn't that the truth? I was married for eight months. She's 43. And she has four grown sons who are twenty-eight, twenty-nine and thirty."

My eyes bulged out of my head. "Wow. So you're the nineteen year old step Daddy running shit."

He laughed, and that's what I wanted to see. "She runs me. She runs my paycheck, she runs my car and she is so demanding. If I don't do what she says she doesn't cook or clean up and her *sons rally against me, trying to jump on me. I fought them three times already."*

"That's not love, bruh. When you have to go through that, love is gone."

"That's why I'm getting a divorce…so you go to school here?"

"Yea."

"Cool, how long have you been going here?"

"I started this year."

"Me, too. Do you live in the dorms?"

"No. I'm from here so I don't have to."

"Do you have a number I can reach you?"

And we exchanged numbers.

S ax smiled when Philippe set the bottle on the table, and two small glasses loaded with ice. "You were daydreaming?" Philippe asked chummily.

"Yea. Are you going to ask me what about?"

"No." Philippe sat down, taking off his suit jacket. His chest was a lot fuller than it was in college, when all the women chased after him. Every day Philippe had new pussy on his tongue or on his dick. When Sax and Philippe finally did get an apartment together during their second year of college, Sax had to buy ear plugs because Philippe was fucking Hoes regularly.

And I still haven't had sex yet.

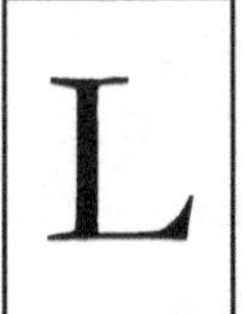

L enny sat in the chair next to Tommy. Tommy, lying in the bed, with his street clothing on, sighed and said, "I had a bad accident, man."

"So that's why you didn't call me and let me know you're in the hospital?"

Tommy wouldn't look him in the eyes. "Yes. I didn't want you to worry."

"Now I'm as worried as ever. Was your car totaled?"

"Yes," Tommy lied.

"So that explains why you lied about being at a party at the hospital…"

"I'm sorry, man. I lied because I didn't want you stressing out over me."

"That's my decision, and you're my best friend. My family loves you and whatever they love I gotta protect at all costs."

Lenny lowered his head, holding back his grief. A lot was churning through his mind and he didn't know what to think about anything. "How long have we been road dogs?"

"A very long time," said Lenny.

"Seems like centuries."

"You are the only man I ever brought around my family. I love you like a brother. In a lot of ways you are my brother. We have always had each other's back. We have always been there for each other. We could tell each other any and everything, no matter how big or small, no matter how good or bad." Lenny looked up, his eyes tired and red. "Want something to drink? I bought some E&J."

"Sure."

Lenny opened the huge paper bag and pulled out two plastic cups. He set the ice in the sink, ripping open the bag. He put in three ice cubes and poured Tommy something to drink. He handed it to him.

"Thanks."

"No problem."

Lenny poured himself something to drink and replaced the cap on the bottle. Sliding the bottle back into the purple velvet bag, he then put it in the paper bag on the floor.

He set his drink on the little counter behind him. "Are they letting you go home tonight?"

"Yea. Even though my head is killing me." Tommy wolfed down the drink, and wanted more. Lenny handed him the other cup. Lenny didn't want the drink anymore, Tommy could have it. Tommy wolfed it down.

"Are you sure you're ok, Man?"

"Yes, Lenny." Tommy turned on the TV.

"I know you like a book."

"Depends on what book you're reading. I'm not the Color Purple tonight. Cellie has left the building."

"Ha. Dear Tommy? What book are you?"

"Dear Lenny. I'm *The Silence of the Lambs*."

"Oooh. Hannibal."

"Yea."

"I gotta get out of here. I have an angry wife at home who keeps blowing up my phone. I told her I was going out to get ice cream."

"And you haven't gotten it?" Tommy asked, laughing.

Lenny fell silent for a brief moment. "No. I said that so I could come see why you're in the hospital. I didn't want her worrying about you."

Tommy's brows rose. "Does Jadish know I'm in here?"

"No," Lenny said. "I didn't tell her."

Tommy was relieved. "Good. Good."

Lenny cupped Tommy's hand. "So I'll see you tomorrow. You are checking out tonight, right?"

"Yea."

"Here," said Lenny, handing him the bottle of E&J. "You can keep this. Drink up. I can't drink all this shit, plus I'm driving home."

"Thanks, man."

L enny was walking to his car, thinking to himself. *Why didn't my best friend call me the second he got to the hospital? That isn't like him. I know this man more than I know myself. I used to be a goon, I know these things. I know the streets; I can be a goblin when I wanna be. I will tote those guns; I will blast those lights if something isn't clear to see.*

Lenny reached his car and unlocked it. When he opened the door his eyes landed on another car and his mouth fell open.

It was Tommy's car.

And it wasn't totaled.

I hate motherfucking liars!

S ax and Philippe had one too many drinks. They were laughing, talking about the happenings in the news. A few people left the bar, heading to their rooms. And once the clock struck ten p.m. they were the last two in the bar.

"So, why didn't you bring your wife down here to great ole Miami?" Sax asked, popping peanuts in his mouth.

"She's back at home, holding it down. She gotta handle our affairs there."

Sax was silently chewing. "So…how's your son? I know he's getting big."

"Yea, he is."

Sax swallowed the peanuts. "I bet he looks just like his Daddy."

"Yea he does. I talked to him earlier. He wants to talk to you."

"Well, call him up!"

"He's sleeping. He has school tomorrow, remember."

"Oh, yea. I remember back in the days Mama made me go to bed at 9 p.m. every night, even on weekends."

"Taught you how to be punctual didn't it?"

"Yea…"

Philippe had a thought. "How's Jadish? I called her tonight, asking for you."

Sax's frown crashed on the table, literally. He hesitated with his answer. "She's…selfish."

They fell quiet. "Selfish, *how*?"

Sax was laughing, but inside his heart was slowly corroding. "I've been married over two years and she still hasn't made love to me."

Philippe's eyes were wide. "What? Are you fucking me right now?"

"I wish I was. Then maybe I'll finally get some ass."

"She hasn't made love to you, man?"

"No." Sax drank his seventh glass of Grey Goose and wanted another. His eyes were narrowed and he felt good to finally get that out.

"So what did you do on your honeymoon?"

"The selfish bitch jacked my dick, made me come and rolled over and went to sleep."

"Why? I didn't take Jadish for the selfish type."

"Don't get me wrong. She's a very compassionate woman. But when it comes to her pussy she's the Queen of the Damned."

"Man…so Akasha ain't coming off the pussy."

"Basically." *Akasha was one of the characters from Anne Rice's Queen of the Damned book.* "And Aaliyah's dead so there goes Jadish's pussy."

"Well, I have a confession to make," Philippe said, looking into Sax's eyes.

"What?"

"My wife and I are getting a divorce."

"Wow. Oh my God. Man. Why?" Sax sat up straight, pouring another drink. He refilled Philippe's glass.

"She's in love with someone she met in high school. An old flame has rekindled in her loins and she wants him. He calls her up and says he has Cancer and it's like she dropped me and our son to rush to his aide, and somewhere along the line they made love and she wants to be with him until his dying day."

Sax was stunned. "Whoa."

"Yea. She traded in our wedding vows for the leukemia patient."

"Wow, man. So I guess we're both…"

"In the same boat. I haven't made love to my wife in ten months. Ten, dawg. I'm faithful to her. Back in college I wasn't faithful at all. I fucked women left and right."

"I know. I was late to half my classes the next morning because of it. A Niggah couldn't sleep because the bitches were 'Ahh, yea, fuck me in the ass, Daddy!' all damn night…"

"You're a trip, Homie."

"I'm in love with a woman who won't let me fuck. Isn't that one of the quirks of marriage? To get pleased at home so you don't have to pay for pussy in the streets?"

"That's what I heard. But men pay for it whether they like it or not."

"I haven't."

"When you pay their rent, lights and water and buy the grocery and buy the gas to cut the lawn and fill up your woman's tank, you're paying for pussy."

"Damn, man. Never thought about it like that…well, I'm done paying. I may be filing for divorce. And I haven't told Jadish yet."

"When are you going to tell her?"

"I might let the lawyer tell her."

"That's the best way to handle it. My lawyer worked out the legalities and everything. I'm letting my wife keep the house so my son keeps a roof over his head and we will split custody."

"Man I know this will be hard on your son."

"It's even harder on me, because I feel like a failure."

Sax took his hands. "What? Why do you feel like a failure?"

"I lost my family. A man isn't a man unless he can build a home and run his household successfully, like a successful business. Sure, sometimes the NASDAQ will drop or crash, but his home is his home and as long as his woman and child is happy and content under one roof then he succeeded. But I failed."

"You're an incredible husband, Dawg. And you are an equally incredible father. Your son loves you. You taught him how to read before he even started Pre-K."

"I surely did."

"And you always treated your wife with love, kindness and respect. I remember when I saw you two get married. Remember?"

"Yea."

"You were glowing, man. You were so happy to be divorced from the older bitch that ran your life that you could barely contain yourself. Your wife has an education and grew up middle class. It doesn't mean she's better than anyone else, it just shows that not all black women grow up in the ghetto."

Philippe rubbed his thumbs over the top of Sax's hands. "Thank you, man. I needed to be reassured…"

"So don't ever say you failed. Your wife failed you. Women want a good man and when they get one they fuck it up with baggage they should have given to the Goodwill before they got married."

"True. And now I'm losing my wife. And I wanna make love. And I can't…"

"I have wants and needs and desires…"

"And fantasies and my wants I have never needed because I never got what I needed and now I am a walking, horny toad and all I want to do is fuck something."

"I want to fuck something my damn self."

"What are you waiting for?"

"What are you waiting for?"

Philippe licked his lips. "The right person."

"But H.I.V. is out there and STD's and I don't have time for all those doctor check ups, unless it's to check my cholesterol."

"I'm getting sleepy, Homie."

"Ok. I gotta get home to Jadish. She cooked me some fancy dinner tonight."

"And you didn't go?"

"No. She stood me up for two plus years. Tonight, she saw just what that felt like."

Philippe stood up, having a little trouble keeping balance.

Sax wrapped his arm around Philippe's waist, helping him to the elevator. *He feels good next to me,* Sax thought quietly.

"I got you, Dawg. What room number are you in?"

"Room 269."

"OK. I'll help you. Then I gotta be getting home."

Philippe's heart dropped. "Thanks, man. I appreciate that."

Sax shook his head. "What are best friends for?"

"Tell that to my wife."

Sax laughed, pressing the elevator button. "Tell that to mine. With her selfish ass."

The elevator doors opened.

L enny entered his home and closed the door and his wife slapped him.

"Are you cheating on me?" she asked, looking a wreck. She'd been crying and she was about to explode.

"No, baby."

She was punching at him. "Where's the ice cream, liar? I thought you wanted ice cream! Who is she? Oh my God, Lenny! I have been nothing but obedient to you and you go out and…"

Lenny hugged his wife. "Baby, calm down. There isn't another woman. I went to see Tommy in the hospital. He was in a bad car accident."

"Oh my God! Tommy! Is he ok?"

"Yes. I just left there. I stopped by the store and bought him some things and I sat and talked to him for a while. He's being released tonight."

"I'm sorry, baby."

"I forgive you, Honey. I'm man enough to handle you. That's why I married you."

She kissed her husband. "What's in the bag?"

"I had to buy some rat poison. I saw a rat behind the washer."

"Make sure you kill it."

I already have.

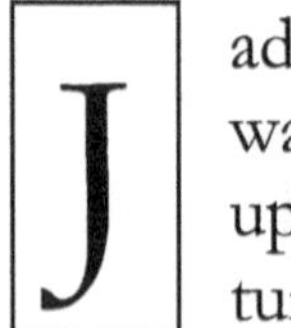adish awakened with a start. She looked at her watch. It was a little past 11:30 p.m. She stood up, stretching. The TV was blaring so she turned it off.

"Sax!" she called out but there was no answer. Annoyed, she went to the bedroom and he wasn't there. "He still hasn't come home. What have I done? Is it too late? Did I lose my husband?"

Her eyes fell down on the door knob, the one that brought her so much pleasure. There was a magnetic force inside the metal, beckoning her to spread her ass cheeks and back up against it so it could slide up inside her pussy. She actually smiled thinking about it. Running her fingers across the brass, she shook her head and decided against it.

Tonight I leave the door knob behind and I fuck my husband. I will finally give my husband his pussy. No more door knobs. I have to stop being selfish and nurture my man. He deserves it. After all I did make vows to love him, to cherish him and to nurse him during sickness and in health.

She called his cell phone.

ommy was checked out of the hospital. He walked to his car, disoriented. Lenny couldn't find out about what he did to Jadish. He couldn't lose his best friend and he didn't want to go to prison or be labeled a sex offender. When he reached his car he unlocked the door and got inside.

It took him a minute to gather his thoughts. He was rubbing his face, his legs trembling. He really couldn't afford to go to jail. Maybe he should talk to Jadish. What if she called the police when he showed up. No, Tommy. Stay away. Leave her be. She needed to calm down and rethink things. Maybe time and patience was what everybody needed. Yea. That had to be the answer. Let sleeping dogs lie.

What can I do? I have to do something.
If I don't I could be looking at serious prison time.
He knew what he had to do now.

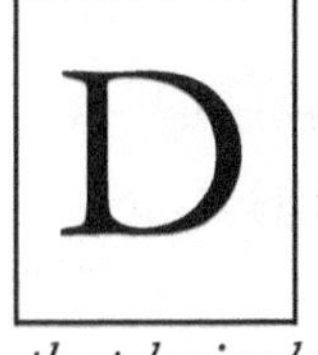

hen Sax got off the elevator, the phone buzzed in his pocket. Philippe said, "Aren't you going to answer that? That's probably your wife."

"I'm getting divorced, remember. I don't have a wife."

Philippe said, "Whatever you decide to do I got your back."

The phone stopped ringing in his pocket.

eeply disheartened, Jadish threw the phone on the floor. *He's not answering the phone. He's probably mad with me. Oh, Baby. Come home. So I can make it up to you. I can be there for you in that lovingly special way. I can finally make love to you and give you all of me. I can make you a man tonight. For two plus years you've been just a male, now you can be a man and come deep inside your wife.*

We'll go half on a baby.

Philippe's head was swimming, but he knew where he was. Feeling the cool air from the AC somewhat mellowed him. The lights on the ceiling fan were very bright. He was glad to be back in his room, where he felt safe. Sax released him, standing up straight. He checked his watch.

"I gotta go, bruh…" His head felt light, and his legs were about to give out. *Oh, God. Can I even drive in this condition? I don't wanna leave Philippe. He's the one bright spot in my life. Maybe I should stay here. Maybe I shouldn't.*

No.

I shouldn't.

Because if I don't leave I am going to fuck the shit out of him.

Wait, Sax. What are you saying?

I'm saying this: I'm in love with Philippe, and I don't know how to tell him.

No, you're not. You're just hurt. You're not thinking logically. You are making rash decisions based on the weakness of your flesh.

No, I'm not.

Yes, you are. You need to leave, go home to your wife and beg for her pussy if you have to.

No. Why should I beg for pussy when she's my wife? It should be easy as 1-2-3.

"I can't let you drive drunken, bruh," Philippe said, taking his hand. Sax looked down at it, his heart hammering. He could barely catch his breath.

Stop touching me, Niggah. I love the softness of your hand. I love everything about you. I wanna taste that ass. "I gotta try to get home."

Philippe snatched Sax's keys, and dropped them inside his pants. They pressed against his dick. Philippe pulled Sax closer to him, breathing his air. He could not take his eyes off him. The flames were ignited. The fire was building. "I can't let you, man. What if you get in a crash or something, then I can't live with myself knowing I let you walk out of my hotel door without attempting to stop you. If something happens to you I will go crazy."

"Why will you go crazy? Life goes on."

Tears built in Philippe's eyes. He hated expressing himself. Every time he expressed himself to his selfish wife she laughed at him and made him feel foolish. *Please don't make me feel foolish, Sax!* "I don't want life to go on without you, baby."

I love your height, your face, and your sincerity. "I don't want to live without you, either…"

Go for the juggler, Philippe. Do it, Niggah. He's right here in front of you. He's the reason you boarded a plane spur of the moment and came to Miami. Sax is the reason you don't want to be with your wife anymore. So go for it, goddamn it! "Stay with me tonight…if not the entire night, just stay for a little while. Be my singing group Jodeci. Let me be your group member, Devante Swing."

Sax was falling deeper into a vortex. *I love the sparkle of your eyes; I love the sun of your smile. The way your dimples form when you lick your lips. The way your lips bend over the tip of the glass when you're drinking.*

"I gotta go, man. Jadish is waiting. Thanks for your concern."

Abruptly, Sax yanked his hand back and turned to face the door.

I gotta get out of here. Run, Sax, Run! Bubba Gump wants your shrimp and you don't have a shrimp boat, Niggah. You want Jenny, but she's at home, biologically named Jadish Houston. And she has sweet, sweet nectar between her legs. That gushy stuff that makes you a man.

His tie loosened, Philippe walked in front of him, blocking the door. "Look me in the eyes and tell me you truly want to leave."

"Man, trust me. I don't wanna leave but I have to go. I have to get home to my wife. I made her wait enough. I love her."

"But she doesn't love you. If she loved you, why wouldn't she make love to you on your honeymoon?"

"Because she was making me suffer for another man's mistake."

"That's not love," Philippe said, his lips getting closer to Sax's.

"What is it then?"

"Selfishness. Baggage."

God, move this man from in front of the door. If his lips touch me I am going to beat his ass to a pulp. I have to do that, Lord. Because I want my dick so far in his ass I want him screaming from the excitement.

Sax looked away from him. "I'm not going to rush home. I will drive slowly. Why should I rush home to a loveless home? My wife will never make love to me. I will officially die a virgin."

Philippe said, "Sax...Look at me."

"No."

"Come on, Man. Don't do me like this."

"Just leave Jadish out of your mouth."

"I can't. I respect her, yes. But she doesn't respect you, Sax."

"Please!"

Philippe stroked Sax's cheek. "Aren't we boys?"

"Yes, man." *Lord, his touch is setting me on fire. I want his fingers in my mouth.* "Get your hand off me, goddamn it!" *I'm sorry, Philippe. I didn't mean to yell at you. But I will never tell you that.*

Initially hurt, Philippe walked past him, and paused by the bed, taking off his jacket. He dropped it on the floor.

Philippe was shaking his head. *What was I thinking,* Philippe wondered bitterly. *He doesn't want me. Sax isn't even bisexual. I'm the weird one. I shouldn't push my lifestyle on him. And even though I'm not out the closet and my wife doesn't know, I love him too much to lose him.*

Sax closed his eyes, biting back tears. *I can't cry. I'm a man. I have to fight temptation. Philippe is a very gorgeous man. I can't lie. I fantasized about him years ago in college. I once masturbated while I called out his name, but I never acted on those feelings. I was never abused as a kid. I was never raped or anything like that. I had a good life and a very good upbringing. So why did I want to make love to my male best friend?*

Philippe cleared his throat. "Sax, please. Look at me."

Slowly, Sax opened his eyes. He was surprised that the ceiling fan lights were turned down very low. He turned to look at Philippe and his mouth fell open. Philippe stood there.

Clad in his boxers.

His clothes were at his feet. He was smiling, his eyes sparkling. He'd rubbed baby oil all over his amazing chest, his nipples erect and mouth watering. He looked like a helpless dog searching for food and never finding it.

Sax was blown away.

"Philippe…" I want him, Lord. Forgive me, Father. I have to have him. Just once. Just for tonight. One night, God. One time. The recital and the encore all in one nutshell.

Desperately, Philippe wrapped his trembling arms around Sax and their lips anxiously and awkwardly touched…then they fell into each other like well-mixed paint. Sax felt vulnerable, melting underneath Philippe's sweet touch. He taste good, the inside of his mouth warm. Sax greedily held Philippe's buttocks, and his tongue dipped from his mouth and trailed his neck. He gave him a few passion marks, taking his time. Careful not to rush or appear needy.

Philippe took Jadish's prize. "If your wife won't give you some ass then I will," Philippe said, smiling inside. "I will give you what you've desired all night long, baby. I am your ocean, give me the shore."

The flood gates inside Sax's flesh burst open. He could no longer contain himself. A sudden sexual knight in shining armor, Sax picked him up and walked to the bed. He was tired of being Repunzel. He was tired of being trapped in the tower. He was going to let down his zipper and explore. He wanted to know what his feet felt like on new soil. He wanted to blaze new terrains and slay new jungles.

Sax gently lay Philippe down and used his teeth to take off his boxers. When Sax saw his penis he was hesitant. He cracked a smile.

My God! I've never been this hard for my wife. My dick is on brick status. I can actually feel it throbbing in my briefs.

Then reality struck.

Sax stopped smiling. "What am I doing?" he asked, sitting on the bed, his head hanging low.

"What's wrong?" Philippe asked, putting a pillow under his head.

I've broken my vows, Lord. I've betrayed you and my wife. I should be stoned do death. "I've never been with a man before. Where is all this coming from?"

"Maybe it comes from your heart."

Sax looked back at him and couldn't help but smile when he looked in his heavenly eyes.

But I love him, God. How long have I loved him, who knows? But why was being with another man wrong? Was it really wrong, God? You said in the Bible you want us happy. Well, my wife hasn't made me happy. Philippe has made me happy. I want to cry when I look at him. I want to tell him all my joys, pains and sorrows when he blinks. And now I want to feel his warmth, his tightness. "Maybe I'm just hurt because my wife doesn't accept my true worth."

"Maybe she doesn't know how to calculate your true worth…"

Sax said, "I should go. I already went too far."

Philippe sat up, unbuckling Sax's pants. "Then I will take over."

Philippe pulled out Sax's humongous dick and slowly put it in his mouth, slurping and pulling expertly. Sax died in his stroking ability. His eyes rolling to the back of his head, he licked his lips, spreading his legs as far as they'd go. He couldn't believe Philippe felt like this.

Work it, baby. It's yours if you want it. My wife abandoned it. Shit. Abandoned? She never really had it inside of her.

So what was he truly missing from his wife? A thought? A dream? A fantasy? They were moaning together and kissing seconds later. They couldn't keep their hands off each other and why should they? They were both on the verge of divorce. They both wanted and needed each other. Sax actually relaxed, telling himself that if Philippe hadn't come to town he probably would have chocked Jadish for toying and boxing his emotions like Barbie dolls, to be consumed commercially. Sax was rubbing, needing and desiring his best friend in ways he never knew existed.

"I wanna fuck, Philippe. I wanna lose my virginity, tonight. I can't take it anymore. Too much is built up inside of me. I am about to loose it, baby…"

Sax lovingly turned Philippe on his stomach and got on his knees. He admired the view from the back.

I can't believe a man is this beautiful. Philippe, you are so gorgeous to me. I love your body. I want to explore. I want to do to you what my wife didn't let me do to her. You're going to love it. I will spend all night stroking you, fucking you, massaging you and tasting you if I have to. I just don't want you to leave me.

Stay with me.

Spreading his ass cheeks, he slowly ate Philippe out, bringing him pleasure. He loosened him up, getting him to match his rhythm. Philippe couldn't believe that it was finally happening.

After years of imagining what it was like, he now found out.

Sax slowly put the tip of his dick on Philippe's warm opening, pushing inside him slowly and cautiously. Philippe bit the pillow, slowly pressing his ass back.

Once Philippe's butt cheeks connected with Sax's torso they rocked and fucked the next few hours away, trapped in their secret sexual bliss. Sax pretended the outside world didn't exist. He needed nourishing and Philippe made him feel godly, made him feel whole.

What have I been missing, he pondered, thrusting himself inside Philippe. *He feels so good. I love this man. I want this man every day. I'm addicted to his body already.*

Philippe was receiving him without packing slips.

Sax flipped Philippe on his back, his dick still inside of him. They looked into each other's eyes and continued to rock the boat in unison. Philippe wrapped his legs around Sax's waist, holding his amazing ass.

"I love you," Philippe said.

Sax gave him some tongue. "I love you, too…"

"You feel so incredible. Just the way I imagined."

"Imagine no more, baby…Kiss my lips."

They kissed, slowly building themselves into a crescendo of lust. Sax didn't want the night to end. Philippe pushed all thoughts of his wife from his brain. If this was wrong, Lord they didn't want to be right. Selfish pleasures overshadowed logic and thought. Sax suckled on Philippe's nipple, softly biting it. Philippe was grinding all over Sax's thick stick, about to explode all over himself. They were face to face, breathing and panting…huffing and puffing.

"I'm about to come, Philippe."

"Come inside me."

Sax's body locked up. Philippe's warmth took him captive, kidnapping his spirit and gave him relief. Sax felt himself throbbing, his seeds pumping inside

Philippe's warm flesh. He screamed out from the pleasure, not believing it felt like this. He was sweating so hard he lay on top of Philippe and they fell asleep in each other's arms.

In love.

There was a knock at my door. I didn't know who it was, and whoever it was they were going to get cursed out. For one, they didn't call. I liked for people to call me BEFORE they come over. Not AFTER they arrive. What if I was sucking Sax's dick? Do you think a doorbell will stop me?

I was already upset. Past upset. Sax hasn't called me. I tried calling him again and nothing. My father called me and I didn't answer. Mama called me and I ignored it. I wanted to hear from my husband. I couldn't find him and this worried me because he has never been this late coming home. Never.

I checked my hair in the mirror. I didn't bother with putting on a coat to cover my lingerie. Why should I? This was my house.

I opened the door, shaking my hair behind my head and when my eyes landed on Tommy I had heart failure trying to slam the door.

But he grabbed it.

"Jadish, *please*. I need to talk to you."

"Talk to me about what?" I stammered, pressing my body against the door, using everything I could muster to push it closed. But Tommy was too strong.

"Baby, please."

"Baby? I hate you! Get away from me."

"Please, allow me to explain."

"Explain what?"

He pushed it so hard I fell on my ass, disoriented. He came inside, closing the door. He stood there with a box of chocolates and a dozen roses. Bitch. He knew I loved chocolate and roses. But I loved my virginity more and he raped me on my graduation night. On the night everything came together for me. When I was celebrating my achievement with my friends he plotted the demise of my pussy. He took that from me and I didn't have a clue. I remembered waking up with blood everywhere and my body on fire. Maybe I did know what happened. Maybe I was just in denial.

He extended his hand, but I averted my face.

"Can I help you off the floor?"

"I feel safe on the floor. Away from you!" I spat icily. My heart beat out of my chest. I was so afraid of this man. I feared him to the point I think I was starting to break out in hives.

"Jadish."

I staggered to stand up. He had sad eyes. I loved this man. He was my God daddy. How could he betray me? I was having a hard time with this. I wasn't going to be able to eat or sleep. Because of Tommy I made my husband suffer.

"What do you want, Tommy?"

He handed me the roses and chocolate. Absentmindedly I accepted the flowers. I tossed them by the front door. He watched them separate from the bunch.

"Forgive me."

"Forgive you for what?"

"What I did, Jadish."

"I want you to say it. Tell me what I should forgive you for."

"For having sex…"

"Having sex? That's what you call it?" I asked, putting my hands on my hips. Tears fell from my eyes. It really felt like I was against the world. Like I stood on my own. I had a husband and a father. But I felt so disconnected from them. Like somebody turned my computer off and no information surged through my fucking hard drive. That's how I felt right now.

"Yes, Jadish."

I had to sit down, my face in my hands. I was rocking back and forth. "When you say 'having sex,' that means it was an act agreed upon by two consenting human beings." My head snapped up. He walked up to me, sitting on the low-table, careful not to make me cut his ass. "You consented. I didn't. Did you have fun, Tommy?"

"No, Jadish. I was being greedy. I was in love with you and I didn't know how to tell you."

"You were in love with whom? You?"

I saw the love in his eyes. It was undeniable. I couldn't turn from it. I loved him, too. But in an Uncle kind of way. I used to be in love with him, back when I was a teenager and I didn't know love from the hole in my pussy. But now, too much has been done.

"Please…I'm not trying to pressure you."

Girl, good or bad he's your god father. He has been there for you during some trying times in your life.

But he put drugs in my drink and when I was out of it he fucked me left and right. How do you explain that?

Forgive the man. Men are creeps. You know that. Men are uncontrollable motherfuckers. You know that, too.

Sax is perfect.

Sax is falling out of love with you.

"Jadish. Did you hear me?"

I broke open. I couldn't take it. "I should tell my father."

"Please, keep this between us."

"Keep what between us, Man? I still want to hear you say it."

"Fine. I was so in love with you I thought you'd reject me if I came out and told you I wanted you to one day be my wife. I watched you from a kid grow up, develop and mature before my very eyes. You were like those roses. Red with love. I wanted you. I desired you. I wanted to take you to your prom…"

I was stunned he felt that way. "So I guess being there for me when I was young, giving me what I wanted and giving me money was your way of grooming me before you pounced."

"No."

"YES! They call that grooming the victim. You groomed me well. I can't look past the fact that…FUCK! You still haven't said what you've done!" I jumped up to my feet and slapped him so hard his head snapped back. He closed his eyes, sucking down the pain.

"Go ahead. Shoot me, lash out at me. I'm in love with you. I've already lost you."

"SAY IT! SAY WHAT YOU DID TO ME! WHAT DO YOU WANT ME TO FORGIVE YOU FOR?"

"I loved…"

"Tommy!" I snatched him by the shirt and he stood up, standing face to face with me. Our lips were inches apart. My body cried out for him. I felt the heat radiating from his skin. Why did I let him in? Why didn't I call the police the instant I saw his face? Why was I in a catch 22? Why didn't I want to see him suffer?

What do I do, God! You forgave me so many times. Sax has forgiven me so many times. We're not perfect.

I inhaled deeply. "Tommy. Tell me what you did. Without all the *I love you* and *I did it because…* I want to hear you say it. Be a man. Own up to what you did. Be like Ilyana Vanzant and acknowledge your mishap."

He inhaled also, looking at me. He took both my hands and I melted. My pussy was so wet my panties threw a block party on my clit and invited my ass cheeks for drinks because no matter how much shit they go through my ass cheeks are loyal motherfuckers. They always come back together.

"Fine, Jadish. I watched you in your cap and gown. Your smile set me on fire. Your eyes held me hostage. The sight of your amazing body made me lose it. I got you a martini and when no one was looking I slipped crushed pills inside, stirring it with a miniature red straw. I handed it to you. You took it to the head. I urged you to have another drink. I put another crushed pill in it. Slowly but surely I lured you from the party. I told you to go to your room. You did. I beat you there. When you came inside I closed and locked the door. I was already naked. I had rose petals on your bed. You were zonked you didn't see the lit scented candles. I slowly took you into my arms. You were disoriented. You started moaning piteously, saying you had a head ache. I gently lay you down…"

I couldn't believe I was hearing this. Why did my heart skip a beat? Nowhere in this did he say he was a beast, that he rushed and fucked me and left. He had rose petals on the bed?

He kissed both my hands. "I then…"

I leaned up to him and our lips touched. Sax didn't want me; I didn't want myself if Sax left me. He didn't come home and Tommy was my God father. But for some reason my body responded to Tommy in ways it hadn't for Sax. Maybe my body had a memory cell. Maybe it remembered Tommy gave me my first string of dick. Our tongues danced slowly. He was awkward, opening his eyes. He didn't trust me. He cringed inside, backing up.

"No, Jadish. I can't do this to you. I violated you. I am an asshole. I'm a sick individual and I should be dragged in the street and shot."

He pivoted on his heels and raced to the door. Scooping up the roses, he opened the door and I pushed it closed, grabbing him by the shirt. I pushed him on the floor and I got in his lap, pulling my titties from my bra. They sat there like two famished fat bitches ready for some goddamn cake.

"Jadish. Please…let me go."

"Make love to me. Recreate in this room what you did in my room on my graduation night."

"I can't…I am trying to atone for what I've done. I don't want to go to prison. But if you do call the cops then I will accept my fate."

I brought my quivering lips to his, and we tasted my tears. Gradually his hands explored my body, his fingers firm and polite. He was being a gentleman. He closed his eyes, finally relaxing. My pussy was so wet a huge wet spot was on his pants.

He picked me up and carried me to the couch. He gently laid me on it. I spread my legs and he got on his knees, tasting my pussy. He took his time. While he tongue fucked me he pushed both my legs back, grabbing one of the roses with his other hand. He pulled his tongue out, and told me to hold my legs back.

"Don't let them go."

He went into the kitchen and I quivered. I was about to pull my hair out. If Sax was here this was what I wanted him to do. But he couldn't hold his temper in place. He didn't come home. What if he's fucking another bitch? I couldn't even be mad at him if he was and I'd forgive him, this once.

Tommy appeared with a bottle. He got on his knees and removed the cap. Setting the cap on the table, he poured the virgin olive oil all over my pussy. Now this was hot. He slowly massaged it in, careful to drape my clit with it. Wow. What a feeling. This has never been done to me before.

"I'm sorry, Jadish. I shouldn't have done that to you. But I want to do it right."

"Baby, I'm tired of getting head. I want to make love."

"I want to taste you."

"TOMMY FUCK ME NOW!"

He smiled, standing up and unzipping his pants. He pulled them below his waist, his dick hard and ready. I looked for my teeth marks. Could he make love to me after I tried to bite his dick off?

He got on his knees and told me to spread my lips. I did with urgency. Into my pussy he dove. Swimming for the Olympic gold and finding the silver metal on my pussy.

I held him, indulging in his powerful arms, his powerful hips. He moved like pistons. I enjoyed every second. Dick felt like this?

Oh my God! I didn't know it would feel so incredible, so wonderful. I spread my legs and he pushed them back, like a huge V on my couch. The olive oil gave his dick the lubrication, and it was then I thought about a condom. God, what was I doing?

Girl, he's in the pussy now. Just enjoy it.

"Jadish…you feel so good, baby…goddamn, baby…"

"Get it, Tommy. Get it, baby."

"…What about Sax?"

"Fuck Sax. Just fuck me and shut up."

"Your wish is my command."

Tommy was excited; finally getting to make love to a woman he's been in love with for years. Jadish trusted him again. She had to. Part of him didn't want to go up in her pussy raw but this was Jadish. A girl who kept her legs closed all through high school. A girl who was almost raped by friends and he and Lenny saved her.

"Jadish, I'm about to come. I don't want to come yet. It's too soon…"

He tried to pull out but she wrapped her legs around him and held him there. The minute she did her body tensed up and she twirled her hips for dear life.

It built up in her body, swirling in her loins, tossing in her skull, burying in her pussy and she exploded, coming all over Tommy's dick the instant he started to come deep inside her, her pussy receiving the nutrients and her tight walls remembering the scent.

She was panting, her eyes wide open. Her mouth ajar. It felt so good she couldn't talk.

This feels better than my door knob, she thought jubilantly. *When Sax comes home we're fucking every day. I know he'll love it.*

Girl, you can never tell him you just fucked Tommy.

Sax and Philippe lay side by side. Listening to Sade. The covers pulled up to the start of their abdomens. Philippe was gently stroking Sax's upper thigh. Sax loved his touch. He wanted to call Jadish but he made up in his mind that he was getting a divorce.

"So where do we go from here?"

"Nowhere," said Sax, turning to look in his eyes. "I don't want to leave here yet. I can stay here forever."

Philippe smiled. "*Really?*"

"Yes. Thank you."

Philippe kissed his lips. "For what?" He rolled over, opening the nightstand. Pulling out a rolled blunt, he closed the drawer and lit it.

Sax kissed his forehead. "For taking my virginity. For letting me play in your body. For making me come. You felt so good."

Pulling on the blunt, Philippe looked at it for a brief second, passing it to his lover.

"I didn't *take* your virginity, bruh," Philippe said with love and admiration in his voice. "I simply pulled back the curtain on your virginity and showed you the man you are. The incredible, committed and loyal man you are. Jadish doesn't deserve you, bruh. What woman makes her husband wait two plus years to make love? No man would have stuck around for that, unless she was battling cancer or something. And you were the best lover I ever had."

Sax beamed like the morning sun. A huge cloud of smoke gravitated around their spent bodies. Philippe pulled hungrily on the blunt once more, setting it in the ash tray. Sax tongue kissed him, getting a contact high. They talked between lip locks. "I'm curious." Kiss, kiss. "How many men have you been with?"

Kiss, kiss. "*Two*," Philippe said truthfully. Sax believed him. They have always been honest with each other about everything.

Sax smiled, pulling away. "So I'm number three."

"No. You're number two…And you were the *best*! You are everything I ever imagined."

"I have loved you for years, Philippe. I misplaced it as brotherly love."

"How did you know it wasn't brotherly love?'

"Because I used to get hard when you came around. I knew then. I just never said anything."

"I know. I did, too. I was too scared of losing you as a friend."

"I wouldn't have turned on you."

"I know that now. But back then I was terrified. I didn't even like gay people. And when I turned out to be bisexual, I thought I was the weird one."

"You're not weird. But we both have wives."

"And I have a son."

"So what are we going to do? I'm not ready to come out and I never will.

"Me, either. I mean, I respect those who have. I respect those who keep it real and they are who they are but I have to think about my job, my reputation. I do want to leave my wife and be with you."

"I do, too. You have always made me feel so good about myself. You always believed in me and offered me advice and hope."

"And I always will."

Sax kissed his lips. "I hope you're ready."

"Ready for what?"

Sax turned him on his stomach and began to taste him all over.

Philippe's cell phone rang.

I couldn't believe it. I just fucked Tommy. Bitch, were you crazy? Was I that vulnerable that I had to give in to the man who raped me? Was this normal? Was I normal? I just violated my own self. I stood up, running my shaking hands through my hair. I truly didn't know what to do or what to say. Should I cut his ass? No, how could I? I got on my knees every night and asked God to forgive me for my mishaps. So why couldn't I forgive Tommy? If I wanted God to forgive me I had to forgive others. But I thought I could forgive on my own time and on my own terms.

I just cheated on Sax. What is going on with me?

Tommy was pulling up his pants, quiet. He refused to look at me. He was shaking his head, cursing himself.

"What's wrong, Tommy?" *Bitch, did you care what was wrong with him? Tell him to get out! Call the police! Have him arrested.*

No, girl. You're talking through your obvious hurt.

Bitch, you can't be too hurt. You just fucked him without a rubber, a Jimmy, a condom or whatever you wanted to call it.

Oh, Well. He had some good dick.

Are you insane?

"I have to go, Jadish."

"No, Tommy. Stay…Are you hungry?"

"A little. But it's cool." He was walking to the door. "I'll grab some McDonald's."

"Don't be silly. Go sit to the dining table. I'll warm you up some food I cooked for Sax tonight."

"Where's Sax?"

"He never came home. I think he wants a divorce."

Quietly, Tommy slipped out the door when Jadish opened the fridge.

D riving home the entire episode played out in Tommy's head. He was deadly tired, yawning what seemed every five minutes. He didn't understand why he was so tired. Maybe because he had a long night. A night of worrying, praying and dreading. He worried about Lenny. Maybe he shouldn't have drunk the liquor his best friend bought. He smiled to himself, trying to manage his automobile on the road. Small specks of rain fell on the windshield. His cell phone rang. He looked at it and it was Jadish. He kissed the phone, and put it in the glove box. Tonight had been wonderful. It would be a night he would never forget. He loved her. Yes, she forgave him. But he didn't understand why she gave in to him. If she would have stabbed him he would have accepted it. He was dead ass wrong for drugging her drink. He was dead ass wrong for violating her trust. She trusted him and he took full advantage because he thought he could get away with it.

God, forgive me Lord. I was wrong. I made a bad decision. I was out of pocket and out of line. But I'm a man and I have weaknesses. I am not perfect.

God I'm asking you to forgive me. Why am I so tired? I am getting painfully sleepy. I need to pull over on the side of the road. Yea.

I'll do that.

Tommy slowly braked, pulling over to the shoulder of the road. He turned off the engine and turned off the lights.

"I'll just get a little rest. I'll drive home in an hour or so." He set the alarm on his phone for an hour. He set it on the dash and leaned the seat back as far as it'd go.

"It's better to be safe than sorry."

As the passing cars continued to zoom by him, Tommy fell asleep within minutes, silently praying to God to forgive him for raping Jadish.

The woman of his dreams.

The next day Sax was heading to the shower in the hotel room. Looking at his watch, he realized he was late for work. But he didn't care. He loved his job and he loved his co-workers and his boss. But he loved Philippe more and now that Philippe opened the Candy Shop in his ass, he wanted to taste all the flavors. Philippe had hooked up his Xbox 360 to the TV and was playing *Halo*, a game he loved. Sax wasn't one for games, just football games on ESPN.

Sax smiled, grabbing a towel from the chair by the small dining table. "I don't know how I'm going to tell Jadish I want a divorce," he said, eyeing Philippe. He was pressing buttons so fast it made his head spin.

Philippe was heavily engrossed in combat. "I don't know how I'm going to leave my family, bruh," Philippe said. He pressed "pause," looking at a half naked Sax. His eyes raked his body, carefully noting his amazing ass, his plump dick and his beefy thighs. His calve muscles were just irresistible. "I do know I love you and I want to be with you."

"And I want to be with you." Sax walked over to him, kissing him. They melted into each other again.

"Go shower."

Sax said, "Ok."

P hilippe answered his ringing phone.

"Hello." He resumed the video game.

"Dad!"

"Hey, Son."

He was sniffling. "Tell me it isn't true."

Philippe turned off the game without saving it. His son was more important. "What isn't true?" He narrowed his eyes.

"Mommie said you are leaving us."

His heart dropped. "No, son. I am not leaving you. But I don't…"

How do you tell your son his Mama doesn't make you happy anymore? Why did she tell him about our impending divorce without me present? Silly bitch! She's already trying to come between me and my son and I'll be damned if she comes out the victor!

"But you promised to always be there for me."

"And I will."

"But Mama said you're moving out."

"Son, it's for the best."

"NOO, Daddy! What did I do?"

His heart exploded. "Son. It's not your fault."

"YES IT IS! You're leaving me! I hate you, Daddy! You promised!"

"Son…"

"If you leave me I will never talk to you again."

"You're young, Son. I don't expect you to understand…"

"I'm eleven years old, Daddy! I understand perfectly. You found another woman and you don't want us."

"It's not like that."

"Go to hell!"

His son hung up in his face.

Sax was bathing. On the sink counter his phone buzzed and he answered it. "*Yo!*"

"Why didn't you come home last night?"

"I couldn't face you, Jadish."

"Why? And is that the shower I hear in the background?"

"Yes, Jadish. It's the shower."

"Oh my God! You cheated on me! How could you!" She broke down and he felt guilty.

"I'm sorry, Jadish. I am going to be a man about it. Yes, I did cheat on you."

"But you made a vow…"

"Yes, I did, and you forfeited on the fine lines before I slept with somebody else."

"So now you don't want me? Is that it? You hate me now? I mean nothing to you?"

"Baby. I *do* love you. But you wouldn't make love to me. You made me feel terrible inside. You walked on my manhood. No, it's not all about sex, but two plus years is sheer lunacy. I can't believe I stayed that long."

"Please come home. Let's talk about this."

"I'll be home soon. And when I get there I'm packing my stuff and I'm leaving."

"Why, Sax! Why are you doing…?"

"I have to go."

"Who is she?"

It's not a she, baby. It's a he. Philippe. And I want and need to be with him. And we already decided that we would be together. We were going to get an apartment together and make love all day and get to know each other deeper all night. It's a done deal. I'm just waiting to sign divorce papers. Nothing was going to stop us from being together.

We just had to keep it on the low low.

He hung up the phone.

Before I lose my mind.

P hilippe couldn't stop crying. He wasn't a water bucket, but he never dreamed of hurting his son. He lay on the bed, rubbing his temples. Next to him was a pen and a pad. He shook his head, sitting up. He smoked the last of the joint. Did he really want to leave his family?

Yes.

And he would leave them. He *had* to go. People had to stop using the children as an excuse to stay inside a loveless marriage.

Plenty of adults raised successful children while divorced.

Hell his Mama has been doing that for years. She never complained so why should he? Children had to stay in a child's place.

They didn't dictate what he did and who he did it with.

I got to leave.

I can't stay with my family. I don't love my wife.

He picked up the pen and scribbled a note.

J adish sunk to her knees, sobbing. Her nose stopped up instantly. She had to breathe through her mouth. Her skin crawled and her pulse quickened. She wanted to break something. She opened her counter and shattered her dishes. She screamed to release steam.

"It's all my fault! I did this to him! I drove him to the arms of another woman."

She threw her good China against the wall, basking in the symphony of misery that trickled into her ears.

"I cheated on him, too. We both did something unforgivable. I can't believe I lost my husband. Another woman will enjoy his body and I haven't even enjoyed it yet. She already has leverage over me. Who is the bitch? I'll gut the Ho!"

She vowed it on her life.

T ommy was out of it. The alarm continued to go off, but he didn't move. The sun rose above his car, rays beaming down on his skin. He was clammy and unprepossessing. Cars traveled to and fro. His mouth was ajar. His eyes open to the world. His pupils stale and dry. His eye lashes, curly and disdained. Ants crawled along the hood. Bugs flapped all around the car.

The grass was wet with the morning's dew.

Tommy was dead.

L enny hugged his wife, thinking about Tommy. He didn't understand him. Well, he used to think that he did. But obviously he didn't know Tommy as well as he'd thought. Why would he lie and say he was at a party at the hospital? Why would he say a dead woman told him to say "Hi?" Was it to cover up the fact that he was actually the one admitted into the hospital?

Lenny kissed his wife's cheek and decided to let it go for now.

He already did what he had to do. And he was cool with that.

Next time Jadish…make sure you press the mute button when you say Tommy raped you and you didn't know how to tell me.

Plus I overheard Tommy and Sax's argument at the hospital.

I was standing at the door the entire time.

Devastated.

Holding a bottle of E&J.

Loaded with rat poison.

ax came out of the bathroom. He thought about calling the auto parts store so he could pick up the parts for Lenny's Mustang. He forgot all about it.

I'll do it later. Just because I'm divorcing his daughter didn't mean I turned my back on them.

They have become my family as well. I love Jadish's parents.

"Philippe…" Sax grabbed a toothbrush. He did a quick job on his teeth then gargled. He had to see Philippe.

Turning off the water he checked himself over in the mirror. He was fully clothed, ready to go to work.

He walked out into the room. The TV was on.

"Philippe…"

Oh, he probably stepped out to grab a bite to eat.

Sax sat down, putting on his shoes. He smiled to himself, thinking about his man. His baby.

"Why did he wait this long to make a move. I wish he would have done this years ago. But do I truly want him? Or am I infatuated? Nah. Must be lust mixed with love. Had to be."

Sax looked forward to his new life. That was short lived.

He frowned when he realized the drawers were open and empty.

The suit cases were gone.

"What the fuck? Did he leave? Without telling me bye?"

He felt like a cheap hooker that wasn't compensated. He snatched up his cell and called him.

"How could he just up and leave? Nah, bruh. You don't treat Sax like a piece of meat. Little bitch!"

When his eyes fell on the note on his pillow he hung up the phone.

The note was in Philippe's handwriting.

D ear Sax,

I love you. I love you like I have never loved any other man. You fulfilled a fantasy, a dream I long ago had. I actually asked God to let me have one night with you years ago. I think Satan heard my prayer, because my son called me this morning and told me to go to hell. He told me I made him a promise that I would never leave him. And, yes, I love you, bruh. I would die for you. But my son comes first. I have to make him feel safe and secure. He's a Mini Me. I can't make him with his mother then turn and leave. It's more complicated than I thought. I'm going back home to work it out with my wife.

Please work it out with yours. We will never be. We could never be. You felt wonderful last night. Your body against mine reminded me of doves in flight. They flap and they fly. They gawk and they sigh. But eventually wings get tired. Famished, they must land to reevaluate the next travel plan. South for the Winter or East in the Spring? You tell me, bruh. I'm not ready to leave my family and exchange my house, life, and child for a life living in the shadows. That's for the trees and the sun when it changes course in the sky. Whether that sky is sunny, blue or dark. Clouds have the type of wetness that either cleanses or floods. My job is done. I was to come and show you something. To pull back the velvet ropes and show you the man you are after your first sexual experience with someone who truly loves you for you. I want you to go home and patch it up with Jadish. You both hurt each other. I should be on the plane by the time your pupils slid across the last word on this page. I prayed to God about it. My conscious told me to go save my family.

I have to save my son. I made him a promise.

I'm a man of my word.

P.S. What we did and what we shared stays in the Marriot Hotel. I will never destroy your reputation. I will never cause you harm. Please don't destroy mine. If you do, I will man up and own it. But I know you're too good a man to destroy a life. I should know. You were married to Jadish Houston for two plus years, saving a woman who wasn't ready to be saved. But now that she knows of Tommy's deception, maybe you two can truly be happy. Now's the time to go home and get your pussy once and for all. I love you. I love Jadish. Us sleeping together was meant for one thing. Mending. Healing. Fixing. Building bridges. I love you. You love me. I love my son. You love my son. You're his God father. You want him happy. You want him nurtured. We must build our village and raise my child. You. Me. My wife. Jadish. We were two vulnerable black men coming together to make beautiful Love, not War. Please Inspector Gadget this letter when done reading. And even if you keep it, please keep this sacred and private. I want to cherish feeling you inside me. It's not for public consumption. It's not meant for office fodder. I trust you, the way you trusted me last night to show your virginity the door.

    I love you.

    P.

Sax closed the letter and stood up. He read over it a few times, understanding why Philippe left. He couldn't blame him. Sax was at the hospital the day little Phil, Jr. was born. He held him and took pictures with him. Philippe was on cloud nine. Nothing was bigger than his son. There have been times Philippe and Sax stayed up for hours on the phone talking about his son. His expectations. His dreams. Sax was very envious, one day wanting a son of his own.

    I will never have a son. I'm divorcing you, Jadish.

    He took out his lighter and opened the letter. He held it up, tears falling. He was burning the evidence. He was burning his love. He was burning his infidelity. As long as the letter existed, the infidelity on both their parts was immortal. It lived on. It was the Last Emperor. It was life threatening. It could destroy lives.

    Sax walked out of the room, wallet and keys in hand.

    The letter turned to charred ancient ruins seconds later.

There was a knock on Jadish's door. She had showered, changed clothes and decided to pull herself together. She was done crying. She couldn't change what happened.

When she opened the door five men in suits stood before her, holding roses and huge teddy bears. She melted into a smile. A small band walked past her, standing in her living room, clad in silk suits. They played Blackstreet's "Don't Leave." Jadish loved that song.

"*Oh my God!* What is this?"

The men set up the roses and set the teddy bears on the living room couch. One of the men handed her a bottle of Dom and two flute glasses.

In the glass was a ring and a small note.

Her hands shaking she took out the note and read it.

I love you.
Let's get married again.
Sax.

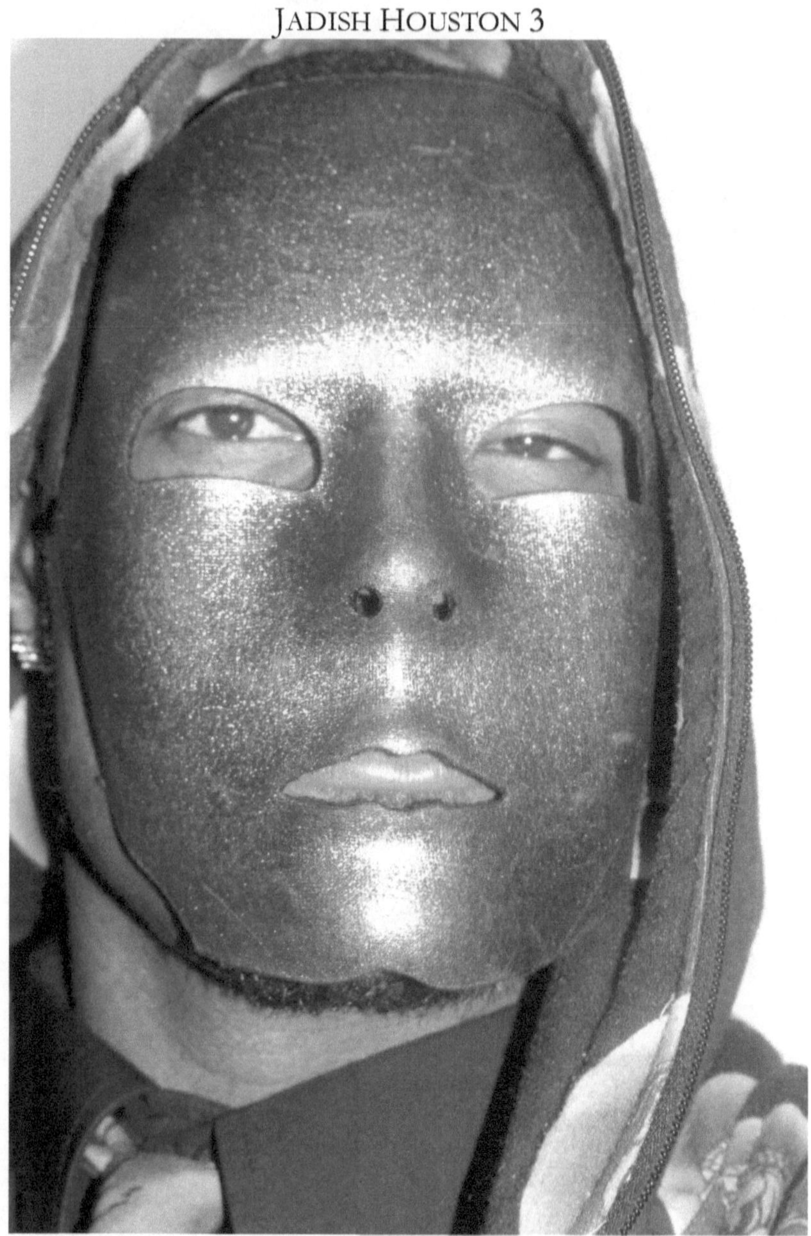

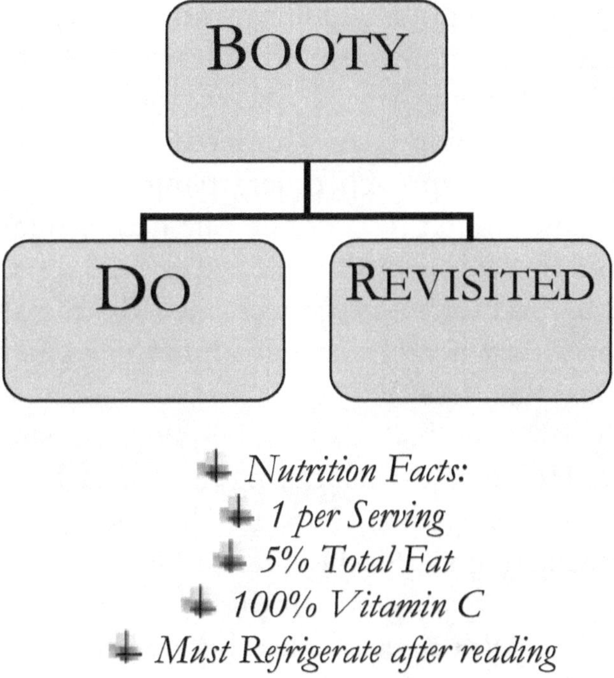

Nutrition Facts:
1 per Serving
5% Total Fat
100% Vitamin C
Must Refrigerate after reading

*G*od, I don't even know if I'm coming or going! I'm about to lose it. I'm about to go crazy. There's only so much a woman can take and right now my heart isn't the limit and love seems to be spending outside of my budget. My entire soul has been compromised because love has blown up in my face.

Hot tears streaming down her beautiful face, Georgia, sitting on the floor in her huge walk-in closet, looked over her beloved school screenplay. She remembered when she wrote it. She was sixteen years old and she was going through something in her life. She had just lost her virginity with a disrespectful asshole named Eduardo Rodriguez. She thought she was in love with him. She waited her whole life to give her body to a knight in shining armor and when she did, after saying he was, she found out that he had sex with half the girls in school. She was nothing but a traffic stop. Her name was slandered and scandalized.

Other boys approached her, trying to get in her panties. They didn't respect her. She had to fight other women to get her respect back and she did. Her red light didn't last long enough to make Eduardo stay with her. And when her clit gave him the green light he did just that: left her.

Eduardo then had sex with her close cousin, Priscilla. He told Priscilla, during their sexual romance, that she felt better than Georgia. That Georgia was a prude compared to Priscilla's feistiness.

When Georgia found out through the rumor mill that Eduardo Rodriguez fucked her cousin she was so upset and betrayed she jumped on Priscilla during her Sweet 16 party, stabbing her with a huge kitchen knife in front of other family members. Once the shockwave swarmed throughout the event, she turned the knife on Eduardo, stabbing him so deeply in his arm he almost bled to death on the way to the hospital. Priscilla was in the same paramedic truck with him.

When her parents lashed out at her in confusion and anger, she ran and locked herself in the bathroom.

If only they understood what Eduardo and Priscilla did to me, then they wouldn't be so quick to jump on me.

"Open this door, Georgia!" her father raged, pounding on the door. Her Asian mother was calling her all kind of names.

"How could you stab your own cousin? You little bitch open this fucking door!"

"LEAVE ME ALONE!" Georgia spewed, opening the medicine cabinet.

Eduardo didn't love me. He loved Priscilla. They went behind my back and had sex. I am so embarrassed. No one will ever love me. How could my cousin betray me?

"Georgia." Her father pounded on the door again, the door about to break free. "Open the door!"

"I DON'T WANT TO LIVE ANYMORE! FUCK PRISCILLA! SHE FUCKED MY BOYFRIEND BEHIND MY BACK!"

"Baby," her mother reasoned, touching her husband's arm. He settled down. "Open the door. We can talk about this…"

Georgia sunk to her knees, eyeing the bottle in her hands. The razor was by her legs. Her hair hanging in her face, she started to perspire.

Eduardo lied to me. He told me what I wanted to hear just to fuck me. He got what he wanted. People bash me in school. The boys think I'm easy. I hate life. I hate love. I hate men. I hate myself.

Georgia opened the pills and poured them into her mouth. She struggled to swallow them. The bitter taste in her mouth nearly made her gag. Once she swallowed them, she took the razor and slashed her wrists. She lay in the fetal position and welcomed the pain. She welcomed the embarrassment. In her mind she saw herself stabbing her cousin and Eduardo. She kept her eyes closed tightly.

Good bye Mom and Dad. Good bye to everybody. I won't be missed. No one will mourn me. Death is the only option.

"Georgia…" Her father listened. Nothing. Her mother called out her name, knocking.

Nothing.

"Why is it so quiet in there?" he asked his wife.

Before she could answer they heard banging sounds.

"What's that?" he asked, looking confused. Other family members started forming a crowd behind them.

"Oh, *God!* BABY, OPEN THAT DOOR! GEORGIA! NO, BABY!" her mother was covering her face, backing up from the door.

Scared for his child, her father kicked in the door. When he saw Georgia twitching on the floor, blood everywhere, he picked her up, screaming at the top of his lungs, and he ran past family and put her in his truck.

Her mother was right behind him. Before she could open the door he sped off. He put the pedal to the metal getting her to the hospital, her mother speeding behind them in her car, her heart hammering.

G eorgia pulled through. She would spend two weeks in the hospital. Her parents were right by her side. They didn't care that Eduardo made it and that Priscilla pulled through.

Georgia had to go to counseling. She didn't love herself. She didn't want to live. She wanted to die. She didn't want to go to school. She didn't want boyfriends. She didn't want the very air she breathed. Her parents convinced her to go on living, that they would love her and be there for her. They told her to finish school and Georgia, after a lot of hesitance, agreed.

She vowed that if she gave her body to another man he would have to be in love with her, cherish her and be there for her when she wanted. He couldn't have eyes for another woman. She vowed to never get close to another female.

But God had a different plan for her. Her father had a friend who was in the Marines with him. He had a daughter named Princess Webster. Mr. Webster was a warm, intimidating man. She met him and Princess during her junior year at Spellman College. She liked Princess instantly and they started to hang out and be there for each other and stay up on the phone talking about fashion, boys and life. She felt in her heart that she would not make Princess pay for Priscilla's mistakes. Not all women were whores.

When Georgia met Ed her life changed forever. In the beginning he dogged her, talked shit to her and he used to hit on her. She didn't know what it was about his eyes and the warmth of his smile, but as she got to know him and finding out that he went through a lot of emotional abuse as a kid, she grew closer to him.

She never gave up. Ed asked her to marry him over pasta at an Italian restaurant. She said yes, despite everything he'd put her through.

They were married two weeks later. Princess couldn't attend the wedding because she didn't believe in them.

Thank God for Princess Webster's father. He single-handedly got a hold of Ed and beat some sense into him. Ed was like the son he never had, and he got it together after marrying her and showed her that he could be loving and sensitive and attentive and caring.

Now Ed is in love with another woman. Call your lawyer and get a divorce. Thank God Ed and I don't have children together, even though we were going to start trying in a few weeks. He wanted a son and he told me he didn't want to die and not leave behind a child to carry on his name. I wanted to give him what his heart desired.

Now I never will.

Tears fell on the play. Several words looked smeared. This was the play that won her rave reviews and a scholarship to Spellman College.

If it wasn't for this screenplay, I would have never gone to college. I didn't even want to go to college. I just wanted a high school diploma because my Daddy never earned one and Mama did, but she never put it to use or use it to its full potential and I wanted to be different.

I wanted to be better than my parents. This play did just that.

That was the play her parents were proud of. That was the play her high school would use for future reference for other drama students. That was the play Priscilla and Eduardo attended and loved.

That was the play that changed her life for the better and gave her high self-esteem and self-confidence she didn't have growing up in a loveless home with an overbearing father and a mother who let her husband walk all over her like floor mats.

That was the play that detailed a lonely wife who cooked dinner and was having an imaginary phone conversation with a friend to keep her mind off of what she didn't have in her life. The very same play she reenacted when she caught Princess and her husband having sex in her guest bathroom the morning after Ed's very successful and much hyped and talked about party.

Georgia remembered that morning well. It has played over and over in her mind like a movie she hated.

She remembered standing at the guest bedroom door, her hands flatly pressed on the paneling…her eyes locked on Princess sucking her man's dick in ways she never had…while he sat on the toilet. Loving it. Needing it. Craving it. In ways he never craved Georgia.

Georgia didn't see the Bob Marley pictures on the wall that were gifts from her mother, when she attended a reggae festival in Jamaica six years before.

She didn't see the black carpet she bought online from Indonesia a few years ago and paid over $75 to have shipped UPS to her house. She didn't see Ed's $3,500 big screen TV mounted in the wall, a TV she has, with Ed and friends, watched numerous Super Bowls and NBA Championships on.

Her heart crashed and burned when Ed ran his hands through her hair and was moaning her name and his deeply rooted love and affection he claimed he always had for her.

This was before they closed and locked the bathroom door. Georgia was about to go crazy. Her world, her home life, her household and everything she invested exploded in her eyes and reconstructed her face.

Georgia moved like a zombie across the room. She pressed her hands on the door, silently sobbing. She turned her face to the side, and put her ear to the door.

She heard them moaning in unison. She heard the suction sounds of Princess's lips on her man's dick.

"I gotta pee," Princess said to Ed.

The door opened a tad. It wasn't locked! Oh, God! Did she really want to see what lied behind the door?

She opened it slightly, enough for her to peek inside. She saw Ed eating Princess's pussy. She was sitting on the toilet, pissing into it. Ed took some of her urine and wiped it on her nipples.

She wanted to puke.

Burst in! Kill them both! Do it, Georgia! Kill them! Do something, bitch! Stop acting helpless and show these two fucks that no one crossed you. You made a vow to yourself, after what Priscilla and Eduardo did to you. You wouldn't love a man unless he loved you for you and he couldn't have eyes for another woman.

Her soul died when Ed got on the floor, guiding Princess's pussy on his dick. She took his Nike hat from his head and slanted it on her head.

Georgia softly closed the door and ran down stairs, vowing to kill them. But in her heart she had a conflict. She was in love. She loved her husband. She loved Princess like a sister.

What would she do?

Before Georgia caught Princess and Ed having sex, she was initially walking up the stairs. She was on her way up to tell Princess that she wanted to cook her breakfast. She knew Princess had the Hennessy and Coke drink at the party and she was out of it.

She wanted to make sure she was ok. She looked out for her friends when they stayed over and that rarely happened because the only person she and Ed allowed in their home was Princess.

On her part, she knew that allowance came from her loyalty to her friend.

On Ed's part, she had to wonder was it because he truly wanted to fuck Princess?

No time for that now. I gotta do something. I can't go on pretending like I don't know what's going on between them. That's why Princess ducked me for months. She didn't take my calls. She didn't return them, either. She totally avoided me. If she would have been a woman and come to me on the morning she fucked him would have made all the difference. Friendship over dick.

Georgia shook with rage putting her play, which was neatly and meticulously formatted on 8.5"x11" paper, back in the suit case and returning it to the top of the closet.

Why did I cook that morning and pretend to be talking on the phone? Why did I redo my play, a play I did on stage in high school?

Why didn't I stab the bitch when I caught her crawling out of my kitchen?

Do to her what I did to Priscilla?

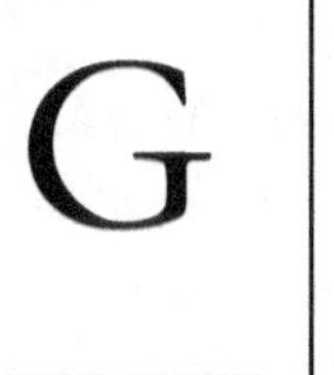

Georgia was in the shower, wondering why Tina, Thomas's wife, didn't show up. Her cell phone vibrated on the sink counter. Wrapping a towel around her, she got out, the shower still running, and answered it amongst steam.

"Hello."

"Hey, Girl. I know you think I forgot about you."

"Hey, Tina. How could I?"

"I won't be coming over. I can't meet the woman who is pregnant from my husband. I will probably gut the bitch."

Believe me; I want to gut her ass myself. She fucked my husband, Girl.

"She's gone, anyway. I don't know where she went. And right now, I got my own dilemmas. I don't have time to be getting involved with other people's problems."

"What's wrong?"

"Nothing." *Ed cheated on me with the bitch that is pregnant with your husband's baby.* "Look. I'm in the shower. Call me later."

"OK. And Georgia?"

"Yes?"

"Thanks for the organizer. I appreciate the gift."

Organizer? Bitch, what fucking organizer? I didn't buy you anything.

"No problem, Gurl. Bye."

Click.

A few hours later, Georgia quietly sauntered into *Johnny's Fuci-Fino's Sport's Bar and Grill* on *Oakland Park Boulevard*, and hesitantly sat at the bar. She had tried to call Ed, but he didn't answer. She also tried to call Princess, wondering did she go to Thomas and tell him who she really was.

The girl is in love. That much I will admit. I don't know what kind of magic Thomas had on his dick, but Princess is hooked on him. I have never seen her so happy. And she's pregnant from Thomas. That's another thing. What is she going to do? Thomas is still married. And why didn't Tina show up? I waited on her and she never came over to meet Princess. Not that it mattered. Princess bolted on me to go after Thomas.

Gorgeous in an ankle-length dress with a lily in her curly hair, she smacked her lips and decided that she made a mistake coming to a bar to alleviate her inner turmoil.

Why did I put that lily in my hair? Ed used to love when I put flowers in my hair. He said it brought out my eyes. He used to stroke my hair and say he loved me. I used to die from his touch. Now I don't want him looking, touching or thinking about me.

It was after 6 p.m. and Happy Hour was from 4-7. She didn't care about the free buffet, either. She wasn't hungry and she didn't have a craving for food. Her craving went deeper than well-prepared dishes. Her craving tied in to her husband and trying to love a man who didn't love her.

The place had great dining; drinking, people, laughs, fun, and dancing yet her heart didn't want to be there.

Then why did I even come?

She loved coming to that particular sport's bar because it wasn't like all the others. It was very people-friendly and it catered to her needs in ways she wished her husband would.

Maybe I should go home. I really don't feel like being around people. Not today.

She wasn't like most women yet she needed and desired and wanted a solution to her burgeoning problems.

Looking at her pricey watch, she tossed her bang from her lightly made-up face and looked around.

There were a lot of black folks in there doing what they did best: trying to take each other home and fuck each other's lights out.

She grooved to Marvin Gaye. "Let's Get it On."

I don't think so, Georgia thought.

A few men tried to hit on her but she wasn't interested. A tall fellah grabbed her hand, trying to get his game on and she shot her buzzer before the game winning shot.

"I'm married. Release me or catch a rape beef."

He had never run so fast in his life. She rolled her eyes, and set her small Chanel purse on the counter, lowering her head.

I love him. God, I took vows. I meant them, too. Did he? Why did he turn on me? I can't believe this. And Princess. God. I love that girl so much. With everything in me. She's my partner in crime. I trusted her with all of my secrets and my fears. I know all of hers. I know she is afraid of the dark. I know she hates being alone. I know she was picked on throughout her twelve years of school and when she was a teenager she used sex to validate herself and that quickly turned into a profitable business.

Why would she turn on me and take my husband?

"Ma'am," said the bartender, looking as good as he want to be. "Can I get you something to drink?"

Marvin Gaye ended and Barry White started. She loved that song. She and Ed made love to it a million times. I Wanna Do it Good to Ya. *God.* Shoot me. Snatch my hair out.

"Ma'am…"

She focused on him with a frown. "Oh, sorry. Yes. Give me a Husband on the Rocks."

"I'm sorry?" he was shaking his head, placing his hands flat on the counter.

A few other women were trying to get his attention but he only had eyes for the pretty lady who was obviously going through something painful.

She wiped tears away. "Never mind."

"I'll get you something to cheer you up," he said. "I'll make you something you have never had before."

"What will that be? You'll make a Good Man? Make that, since you fucking men think you know what women has never had. I never had a backstabbing best friend who fucks her friend's man. She's pregnant with another man's child."

"Wow. You are really going through something."

Georgia jumped up to her feet, grabbing her purse.

"I shouldn't have come here. I need to call my lawyer. Why am I telling you this?"

He held up his hands. "Wait, ma'am."

"This was a mistake. I'm so sorry. And don't wait on me. You won't ever see me again in this bar. And this is my favorite place in Fort Lauderdale…"

She rushed out of the bar, running to her car.

God. I'm about to loose it.

Get me home before I go completely ballistic.

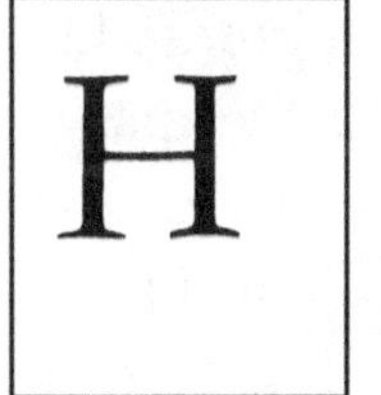

Heartbroken, Georgia lay in her bed hours later, her soul shattered into a million little fragile pieces. She couldn't think straight. On her nightstand, next to Ed's picture (He was so handsome. Lord, his smile radiated, even after all these years) were empty beer cans. Georgia didn't drink. In fact she hated people who did. She couldn't stand people who put their problems in beer bottles. She detested people who went to bars and told all of their business, right on down to bra and dick sizes, to the bartender and *he* didn't even know how to get himself out of a bind.

That's why I left Johnny's. I was turning into one of them. A lonely woman who couldn't decipher men from pigs.

Yet she has succumbed to doing just that: drinking away her derision for her husband's decisions. She was paying for her husband's mistakes. His lack of judgment has left her hearing impaired. She wasn't trying to understand anything about him any longer.

But I have to. I'm his wife. We are still married. Is it me? Did I do something wrong? Did I suck his dick right? Didn't I swallow him enough? Didn't I let him come inside of me the way he loved? Wasn't I his bitch in the sack? Didn't I roll his joints fast enough? Didn't I cook fried chicken for his friends on game days? Wasn't I faithful enough, Lord. Why have you and my husband forsaken me?

Cigarette butts were all over the floor. Georgia didn't smoke. Now she was. She was too stressed. She tried playing with herself, thinking about her husband but before she could insert the dildo she dropped it and the lube on the floor and she started crying so hard her nose stopped up. How could he betray her? How could he give himself to another woman? How could he look her in the face, smiling and laughing, like everything was alright? Didn't he have a heart and a soul? Hadn't they been through enough together?

It was a few minutes past 1 a.m. Ed still hadn't come home.

Where are you? With Princess?

No, you can't be. She is probably with Thomas, where she belongs.

Stay far, far away from here.

She was listening to every sad song imaginable. She had erased all of the songs on her iPod and she downloaded the sad shit. Aretha. Patti. Whitney. Janet. Beyonce. Scratch Beyonce. She's *too* young. A grown woman of Georgia's stature didn't need to be listening to little girls giving it to Mama and wearing Freakum dresses to get back at a man. Every woman didn't have that kind of dress in the back of their closets. Hell, she had clothes she couldn't fit all through the closet. And getting a new man was not the answer. When you were a whore, sure, you could go out and fuck whoever you wanted. But when you're married and you wholeheartedly stood before God and family and told a man how much you loved, adored and admired him, then the stakes were higher.

If her marriage was on the Dow Jones the stock market would have crashed the minute she realized Ed's phone switched to vibrate status.

It would have exploded when she realized she was a married woman and a Freakum dress would not bring her husband back.

No, she hasn't thrown him out and no, his shit was still in the armoire, dressers and in the closet. But in her heart and in her mind, body and soul Ed was out on his natural ass. And he wouldn't be coming back.

Where are you, Ed? Why are you not home yet? The least you could have done was call me. I am so worried about you. Well, maybe I'm not.

I already know the deal. I know what's going on, but you're a man and men think they have all the fucking sense and when it comes to sex and their dicks they don't have the sense of a freaking bird.

You are in love, yes I know. Your heart isn't pure, which is another matter I won't get into. When are you going to be real with yourself?

This was unusual. He always came home around 9 p.m. He never stayed out late. And when he happened to get off work late he always phoned her and insured that he was ok.

She reached over and picked up her cell phone. She closed her eyes. Should she call him? Nah. She wouldn't. She had her pride.

Husband or not she wouldn't sweat him.

Why should she sweat him anyway?

He's in love with an ex prostitute.

Ed was in a myriad of thoughts. Inside his heart was a Hurricane and it spelled disaster. He wanted a woman who was in love with another man.

I can't live without Princess. I love her. But how do I tell my wife that I don't want her anymore. How do I tell her that I love her like a sister?

He was driving his Mustang along Campbell Drive. He has passed the Big Lots store. He could barely keep his eyes open. If he lost Princess he didn't want to live.

She was his soul mate.

But does she know it? Does Princess know she is my missing rib?

He knew it in his heart and in his soul and he would fight Satan for her love and her time and her devotion.

The thought of another man getting the pussy killed him inside.

I know it's late. It's after 1 a.m. But I couldn't come home after work. How could I?

I have been camped out at the Motel 6. I watched Princess throw herself into Thomas's arms.

She's pregnant with his child. How could she ignore my love for her and go with another man?

Hell, how could I cheat on my wife?

Why did I drink myself into a stupor? Why didn't I call my wife and tell her I was going to get home late.

Why didn't I give a fuck?

Niggah, the least you can do is call Georgia. She's a loyal woman. She has never hurt you.

So what? And?

d phoned Georgia. He braked at a stop light. No other cars were on the road.

How do I tell you I don't love you?

The cell phone vibrated on Georgia's nightstand.

She was fast asleep, Toni Braxton's "Seven Whole Days" playing.

Georgia was holding Ed's picture in her arms.

The Bible opened and on the floor.

The phone vibrated off the nightstand and onto the floor.

A few seconds later it stopped vibrating.

d parked his car next to Georgia's Toyota Camry.

She's home.

He looked at his room window. The

lights were out.

She's sleeping.

Unlocking the door, he slowly walked inside, the cool air hitting him in the face. Closing and locking the door, he activated the alarm.

Making his way upstairs, he paused.

Princess. I need you. Make love to me. Have my children. Replace Georgia in this house.

I don't want Georgia living here anymore.

Why am I such an asshole?

d entered his room. Music was playing at a moderately considerate tone. The glow of the moon illuminated Georgia's gorgeous face.

I love you like a sister now. I think I always loved you that way.

He took off his leather coat and his jeans.

I don't even want to lay next to you.

He crawled in the bed next to her. He noticed it. She held his picture in his arms.

She's so in love with me. How do I get her to understand?

He put his arm around her and went to sleep.

hen his arm went around Georgia she inhaled, and her eyes opened.

Please. Stop touching me. Get your arm from around me.

I hate you.

I know you wish I was Princess.

eorgia was sitting at the dining table, across from Ed the morning after. On the table was her wallet, the cordless phone and her purse.

Stupid prick. He sits there like nothing has changed. Everything has changed. Nothing is the same.

The silence fell on their ears and they didn't know what to do or how to deal with it.

Ed was thinking about Princess.

I wonder what she ate for breakfast. Is she happy? What is she wearing? I want to buy her roses. I want to massage her feet. I want to taste her sweet pussy and make her titties chameleons to what I feel inside.

He wanted her slithering all over his chiseled body, riding his dick. He wanted to make her come day in and day out. He wanted to wax on and wax off the pussy but how could he? She was avoiding him. She refused to talk to him. She didn't take his phone calls. She ducked and dodged him when he went over to her father's house. Didn't she love him as much as he loved her?

What are you thinking? Georgia wondered, sipping some water. Her throat was parched and her heart with it.

Or do I already know. You're thinking about my best friend. My best girl. Princess. The woman who fucked my husband. She was supposed to be my girl. My ace. Which is why I should have never trusted a bitch around my always-hard husband? He couldn't go throughout the day without whacking off to porno tapes. If I heard Janet Jacme moaning one more time, "Put it in my ass, Niggah," I will freaking scream!

"Baby." He spooned rice and beans into his mouth, careful not to drop food on his white pants.

Her brows rose.

I'm not your baby. And I don't want to have your baby anymore.

"*Yes,* Ed?"

He gave her a heartwarming smile. It did nothing for her. "You haven't said anything since we've been sitting here."

Want to talk about business? Hmm, ok. Stock is up three points in Princess's pussy. "Is there something you want to talk about?"

He wiped his lips with a napkin. "Yes. *Us. You.* What's going on with *you?*"

You fucked Princess in my home! That's what's going on with me and both of you looked me in the fucking face and lied about it! Prick!

"I'm fine, Ed."

"I'm fine, Ed," he mocked. "Since when did you call me Ed? You always call me *baby*."

Bitch, fuck you! "Not tonight." She toyed with her food, her head hanging low.

"Baby. Something is wrong."

Her head snapped up. "Ed. *Please.* Just drop it, ok? It's not that big of a deal and I really don't feel like dealing with it or talking about it."

"I'm your husband."

He remembers! Gee golly wow! "Oh, you remember."

He slammed the fork on the table and the table shook. Georgia wasn't rattled and she wasn't intimidated.

"Slamming forks isn't going to get me to talk."

What is her malfunction? "What will get you to talk, Georgia?"

Stab yourself in the eyes and fart out my alimony. That'll do, Ed! "Leaving me the fuck alone."

He released a large gush of air. He wasn't hungry any longer. She spoiled his appetite. "I can't do that. I'm your husband."

"You say that like it's a badge of honor."

He looked into her eyes. She averted her face. "It is."

"I don't think so, Ed."

"STOP SAYING MY NAME LIKE THAT!" he exploded.

Defiantly, she threw water on him. It splashed in his face, and dripped from his puffy cheeks. "I can say what the fuck I want."

"Don't make me slap your ass. I'm the man of the house."

"With the two ton balls. Yea, yeah, yeah. Don't I know it? Poor, poor Ed. He does what he wants, when he wants and how he wants. He stays out all night and crawls in the bed after 1 something in the morning and think by wrapping his arm around me I am going to let it slide. And when I try to do something for myself you tell me that I'm being selfish."

Damn it! Princess would never talk to me like I'm a peasant. She's making it easier for me to leave her. "Right now you are."

She shook her head, glaring at him. "I'm selfish? I cook your food, wash your clothes and let you fuck me to your heart's content. But as of late we haven't fucked because you fucked up, Ed."

"How did I do that?"

"When we fucked around three a.m. this morning, my heart wasn't in it. I cringed the entire time."

His ego took a nosedive. "Really?"

"Yes, really. You were so into my pussy you called me something I don't approve of. And I don't understand why you called me that."

"What? Calling you my whore? My dirty little slut? In the bedroom you are those things to me. As long as you're my dirty little harlot in the sheets but a lady in the streets that shouldn't even be a problem."

"But it is a problem, man."

"Why? What do I look like saying, my dirty angel? Or 'Oh, yea, baby! Take this penis. Yea. Let me screw you in the booty.' That doesn't move me. I want to grab those ass cheeks and be like 'Ho, take this dick! Throw that pussy back on my shit, bitch!'"

She was repulsed. She was waving her hands.

"Not at the dinner table, man."

"It's *my* table."

"It's our table. I *bought* it, motherfucker!" They stared each other down like Gladiators. "And I don't want to eat my food imagining your dick in my ass, Man. Have some fucking respect."

"You're barely touching your food."

"Because you won't shut up. And for the record I don't have a problem with you calling me names in the bed."

"Then what's the problem?"

"Your mouth wrote a check your dick can't cash."

"Meaning?"

"What do you think it means? It has meant the same thing for months."

"You aren't making any sense."

"Oh, Ed. It makes perfect sense."

"I'm tired of this…" He stood up, stretching. "I'm going to work."

"Sure. Go ahead. Go to work, Plumber."

"Plumber? I am not a *plumber*."

"Sure you are. I heard you lay good pipe."

He was suddenly guarded. "Baby…"

"It's Georgia, and I am no longer your baby. Nor do I want to ever have your motherfucking child, dumb ass!"

He was angry. "You're going to have my child. You know how much I want one…"

"This is why I'll never have your kid, bitch. When you came inside me this morning, you called me 'Princess.'"

The blood left his face.

Thomas and Princess were lying together in bed. Their legs intertwined and their toes wiggling all over each other. She was laying on his chest, listening to his heart beat. She smiled, biting back tears. She was in love with this man and he loved her.

"So what are we going to do?"

"We are leaving town, Baby," he said. "My wife filed for divorce today and when I'm served the papers I will sign them. She double-crossed me anyway."

"How?"

He kissed her forehead. He tried to forget about it but the more he thought about her deception the angrier he became.

"Do you want to know why I'm not a father?"

"Why?"

He was silent. Maybe he shouldn't talk about it. Yes, he loved Princess and yes he was happy that she was pregnant with his kid, but he wasn't used to people wanting to know his problems. He was too busy helping others with theirs.

"Maybe I shouldn't say."

Princess kissed his lips. She still could feel Thomas's dick in her. His come had long ago dried on her titties and on her ass.

"Tell me."

"OK. Here goes. She was taking birth control pills the entire time, preventing herself from getting pregnant. She was convincing me that she was trying. I thought it was me. Maybe I was shooting blanks. But when she revealed those pills to me I was crushed."

"How could she do that to you?"

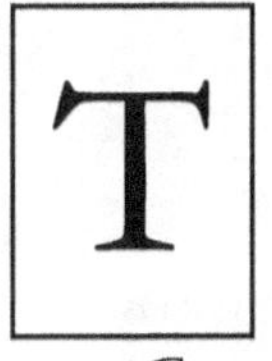The force of Georgia's words knocked the earth from beneath him. He had to sit down and shake his head for a second. *Damn it. Damn it. I fucked up. I fucked up badly. Gotta do damage control.*

Ed reached across the table and took Georgia's hands. He rubbed the top of them with his hairy thumbs.

Damn. How could I have slipped and called her Princess? I wonder what she's thinking. Thank God she doesn't know that Princess and I had sex. She's all I ever think about.

She pulled her hands away and ran a shaky palm through her hair. He didn't understand what was going on.

"You smell nice, Ed," she said. "I see you're using Dove soap now."

He smiled, remembering when he first used it. It was when he fucked Princess in the shower in the guest room a day after his party. Princess had the hottest piece of pussy in Dade County. From day one he always wanted her. He really wanted to date Princess but she wouldn't give him the time of day. And being married to a woman he didn't love was the true crime but he could learn to love her.

"Ed."

He snapped out of the daydream. "Oh, yea. I use the soap now. Smells good, huh?"

"Yup. When did you start using it?"

"A few weeks ago."

"A few *months* ago?"

"Weeks."

"It's funny. When I wanted you to use the soap you vehemently denounced it. And now you are using it? What was the catalyst?" Georgia's eyes rose. "Something I should know?"

"No, baby. I use the soap now. Big deal."

"You're right. It is a big damn deal. And call me Georgia. I am not your baby anymore, Ed. I haven't been your baby in months. *Tell* me. What made you start using it?"

Princess. "You."

"*Me?*"

"Yes. I got tired of you bringing it up so I started using it. There. Happy?"

"No. I'm *not.*"

"What can I do to make it better?"

"Nothing, Ed." She stood up from the table and he rose also, walking around the table and wrapping his arms around her. She clammed up and he felt it.

He slowly pulled away from her. He slid his hands in his pockets to hide the fact that they were shaking.

"You just cringed when I hugged you."

"I did? I didn't notice."

"*Yes* you did. Now I know something is wrong."

"It is, Man. It is."

"What?"

I can't hide it anymore. "Let's just say the morning you started using Dove soap I found your wet boxers by the shower."

"OK." He was shaking his head. "And?"

"Princess's earring was next to it. The morning after your party."

God! She knows!

In good spirits, Princess was holding Thomas's hand while he drove his Monte Carlo over to Georgia's house. She couldn't believe her good fortune, that God has blessed her and changed her life. In the blink of an eye her life has been shifted heavenward, showing her everything she has been missing. The only problem was that Tina now knew she was pregnant with Thomas's child. Was she ready to deal with the nuclear fall out? Maybe. Maybe not.

Plus she still harbored a secret hurt for allowing herself to sleep with Ed behind Georgia's back.

I should tell Thomas? No. I can't. I can't do that to him. I'm pregnant and I am happy. I want to be with him and I can't risk losing him again. I can't breathe without him. I can't hurt Georgia. I can't do it to her. She's so sweet. But the hooker in me wanted Ed's money.

Who knew that the man she once cursed out was the father of her child? Who knew that her prostitution days were finally gone? It wouldn't even be hard to let go because true love has pushed all desire to be with other men from her heart and soul.

She told herself that she would read the Bible and go to church and nurture the good things that were happening to her. The times she slept with men and charged them for it would forever be a part of her. She would always remember the misery she faced when giving up her body for money to feed a sick need to be loved and to feel special.

Thomas smiled, turning up the radio. An old Aretha Franklin cut was on. "Giving Him something He can Feel."

He could remember his mom and dad used to dance to this song when he was growing up. He used to sit on the couch; eating his candy and watching them love each other and stroke each other's hair.

He told himself that when he was older he would treat his woman the same way.

Ed and Georgia weren't looking at each other. He has made several attempts to talk to her but Georgia shut down. What he didn't know was that she relived what she went through with Eduardo. All the hurt, all the pain and embarrassment was getting to her, slowly breaking her down. Her eyes were out of focus. *Does Princess feel better than me, Ed? This is my fault. I should have left you years ago. But no. I believed in forgiveness, giving you a second chance.*

"Georgia, Baby." He reached over and took her hand, squeezing it fondly.

She didn't squeeze it back. "What, Ed."

"We can make this work."

"How?" She looked at him, trying to keep the sting from her words. "How are we going to make this work? You cheated on me with my best friend. I feel betrayed, man."

He leaned over and kissed her cheek and she wiped it off. "I don't want my cheek smelling like Princess's pussy."

His mouth fell open. "Baby, you're being unreasonable."

She glared at him. "Unreasonable? You stick your trashy dick in another whore and I'm being unreasonable?"

"Yes. Baby, I'm not perfect."

"No, you're not. But you have common sense."

"Georgia."

"Am I packing my shit or are you going to pack yours?"

"What are you saying?"

She snatched her hand back, turning her back on him, pressing her feet on the floor. Her head hanging low, she remembered. Slitting her wrist after swallowing the pills. Her father kicking down the bathroom door. Rushing her to the hospital.

"I want you to pack your things. If you don't, then I will. I will go live with my cousin until I decide if I want to divorce you or not."

Ed jumped out of bed and raced around it, getting in her face. "You can't leave me."

She picked up the phone and called Princess. It rung a few times. Ed sat on the chair, looking into his wife's face. Too much has been done to turn back. Georgia couldn't stand the sight of him. Men were liars. They couldn't be trusted. They were pricks. *I gotta get out of here. I can't stay another second. He can have the house, everything. Maybe he'll give it to Princess. How could she betray me? I loved her. I would give her the world. She was my sister from another mother.*

"What's up, Georgia?"

"Could you come over? I want to ask you something."

"Are you ok?" Princess asked, tapping Thomas's leg. He looked into her face, wondering who was on the phone.

"Yes. I'm good. Can you come over now? I would appreciate it very much. And bring Thomas."

Ed lowered his head.

"I'm so glad you found true love. You deserve it, Girl."

Princess kissed Thomas's lips. "Thank you. We're on our way."

Georgia kissed through the phone, tears falling from her cheeks. "See you soon."

She slowly replaced the receiver.

Tina was on the phone with her lawyer. She wanted to get the divorce over with. Sure, part of her loved Thomas. But the other part didn't want to give him children. The thought of it killed her inside. She had an explosive career as a Journalist. She didn't have time to walk around barefoot and pregnant. She didn't have time to play desperate housewife. She didn't feel like being at his beck and call. So sure she took birth control pills and didn't tell him. Why not? Who said you had to tell your man every damn thing about you. Sometimes you had to keep things to yourself. Sometimes you had to put yourself first. Sometimes it had to be all about you and not your man because when it was all about your man they bragged about it to their friends, they talked bad about you and let their boys know that "Hey, she does what I want her to do," and she burst his fragile, egotistical bubble.

"So how long will the divorce take?"

"When he signs the divorce decree it will take up to six months."

"Why so long?"

"Well, its very heart wrenching. Assets have to be split up, bank accounts frozen until the judge works out the legalities. If you own houses and cars, the judge also deals with that."

I just want it to be over. "He can *have* everything. I just want him out of my life. I don't want to be attached to him at all."

"But what about your son?"

Tina thought about it all of three seconds. Her mind wasn't changing. "He's *not* the father."

"But he signed the birth certificate."

Tina frowned. *Lawyers are always trying to milk your piggy banks!* "Because he felt he had to. He was in love with me. But he's not the father. I tricked him in the beginning and made him think he was."

"I'll look into that for you. Don't just walk away from everything. You said he cheated on you, right?"

Tina needed a tonic. "Yes."

"And you said this Princess girl is pregnant with his child?"

Tina burned up just thinking about it. *The whore needs to die a horrible death!* Tina's heart blackened, and in her mind she wished every ill, inconceivable thought against Thomas and Princess. "Yes."

"Well lets play *our* cards right. The proof is in the pudding. If Princess's baby comes out and DNA proves *he's* the father then, *baby*, you walk away with alimony, the house and his car and the bank accounts, too. Adultery is frowned on."

Tina thought about it. Yea. I'll be damned if I see another whore living in *my* house.

Tina's eyes clouded over with evil. "I agree. Let's do that."

"Can you get them to take a paternity test?"

Tina thought about it. *I don't know about this.* "I doubt it."

"I got you, Tina. I'll have the judge subpoena the test. That way if they refuse it makes them look bad, holds them in contempt of court and they could be facing jail time."

Tina said, "OK. I'm in."

P rincess looked over her dress, tugging on the waist part. Thomas hugged her, kissing her lips.

"I can't believe you're mine."

"This feels like a dream."

"And you're pregnant with *my* baby. I am *so* excited about becoming a father." He held her booty, giving her some tongue.

"I can't wait to give you a son or a daughter."

Thomas reached past her and rung the door bell. He kissed Princess's neck, drawing heat from her titties.

The door opened and Georgia smiled at her. She hugged Thomas, kissing his cheek.

"Hey, cousin! You look happy."

He looked at Princess, winking. "I am."

Georgia reluctantly hugged Princess. "Hey, Girl."

Princess felt the tension. *What's wrong with my girl?*

"Hi, Georgia." They pulled away from each other.

"Come on in. I hope I didn't disturb you all."

"No, cousin. You can never disturb me," said Thomas, coming inside. He saw Ed smoking a blunt, sitting on the couch.

"Hey, Ed!" Thomas said, giving him some skin.

"Hey, Dawg…" He held up the joint. "Wanna hit this?" Ed seemed to be in another world.

"*Hell*, yea…" Thomas pulled on the joint, holding it in his lungs. "What is this?" he asked with a strained voice.

"That's Louisiana Kush, Dawg. Chronic don't have shit on this!"

"I heard about this shit…"

"So Princess is pregnant with your baby, 'ey?"

Thomas sat next to him, blowing smoke in the air. "Yea. I'm so excited, Dawg."

"Oh, yea?" Ed asked, torn up inside that Princess carried another man's baby.

Princess barely looked at Ed. "Hi, Ed," she whispered.

Ed's eyes sparkled like diamonds. This crushed Georgia. She held her stomach, sitting at the dining table. "I called you all over for a reason," said Georgia. *Keep it together, Chile.* "Can we all sit to the table? I have some Grey Goose and some plastic cups and ice cubes. Princess, I got you some orange juice."

"Thanks, Girl," said Princess, taking Thomas's hand and pulling him to the table. When Ed looked at her Princess gave Thomas the best tongue of his life, pissing Ed off.

Georgia had a huge smile on her face, glaring at her husband. Ed sat down, trying to keep his anger under control.

The door bell rang. Princess said, "I'll get it, since I'm closer to the front door."

"Who could that be?" Georgia asked, thinking about the possibilities.

Princess ran her hands through her hair, opening the door.

She was face to face with a very beautiful woman.

"Is Georgia here?" she asked, clad in leather pants and a leather jacket and the most expensive heels she'd ever seen.

"Yea." She extended her hand. "I'm Princess."

The Leather Bitch stared into her eyes.

"And I'm Tina. Thomas's wife. Nice to finally put a face with the dream he had so many months ago."

The smile was frozen on Princess's face.

"S o we finally meet, Miss Webster," said Tina, eyeing her from head to toe. Princess put her guard up, breathing Tina's cheap perfume. Rubbing her tummy, Princess said, "Yes. We finally meet."

"So I understand you and Thomas are quite the odd couple."

Princess tilted her head, scowling a tad. "I wouldn't call us the odd couple."

"Sure I would. A recovering prostitute and a soon-to-be divorced creep. I think that qualifies you for Odd Couple of the year."

"And what about you?" asked Princess. "I heard you swallow more than just birth control pills."

Tina rolled her eyes, her failures in her marriage evident and written on her face in a way her make-up failed to do. Dandruff flakes were on her collar and this grossed Princess out. "Watch it."

"I did. I watched him hold me, kiss me and protect me at night. I watched him smile, laugh and shed tears of joy when we finally found our way back to each other."

"I guess I should look around to make sure Ashton Kutcher ain't punking me."

Princess tried to slam the door in her face and Tina pushed it open. "Face me. Be a woman!" Tina said and Princess spun on her heel, walking to the kitchen.

"Who's at the door?" Georgia asked, and Tina grabbed Princess above the elbow and Princess snatched her arm back.

"Look, bitch. I don't suck pussy. So don't grab me like you lost your mind."

Dropping his napkin, Thomas stood up and pulled Princess behind him. "Why are you here?"

Tina opened her leather attaché case and pulled out a manila folder, wiggling it in his face. "These papers got more gun powder than Iraq."

"Are you trying to be funny?"

"No. I want a divorce. Just sign the goddamn papers and we can all be happy."

"I am already happy. Princess is unlike any woman I've ever met."

"Do you say that to all the whores you buy?"

Insulted, Princess tried to get to Tina but Ed stood up, placing a friendly hand on Tina's shoulder. "Can we all talk like adults. Princess is pregnant."

Georgia said, "Tina, sit down for a minute."

"I just want Thomas to sign the papers," Tina said, tears falling from her eyes. "He cheated on me with swine. I thought pigs belonged in a pig pen."

"Bitch you got one more time to insult me," Princess said, sitting down in the chair. She was opening and closing her hands into fists.

Tina dropped the papers on the table. "Sign them."

"After I read over them I will."

"You can read them now!"

Georgia stood up, walking to the fridge. She needed a stiff drink. It seemed that divorce was the big theme tonight.

"I want my lawyer present."

Tina wasn't hearing him. *"Sign them now."*

Thomas hated being embarrassed in front of family and friends. "Bitch, fuck off! I'm a grown man!"

Tina raised her hand to slap him but she refrained. *I'm going to make him look like a pussy in front of a pussy ass bitch!* "I don't want you!"

"And I hate you, whore! Go swallow some more birth control pills and hide the fact that you are a deceitful bitch!"

Thomas sneered, throwing the divorce papers across the room. Ed's mouth fell open. Georgia, an open beer in her grasp, sat back at the table and said,

"Look, Tina. We all need to talk. All parties here are guilty of something. No one in this dining room is exempt. We all need to calm down. We're acting like children." When she said it she wanted to take it back. Georgia wanted to bash Princess's head in and watch the bitch bleed to death.

Tina ran her hands through her hair, shaking. She was about to explode. Princess stood up and walked over to the dining room window, looking outside. Thomas looked over his shoulder, making sure she was all right.

Ed didn't know what to do. Part of him wanted to hold Princess and protect her and kiss her face and tell her that he wanted to spend his life with her but another part of him respected Thomas.

Georgia set the beer down. "Princess. Why."

Princess looked at her. "Why, what?" *Damn, I hope she hasn't figured it out. God, no. Please don't let that be the case. I'm so not ready to reveal it. I can't deal with it. I'm pregnant for God's sake and if anything messes up my chances of being with Thomas I'd rather die.*

Georgia slowly stood up, cautiously walking over to her friend. She looked her over, trying to find the words. She hurt inside. "Why did you do it? I loved you like a sister. I thought I could *trust* you."

Thomas said, "Georgia, *she's* pregnant. She is dealing with *enough* stress." Thomas wondered what she was talking about. His mind worked overtime.

Georgia looked at him blankly. She felt nothing inside for anyone at the moment. "Do you *love* her?"

Thomas said, "Yes. I will die for her. She carries my child." He wasn't too sure of it. He was still getting over the fact that the woman he fought turned out to be the love of his life.

Georgia was skeptical. You didn't meet somebody and boom, fall in love. Love wasn't a nuclear bomb. "You don't *know* that."

Everyone fell silent. Ed's mouth fell open. Thomas looked at Princess.

Tina said, "If this was Maury Pouvich, he would open the DNA test and say 'Thomas, you are *not* the father…'"

Thomas snapped on her. He wrapped his hands around Tina's neck and tried to rip out her esophagus. Ed grabbed his arm, and used all the strength he could muster to pull him off. Princess simply looked out the window and Georgia snatched Princess by the arm. Tina sat down, trying to catch her breath. "That's all you can do when I tell you the truth, Thomas? Is attack me?"

Thomas was so infuriated he wanted to bash her face in. "*Fuck* you, bitch! You're turning me really bitter really fast."

Once Ed calmed Tina and Thomas down, Georgia took Princess's hand, fondly squeezing it. She smiled. Princess smiled. Georgia asked, "*Why* did you fuck my husband the morning after Ed's party?"

Princess's mouth fell open. *No, no! This can't be happening, God! Please, not now. Please let this be a trick, Lord. PLEASE! Oh my God! I love my Girl, and now she thinks I betrayed her. Hell, I did betray her.* "Girl. I'm sorry. It was a mistake." *A mistake! Bitch! A mistake? I had distorted thinking.*

Tina said, "I guess when you and Thomas fucked, *that* was a mistake too. Tramps, I tell you. Thomas I hope you're happy."

"TINA!" Georgia spewed, shutting her up. Georgia got in Princess's face. "Talk to me. I was your best friend. We have gone through thick and thin together. And you do this to me. Face me. Grab your titties and face me, damn it!"

Princess was breaking apart at the seams. "Georgia, *please*…"

Shocked beyond his wildest dreams, Thomas said, "When did you sleep with Ed?" You could hear the hurt in his voice. If it was one thing Thomas believed in it was Georgia's and Ed's marriage. He rooted for them. He could remember when they got married. He attended. He remembered what he bought them: sexy underwear for their honeymoon.

Ed said, "You two don't have to gang up on her."

"Oh, God," said Tina. "What a love triangle this is. Now Ed loves the prostitute."

Princess rubbed her arms, wanting to run. "I can't do this." She sped past Georgia and Georgia was on her ass. When Princess whipped open the front door Georgia pushed it closed, standing in front of it. "Don't run. Talk to me. How did you suck his dick?" Georgia sunk to her knees, holding Princess's hips. "Were you this close from it? His boxers on my guest bathroom floor and your earring by the toilet?"

"Georgia, please…"

"How did it taste? Did his dick taste better than Thomas's? Or what about his brother? He paid for it, didn't he? Didn't you try to steal Thomas's phone number out of his brother's phone when ya'll had sex in your Daddy's house? Maybe I should call him and let him know you ran a whore ring from under his roof!"

Thomas rushed over to Princess, burning up inside. He didn't know who to believe or what to say. The rug felt pulled from beneath his feet. "Is this true? You fucked my *brother*?"

"Seems like this tramp can't keep her lips closed…Is this who you want to spend you life with, Thomas? You messed up our happy home for the Whore of Babylon?"

Thomas said, "Did you sleep with Ed?"

Princess said, "Yes."

"And when were you going to tell me, Princess?"

"Everything is happening so fast! I was going to tell you!"

Tina looked at Thomas. "I want a paternity test of that baby. You will get a subpoena. I am going to prove that you committed adultery and when I do I am cleaning your ass out."

Princess watched Georgia stand up. "Princess. Who's the father of that baby? Is it Ed?" Georgia watched Thomas cringe inside. "Or is it Thomas?"

Princess tried to hug Thomas but he backed away from her, shaking his head. "Answer the question, Princess. Who's the father?"

"Thomas. We can talk about this in private."

"Seems like doing shit in private is what got you in a world of shit. Can you not control your pussy, whore?" Tina asked, clearly devastated.

Princess said, "I gotta go!" She opened the door, rushing outside. Her heels clicked against the sidewalk, heading for the car. She had the keys in her purse. Thomas could find his way home.

"Princess!" Ed called out, running behind her. He wanted to wrap his arms around her and protect her from the cold world.

"GET AWAY FROM ME!" *Oh, God! I'm losing everything. Every bed I made I gotta lay in. I only have one body. I can't do this. Who is the father of my child?*

Georgia brutally snatched Princess by the hair. They started fighting. Georgia slapped Princess so hard she fell to her knees, the pain from the sidewalk making her mouth fall open. She kicked Princess in the chin, and she fell back, her head slamming into the pavement. She moaned piteously. Georgia started remembering. Eduardo. Her cousin. Fucking him. The suicide attempt. The knife. The party. The family.

"You fucked my husband in my house, you trifling bitch!"

Thunder boomed and out of nowhere it started to rain. Tina tripped over her own feet trying to get a piece of Princess. Once she did, she kicked Princess in the face and she fell back on the wet grass. Staggering to her feet, Georgia and Tina double-teamed Princess, their feet crashing into her skull, titties and face. Blood began to openly pour into the lawn. Princess had never known so much pain in her life.

She began twitching where she lay, her legs thumping against the ground. Crazed, Tina had completely lost it. She blamed Princess for taking her husband; she blamed Princess for all of her faults as well. In her own sick way, Princess was to blame for everything that has gone wrong in Tina's life. At least that's what she told herself.

When Tina picked up a cinder block, trying to smash it into Princess's face, Thomas grabbed Tina and she turned and dug her nails into his face.

Thomas punched her so hard in the nose Tina lay unconscious on the grass.

Georgia was kicking Princess in the side. "I hate you, bitch!" She was a monster. "I loved you! I trusted you! And you took my husband!"

Pain skyrocketed throughout Princess's body. She curled in the fetal position, blood pouring from between her legs. She started screaming, holding her stomach as the rain continued to pour. Thomas panicked.

"Oh, no! No! The baby!" he yelled, about to lose his mind.

All the blood left Georgia's face.

What have I done?

Terrified, Ed picked up Princess, rushing to his car. She was heavy but he didn't care. He'd carry her all the way to the hospital if he had to.

He didn't bother with calling 9-1-1. She might be dead by the time they arrived. They always took their time to answer calls in the black neighborhood of Florida City.

"Hold on, baby! Hold on!"

Thomas ran behind Ed. "I'm going with you. I'll drive." Thomas heart beat out of his chest, his breathing coming in short spurts.

When it dawned on Georgia that Princess could lose her baby she ran inside the house and grabbed her car keys. Her head spun so fast she nearly vomited on her carpet.

"What have I done, Lord? My anger has gotten the best of me. God, I don't want the baby to die."

It may be too late.

P rincess ached all over. She was distraught, clearly out of her natural mind. She did know that lights sporadically passed over her face. The truck was silent. She felt Ed stroking her face. He was rocking back and forth, scared out of his mind. Tears dripped from his chin and onto her face. Thomas kept looking at them through the rear-view mirror. He blamed himself. He shouldn't have cheated on his wife. He shouldn't have brought Princess into his life when he wasn't even divorced yet. What was he thinking? Did he truly love Princess? He battled his emotions. He didn't know what he wanted. Everything happened so fast. Everything was so convenient. His father once taught him that if a foundation wasn't met then a relationship couldn't be built. The house would topple like sticks. The debris would be washed out to sea with the current. Why didn't he listen? Now Princess might be losing the baby. His baby.

Or Ed's baby.

E d was sitting in the Lobby at Jackson South, on 152nd Street. Princess's Daddy wasn't a happy camper. Once Georgia explained to him everything that has been going on he was in shock. Thomas was trying to focus on the news but he couldn't. His eyes were so red you couldn't see his pupils. Georgia was pacing around, the Pepsi soda going warm in her hand. She tried to sip it but she felt like throwing it up. They have been waiting for six hours, and nothing. When Thomas went to the circulation desk, asking for a check up on Princess, the nurse didn't offer him any information. Ed was about to go crazy. He loved Princess with all of his heart.

Georgia decided to sit down. She wondered about Tina. She was brought to the very hospital by the ambulance. For some reason she really didn't care if she was all right or not. She worried about the baby.

Ed looked at Georgia. "I hope you're happy."

"No, Ed, I'm not," Georgia snapped, a few people listening in on their conversation since there wasn't anything exciting on TV.

Thomas said, "Ed, no one is happy about this."

Princess's father stood up, walking outside. He wasn't in the right frame of mind to hear their bickering. His daughter was pregnant and he didn't have a clue. Finding all this out in one night did a number on him.

"You should have thought about that before ya'll gang up on a pregnant woman. Now she could lose her baby."

"I feel bad, man. Trust me I do. I love Princess."

"Really?" said Ed, standing up and getting in his face. "*Really*? You love her?"

Thomas looked up at him, trying to remain calm. "I am confused, Ed."

"Confused?"

Georgia said, "So am I. I'm losing my husband. I'm losing my marriage. I don't know if I'll ever forgive you and Princess for what you did."

"OK, Georgia. I fucked up. There. Move on. Princess is in the hospital. Because of you and your uncontrollable anger."

"I had to make her pay."

"And you see what payments can do, right?"

"Don't try to chastise me in front of people."

"Fuck you, Georgia!"

Her mouth fell open. She couldn't believe her marriage has resorted to this. "Whatever, Ed."

A tall doctor, early forties, suddenly appeared, trying to get Georgia's attention. When he finally did, she rushed over to him, looking scared. Thomas ran outside to get Princess's father. Ed's heart seemed to stop beating.

"Doctor…how is she?"

Before he could answer Princess's overbearing father rushed into the hospital, and up to him, with Thomas at his side.

"How is my daughter?"

Dr. Beckman reached out and took his hands.

"There is never an easy way to say this…"

"Say what?" he snapped, about to go crazy.

"Doctor…" Georgia's legs were shaking so bad she had to sit down. Ed's heart fell out of his chest.

"I'm sorry. Princess…neither she *nor* her baby made it."

Princess's father grabbed Georgia by the neck and started squeezing. "YOU BITCH! YOU FUCKING BITCH! YOU KILLED MY DAUGHTER!"

Thomas grabbed him, on the verge of breakdown himself. Ed grabbed Georgia and pulled her outside. Georgia was weeping so hard she couldn't breathe. She was in denial. God, Princess couldn't be dead. And the baby, too. God, help her. Save her. God why was this happening. As Ed put Georgia in the car, closing the door, Princess's father broke free of Thomas's embrace and he sprinted outside. Looking around wildly, he didn't see the security guards running at him. When he saw Ed's car he picked up a brick and ran full throttle for the car. He threw the brick through the windshield, and it hit Georgia in the face. Glass cut her across the cheek and neck. He dived into the windshield, chocking her to death. Blood was everywhere. Ed opened the door, grabbing him by the arm, trying to pull him out. Security guards intervened. Once they pulled him out of the car, he wouldn't stop screaming. Georgia was losing a large amount of blood.

Police officers thundered from the hospital. They apprehended Princess's father and Georgia.

They read them their rights.

They were co-defendants. Georgia and Tina. They were whisked into a public nightmare. Their faces splashed across every newspaper across the country. On the TV their lives played out. They were being talked about in businesses and hospitals. Both of the women, once very good friends, were pitted against each other. They were looking at life in prison for the murder of Princess Webster and her unborn child. Princess's father wasn't fit emotionally to come to the trial. Temporarily, he checked himself into a mental ward. He said he would kill Tina and Georgia if he hadn't. He was under 24 hour surveillance.

Georgia's lawyer was a recently graduating scholar from Yale. Coming from a family high on the pedigree chain, she was white, blonde and knew her shit. Georgia paid out the ass to get her on the case. But from how it looked, Liliana Gray said, point blank, "We have to enter a plea. Because if you fight this you will lose. Thomas and Ed are testifying against you. Both of these men were obviously in love with your ex best friend and their passion alone, their hurt and grave pain will be enough to get you convicted."

"I don't want to plea. I want to go all the way through with it. I wasn't in my right frame of mind. And I hate spending time in jail. It's horrible in there."

"I will see to it."

"I hope so. I want to win. She shouldn't have taken my husband," Georgia spat icily. Tina, sitting next to her, was trapped within herself. She was already raped in jail and she was threatened. Big Pussy Dropper told her that if she snitched her out she would die a horrible death. Tina knew she was being punished, and she couldn't believe she lost custody of her son. The Department of Children and Families was set to find a deserving family for the boy if she was found guilty. And even if she by some twist of fate beat the charges, the Department would keep the child with an adoptive family until they saw Tina fit.

Liliana sat next to Georgia, opening her brief case. She pulled out some files and set them on the table. The courtroom was filled to capacity. Several news programs were interrupted across the country with this harrowing tale. When the Honorable Judge James came from his chambers, the bailiff told everyone to "rise."

Everyone did. He was a burly man with a thick mustache and an overbearing, piercing gaze.

He sat down and began his opening remarks.

Georgia couldn't sleep. A week has passed and nothing went right in court. Watching Ed testify against her devastated her. Hadn't he betrayed her enough? When Ed looked her in the eyes and said, "Georgia and Tina stomped her on the ground, in the rain. I stood helpless, like I couldn't do anything…" Georgia lost it. She jumped up to her feet screaming.

"You fucked that slut! You were my husband! What happens to you for your infidelity?"

The judge ferociously beat his gavel.

"Order, Georgia! *ORDER!* One more outburst in my courtroom and I will hold you in contempt of court."

Reluctantly, Georgia sat down, covering her face. Tina didn't say anything. She already entered her guilty plea. There wasn't anything she could do. She wasn't going to be like Georgia and publicly embarrass herself.

Princess's doctor testified. Pictures were shown of her brutalized face. The members of the jury cringed, some of them lowering their eyes. Georgia turned away from them, sobbing. Tina put a huge smile on her face, shocking the entire courtroom.

I'm glad she's dead, bitch!

The day had come for the verdict. Georgia kept her fingers crossed. She was still dazed that she threw her life away. Everything that she was as a woman, everything that she accomplished has gone up in smoke. Ed sat behind her, refusing to talk to her. He didn't even acknowledge her.

You're making me suffer. You killed the one woman I loved with my heart. I would never know if she was carrying my child. You robbed me of that, Georgia. I never knew you had blackness in your heart.

Thomas didn't say much. During the entire trial, he didn't say one word. He didn't talk to family. With his brother present, he didn't talk to him, either. He didn't talk to friends. He quit his job. A thick beard has grown on his face. He was slowly letting himself go.

When the "Guilty" verdicts were read Georgia had gone deaf. A loud sound filled her ears and she covered her face, screaming.

Tina remained quiet. She smiled, standing up. Police men handcuffed them.

Georgia and Tina got life in prison, without the possibility of parole.

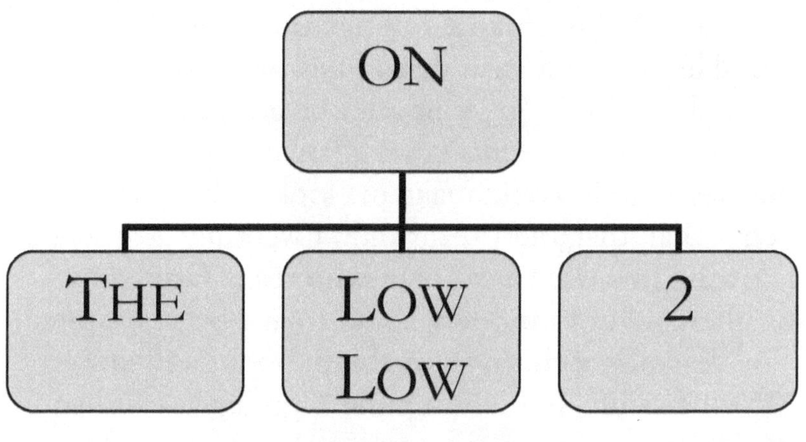

Nutrition Facts:
345 Calories
100% Fruit Juice
100% Natural Sugars
89% Saturated Fat
Not a significant source of calories
From saturated fat, trans fat
Cholesterol and dietary fiber,
D.Phar.69

Now see, I was mad! Deeply upset. I was so damn pissed off my bladder jerked and it wasn't pretty. I was going through a bitter divorce from a very selfish man. I never imagined that my wedding day so many moons ago would turn into the onslaught it has become. I have been separated from my husband, Terrance Jo'Shawn, for about nine months, with his punk ass. How could he fuck my brother and not tell me? Hell, how could my brother betray me like that? Fucking my husband in my bed when I worked. I thought I could trust him, like any big sister would.

I bought his broke ass things and I was there for him. He's the only man that I knew who had a good job and was broke an hour after he got paid.

I could have been a cruel bitch and spread his business, but it would make me look bad. I was raised better than that and I really didn't want my girlfriends knowing I married a gay man who really wanted my brother and not me. How could I have been so stupid? You read about this type of shit in books and in Terry McMillan's life, but not in mine. Ugh! I swear! I had the best pussy in town, yet my husband left me for the best piece of ass in the United States. Who knew my brother loved a banana in his tail pipe instead of in banana pudding?

Thank God we didn't have kids. If I had a son or daughter I would have to tell them their father was gay. And who gave a shit about Clay Aiken coming out on People magazine saying I'm Gay with his newborn son? I didn't believe in gay people raising children. That was just me. Who would be the daddy? Seriously?

Before I go any further I should say how I caught my husband playing around dookey chutes. I had come home months ago to my man waiting for me, or so I thought. We kissed and all that jazz. I didn't even know that he was fucking my brother prior to me coming home. My brother was hiding in the guest bathroom, half naked, his heart beating out of his chest. Of course I was the dumb bitch. The joke was on me. So my husband told me to go shower and I did. I was washing my body, playing with my pussy, trying to get a quick nut so when he pulverized my pussy with his incredible cock it would take me a long ass time to come the second time.

When I come I come harder than 50 Cent riding a tricycle balancing Ja Rule on his magic Stick. My knees buckling, my weave was wet from the shower. I didn't care. I was about to get the royal fuck down from my husband and sweat my hair out anyway.

I turned off the shower and I heard my man fucking my brother through the wall. I was so in shock I stood there for a minute, hoping it was a porno tape. And even if it was a porno, why would my man have gay flicks?

I sat on the toilet, about to pull my hair out. I heard them. Oh, yea. Feels good. Fuck me, Terrance and all that jazz. I couldn't move, I was nailed to the floor, my life blowing up in my face like a bad face lift.

By the time I walked out of the bathroom, leaving the towel on the floor my brother was long gone. I went in the guest bathroom and smelled sex in the air. They didn't clean up very well. I wondered where my man was. I looked for him. He was in the kitchen, with a towel wrapped around his waist, looking good enough to eat. But I wasn't hungry. My eyes were so red I couldn't cry. Why should I cry over a gay ass motherfucker? If he would have told me before I married him that he experimented with men I would have still married him because he was compassionate, kind and loving and you never knew what a person went through in his life that turned him towards guys. He treated elders like Gods, held gainful employment, and fucked a good meal when he cooked it the way he got this pussy in the sack. But since he decided for me, choosing to lie to me, taking his vows under false pretenses, all wouldn't be fair in the game of divorce.

Absent-mindedly, he poured me a cup of coffee. I held the Styrofoam cup, simmering. I refused to look at him. It took everything in me not to gut his dumb ass.

He smiled like everything was all right. Was he really that heartless? Was it that easy for him to lie? Did he think about me when he fucked my brother? Did they bash me? I thought he was my partner as well as my best friend. I guessed I was wrong. He tried to hug me and I walked past him, groaning.

"Baby, I wanna make love to you."

I paused by the stove, setting the cup by a huge bowl of fake fruit. The fake bowl seemed symbolic to my fake ass husband.

Baby, I wanna make love to you. "You do?"

"Yes." He traced invisible shapes on my cheek. Felt so good, but I had to force myself to become stone. If I gave in to him it would mean that I condoned what he did in the darkness. Didn't he understand that what's done in the dark will come to the light?

He took me in his arms, and I welcomed it, reminding myself of what I *wouldn't* be missing when I left him. Should I leave him? Shouldn't I stay and try to work it out? How could I work it out with someone who didn't even love me? That would be a complete waste of time to even try to save something he ruined when he slid his dick inside my brother.

He kissed my neck and I was self-consciously rubbing his back. My pussy was wet. I tried to go numb but I *couldn't.* I loved the way he touched me. I was obsessed with his body and his hands. This body loved him and oh how my heart missed him like a Janet song.

Kick his ass! Kick his ass!

"Let's do something different," I told him, my tits bouncing as I opened the cup board and took out the duct tape. He was getting excited. I didn't know what I had in mind, but I did want to immobilize the bastard so I could do what I had to do. And it wasn't going to be pretty. Not by a long shot.

"Damn! You wanna get freaky?"

I giggled like a white girl. "Yea-uh! Sure, why not?"

"Add some spice in our life!"

"Sit in the dinette chair…"

He sat down, putting both wrists on the arms. I ducked taped them one by one. I then duct taped his ankles together. I started sucking on his dick and his head leaned back with pleasure. His dick grew in my mouth, and it tasted so sweet.

I stood up and went into my bedroom. I told him I'd be back. I took the blindfold from his side of the bed and waltzed my hot, upset ass back into the kitchen. I blindfolded him. I straddled his waist, lowering my pussy on his dick, tossing my hair like Hurricane Ike.

He moaned obscenities. His dick filled me up like a glove, taking me away once again.

Every time he fucked me it was an odyssey, an epic adventure of hair pulls, toe curling and ass slapping.

I held his head, bouncing on that dick, like a real bitch. I was Heather Hunter and he was Sean Michaels.

"Baby I'm about to come!" he said. I stopped riding him, standing up. He tried to break free of the tape to finish him off and I sucked my pussy off his dick.

"Suck it, baby…make that dick spit."

"You want to come on Mama's pretty face?"

His hips were moving a mile a minute. His scent, heavenly, just the way I loved.

"YES!"

"Oh, yea! Give it to me!"

"I'm coming!"

When his come spurted from the head of his dick, I snatched up the huge coffee pot and dumped it all over him, scorching his faggot ass.

Die, bitch! You cheated on me with my brother in my house then suffer the consequences!

Experiencing excruciating pain, he savagely tried to break free of the duct tape, trying to get out of the chair. He fell on his face, his ass in the air. He twitched on the floor like a fish outta water and I didn't feel a twinge of remorse. Why should I? I'd rather be gouged with hot coffee than go out and knowingly cheat on my man.

I brutally beat him in the head with the glass pot, the pot cracking in four different places.

"YOU BEEN FUCKING MY BROTHER, FAGGOT!"

He laid still, his body unmoving. I stared at him, dropping the pot.

I lowered myself to my knees, sobbing over his body. Was he dead? Did I care? I hope he had some decent insurance because I wasn't paying for his burial. And when I was done I called the police and told them if they didn't get his faggot ass out of my house I was going to call Miss. Bobbitt and cut up another dick.

BITCH!

That was months ago. I couldn't say that I was glad for winding up in the slammer. I had to do two months and I was on three years probation. The only reason why I didn't get three years for assault and other charges was because Terrance felt guilty for being caught and he asked them to go easy on me. I didn't care, honestly. My brother skipped town and refused to talk to me. I didn't lose any sleep. The day was coming when he had to face me and deal with the aftermath. I was going to royally fuck him, and not in the way he liked. Terrance and I were in court when he made the "go easy on her" remark. Angrily, I jumped up from my chair and shouted, "If you didn't go easy on my brother's asshole, why go easy on me? You don't think I'm woman enough? I'm not *tough* enough?"

My lawyer told me to calm down and the judge was going through a divorce herself so she didn't say too much. Terrace, half of his face fucked up for life, refused to say anything else. He had to go to physical therapy, and he had to see a shrink. Initially, the courts recommended that we go to marriage counseling but there wasn't enough marriage counseling in the world that would make me forget a dick in his goddamn mouth and ass. So the court ruled that possibility out.

Bottom line: my marriage was over. And they were all going to laugh at me.

The hating bitches who said it wouldn't last.

Now I was getting my life back together. My divorce would be final next week and I couldn't wait. There was no love loss between us, but there would be no love gained with his stinky ass around me.

I walked away with the house, the car and a nice severance package from our business transaction of a marriage.

Shortly after my court room drama I met a man named Andrew at the grocery store. He seemed promising. I asked him where did he work and he said he was a correction's officer. It was all good. I did see a nice pair of pumps and a few wigs I wanted from the Mall.

I think I just found my cash cow. We hooked up, fucked in his van and we started seriously dating. It didn't last very long. I put my all into the relationship, but he didn't.

It was what it was.

MySpace has come into my life. I sat behind the computer, looking at those fine ass men! Damn! The candy store was right in my face. Shopping for dick has never been so easy. Part of me missed my soon-to-be-ex husband, but my heart told me the separation was necessary. I didn't want to be with a man who didn't love me. Terrance and his ordeals have drained me and the only thing I needed a man for was to suck this pussy like a Tootsie pop and fuck me to sleep. I could handle the rest when I sent his ass home. I wasn't ready to be a kept woman. I wasn't interested in one woman men. Fuck it. I was going to do me and do me well.

Sending messages to all those hunks online was a cinch! In ten minutes I must have sent out eleven of them. Online now icons flashed under their default pictures. In no time I got a response.

Hell, I was bending over in my main profile picture, clad in pink high heels and a huge afro wig. What Niggah wouldn't look at all that ass and get at me? They better get into it because time was limited.

I read the message from someone who called himself the Pussy Bandit.

Hey! Get right on down to business, shall we!

SUP WITH YOU, PRETTY LADY? I
AM DIGGING THAT PROFILE PICTURE.
BUT CAN I DIG YOU? I AIN'T G'ON LIE.
I JUST WANNA FUCK, SO WHAT'S UP?

Hell, yea! There was nothing wrong with a little premarital sex. My blood boiling from the anticipation of getting my boots knocked, I thought up a quick response. I sent him a message back.

I WANNA DO THE DAMN THING.
SO WHAT'S UP. SHOOT ME A NUMBER OR
SOMETHING AND WE CAN MAKE THIS HAPPEN.

I decided to hook up with The Pussy Bandit's fine ass. He had a gorgeous face, fabulous chest and I remembered I played with myself while looking at his photos. On his Top Friend list were big booty Ho's. Ego problems, Sir? I didn't care. Just as long as he fucked me good, licked my pussy and my crack then we would be fine. When I called him (finally) I asked him why he didn't smile in any of his pictures. He told me he didn't like smiling, that people ran him over and assumed he was nice when he did so I was like "OK, we gotta meet." I was fresh out of a relationship with Andrew.

Men and I weren't hitting it. I was still waiting for my divorce to be final. Andrew was too controlling, too contrived and lied more than Eddie Murphy in *Beverly Hills Cop*. And the bad part about it was that he lied with a straight face.

I should have known that fucking a correction's officer wasn't going to cut it.

I got all dolled up. I shaved my pussy with a dull ass razor, to give it that…edge and I wiped baby oil all over my lower half so it shined when I pulled down my panties. Nah. I'd let him use his teeth to take off my panties.

Maybe I should clit ball. Clit ball meant leave the panties at home and let the fabric of my clothing brush the kitty and keep it purring. I wanted to call my girlfriends and tell them of my new find.

But I quickly decided against it because I didn't need them Clit Blocking. Clit Blocking was when they found out about your man and went behind your back trying to fuck him.

Mama called me and told me that she wanted to take me out but I declined because my pussy was hot and my breasts wanted to be out and about some action so I pulled up my panty hose, crawled into a long, flowing black skirt with ruffles on the ass and a breathtaking black blouse with golden Chinese art on the sleeves. I had to put Mama on speaker phone so I could use my hands.

"Baby, we should really go out to the Olive Garden."

To top off my outfit, I rubbed cocoa butter on my face and decided against make-up.

"I don't like the Olive Garden, Ma. I'm black, not Italian."

"I know you're not Italian, dumb ass. I'm just saying…let's go out. Mother and daughter bonding. We haven't done that in such a long time. Plus you're getting divorced. You don't need to be alone."

"But I am alone, Ma. And I'm a big girl. I can take care of myself."

"Whatever. Look, I'm about to go. I gotta quilt I need to finish knitting."

"I got you, Ma. I love you. Bye."

I hung up.

The reason why I chose to leave the make-up alone was because I wanted to show his fine ass that I didn't need the pyrotechnics of make-up to pull a man.

It was that simple.

I should have asked his name. I wasn't about to call him the Pussy Bandit.

What if he couldn't fuck? I didn't wanna jinx the dick so I kept my eyes wide shut.

My lips were chapped. I took a trick from my cousin Melissa Jackson's playbook and wiped pussy all over my lips, so I didn't have to bother with lip-gloss.

OK. I looked the finished product over in the mirror. Ah. Yes. I'm the shit, believe that, Ho.

So I locked my house, my purse under my arm and I smelled pussy on my lips all the way to his crib. I chewed some Winter Fresh, to give it some attitude.

I heard on the radio that people needed to register to vote. I knew I was.

I'd rather see Obama than George Bush in the Presidential seat.

When I got to the Pussy Bandit's home I parked by two garbage cans. His place wasn't anything extraordinary, but I actually liked it. Cozy little place. OK. I could fuck in there. I could tell he did his own landscaping. His car, a Chrysler, was polished to a shine. The tires gleamed like diamonds. The expensive rims glittered like gold. There was a rose garden growing under the window, and as I approached the door I heard some Erykah Badu. So the brothah had some flavor. Hell, yeah.

When I got to the door I pulled the compact mirror from my purse and looked myself over. I could have done something different with the hair but why do *that* when I only came over here to get my hair pulled while he fucked me? I wasn't auditioning for America's Top Model.

Before I could knock my cell rang. I loved running my trap on the phone so I answered, wishing I stopped by my cousin Sted's house in Florida City and bought a few dime bags of weed.

"Yes, Ma…"

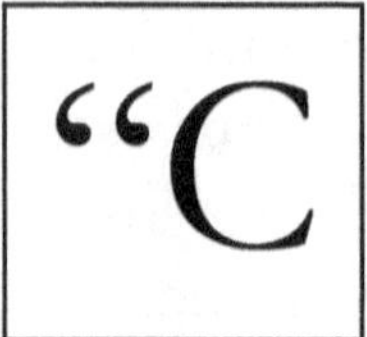

"**C**an I use your washing machine?"

"Why, Ma? Don't you have your *own*? Sure you do. I bought you the most expensive dryer and washer combo Best Buy had to offer…"

"Yes! But I wanna wash my clothes over your house because my light bill has gone up a hundred dollars."

I stomped my foot, my hand on my hip. "So you want to run mine up? No, Ma!"

She sighed audibly. "Come on, Girl! It's not fair! I'm your Mama and I…I have been there for you and taken good care of you; and when you were growing up you didn't want for anything. And I paid for your

Prom and bought you your first car. As a matter of fact you are still driving it around town like you're grand and I can't wash my clothes at your house, Girl? God don't like ugly…"

"And God don't like you washing your Granny panties in my washer, Ma! The *last* time you washed clothes at my house your thick, synthetic bloomers stalled my shit and smoke set off the smoke detector. You waste detergent all over the floor, didn't bother to clean it and you secretly washed my *brother's* clothes without telling me and you *know* I can't *stand* his ass. You violated my trust and I don't want you doing that to me again, Ma!"

"He's your brother, good or bad. I didn't raise my children to be at odds and ends with each other."

"You should have said that before my brother fucked my man! Did you raise him to be gay? I don't remember pussy looking like a dick."

"Girl, watch your mouth. He's my son."

"And you love him more than me."

"I love you both equally."

"*Imagine* coming home and finding your man playing Barry White. You think he's naked for you and your brother is hiding in the guest bathroom, having just had sex with your goddamn husband, faking like he was taking a shower. Are you *serious*? Then on top of *that* I heard them through the bathroom wall, trying to keep it all quiet and shit. He didn't *remember* that *our* bathroom was on the *opposite* side of those cheap tiled walls." Tears fell down my face. It still hurt to think about it. "…I was devastated! And then I meet *Andrew* and dumped his sorry ass because he *also* fucked my brother and he had the nerve to *lie* about it."

"That's hasn't been proven. I'm not going to let anybody bash my son. Not even my own daughter."

"Oh, *yea*? It hasn't been proven? Then *why* was Andrew wearing my brother's draws? I bought my brother that underwear for his birthday a couple years back and Andrew came home with them on. He mistakenly put on the wrong draws after he fucked my faggot ass brother. So for that reason I don't want you washing clothes at my house because I know you're going to try to wash my brother's clothes."

"Baby, *please*. Can I wash clothes at your house? I don't have time for all this back and forth. My nerves are bad and I'm wearing my bad wig so my head tingles when I think too much. Goddamn!"

I waved my hand. "All right, all right. Come by in a few hours and I'll wash your clothes."

"Too late. I just poured in the Tide with Bleach. And you didn't tell me you knew how to bake peach cobbler. You got a lot of food in your fridge. How did you get all of this food, they don't load the food stamp card until the first of the month and it's the middle of August…"

I tucked my chin back. "I'm grown. I stopped explaining myself when I got my first taste of dick. Good bye, Ma. And keep my house clean!"

I hung up.

I knocked on the door because I didn't see a door bell. I was already hell bent on that because I wasn't trying to chip my nails by knocking. When I got my acrylics done by the Asians my fingers were accidental prone. I paid over $40 dollars for my nails and I'd beat a bitch's ass over them.

No one came to the door. I knocked again, holding my purse, sucking my teeth.

Again, nothing. OK.

Was anybody home? Did I make a blank trip?

I called his ass on my cell and he answered. The music blared through the receiver and I yanked my head back from the phone.

"HELLO?" he was screaming.

"I'm at your door," I said politely.

"WHAT? I CAN'T HEAR YOU! HELLO!" he said louder.

"I'm at the door," I said more sternly.

"WHAT?"

"MAN I'M AT THE DOOR!"

"WHAT! STOP PLAYING ON THE PHONE!"

"I'M NOT PLAYING MOTHERFUCKER ANSWER THE DOOR!"

"YOU'RE BREAKING UP, *WHAT*?"

Fed up, I bammed on the door, my nail snapping on my index finger. It popped me on the forehead.

Damn it!

God*damn* it!

After a few moments, he turned down the music. He opened the door, smiling like a Cheshire Cat.

He engulfed me like we were long lost friends, his dick pressed against my pussy.

"Hey, Girl! I didn't *know* you were out here."

I closed my eyes, inhaling, my pussy getting dryer than the sun.

I *now* knew why he didn't smile.

I stared at Gumby with a fake smile. He extended his hand and I shook it, wanting to run. He was a gorgeous man, but his grill? Oh my God! He probably didn't have a dental plan with his current employer. My clit seemed to pull back deeper into my body.

"Would you like to come in for a drink?" He was trying to grab my hand and I was snatching it back, clearly annoyed.

"*No*, Gumby…I meant, no, no I'm ok. My Mom called. She wants to wash clothes at my house and…I gotta get home."

Gumby smiled again. Ugh, God! Shoot me. I half covered my face. I wasn't trying to be rude but his mouth made his face look like shit. I didn't want to play this game anymore, Gumby. Game Over. You win.

"She can wash clothes over here. Damn you're fine. I know you can't wait to take this dick," he went on, his breath smelling like somebody bathed his tongue in pure shit. He wore baggy jeans, with his boxers in plain view.

He started slowly walking around me, checking me out like I was in a police line up. When I saw the shit stains on the back of his boxers it was a wrap. Now if you knew you wasn't going to wipe your ass at least wear black underwear. I was about to puke. One of his nipples were shorter than the other, he had jacked feet and he had so much dirt behind his nails you'd swear he was clawing through dirt.

"No, I don't want my mother washing clothes over here…she doesn't know you like that."

He kissed my cheek and it took everything in me not to spray Lysol disinfectant spray on my face to kill the germs. Ugh, man!

"She can get to know me."

He was trying to touch my booty and I slapped his hands. He didn't have any finesse. I guess I was getting what I asked for. "You're gonna be my bitch. Goddamn, how did I get so lucky?"

I looked behind him.

He had two other men inside.

They were snickering, looking at me. They wore baggy jeans and Young Joc T-shirts that were about eight sizes too big. I hated when men didn't wear clothes that fit their asses. Plus his house was filthy. The air trailing up my nose wasn't very flattering. And if his house smelled like baby shit then his dick had to smell worse.

Empty Colt 45 beer cans were on the floor. Who the hell drank Colt 45? Roaches were crawling along the wall beside him, like they were getting ready to bungee jump.

Now I had to go.

I was running to my car, my heels clicking against the side walk. I hit the alarm button and the car unlocked. I couldn't believe I drove an hour across town to get my clit pierced with his tongue and I wound up coming face to face with Gumby.

MOTHERFUCKER!

So now I'm in my car, speeding on the expressway. I was shaking my head, cursing myself out. Could you believe the nerve of that man? Shitty breath, dirty underwear and an unclean house were three things a black man should never do. I didn't think men were capable of shit like that. For real. He had more gums than teeth. If I wanted some goddamn gum I'd buy some Bubble Yum, for real. That fine ass man with baby teeth. I *knew* the Tooth Fairy must have gone out of business because he didn't shed his childhood teeth. Ugh. I should have known it was too good to be true. Why did God ruin such a glorious body with too many gums and little reptilian teeth?

My cell rang and I refused to answer. It was him. Gumby. I put it on silent. He kept calling me back to back. By the time I got off the turnpike forty minutes later, I had thirty five missed calls from him.

I was just happy to be home, looking forward to my divorce. Shunning away online and grocery store men forever.

Now if only I could get Mama to take her ass home.

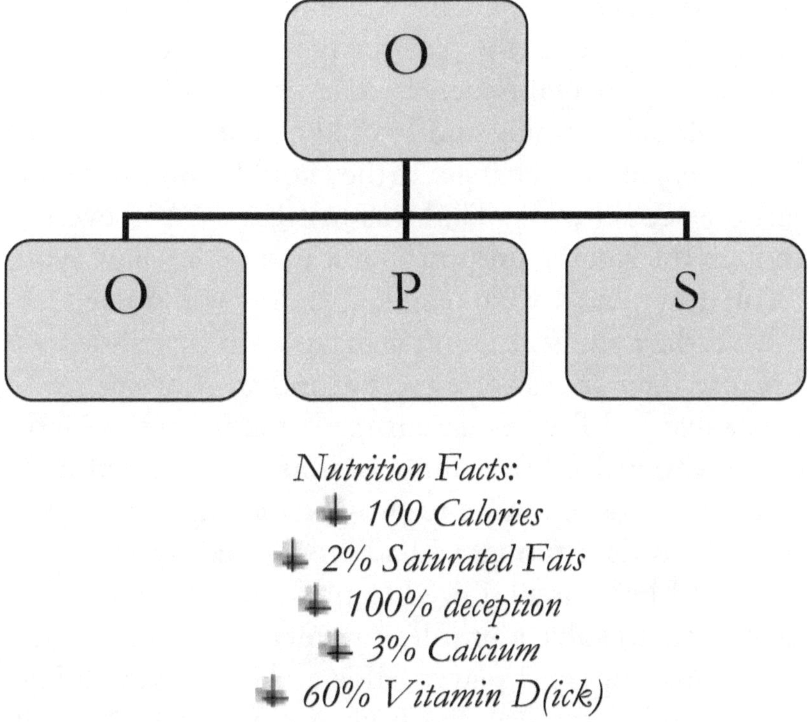

My name was Ted Oxford. And I was depressed. Nothing in my life seemed to be going right. I longed for my childhood. A time in my life my parents' home was filled with bluegrass music, apple pies and good Caucasian cooking. I didn't have to pay bills, I didn't have grown man problems and I didn't have to work a 9-5 job to keep the water on and food on the table. Things seemed to be so much simpler than they were now. I was a cut-around-the-edges white man who loved all kinds of music, people and places. Completing my physical package were blue, piercing eyes that made women buckle at the knees, a nice body and Southern views imposed on me by myself and the standards I set back when I was a teenager in high school. I was never the playboy type, and I was never into environmental issues. I could give a rat's butt about global warming and I could care less about bums begging for change. If they could blink, shit and fart they could work. That was my theory. And even though the singing group Everclear sings a song saying "You don't know what it's like," unless you walked a mile in their shoes, I didn't want to *wear* their shoes because their shoes were too big and *my* shoes were expensive and I didn't care to get a toe fungus behind those who walked five hundred miles and wanted to walk five hundred more to prove a fucking point. By many accords, I thought I had life figured out. I thought I knew it all. I used to pride myself on this, being able to solve a murder mystery on TV in record time. Growing up, I played Hide and go Seek with my friends and nothing and nobody got past me. My uncle Paul, my Mom's loving brother (they were closer than white on rice) used to watch us from her living room window. He was a quiet man, who never got into much. He didn't like my father very much, but he always treated him with respect. Paul once told me I had cat eyes and a dog's sense of smell. I would lure you from the darkness like I was rays of sunshine in Summer. He also told me I was very intelligent. That when he was younger he was equally smart, but when he went to jail for trying to shoot one of his ex girlfriends (for cheating on him), all of that intelligence went out of the window. He lost his job, lost his reputation and he moved in with Mama, since she was the oldest child, and focused on family.

I was in Pre Calc by the time I reached the ninth grade. My way with numbers would stun you. That's why I was now trying to go to accountant school. And with my impending divorce from my wife, I would now have a lot of time on my hands to do so. Why not enroll in college to preoccupy myself?

Most of my peers hated my high I.Q. And because of it I was sometimes ousted from the group, becoming the outsider. When they did this I felt alone and abandoned and deserted and I developed thick rhinoceros skin that was unperturbed. When I was a lad, my loving Christian mother, Stacy Oxford, born and raised in Illinois and my father, Phillip Oxford, used to brag about me to their friends. "I have a smart son," Papa used to say. "Nothing gets over his head."

And he was right. When our home was broken into when I was ten years old, my parents were devastated. So was I, considering my favorite sweater had been pissed on by said robber. My valuables were gone, couches over turned and insulation ripped from the roof. My uncle Paul had been kidnapped for ransom. I knew this as fact because the robber left a half-assed scribbled note on the dining room table, next to a magazine. My parents called the police, as they should have. But something didn't sit well with me. Why would my sweater have warm piss on it? It hadn't dried up, it was still wet and it was still warm. When the police arrived I sat out in the living room with them and my parents. Mama cried her heart out, Frank Sinatra playing at a low volume from the stereo. Daddy was aggravated. Not only was he upset about the break in, and the robber taking over $700 of his money from his drawer, but he hated Frank Sinatra and he wanted to put on his favorite bluegrass CD.

The two cops weren't very "seasoned," as I liked to say. They seemed to be zonked, like they were on drugs. The taller white guy, named Officer Ways, had a huge mustache and you couldn't see his lips when he spoke. His eyes narrowed too much and he obviously was chewing on tobacco. His breath reeked of something foul. It turned my stomach and made me want to barf. Officer Simms, a five feet 4 inch midget of sorts, kept cutting his eyes over to my mother, questioning her. At first I dismissed it as standard procedure. But every time Mama's ample tits shook Officer Simms was asking another question, as if giving himself an excuse to look at them. His hard on, suppressed with a folder, was evident. I dismissed myself, because I didn't really have a place in grown folks business, as Papa liked to say.

It was when I stood up, yawning, that my eyes cut over to the hallway closet. The door was ajar and I saw a pair of eyes glittering. I didn't make a sound, I didn't blink. I pretended like I didn't see them. I sat back down and said, "I'm tired."

Mama signaled for me to come over to her. When I sat in her lap, her sparkling blue eyes shined down on me. "Are you tired?"

"Yes," I said, Daddy rubbing my head. "I'm very tired."

"Well go on up to bed," Papa said, picking up his beer from the low-table.

I looked at the cops. "Thank you for responding to my parents call so quickly."

Officer Simms grinned. "He looks like a little detective," he said offhandedly, Officer Ways agreeing.

Mama beamed, despite her grief. Papa smiled.

"I will make a good detective," I said, taking Officer Ways' pen from his uniform shirt pocket. I took his pad and I said, "I am going to write something and let's see if you all can guess what it is."

"Son," said Papa, not in the mood for games.

Mama said, "Honey, its ok. He's just a child. We should encourage him."

Papa grunted in defeat.

I wrote something and handed it to Officer Simms. When he read it he sat up stiffly, handing the pad to Officer Ways. Officer Ways was confused. He didn't understand Officer Simms reaction. Now my parents were alarmed, but tried their best to hide it from their faces.

Officer Simms looked at Officer Ways.

"Well, I think our work is done here," Officer Simms said, standing up. He picked up his hat from the end table and put it over his blonde, unruly hair.

"If you all have any questions or wish to give some more information…" Officer Ways handed them a slip of paper with his writing on it. "Don't hesitate to call."

Somber, Papa's eyes clouded over. "So that's it? Our home gets broken into and you do *nothing*?"

Unshielded, Mama began weeping. I hated to see her cry. It unconventionally cracked my soul in unexplainable ways.

"We'll be in touch," said Officer Simms, hurriedly heading for the front door. He took a pack of cigs from his pocket, extracted one and lit up. Officer Ways was behind him. When Officer Simms opened the front door, Officer Ways snatched the closet door open, quickly and expertly drawing his pistol.

Fire was in his eyes. "FREEZE! DON'T MOVE!"

The perpetrator was so caught off guard he couldn't blink, smile, fall or react. Mama and Papa couldn't believe their eyes. The perpetrator was handcuffed. I studied him. He had a ski mask over his face, was about five feet 7 and had blondish hair peeking from under the skull cap. His black pants were rugged, his black fleece jacket a little on the worn-out side and his tennis shoes had mud caked on the bottom.

After his rights were read, Officer Simms looked at me. "Son. You are going to make a great detective one day. I can truly see nothing gets over your head."

Papa hugged me. "That's my son."

Mama said, "We're pressing charges. But before you haul the creep away, I just want to see who it is."

Mama snatched the ski mask off his face. Her mouth fell open in shock. Papa had to sit down and my world became an appendage.

"Do you know him?" Officer Simms asked.

"Yes," I said. "That's my Mama's brother Paul."

The last thing I remembered, before Papa whisked me to my room, was Mama taking the lamp and brutally slamming it over Paul's head, instantly knocking him unconscious.

T hat was many years ago. Now I was a grown man trapped in a situation I didn't know how to control. Silently driving in my truck, I was on my way to my best friend's wife's house. I called her earlier and let her know what her husband Dexter had been doing behind her back with my wife. I was still numb inside, feeling betrayed by two people I loved and trusted most in the world. My wife Bianca and my best friend Dexter. When I met my soon-to-be-ex-wife at the Muvico Theatres in Fort Lauderdale (I was going to see the Tom Cruise flick *Mission Impossible 3*), I really thought I had found someone genuine. She was the most beautiful woman in the entire establishment. When I lay eyes on her, I knew then that Papa telling me nothing went over my head had to be correct. She had an Apple Bottom ass, Janet Jackson wash board abs, ample breasts and perky nipples. She had short, croppy hair, loved poetry and loved eating the best foods. She turned heads, I tell you. Clad in tight snakeskin print pants, long leather boots with spiked heels and cowboy golden spinners on the back, long-sleeved gold blouse with a huge oval button holding her tits in place, I was in love. Initially, I wasn't going to say anything to her. She seemed stuck up. Plus my wearing a pink IZOD shirt, blue Dockers pants and pink banana Republic shoes didn't sit too well with me. I thought she would turn me away. But she didn't.

I didn't even think I had a chance in hell with her. Being that I was a white man, I tended not to believe the rumors I heard about black women from my colleagues.

All of the rumors skyrocketed in my skull, watching her in motion.

    + They were finger-snapping, head rolling trolls who was all about money and being independent.

- They loved weave and make-up more than life itself.
- Fried chicken was the ritual.
- They all went to the clubs on Saturday and then to church on Sunday.
- They liked big cocks and were size queens.
- They had two or more Baby Daddies
- They spent their child support checks on anything but the children.

One of my friends who worked security with me, Kamal, told me, "You better be careful. Black women buy their own diamonds and they buy their own rings now."

I used to laugh it off, brushing it off as stereotyping.

Now my world was destroyed. I was still in love with Bianca, but I was caught between a rock and a hard place. Since I've been a work-o-holic, she has been sneaking my best friend into the house, fucking him senseless in my bed, on my sheets. My insolence got the best of me. Their images sped through my brain like Speed Racer…I nearly ran off the road thinking about it, punching the dash board didn't help matters and blaming God was irrelevant.

Boom.

There I was. In my doorway. Frozen. Dexter was tagging Bianca from the back. Bile rose in my throat. She was inefficaciously riding his dick…Dexter was selfishly dancing inside her declination…spreading her ass cheeks apart. His dick was light years bigger than mine. I felt insecure in my own home watching my own best friend, my partner in crime fuck my wife. She started to come. Thick, gooey nut was all over the shaft of his condomless dick.

"You like it, Bianca?" he asked seductively.

"I love it Dexter." Getting off him, she sucked her come off his dick. I had heart failure. She then tit fucked him. After that ended, he stood up and slid his dick deep in her ass. She went haywire, saying she loved when he fucked her in the ass. She loved when she snuck him in my home to have sex. Seething with rage I raced downstairs and put on a pot of grits. The minute it started boiling I snatched the pot off the stove, ran up stairs and burst into the room. They were in the shower.

After Dexter said he never liked me and issued sexual demands from my wife, I snatched open the shower curtain and all she could say was "Oops." I dumped grits on them. As the grits ate away at her pretty face, I beat Dexter to a pulp with the pot and my feet. When I married Bianca he was my best man. And it all blew up in my face.

I guess I had to blame myself. I believed everything she said when we met without investigating any of it. She told me I looked like Brad Pitt. I was flattered. She also said she was a direct woman, that her zodiac sign was Scorpio. I told her I loved shrimp scampi and she nodded her head, saying "Same here." Why didn't I notice that? If I would have said "Spaghetti," she would have said, "Same here." She said "Wide Open Spaces" was her favorite song from the Dixie Chicks, yet couldn't sing three words of the song after we got married.

She also told me that she wasn't raised in the projects. She wouldn't know what one looked like. She said she was adopted when she was 3 months old by an Australian family. She was a crack baby. I had chocked on my Coke soda. She had me emotionally from that point on. She knew just how to lure me in. And it worked. She then said she was raised in the suburb of Miami, but never said which one. She went to the best catholic and private schools. She graduated from Palmetto Senior High with honors and did four years in the Airforce, did a tour in Tokyo and another in China. She got the Montgomery G.I. Bill and attended college. She went to USC off and on. She did another 3 years in the Airforce Reserves. Once she got tired of wearing blue she finished law school, gave up on that dream, and got into TV Production. She wanted to be an anchor woman. That dream failed. She said she (at the time) worked at Channel 7 News as a sound editor.

She was everything I wanted in a woman. After she sucked my dick in the back of the theatre and swallowed my come, I still didn't see her for what she was. I was blinded by the head she gave.

What classy woman sucked dick in a theatre and swallowed instead of spit?

She didn't know my ball bag from a sack of grocery at the time. But I was so alone, so tired of sleeping alone in bed that I didn't care. Things intensified.

She drove her Benz back to my crib and we went out to South Beach. We wined and dined, went to Club Deep and hours later I beat the dust off the pussy in my bed, which became her bed shortly after when we married. I sent her flowers four times a week, gave her keys to my place and she introduced me to her friends and adoptive parents.

I would later propose to her in front of her family and she would accept. They ate my food, tarnishing my image and they drink up my liquor bashing me, then once I did get home they smiled in my face like everything was ok. I was the dumb cracker. I was the man who believed in his woman and his friends. I was the empathetic fool who loved sports but loved life even more. I was the man who would give the coat off my back to protect a woman's high heels from getting water on them.

But the day I caught them together in the shower, she told Dexter, "I'm divorcing Ted. We (meaning she and Dexter) can build a life together. What was I thinking marrying that punk? I mean I don't listen to the Dixie Chicks. I just told his ass that so I can get in his wallet. I was never adopted. Can you believe he fell for that shit? My parents still live in the ghetto. I was never a suburban chick."

What was I to do?

I turned off the truck when I parked in Karen's driveway. She was Dexter's wife. She was expecting me. I was having second thoughts. Two wrongs didn't make it right. I was better than this but I was one hurt motherfucker. Logic was the last thing on my mind. When I initially called her and told her of her husband's infidelity she told me that her husband hadn't fucked her in months. She told me to come over and take care of her sexually. Since Dexter fucked my wife I was going to fuck his. We were both consenting adults, why not? I was mad, angry and vulnerable. I needed a woman's touch. I needed Karen more than she realized. She said she'd even change the locks so Dexter's keys failed him.

I licked my lips, knocking on the door. For a moment I didn't hear anything. I knocked again and Karen answered, clad in a bathrobe. Her skin was milky white. We were of the same breed. *God, she's so beautiful.* We looked in each other's eyes and saw the hurt and the betrayal. *I need you, Karen. But I don't want to appear desperate.* She wrapped her arms around me and openly sobbed. *Let it out, Baby. I'm here. And once you're done I am going to give you the best cock of your life.* I held her and refused to cry over an unfaithful bitch. *Bianca can rot in hell!* I was shaking where I stood. Karen's skin felt good against mine. She smelled of light lotion, and her perfume was gentle and sweet.

She didn't want to let me go. "Come inside," she said, pulling away from me. I walked past her. She put her hair in a ponytail, her eyes casting to the tile. She closed the door and rested her hands on it.

I know you're hurting, Karen. So am I. What are we to do? I know why I'm here. But do I want pussy that badly? Well, yea. Getting pussy was always the brass ring. But you are a very dear friend. And you have always been there for me over the years. Maybe this was bigger than sex.

I was reluctantly looking around. On the low table was her wedding picture. She'd torn Dexter out of it. His image lay in shreds on the floor.

"Karen…" I walked up behind her, carefully putting my hands on her shoulders. She looked over them, faintly smiling. She felt so soft.

"Yes."

"We don't have to do this."

She faced me, giving me some tongue. "I always wanted to do this. I've wanted to kiss you for years"

"Why didn't you?" I asked, unsure of what she said. Women always gave false hopes and blinking dreams when they were hurt.

Our lips danced in unison. I was on fire and I didn't want to be smothered. I was about to combust. I felt the smoke rising in my loins and pushing the blood to the head of my cock. Her breathing increased, and she released little moans that turned me on. I held my breath. She was a beautiful woman. Why would Dexter cheat on her with my wife?

She untied the robe and it fell to the floor. She looked into my eyes and seemed to be hesitant.

"What's wrong?"

"I guess I can't be upset at my husband for his betrayal."

"Why do you say that?" I asked, taking off my shirt. I wasn't leaving here until I fucked his wife.

"It's my fault," she said, falling to her knees, her face in her hands. "I loved him so much."

"And I did, too. He was my best friend."

"It's deeper than that."

I got on my knees in front of her. "Look at me."

"No."

"Karen." I lifted her face. Her eyes were dull and sad. I wanted to protect her.

"Yes."

"Kiss me."

"I don't know…" I stood up, taking her by the arm. When she stood up I picked her up and lay her on the couch. I spread her legs and started to taste her pussy. She exploded with jubilancy. She shook out of her skin. I spread her salty pink walls and thumbed her clit while I pushed my aching tongue in and out of her twat. She sunk her nails into the leather of the chair.

"Yes, Ted. I love it."

I ran my tongue all over her thighs, carefully pleasing her. I was erasing her hurt and alleviating her pain. This wasn't the first time I was there for her. Even though we never had sex, we were always attracted to each other. I just never went across the line because Dexter was my best friend and I would never betray him by fucking his wife. I was there for her when she came to me, one day last year, and told me she didn't want to be married to him anymore. That her family disowned her when she married the "Nigger." She loved her family. They were the core of her universe. But I defended my boy and told her she could marry anybody she chooses and if she lost her family because of it then oh, well. Life went on and life was bigger than friends and family.

Suffice it to say her parents cut her off. She went through depression. Dexter came to me in tears, not understanding why his wife turned to the liquor bottle. She closed up. She would not tell him. He grew further and further apart from her. He told me he didn't want to be married to a woman who didn't trust him enough to confide in him. I should have seen the signs then, but I was in serious denial.

Pushing the memories away, she held my head, telling me to suck her clitoris. I gracefully obliged. I told her to hold her legs back. I sucked all over the pussy, loving her scent, loving her taste. If my tongue was a cock her pussy would be a chanticleer.

After an eternity I felt her body tense. I smiled, chewing on her walls. She was trying to push me away. I took my tongue out of her and put my dick so far up in her pussy she gasped for air, wide-eyed. I slowly grinded in her tunnel as she continued to rise above the clouds in search of the mountains. They weren't there. Just a ledge. The waves crashed below and her clit was man overboard, drowning in the seas. I wanted the clouds. She wanted the waves. Swoosh, I pinned her legs as far back as they'd go and I gave her every inch of my cock. Holding my back, she was moaning my name in ways she never called out for Dexter. So I took her higher, dancing in her dripping pussy like a game of tic-tac-toe. She wanted the X and my dick formed an O with her cunt. My cock sliding in and out, I started fucking her harder, giving her what she wanted. I was tired of playing around. I was getting a divorce. I lost my wife. I lost my best friend. I wanted her pussy to heal me, take me past the hurt and the pain and show me the way. Show me the light. Show me how to get up and get beyond deceitful people. I needed her pussy because I hated my wife. Her pussy was the deterrent. Her pussy was everything I needed and wanted. I was a man. I needed pussy to heal my open sores. I needed pussy to get me through the day. When I had a bad time I played in pussy. Most men called up the "boys" and played a game of ball. Fuck the boys. Give me some pussy. Her pussy was the Band-aid. Heal my wounds. Her come would be the antiseptic. Heal my sore heart.

When she came I felt her pussy throbbing on my dick. It felt like a hand was gripping and releasing. I pushed it all the way in and froze, looking deep in her eyes with our mouths agape.

Her breath was hot on my face. I had to pull out because, I didn't know what it was, but I started to come. I didn't want to come in her.

We lay next to each other, drenched in sweat. I was ready for round two. She was ready to shower. She faced me, playing with my navel. I rubbed her arm, looking at her.

"I have a confession to make."

"Yes. What is it?"

"I am a family-oriented woman."

"That's your confession?"

She laughed and so did I. "No, that's not it. But it's part of it. When my parents cut me off I could not live with myself. Ever since I was a little girl, I loved having family around. I was always different."

"Different how?"

"I included my family in everything I did. They supported everything, except my love for blacks."

"So they are racist."

"Very."

"So how did they take it when you got married?"

"They cut me off. You know that. They didn't even come to the wedding, and that hurt. My Dad said he wasn't going to give me away to a nigger. Mama told me to die with him and go to hell. She said that if I had mixed kids she would have nothing to do with them."

"So why are you telling me this?"

"You are a good man, Ted. You always have been. Ever since the first time you listened to me vent I've had strong feelings for you. Dexter doesn't listen. He dictates. He tells you what he wants and that's what he expects."

"But you knew that before you married him."

She was massaging my head. That felt good.

"He wasn't that bad when we got married. He was stubborn, yes. But not over the top rude." She grew silent, struggling with her words. "I love you, Ted," she finally admitted and I held my breath. I felt like an episode of *General Hospital*. "And I want to be with you."

"We're rebounding, Karen. And you know that. This is too convenient."

"Who gives a damn? I know what I want."

"And how do you know that? You only recently found out your husband is cheating on you with my wife."

"Actually…"

"Actually, *nothing*, Karen. You are confused. You are stunned. You don't know if you're coming or going."

She was trapped in her own existence. "I do know I love you. That's why I took action."

Took action? What is she talking about? "In what way?"

She sat up and got between my legs, foreign territory. She took my arms and wrapped them around her…her body was so warm. Her skin was so soft.

"Like I said. When I lost my family I think I died inside. And I wanted them back. I loved Dexter, yes but I had to do something that would make everybody happy. So I played Devil's Advocate."

"OK."

"You worked long hours. Bianca was always over here talking about it to my husband, like you and I used to talk. We got our secrets, Dexter and Bianca had theirs. I set them up to meet one on one. I would call her over, and then I would call Dexter. I would tell them I needed help with so and so. So by the time they got here I was long gone and they were alone."

I didn't like was she was insinuating.

She stood up, taking her hair loose. She gave a smile, a sad smile. "My plan worked."

What are you talking about? "How?" I slowly stood up, facing her.

She was rubbing my arms. "They weren't initially cheating on you. I wanted my family. So I kept setting them up to meet by chance. Bianca was hurting because you worked long hours and sometimes I cursed her out. I treated Dexter like shit. He didn't fuck me in months because I told him I didn't want to have sex. I kept faking my period and a head ache. I drove them two together."

"YOU WHAT?"

"And now Dexter and I are getting divorced. I knew they were cheating on us before you walked in on it. I wanted an excuse to divorce him so we could be together and my family would accept me. If they saw two whites married in Holy Matrimony my father would walk me down the aisle and give you me. My mother would be there and all my brothers and sisters. Being married to a black man has driven a wedge between my family and I. I can't deal with it. I want a happy marriage and my family to share it with me."

"Do you realize what you're saying to me? You are playing God. And here I blamed my wife. Yes, she is to blame but I didn't know about these chance meetings. I thought you cared for me as your friend."

Desperately, she hugged me. "I do."

I pushed her on the floor, spitting in her face. She was disgusted.

"*You motherfucker!*"

I exploded. "You bitch! Did you think it would be that simple? Did you think I would pick you up with my white horse and ride off into the sunset? You destroyed two marriages with your selfishness and greed. You love your family so much you would ruin your marriage? You would drive Dexter into the arms of my wife? He was probably hurt because you kept faking head aches and periods. I know Dexter like the back of my hand. You tell him no too many times he's gonna go out and fuck another woman. You made sure my wife was available."

"I'm sorry," she said, standing up. Shaking her head, she wiped saliva from her face. "Sometimes you gotta do what you gotta do."

"I can't believe I'm hearing this."

"*Believe* it." She was approaching me. "We will be happy together and my family will love you."

"You're sick."

"I called my father this morning and told him my husband cheated on me. I also told him I met a good man. I told him all about you. He wants to meet you."

I said it slowly. "*You* are insane!"

She touched my arm and I slapped her. She held her jaw, looking at me sadly. "I'm sorry."

"Stay away from me. I can't believe you would do this to me. I guess you think you're the only one who is supposed to be happy in this life. I lost my wife. She was my earth. I rotated on her axis. You talk about racism but you're one yourself."

"I love all people."

"You love all people as chess pieces on your chess board. You castle the rooks and blind the queen to get to a King. I don't want to be a stalemate move on your game board. Do you hear me?"

"We can learn to love each other."

"I'm leaving."

I walked past her and opened the door. I heard two clicks and I froze.

"If you walk out of that door I will kill you."

The cool breeze blew across my face. I closed my eyes, sucking in air. I could smell the earth. I also smelled rain in the air.

"Come back inside, Ted."

"Why should I? You're going to shoot me anyway."

"I will if I have to."

"Why are you doing this?"

"I want my family back. Ever since I married Dexter my life has gone downhill."

"You made the choice. No one put a gun to your head."

She pressed the gun against my temple. "I'm pressing one against your head. Come back inside."

"Guns don't scare me, Karen." They scared the living shit out of me, but I wouldn't show it on my face.

"They should."

"I'm leaving, Karen. I can't be a scapegoat in your scheme. I really thought you were a friend."

"I am your friend. I just want a husband and a family and…"

"You had that with Dexter. You traded it in for selfishness."

I turned to face her. I didn't want to meet her demanding gaze. She looked weak standing there with the gun. Guns were not her thing. Her arms shook like Julia Roberts in Sleeping with the Enemy. I shook my head, putting both hands on the gun.

"You don't want to do this. You really don't want to shoot me. If you do you will go to jail and you won't have anything. Your world will cease to exist. Dexter left you for my wife. I fucked his ass up, too. Right now he should be checking into a hospital. I threw hot grits on him and Bianca."

"You did?"

"Yes. I did. And I come here thinking I was going to get revenge on him by sleeping with you and I find out you was the Master Puppeteer."

I took the gun from her and took out the bullets. She hugged me. "Please. I need my mom, my dad and my siblings. I want you, Ted. We can divorce our lovers and get married and have one big happy, kosher ending."

"A kosher ending. For whom? This is absurd. Are you crazy?"

"TED!"

I knocked her unconscious with the butt of the gun and looked at her body as it slumped to the floor.

I openly sobbed because I wasn't a violent man. I didn't like causing another person harm. But I had no choice. She was a sick bitch. There wasn't anybody here to watch me cry. No one was here to ridicule me…or to criticize me.

Fitting.

Stuffing the gun in my pocket I walked to my truck.

I got inside, put the key in the ignition and turned it on.

It cranked silently. Putting it in reverse, I backed out the drive way. I put it in drive when I got in the middle of the road.

I drove off. I was going through with my divorce.

I was going to move out of town. I was going to pack my things and be done with it. I would never get married again. I wasn't going to go that route. Love didn't live here. Love didn't live with friends. I couldn't trust anybody after this ordeal. Karen. Sweet Karen. The orchestrator of my doom. The catalyst.

After tonight they were all dead in my life.

Forever.

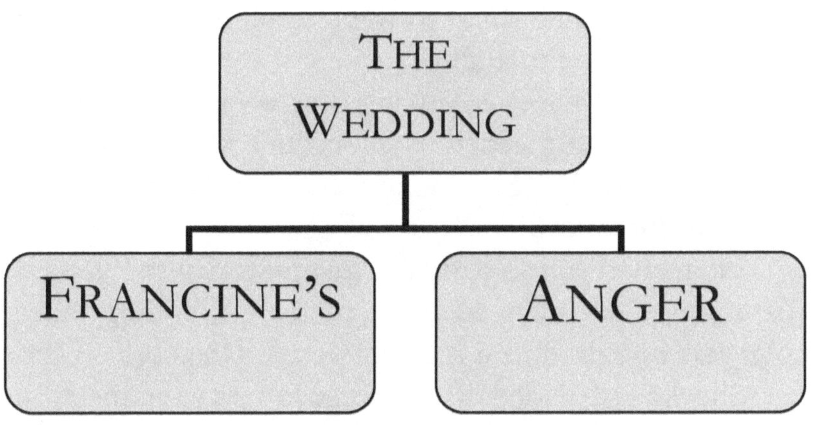

Nutrition Facts:
Contains 5% Juice
120 Calories
34% Sodium Benzoate
43% Thiamin
Shake Well before each serving

She was quietly riding in the back of the cab, trying to convince herself that, despite what Samuel had done to Chandra, she still loved him. Feeling like a zombie, she asked the cab driver, Manuel, for a cigarette. He smiled at her through the rear view mirror, handing her one.

Manuel turned on the windshield wipers. It was starting to rain. He cleared his throat. "Pretty women shouldn't smoke," he said, brushing cookie crumbs from his jacket. "Doesn't make you look good."

Absent-mindedly lighting her cigarette, she hungrily pulled on it. "Well, I'm not pretty today. I'm a pissed bitch in a wedding dress…"

He humored her. "Getting married I see? You wear your wedding dress to the church in a cab? Why? Shouldn't you be in a limo?"

She rolled her eyes, pulling on the cig again. "For one I am getting married in my home. And *fuck* limos. They're *too* costly." She looked at him more fixedly. "Why all the questions?"

He turned onto Florida's Turnpike, South. "I was just asking." He glanced at the meter. "You don't have to get so uptight about it, Lady. Jesus. Breathe."

She was offended. "Just because you gave me a cigarette doesn't mean I'm spilling the beans about my life. And you need to drive this cab and stop trying to sniff my panties. You're not driving Miss fucking Daisy, goddamn it! I don't care what you say or do— don't look at me like you lost your dog. All you men are the same—you meet a pretty girl and the first thing you think about is our pussies." She was heated. Crossing her shaved legs, she said as politely as she could. "Now get me to the church...I meant to my house. I'm running late..."

Well fuck you, bitch! he thought gravely. He was annoyed. He hated lippy broads.

"Look, for you to be engaged you are an uptight..."

She flashed angrily. "Don't say it, don't go there. If you call me a *bitch* I will curse your ass out. You don't fucking know me to be bringing the bullshit. Where's the goddamn customer service?"

He sucked in stale-clad air. "Whatever..."

"You must not be getting any at home," she stammered, directing her anger on him. "That's why you're trying to talk up on this. Look, dude. I have a sour taste in my mouth when it comes to men. If your money ain't right you're talking French to me."

"Don't worry about what I'm doing in my home…" he snuffed, shaking his head. He was embarrassed. "And I wouldn't pay for your snatch if it was the last piece on earth."

"I'm about to *snatch* your ass by that fake ass toupee if you don't shut the fuck up…"

Her cell phone rang, saving him from a verbal beat down.

Glancing at the caller I.D. she said to herself, "Damn…"

She answered.

"W here are you?" Francine's iron-fisted mother asked with an attitude, walking away from a group of people at her daughter's house. She walked into one of the massive bedrooms and closed the door. She sat on the edge of the bed, her mind moving a mile a minute.

"I'm on my way back to the church." She smoked the cigarette, crossing her legs. A heel dangled from her big toe.

"How are you getting here?" she asked, sitting on the edge of the bed.

Francine reached over the seat and stubbed out the cig in the ash tray. "In a cab."

Manuel said, "You …"

She slapped him in the back of the head and put a finger over her lips. He brooded like a child.

"A *cab*? Have you lost your *mind*?" her mother asked, jumping up to her eight-inch-heels.

Francine rubbed her lips together, smoothing over her lipstick. She didn't have time for the bullshit.

"Nah. But you lost yours. This is supposed to be my wedding day."

"I knew something was wrong with you today. I felt it. You have two families sitting in your house, waiting to see a marriage and you get cold feet and skedaddle out of here like you're going to a Van Halen concert."

"Van Halen? Who the fuck is *that?* And I don't give a fuck about two families sitting there, eating my fucking food, running up my light and water bills, sneaking eight, nine plates of food home for relatives I never heard of. Don't talk to me about family…"

"You…"

Francine interrupted. "When I get there, meet me in my bedroom. I have to talk to you about something. If you're not there you can get your ass outta my house. I am getting tired of you. Get your own goddamn life and stay outta mine. Today's the day I tell a bitch off, and you're first on the roster."

"Who in the hell are you talking to?"

"*You!* I'm a grown woman. If you don't like what I have to say GET THE FUCK OUTTA MY HOUSE!"

Click.

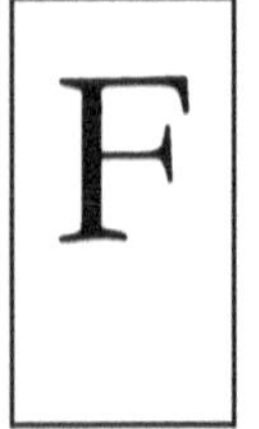

Francine called Chandra. There was no answer. *Damn, girl. Are you okay? Answer the phone. I'm getting worried about you. I know you're going through a lot and it doesn't seem like you'll make it through. But baby girl we've weathered the storm together and I won't abandon you now. We are*

friends till the end. I will never turn my back on you!

"Seems like you're having problems," Manuel said.

"Damn. Are you *still* alive? You haven't died yet?" Francine shot icily.

Manuel laughed. "I love women like you."

She sucked her teeth, averting her face. She watched the scenery zoom by, looking more like blurs. Ghosts with untold stories. She wondered did any of those ghosts have a sick fiancé who deceived her. *Sure,* Samuel got her best friend pregnant behind her back, put a gun to her head and her stomach and made her do drugs, but what did she do? She loved his money more than she loved him. Everything they owned was split down the center. Leaving would be hard. Most black women would have cut his ass off. But for her it wasn't that simple. She tried calling Chandra again.

It went straight to voice mail.

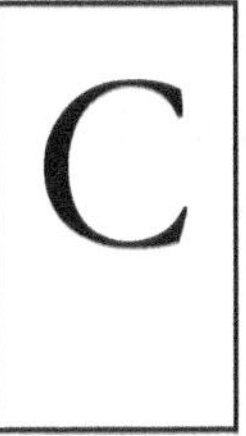

handra tightened the rubber band around her upper arm, hot tears streaming down her face. Finding a hit at the hotel proved to be impossible. Luckily, when she got dressed and went to the bar, the bartender mentioned to a tall, black man that he had a supply of heroine. She eavesdropped.

When the tall guy walked off she made her move. She paid him handsomely, using Francine's money and now, sitting in her room, dead to the world, she inserted the syringe into a fat vein, her eyes fluttering to the back of her head.

She lay back against the wall, staring blankly into her reflection. Nowhere on her beautiful face was the sweet, innocent woman she used to be. Samuel had drugged her, raped her and pumped her body full of heroine so by the time she came to, she craved a drug she didn't know about.

Then she found out she was pregnant. He was very possessive and controlling. Beat her ass from sun up to sun down when Francine thought he was working. Made her have sex with him. Supplied her drug use. He was jealous of Francine being best friends with her. He tried to destroy Chandra before Francine could ever find out.

So she could *never* find out.

But now Francine knew. Shame on Francine's mother—Satan's bastard child—for taking Samuel's side. She was a very deceitful, controlling woman. She never cut Francine a break. No matter what Francine did it was never good enough. Or she could do better. Or she should have done this.

It would drive anyone mad.

Her body felt like it was on fire, her heart pounding. She knew she was destroying her child, but what could she do? She didn't knowingly do drugs, a sick man slipped GHB in her alcohol and spent a few hours carefully injecting heroine into her veins.

Now she had a habit, one she couldn't break. The room suddenly turned black and her head spun. Moaning piteously, she lies down and fell into a deep sleep.

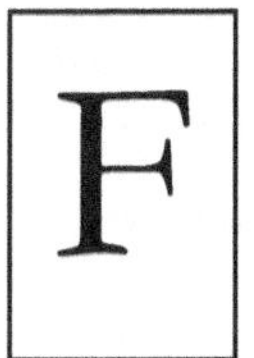rancine hung up the phone.

"She's probably sleeping," she told herself.

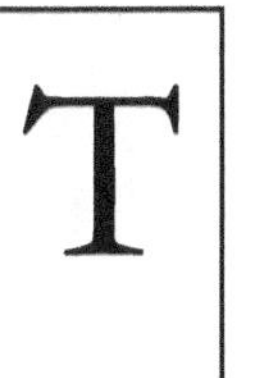hirty minutes later, Manuel pulled up in front of her house. Everyone was still there. Vehicles galore.

She threw Manuel three 20's and got out, closing the door. A few people noticed her and started to smile.

"There she goes."

Francine ignored them, and made her way to the back wooden gate. Unlatching it, she went to the back door and noticed people in her kitchen eating her food.

Niggahs, I tell you! she thought bitterly. *Didn't nobody tell them to go into my kitchen and start eating food!*

She made her way up the back staircase, leading to the balcony. When she arrived, she opened her bedroom door, slipped inside and closed it.

She lowered her head, sucking in air. She shook with revulsion, tears spilling from her gorgeous eyes like rain from clouds. She hurt for herself. She hurt for Chandra. She hurt for her not-going-to-happen marriage.

"Yes, I am marrying him," she told herself.

"I can't wait until you do. This has gone on long enough."

Startled, Francine tugged on her dress.

Turning to face her mother.

S amuel looked himself over in the guest room. His brother Prado, as handsome as ever, said, "Bruh, you're killing that Steve Harvey suit."

Samuel was flattered, rubbing his goatee. "*Really*, bruh?"

Prado brushed off the back of his brother's jacket. "Hell, yea. But of course I do it better."

Samuel shrugged his shoulders. "*Right…*"

They shared a laugh. Prado fired up a blunt and poured a small glass of Grey Goose.

"Pour me some. I'm about to marry Francine."

Prado, the blunt between his thick, luscious lips, poured a second shot, handing it to his brother.

"*Thanks.*" Samuel killed it, slamming the glass on the nightstand with force. Smacking his lips, the pleasurable burn ignited his eyes with zeal. "Pass the Dutch, bruh…"

Prado was in a sneezing fit, his eyes watering.

"Damn. This is some good shit, bruh." He passed the blunt, thinking about Francine. He couldn't get her off his mind. Never has he met a woman that captured his heart the way she had.

Samuel hit the joint, holding the smoke in his lungs until his body reacted with coughing.

He poured another drink.

"Cold feet, bruh?" Prado asked, turning on some Young Jeezy. He kept the volume low.

Hell yea my feet are cold. No, no they're not. They're blocks of ice. I will lose everything if Chandra opens her mouth. I have to make sure the canary doesn't sing!

"*Nah*. I'm ready. I thought she wasn't going to marry me. I love her. I can't live without her."

Prado loved her, but he would never tell his brother. He would keep it a secret. He could still taste Francine's pussy on his tongue. It smelled so good and fresh. He could still feel her lips all over his dick. He would cherish that for the rest of his life. Part of him was jealous Samuel was marrying Francine.

"She loves you, too," said Prado, frowning a little. It hurt him to say the words. He couldn't blame her. She was playing it safe, marrying a man with money.

Samuel's eyes sparkled. "She does?" Samuel asked, unsure of himself.

Prado hugged his brother, angry inside.

"Yea. She does."

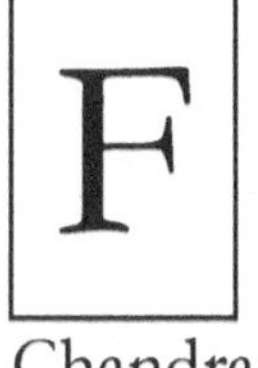 rancine looked at her mother, the woman who gave her life. The woman who controlled her, the woman she could *never* please. *She's a jealous bitch!* She thought about Chandra and what she was going through. A sweet

woman thrown into a nightmarish game of lies and betrayal by two people she trusted most in the world.

Chandra was vibrant and colorful. Full of life and God. She cherished church and family. She loved her friends and was a darling. People loved her instantly when they met her.

Now she's a manufactured heroine addict with no idea on how to save herself.

Now she was pregnant with Samuel's child. She chain-smoked, didn't keep herself up and she bites her nails. She hadn't an iota of God or religion in her mental frame of mind.

And Francine had to rectify that. She owed her best friend that much.

"I don't want you to be my Maid of Honor anymore," Francine said, waiting to bash her face in. She was counting from ten to one in her mind, keeping her wits in check.

Mama was furious. "What?" She huffed, snapping her fingers like she'd gone crazy. "I have on this fabulous dress and I called all my girlfriends, Chile. They are here and want to see me sport my Dolce and Gabana pumps, Chile. *Please.* You must have gotten drunk or something." Francine tucked her chin back. "Girl, give me some of what you're on so I can act out of whack with you. Ain't nothing and nobody stopping me from modeling this amazing dress."

"This is a wedding, not America's Next Top Bitch. Tyra Banks isn't the emcee and fuck that ugly ass dress!"

Mama tucked her chin back. She just about had it. Image was everything to her and Francine just destroyed it.

Dangerously, she said, "You will not talk to me…"
The little girl inside Francine called out to her.

Don't upset Mama! She will whip you. She will talk down to you. Please, Francine…she will lock you in the closet again when she doesn't get her way! She will call all your friends and tell them you're a bitch and tell all your business.

Francine held her stomach, bile rising in her throat. Frightened, she stood her ground.

Francine, don't do it. Don't talk back to your mother.

Exploding inside, Francine walked into her Mama's face, her hands on her hips.

"Don't look at me like that, Ma. You don't fucking scare me anymore."

Francine! Please! PLEASE! She is going to lock you in the closet! And leave you there all night to fight the darkness! Like she did when you were nine years old!

"Ever since I was a little girl I always tried to make you happy. I did whatever you said. You used to lock me inside the closet for hours. If I didn't clean your house right you locked me in the closet. If boys talked to me you'd whip me until you drew blood. I remember when your cousin called you and said I had lost my virginity…"

"Your point…"

"SHUT UP! And you snatched me by my braids and shoved a hot sauce bottle up my pussy! What kind of mother does that to her child? I couldn't piss straight for weeks. I lied to the doctor for you and told him I tried to masturbate with said bottle just to keep you out of jail. And it turned out that your cousin lied. I hadn't lost my virginity yet…"

"Grow up. You're still singing that sad OH GOD LIFE IS UNFAIR song and quite frankly you remind me of Patti Labelle trying to will another hit. *Ain't interested.*"

Francine gritted her teeth.

"I'm sick of you…"

"Take some Advil."

"I'm no longer scared of you."

"Whoopee!"

"Go to hell, Mama! Burn for an eternity. I can't deal with this anymore."

"I should have had an abortion. I was sick of you years ago…"

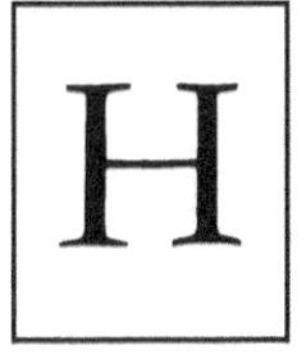urt beyond belief, Francine pushed her mother against the wall and snatched her by the hair. Her mother was shocked by her attack.

"What in the living fuck did you and Samuel do to my best friend?"

Mama footed her in the shin and she doubled over. Mama kicked at her and Francine, tired of being locked inside the little girl in her heart, grabbed her foot and snatched the dick-loving bitch to her knees. They tussled.

"She's a druggie bitch!"

"Oh, yea! You and Samuel orchestrated the entire thing! How could you do such a thing, Mama?"

They slammed into the closet door, painfully pulling each other's hair. Neither would relent. The room door opened and Prado rushed inside, grabbing Francine and Samuel grabbed her mother.

"What is going on in here?" asked Samuel, wanting answers.

Francine said, "Get the bitch out of my house or I will kill her. I no longer have love for the trifling bitch."

Samuel could hardly hold his mother-in-law. She growled, flinging her arms towards her daughter. Huge tears ran from her eyes.

"You two can get over this," said Prado, pushing Francine to the bed, putting his weight on her. She was a beast.

"GET THE BITCH OUT MY HOUSE NOW OR THE WEDDING IS OFF!"

Samuel looked at his mother-n-law and said, "You have to leave…"

"But she knows…"

"OUT!"

"LISTEN TO ME, SAMUEL!"

"BITCH GET THE FUCK OUT BEFORE I THROW YOU OUT!"

Mama was defeated. She swallowed her words, looking them all over for a brief second. She huffed.

Mama stamped from the room, slamming the door closed.

Francine said, "Prado. *Get* off me."
Prado stood up, fixing his suit.
Samuel helped her off the bed.
"Tell everyone we are about to get married. I'll be out there in a second. Leave me to myself right now."
Samuel said, "Are you sure?"
She faked a smile. It hurt her to look at him.

"*Yes*, darling. I can't wait to be your wife. I just don't want my mother being a part of my big day. In fact she is no longer welcome in this house…"

Samuel said, "I understand. No argument from me."

"I hope not. I'm calling the police and getting a restraining order. Her purpose in my life has been fulfilled. I'm a woman now, and I will not live the next thirty years being controlled by that bitch!"

Prado kissed her cheek and her panties were wet. "You look beautiful, by the way…"

She touched Prado's cheek. "Thanks," she said appreciatively.

Samuel kissed her lips.

And she felt nothing.

The music cued up and everyone smiled, clapped and a few people said, "Well it's about damn time!" Samuel took his place at the altar. His mother and father stood behind him. He smiled so big sunlight seemed to pierce through his teeth.

Samuel, Sr. was proud of his son and all he accomplished. He showed off, holding his cane and hugging his wife.

Samuel inhaled; *thankful* Chandra didn't get to Francine. He was ecstatic that maybe she'd overdose and be rid of her all together. Maybe the baby would die with her.

He wanted to control who and what came around his wife. Give her a false security; make her think it's all about her. But in all actuality, he wore the briefs and the fucking pants. He built his fortune from the ground up. He'd be damned if a woman compromised it all.

He was like Tru TV.

Not reality.

Actuality!

P rado was in the bathroom, torn inside. When he heard the music playing his heart shattered into a million pieces. Never to be put back together again. He never cried over anything, let alone a bitch. Jay Z said he had 99 problems but a bitch ain't one. Prado used to say the same exact shit. Now a woman was a problem, a woman that was his habit.

Licking his lips, he savored the faint taste and smell of Francine's pussy. When the marriage was final he'd never wash his lips again. If he died right now he'd be the happiest man alive. He had the opportunity to make her come on his tongue. He was blessed to feel her warmth...He loved breathing her and touching her on her wedding day, when she was about to give herself to his brother.

He loved Francine with all his heart and to lose her to Samuel killed him inside. He could still remember what she wore when he first laid eyes on her. His brother was in school, and he brought Francine to the house. Prado was a promising child football star living in his brother's shadow of Honor Rolls and newspaper articles.

She wore a lovely red dress, with her flowing, long black hair tinted and swept from her face.

She introduced herself to his parents. They were overjoyed that a pretty little thing fancied their son.

When she met Prado he was enraptured. He took a rose from his mother's vase and plucked the stem, sliding the rose in her hair. Samuel didn't like that very much but he kept quiet. Staring at his reflection in the mirror, he hated the man looking back at him.

YOU'RE A FAILURE! YOU LOST! SAMUEL HAS THE WOMAN OF YOUR DREAMS!

Prado then started fucking women without a care in the world. Every woman he compared to Francine. Every time a woman got pregnant with his child he harbored a secret hurt because he only wanted Francine having his baby.

And now that would never be.

SAMUEL HAS YOUR GIRL. NAH. SHE WAS NEVER YOUR GIRL. WHY DID YOU FALL IN LOVE WITH YOUR BROTHER'S FIANCE? YOU LOST!

Prado punched the mirror so hard the glass shattered into the sink and onto the counter and floor.

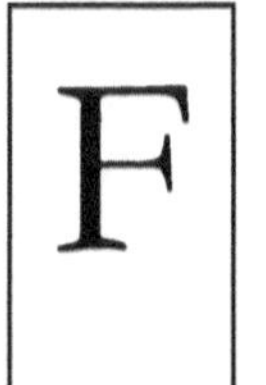

F rancine said into the house phone, "Yes. Is it completed now?"

"Yes, Francine. Everything is taken care of."

Francine smiled. "Good. Because tonight is my honeymoon. Everything has to be perfect."

"Congratulations on your wedding," the woman said through the phone.

Francine hung up.

She sang, *"Goingggg to my living room because I'm goinggg to get maaarrieed!"*

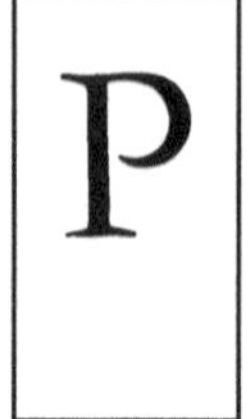 rado paused behind his brother, hugging his mother.

"I like the leopard-print jacket, Ma. Dad, must have cost you out the ass…"

They shared a chuckle.

Samuel said, "I'm glad you're my best man."

Prado hugged him. "I'm glad to be here, bruh."

Samuel pats his back. "Thank you…"

"No problem, bruh."

Prado, hiding his hurt, looked his brother over.

I'm not happy about this at all. Francine, good bye. I will always love you.

When Francine appeared, clad in the most gorgeous dress known to man, everyone rose to their feet with applause. Prado refused to look at her. He stared ahead, holding his breath. He refused to take another breath of air.

He wanted to die.

Samuel's breath caught in his throat. That wasn't the same dress he'd just seen her wear.

Samuel's mother, Mrs. Lester, held her pearls. His father smiled.

"She's wearing my dress," said Mrs. Lester. "And she looks amazing in it."

"No, honey," said Mr. Lester, eyeing Samuel with a secret smile that made his heart flutter. "She looks *better* than you ever did in that dress."

Looking into Samuel's joyous eyes, she stamped Mr. Lester's foot and he frowned in pain.

"Watch it. Or I won't spank you while you suck my high heels…" she whispered conspiratorially.

Samuel said, wanting to puke, "Ma…not here," with a smile, looking at his father coyly.

Prado closed his eyes.

Francine smiled, her hair in a series of curls. She retouched her make-up. Nothing was overdone. She wiped half the shit off her face. Lord knew her heart hammered with both anticipation and excitement for what she was about to do. She made a last minute decision to wear Mrs. Lester's dress. After all it was in the back of the guest closet. She remembered Mrs. Lester had it cleaned and, once it was done, she called Francine and asked her to pick it up from the cleaners. Francine had done so, but when she got to Mrs. Lester's house she wasn't home. So she put it in the guest room closet.

Now she looked radiant. Nowhere on her face was any sign that she'd just whipped her Mama's ass. Nowhere did it say Chandra was pregnant with Samuel's baby.

Prado turned to face Francine.

He smiled so big he couldn't stand it.

She's wearing Mama's dress.

S he was the most beautiful woman he'd ever seen. Wow. Prado looked at Samuel and slapped palms with him.

I can't believe God let this angel escape heaven. Looking at her turns me to mist. I just want to envelope Paris, and touch the metal of the Eiffel Tower.

God, I want to be Moscow while she becomes my Kremlin!

"She is gorgeous," Prado said.

Samuel couldn't wait for the honey moon.

Mr. Lester noticed no one walked her down the aisle. Before he could, Prado walked past him and up to Francine.

Samuel smiled.

"Since your Dad isn't here, mind if I walked you down the aisle?" Prado asked, kissing her hand.

She said, "Sure. I can't wait to become Mrs. Lester."

Prado respected her decision.

He had to let her go.

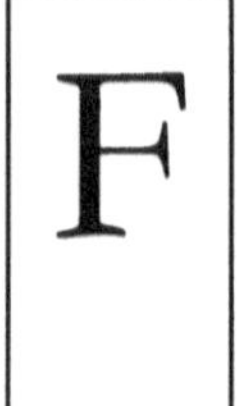Francine took Samuel's hands. He nearly shook with glee. Prado was happy for his brother. He knew deep down he had to let her go. Couldn't get mad over something that wasn't his.

Pastor Reynolds opened his Bible and said, "We are gathered here today to join two individuals together in Holy Matrimony…"

Francine kissed Samuel's lips.

"I love you," she said flatly.

He responded with a breathy, "I'll die for you."

Prado held his brother's shoulder.

Mr. and Mrs. Lester were pleased. A photographer walked here and there snapping professional photos.

"Marriage is sacred and should be cherished," the Pastor said. "It seems these days people get married for all the wrong reasons. Whether it's because of good finances or good sex, building a foundation on deceit and lies corrodes a marriage into the untimely hell of divorce."

"Amen," said Francine, eyeing Samuel, who seemed uncomfortable.

The Pastor closed the Bible. "Francine and Samuel, are you two getting married for the right reasons?"

Samuel looked Francine in the eyes. "Yes."

Francine looked Prado in the eyes, squeezing Samuel's hands tightly. *Don't ruin my big day, Prado! You better keep your fucking mouth closed about our little secret rendezvous. I'll be your Karyn White forever if you shut your jaws.*

"Yes, Pastor."

"I**s there anyone here today who wishes for these two not to be united as husband and wife? Here's your chance to speak. Speak now or forever hold your peace."

Everyone looked around.

Prado sucked in air and thought to himself.

I will forever hold my peace. Congratulations, Francine and Samuel.

His heart hurt.

"May I have the rings," said the Pastor and a very vibrant, handsome little boy by the name of George walked up the aisle, wearing a light blue suit.

People clapped and whispered love and adoration.

George walked up to the beaming Pastor.

Succinctly, Francine said, "Um. Wait, before we go any further. I want to say a few words to my husband to be."

Samuel smiled like the sun.

Francine looked him deeply in the eyes.

"I love you beyond anything. And sometimes love conquers all. Through all the ups and downs love shows a person a road past the crossroads. A door out of hell. A place beyond nightmares and unfaithfulness."

"I love you too, Francine," said Samuel. "I will love and honor you. You are my alpha and omega. I want no other woman but you. You complete me."

Francine turned to Mr. and Mrs. Lester. "I adore you two. You have been married for decades. I hope to share that many decades with your son. I love him. I will die for him. He treats me like a lady and opens doors for me. He appreciates me, doesn't talk down to me and treats me like his equal."

Samuel was the happiest man alive.

Mrs. Lester, huge tears flowing, touched Francine's face. "You have always been a woman about action. Polished military veteran, you wear many hats. I am proud to say you're now becoming my daughter-n-law who I love and admire as if you're my own flesh and blood."

Mr. Lester said, "Samuel got it right. I just pray my other son finds peace, joy and happiness."

Francine hugged Mr. Lester. "He did find peace and love."

Francine walked over to an open microphone and she said, "I wrote a poem for my husband to be."

Prado was about to run out of the room. Everyone seemed to have found happiness and not him. He had children he had to be a father to. He had to get his life together.

Francine said, "I wrote a poem. Called two hearts…"

Her beautifully-shaped lips inches from the microphone she said:

Love is like seeds
water it with hope
And pray for life.
Life is like love
shower it with bashfulness

and sing for peace.
I love love like love love life
shower me with praise
and hope for life
To sing you a song.
I love my husband like love is seeds
I will water him with hope
and pray for life.

A mongst applause and praise, the poem moved the Lesters beyond anything reprehensible. Francine stepped down and walked towards Samuel with a huge smile and was so optimistic about her future being a married woman. Mrs. Lester.

Samuel made his way to his amazing fiancé and extended his arms. Francine walked right by him and wrapped her arms around Prado, sending a shockwave throughout her home.

"Prado, will you be my husband?"

P rado couldn't believe it. He held her tight, showering her face with kisses. *Oh my God! Oh my God! OH MY GOD! There is a God! Thank you, Lord! I won! I fucking won! FINALLY! Samuel lost!*

"Yes. YES!" He couldn't keep the joy from his voice. He nearly had heart failure.

Samuel felt betrayed.

F rancine said, "Pastor, you are right. I loved Samuel because he had money. He was the polished son. He was my first boyfriend, my first everything. I loved him when he was down and out, broke and unpolished. Before he started his business, one I helped build with my own two hands and half the paychecks I had ever gotten."

She pulled Prado to the open microphone and she looked into his eyes. "That poem I wrote for you. I realized last night how much I was in love with you. You open doors for me and treat me as your equal. Samuel never opened a door for me in his life or pulled out a chair for me."

"Francine, are you sure? I want to be your husband, oh God I do…"

"*Yes.* I'm sure. But I haven't been totally honest. Before I take the ring and let you put it on my finger, you have to be a better father to your children. I love you for you. You are everything I hoped a man to be. You're smart and funny. You have flaws that you never hide or sugarcoat. You don't bash people. You love life. Samuel finds the bad in everyone, but you, Prado, you look for the good. I admire your strength and your courage."

"Francine, I have always loved you. In life I have always been let down and disappointed. My own family talks about me and call me outlandish names. I was never as good as Samuel. He did everything right and I was always wrong."

Some people were on their feet, clasping their hands together. Mrs. Lester shook her head, hugging her husband. The look on her face told Samuel that she always knew Francine loved Prado.

Mr. Lester said, "I guess Prado did get it right."

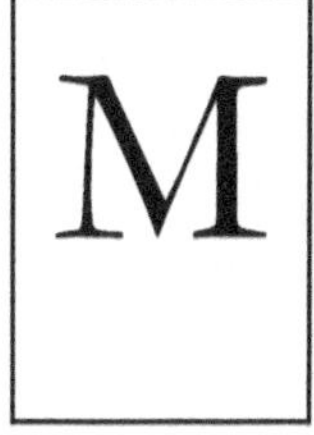rs. Lester walked over to them and she took Francine's hand. She stared at her for a moment. "Francine. I'm glad you listened to the Pastor. About marrying for the right reasons. My husband and I have a confession to make."

Prado lowered his head. He smiled and tried to hide it. His life was about to change.

Mrs. Lester went on, the camera man walking over by them, filming. "I wrote everything the Pastor said today. About love and life. My husband and I were indirectly letting you know that we were aware of your love for Prado."

Mr. Lester nodded at Prado, placing his hand firmly on Samuel's shoulder. Not looking in his face at all.

Mrs. Lester went on. "…To have a decades-old marriage like me and my husband is rare. Black people these days seemed focused on clubs, sex and breasts jiggling in 50 Cent videos. They look to rappers for love and think its fine to marry a woman because her body is sexy or marry a man because he has a hefty retainer from his employers. What happens when the sex diminishes and he loses his job?"

Francine said, "I understand…"

"No you don't. What happens? I will tell you. When the money and good sex is gone then you want to file for divorce. Your foundation has been met and you want out. You want to find another dumb man or woman to marry so you can rebuild your foundation, meet it and walk away pleasured and your pocket's filled. Gold diggers work this way. I knew why you chose to keep it safe and marry Samuel. He was your first. You never really dated and you thought you were supposed to marry the first man you gave yourself to. But, honey," Mrs. Lester went on, wiping tears from Francine's face, "I will tell you the day Prado fell in love with you."

Francine looked over her shoulder at Prado, extending her hand. He cupped and kissed it.

Samuel was brooding. All his anger silently recreated his DNA.

"It was the very first day Samuel brought you home to us. Prado snapped the stem from a rose and he so lovingly put the flower in your hair. Prado had never been so happy, and you were a complete stranger to us. He talked about you day in and day out. Always asking his brother Samuel about Francine. That's the same way his father looked at me the day we met so many years ago. Samuel never had the eyes Prado had and still has for you. I'm glad you found your way home to your true heart's content. Welcome to the family, Mrs. Prado Lester."

Mrs. Lester took Prado's hand and kissed his lips.

"We're proud of you. God is giving you a chance to make it right with your life and your kids by doing what a man should do: honor and protect his family. Don't throw it back in his face the way Samuel has."

"I love you, Ma," said Prado, feeling like he had his family back.

Mrs. Lester held Francine and Prado's hand, leading them back to the altar. They stood in front of Samuel. Samuel took a few steps back and silently watched Prado slide the ring on Francine's finger. Francine smiled and slid the ring on Prado's finger.

Five minutes later the Pastor said, "Now I pronounce you husband and wife. You may kiss your bride."

Prado kissed Francine with a longing and yearning he had never before experienced in his life.

Samuel was pain-stricken. He had stood by and watched this fiasco long enough. His parents deceived him. Prado, his own brother, stole his woman. She was now married to his fucking brother.

Samuel walked past his parents and punched Prado so hard in the face he flipped over the podium, slamming into the Pastor.

He was a beast. He ripped every flower and people starting gasping. A few ran out of the house.

Samuel snatched Francine by the arm and yanked the slut into his face.

"You led me on! You never loved me, Francine? How could…"

Francine said, "I deceived you? I did?" She was shrieking with anger.

Samuel said, "Yes! You married my brother in MY FUCKING HOUSE?"

"This is *my* house, too. Our name is on the papers, you sack of shit. I hate you." She snatched her arm back, getting in his face. "You are the biggest prick I have ever laid eyes on, Samuel."

He said, "I always treated you good. I have never lied to you about anything."

Mr. Lester held his wife, realizing there was some untold story about to unfold.

Prado regained his composure. His mother took some napkins from the table and wiped the blood from his face.

"I'm fine, Mama." He glared at Samuel. Waiting to pounce.

Francine said, "Oh, yea? You never lied? Then *why* is Chandra pregnant with your goddamn baby you sick, twisted freak? Why did you pump drugs into her body? And why, oh Lord please tell me why, you fucked my mother behind my back?"

Samuel lowered his head in shame.

Defeated.

Chandra was dreaming of red lollipops swiveling over a white light. They smiled at her, waving their arms wildly. Then the butterflies burst from a blue spot on her face. She loved the beauty of them, the rare thought of being high as Saturn drove her mad. She rolled over on the bed, smiling.

Francine's mother slid another syringe into Chandra's arm, injecting more heroine. Tossing Francine's cell phone on the bed, she felt alienated. Her daughter attacked her. Over this drugged out cunt! Clad in the dress she wanted to show off, she snatched the extensions from her hair and threw them into the trash.

I was always jealous of you and my daughter's friendship. Even though you two are the same age you were there for her in ways I never was. I hate you for that. She is MY DAUGHTER! I'm glad your life is slipping through the cracks. Even though it's unfortunate Samuel drugged you and now you are an addict, I helped him. I supplied the heroine. I got him the syringes from my job, since I work at a hospital. No one will take me from my daughter. Without you here Francine and I can recover.

All mothers and daughters fight. I got to get through to Francine and make her realize that family is number one.

Too bad you'll be too fucked up to see our reunion.

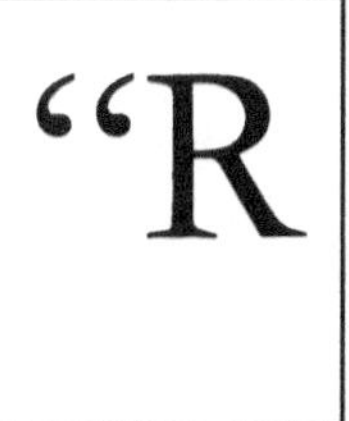

"Room Service!" the French maid called out, slowly entering the room. "It looks a mess in here. Aye aye. This is going to be a long day." She started to pull the sheets from the bed and a body rolled from under it.

"*Madam.* Oh, I'm *sorry.* I didn't know anyone was in the room."

The maid, Matilda, looked at her more closely. She was gasping for air.

"Oh my God!" She looked around and noticed syringes all over the floor.

"She's on drugs. God, not on my shift! Why today, Lord?"

She looked at the covers and noticed a lot of blood. The woman was moaning piteously, hair plastered to her face.

She was perspiring.

"My…my…" She was making gurgling noises.

"I'm calling 9-1-1…"

"My baby…is…coming. To. Early. Help."

More gurgling sounds.

Matilda called 9-1-1. "Please, hurry. A drug addict is in labor she says her baby is coming too early. Yes, ma'am I'm at 564 Biscayne Boulevard, the James Hotel. By Bayside. Thank you. I stay here with her."

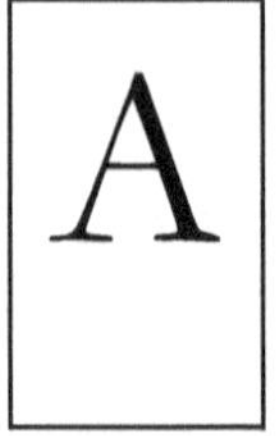 few police men walked into the living room, looking around for someone. People were wondering what was going on. The wedding had been a disaster. Samuel was disillusioned, wanting to retreat into his body. Mr. Lester was rendered speechless. Mrs. Lester walked away from Samuel, averting her face and turning her back on him forever.

Francine snapped at the cops. "There he goes. Samuel. The man who pumped drugs into my best friend."

The cops, with mean looks on their faces, made their way towards Samuel.

When they got up to him the tall white cop said, as politely as she could, "You have the right to remain silent…"

The short, black cop hand cuffed him.

Prado was driving Francine in his car. They were on their way to the James Hotel to check on Chandra. "So where do you want to go for the honeymoon?"

Francine held his hand. "I'm not going anywhere until I admit Chandra into a detox program or something. She's pregnant with your niece or nephew."

"I *still* can't believe he drugged her and all that shit." Anger flashed in his eyes. "Maybe I really didn't know him."

Francine said, "No. I was the one who never knew your brother."

"And what about money? I got a little something. Maybe we can admit Chandra into a program and then fly to Cancun, Mexico for a few days. To get over the shock of everything that's happened."

"I got money. I called the bank before I married you from the house phone and had every red penny wired from all three of our bank accounts to my bank account at Washington Mutual. Samuel doesn't have dime. And from the looks of it he's going to prison for a very long time. I recorded Chandra on tape. She told me everything, even implicating my mother. The cops will be arresting her phony ass real soon. I can pay for Chandra's care with that money. Since he robbed her of life I robbed him of his money."

Prado, turning down Anita Baker on the radio, turned onto I-95 and said, "How is that possible? You got all the money?"

"Yep. I'm on all the bank accounts. And I'm also part owner of his house. I own 51 percent of it. He signed that into the papers."

Prado said, "Wow. I guess Karma is about to teach him a lesson."

"He taught himself a lesson."

They saw the hotel from the Interstate.

Francine said, "We're coming, baby…"

Nobody will every hurt you again, Chandra.

I vow on my life.

Best friends forever!

Samuel was led through the downtown Miami police precinct. Depressed, he avoided the stares. A few men who were being fingerprinted eyed him. They wondered what his story was. A man in a suit being jailed. What did he do?

An hour later Samuel was fingerprinted and booked.

He had court the next morning.

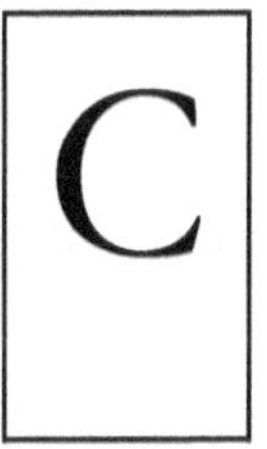handra was in the intensive care unit, hooked up to an EKG machine, an IV drip and two doctors overlooking her. She was unconscious.

Dr. Gristle said, "I have never seen anything like this…"

Dr. Hanks, a short, white man in his fifties, said, "That makes two of us. She's in critical condition. Lost a lot of blood."

Dr. Gristle looked over a chart. "And the baby?"

Dr. Hanks said, "…We did an emergency C-section. Had to try to save Chandra's life. Very risky at 27 weeks. The baby was only 5 pounds, barely five pounds I should say."

Dr. Gristle said, "Wow. My heart goes out to her."

"The cops are supposed to be stopping by. But what can they do? She's out of it, and I don't know if she'll pull through in this state."

"My heart goes out to the baby. How could she do drugs knowing she was pregnant?"

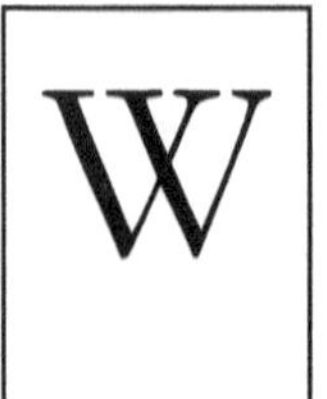

hen they left the room, Chandra flat lined. Never to open her eyes again.

rancine and Prado got off the elevator and approached the room. A team of Coroners and a few cops were there. Francine said, "Uh-huh. Somebody is dead or something on this floor."

Prado said, "Hope it isn't anybody we know."

Francine said, "Probably one of these drug-loving tourists."

When she said it she thought about Chandra.

"Oh, God! They're in her room!"

Her heart dropped in her stomach. And Prado covered his face in shock.

Samuel, what have you done?

rancine pushed Prado out of the way, screaming into the room. She startled the Coroners and the police. The hotel Manager jumped behind the bed.

A crime scene investigation team stopped snapping photos and halted dusting for prints. Another team of investigators put on some rubber gloves and started combing the room, taking things and putting them in plastic bags.

"Where is she? Where is Chandra?"

Two cops apprehended her but she started to fall to the floor and kick at them, flinging her arms.

"WHERE IS CHANDRA? WHERE IS MY BESTFRIEND! WHAT HAPPENED HERE?"

Officer Taylor took her by the arm and said, "Who are you in relation…"

"Where is Chandra? Where is she, goddamn it?"

Officer Taylor, taking off his hat said, "Chandra died in the hospital five minutes ago…"

Francine grabbed her husband and fainted. Prado held her as she fell towards the floor.

Prado thought to himself, *Samuel. You will pay.*

 nurse was writing on a chart. She smiled down at the little bundle of joy. Sadly, he was in an incubator, fighting for his life. Her heart went out to him. "God will protect you," the nurse said with passion. "God will watch over you. Your mother did drugs, little one. I'm calling you Super Man. Because you're a super baby."

She touched the incubator. "You'll get stronger everyday. Those drugs will be flushed out of your system. Huh, what did you say little one? Who am I? I'm family. No, Chandra isn't related to me but she's best friends with my daughter Francine."

Mama smiled victoriously. "Correction, she *was* best friends with Francine. She's one dead little bitch. She actually thought I was going to let her live! I lost my daughter, so I took her from Francine as well. She'll be forgotten in a few weeks. No one will remember her name. She will be just another druggie bitch stuck on heroine."

She scribbled on the chart, and left the room.

S amuel lay in his bunk, tears wetting his face. He couldn't let his Bunkie see his tears. He wiped them away, wondering how long he was going to be in there. He would use his lawyers and every resource in his power to get out. Yea. He had money. And money bought everyone, including judges.

"Yo," said his fat Bunkie, looking down from the top bed.

"The name's Samuel, playah."

"Yo. What time is Chow?"

"Who knows?"

"You should know. I want to eat. A niggah is hungry, you feel me?"

"No, I don't."

"What are you in for?"

He thought about it. "I'm in here for pimping a bitch."

"Playa, playa! So that means you got money?"

"I'm ok."

The fat man jumped down off the bed, grabbed the small golf pencil, and stuck it under Samuel's neck. He was breathing in Samuel's face.

"Since you got money, pay me not to fuck you in the ass. I am getting life. I might as well start by fucking you, bitch."

"I will never…"

He pushed the pencil just under the larynx.

"Think about it. Pay for your life. I want money. I'm doing life! I don't have a family. I have nothing. Mama burned to death in her car. Daddy shot himself in the head."

"I will not…"

The Fat Dude was pulling down Samuel's pants. Samuel tried to yell and the Fat Dude pushed the pencil deep in Samuel's neck. Samuel was twitching on the bed.

The Fat Dude fucked him until Samuel drew his last breath.

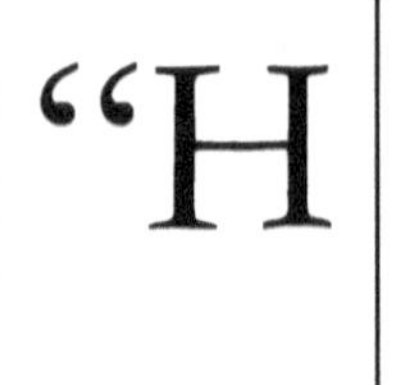

"**H**ow are you?" Roderick asked, pacing the Interrogation Room at the downtown precinct.

"I'm fine." She lit a cigarette. "Why am I here?"

"You should know. Your daughter Francine said you had something to do with Chandra's death."

She chuckled. "She is disillusioned. She doesn't know if she's coming or going."

"But she knows you are involved with Chandra's murder."

"She overdosed."

"It would appear so." The cop looked at the Plexiglas, frowning.

She fixed her hair, crossing her legs. "I didn't do anything."

"So you didn't help Samuel drug Chandra?"

"No."

"When was the last time you seen her?"

"A few days ago."

"Was she happy, sad or shooting up dope?"

"All of the above." She pulled on the cigarette, refusing to cooperate.

"You can make this easier for yourself."

"How? And when is my lawyer coming?"

"Just admit it. We'll give you probation."

"You think you're slick. Why should I plead guilty to anything when I'm not guilty? She was a drugged out bitch. It's my daughter's word against mine."

"Really?"

"Yes," she said, challenging the overzealous cop. "Chandra's dead. She can't talk."

"The dead can talk, if they want to." He sat in the chair across from her, taking a cigarette. "Do you mind?"

"No."

"Chandra told me you drugged her."

"She didn't tell you shit. You're trying to intimidate me."

He leaned over and picked up a wrapped gift. He put it on the desk and slid it to her.

"What's this?"

"An early Christmas gift."

She opened it, humoring him. She took out all the tissue paper. She was laughing. "What is this?"

"You'll see."

She took out her weave. Her face hit the floor. There was also a tape recorder.

"We recovered your hair in the room Chandra was in at the hotel. We ran DNA. You were a perfect match."

"This doesn't…"

"Yes it does. It proves you were in the room when she overdosed. We suppressed tapes from the hotel. It showed you arriving in a Dodge truck. We have you taking the elevator to her room. We seized the camera in the hallway leading to Chandra's room. You're seen going into her room. Oh, yea. Press play."

She pressed play.

She heard Chandra's voice.

"Ah. The dead talks, baby. You are under arrest…"

Mama closed her eyes, defeated.

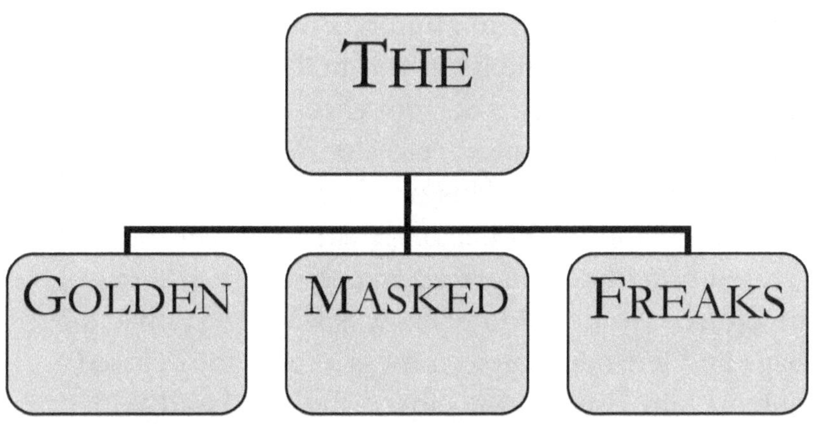

Nutrition Facts:
89% Fruit Juice from Concentrate
1,500 Calories in Melissa's pussy alone
3,400 Total Calories
2% Cellulose gum
87% Vitamin B1
100% Hater Proof

Naygee was on the airplane, twenty thousand feet above Florida. Looking out of the window, he enjoyed the view. The homes looked like Legos cities from afar. Rivers and small little lakes crossed through the land like alleys behind buildings. Breathing a sigh of relief, he thought about calling his wife. But he quickly decided against it because he told her he wanted a divorce when she wouldn't go down on him. It wasn't that he upped and left her. No. He wasn't that cold hearted. He loved her more than the law allowed. He bought her what she wanted, gave her what she needed, fucked her the way she wanted to be fucked, gave her his paychecks when he got paid and played her Bible Boy in church. But he's been asking her to give him some head and be his dirty slut in the sheets for a year, but she kept throwing the Bible at him. It pushed him away, considering he was an atheist. She never met his needs, never did the things he wanted and when her parents came over they treated him like a Hebrew Slave. Enough was enough he figured, so he told her he was leaving, packed a few bags and left her a broken mess as the door closed behind him. Smiling, he closed the blind and leaned back on the seat. *Melissa. I'ma beat that pussy out the frame. I can't wait to see you, with your freaky ass. I want you to tit fuck this dick again. Damn, girl. You're the shit.*

He was extremely tired. He couldn't get Melissa Jackson off his mind. She was the freakiest bitch he'd ever seen. She turned him out without him telling her. Couldn't blow her head up. With a bitch like Melissa, who needed new pussy when she had that good shit? Pulling the thick comforter over his lap, he dry jacked his dick, carefully looking around, making sure no one watched.

He came in a matter of minutes.

A yellow taxi with 305-888-8899 on the doors pulled up into a rain-swept drive way. The driver turned, looking at the handsome customer. A fifty dollar bill was slipped into his hand and a wink of the eye arrested his attention, but he played it off because he was a faggot on the low, sometimes liking it deep in the ass and he was on the clock (with Vodka on his hot breath) and wouldn't be getting off till three a.m. so he didn't have time for a bunch of penile fights.

"Thanks, bruh," the customer said, grabbing his leather bag, smelling of expensive soap and FCUK cologne.

The driver eyed him with a smile. "No problem, bruh. You be safe."

"You, too."

The driver put the car in gear, backing out of the drive way.

The customer looked over the house before him with a huge smile, his eyes sparkling. Glancing at his watch, he realized it was getting late. He'd go inside and shower.

He was thinking about the bed.

I was very in tune with my sexuality. Most women couldn't say that. How could you be called a "woman" yet you weren't woman enough to sometimes be called out your name. Shit, when a man called me a bitch it was normally after I emptied his wallet while I was riding his dick. Yes, ma'am. Give him a shot of pussy to keep his mind off the gold and you'd be the California Gold Rush every time he comes and his ass rolled over and went to sleep. He'd wake up broke as a joke. I wasn't a lesbian, but if a pussy looked scrumptious I'd suck a bitch's clit into remission. I loved the smell of pussy on my lips. If you haven't tasted your cunt yet then what the hell you were waiting for? Pussy did the body good, the hell with those milk slogans. Bitch, Got Pussy? Check, please! If a woman was fine enough I'd dig in her twat and rub her juice on my lips. Which reminded me, when I ran out of lip gloss I'd rub my juices on my lips, saved me about ninety dollars a year. Call me what you wanna, I really didn't give a damn. But give me, me and get the hell on. And leave a fifty on the nightstand, because a bitch had bills to pay and every little bit helped.

I wasn't a greedy chick. I had my share of "moments" with the girls. I called them "lesbian tendencies." Because when it came down to it I'd pick a thick dick over a dripping snatch any day. But I liked what I liked.

I've deep throated a dick or two and I've let two women suck my pussy and everywhere in between. Are you Freaky Deaky? I asked them and they told me they were so when I asked them to eat my ass and let me taste it from their tongues they seemed to be a bit stagnant.

I rode a bitch's face while her husband fucked me in the ass.

I've made him pull it out and I tasted it. I then kissed his bitch while thumbing his balls.

I've fucked the mail man for a hundred dollars, seduced the UPS guy and shipped my clit Fed Ex. The Best Buy Home Installer guy wanted to marry me after I made him jack off and swallow his own come, the Home Depot cabinet installers ran a train on this pussy and my Mama's ex husband fucked me with the plunger because there was a blockage in my loins that Drain-o couldn't suffice. I couldn't lie, Mama's ex boyfriend had a little dick, but sometimes your pussy needed a break from being long dicked. I got tired of banging my head against the wall, shit. Sometimes my cunt wanted some short strokes. Let me stop airing my dirty laundry for all to see. Some things I had to keep to myself.

Illegally changing lanes, I smiled to myself, thinking about New York. I haven't been home for two hours and already I was back on the road.

I had the time of my life in New York, and seeing Janet Jackson on 106 and Park (and getting to hug her) was a treat. I think that's the single most beautiful thing that has ever happened to me. To smell Janet's perfume up close and personal. Outside of that, meeting my thug friend in a department store in Manhattan was another treat. Putting candle wax on his dick and sucking his essence through the shaft like yogurt was the thrill of a lifetime.

I still couldn't believe he let me fuck him in the ass. He didn't have any inhibitions and that was a good thing. He was still a man when we both came. I was a piece of Down South Pussy in the City that Never Slept and the city will never forget Melissa Jackson. I left my stamp of approval, and any bitch that fucked him after I left would read "Melissa's Pussy was here" on his dick when they gave him some head. That's a good way to keep my name in their…mouths. Ho's paled in comparison to me. Fucking him after my breathtaking performance was virtually impossible.

Part of me felt like shit because a few months ago, I turned my church into a lustful playground. At the time I thought I was dying of Cancer and I figured hey, if I was going to die I might as well pussy pop all over the back of the church and pussy pop was what I did. I was clad in a robe with a golden mask on my face. It was so freaky. I could still remember the briefing from Big Daddy Good Dick. You'd swear you were entering the matrix with all of their "rules."

Since that day I haven't been right. I stopped believing in organized religion, and I stayed away from the building. I had to change my phone number because several Golden Mask participants wanted round two and three and my pussy wasn't built to back track. My pussy didn't do piss recalls when I squatted on the toilet so why should it do a church recall? What's done was done and life went the hell on.

It started to rain the minute I got on the Turnpike. Realizing that I left my Sun Pass home, I had to now pay the toll. Damn, Melissa. What were you thinking? Money didn't grow on trees. Tolls seemed to be going up a mile a minute and with rising gas prices and George W. Bush being the bitch he was, I couldn't afford half the shit being sold in stores let alone paying the toll. Patting my weave, I checked over my face in the rear view mirror. I looked a mess. So I opened my knock off Chanel purse I bought from the Indoor Flea Market in Perrine and pulled out some lipstick. Licking my lips, I held the steering wheel with my left ankle, rolling the small clip on the bottom of the tube and ran the thick red stick over my dick-sucking lips. Rolling them together, I tossed the lipstick back into my purse, smiling, making sure I didn't have any on my teeth. The last thing I needed was lettuce or lipstick on my teeth when I sucked a mean dick. Good dick deserved bright teeth so I did the damn thing. Taking control of the wheel, I signaled "left," getting into the left lane. I just passed Coral Way. I still had a ways to go before I got to the airport.

Thank God traffic wasn't the fat bitch it could be. Some days the bitch could be eating cheesecake and drinking Twinkie juice, congesting every lane and every road on the 826, but *tonight* was refreshing because her fat ass was on a diet, Jenny Craig was closed and the lanes were free of vehicles. It started raining harder, and the flash of lightning scared me a bit. I ignored it, of course. Lightning wasn't that bad—BOOM! *Goddamn* it! You see, Lord! You just scared the holy *shit* outta me! Damn! Now my nerves were bad. I needed a cigarette. Nah. Fuck it. I needed a joint to calm down.

BOOM!

Thunder rocked the streets. I covered my face, one eye on the road, my car swerving. *Get a grip, Melissa! Don't panic, Chile.* My heart racing, I was about to panic anyway. Where did all this lighting and thunder come from? A few cars sped past me.

God forgive me for my sins! I know I'm a freaky bitch and you know I keeps it real with you and myself, Lord. I don't fake the funk and you told me to come to you as I am so here I am, Lord. I am a whore, but I'm a pricey whore. But lightning scares the living shit outta me and I know I fall short of your grace but I don't wanna die on this slippery ass road, Lord and I do wanna make it to the airport because when Naygee steps off that plane I hope he brought his snake with him because I'm gonna go Samuel L. Jackson on his dick and put his snake in the plane of my pussy. I love you, Lord. Talk to you soon. Muah. Amen. And a hallelujah good night!

I didn't know why I was about to jump out my skin. I had to take deep breaths to calm down. I always got righteous when God made it thunder. I looked through my purse for my cigarettes. They were behind my iPod. Taking the pack, I shook it. It was empty. Damn. I gotta re-up on the cigs. I was slipping like some good pussy. A bitch like me kept some cigarettes.

With all the pussy I've been giving away, now wasn't the time to be all prim and proper when lightning and thunder scared my ass.

Turning on the radio, I channel surfed. Nothing of interest was on. Mariah Carey. Oh, No, Chile. That's one ditzy bitch. Next. Paula Abdul. "Straight Up." Come on now, radio stations! This wasn't the '80s. *Next.* Rhianna's long forehead ass yodeled all over this cut. Next. Under my Umbrella-eh-eh-eh wasn't cutting it tonight. Fuck it. I turned it off.

I slowed up a bit when a Buick cut me off without signaling. I tucked my chin back. I blew the horn, cursing his ass out. He didn't hear me with the windows up. I grabbed my purse and put it on the back seat. On the passenger seat were two fabulous novels by sexy ass black men I've come to love. I love my black authors. Ty B. Moore's *Liar's Truth* gave Eric Jerome Dickey a run for his money and Michael Mayhem's *Yes…My Retarded Ass Signed Up* novel was glorious. Thinking about his fine ass made my titties rejoice and my nipples repent. I had to rub my pussy a little bit, looking at his picture, trying to keep my eyes on the road. Niggah was gorgeous. I loved military men. Come Search and destroy this pussy and cause it some…*mayhem*, Michael. Now I was horny. What did a bitch do? Simple.

It was time to play with myself.

Spreading my clean-shaven legs, my hot pussy skirt inched up these juicy thighs. Trying to control my breathing, I slowed in speed, the speed-o-meter dropping to 45 M.P.H. but my booty hole remained idle. I loved it in the ass, but right now I didn't have time for ass play.

Desperately wanting to be fucked, I unbuttoned my cream-colored blouse and my tits tumbled free like spilt marbles. I grabbed the left one, suckling on my erect nipple, gently biting it with my teeth. Sensation shot through my body like heat seekers. I knew I was in my car being lewd and lascivious, but if these seats were made for fucking, then fucking's what I'll do… and one day these seats are going to walk all over this pussy because Mama didn't have on any boots, I didn't feel like taking off my stilettos and I looked light years better than Nancy Sinatra.

I noticed a few men in a huge truck were on the side of me, honking their horns, trying to get my attention. Men were always messing up my free time. I turned on the stereo to block their asses out. A bitch needed alone time, and since I was an exhibitionist, fuck men because it was time to get right on down to pleasuring myself. I started to sweat as the smell of my twat filled the air. Turning on the AC, I got a contact high. I did this with weed sometimes. Rolled the windows up and put the AC on full blast. My scent mixed well with the strawberry air freshener dangling from my rear view mirror. I gasped collectively, rubbing myself. It felt so good my legs drummed together.

I glanced at Michael Mayhem's book cover, sliding two fingers into my pulsating hole. Call me your dirty bitch, Michael! Come and give it to Mama. My tits bouncing, I rubbed myself for dear life like I was a camper trying to turn some twigs into smoke and flames. I was cold; Mama needed a heater in this pussy.

I leaned back on the seat, the men getting closer to my car. *Ya'll better not hit my shit! I hope you got some good insurance!* I loved these leather seats because I was slipping and sliding in sweat and pussy juice. I grabbed the baby oil from the cup holder, popped the top and squirted it all over my body, rubbing it into my tits. I felt it trail down my body, mixing with my well-cut pubic hair. I was really sliding now. I just had to get a taste of the strawberry, so I sucked my cunt down my throat with an appreciative smack of the lips.

My foot pressing slightly on the accelerator, I was playing with myself again, thinking about the quickest way to come.

I wanted a nut and I wanted it now! I got it. Impulsively, I reached over and opened my glove box, S.W. 8th Street approaching on the Turnpike. That wasn't my destination, so I could get on with the regularly scheduled programming. I quickly pulled out my vibrator, leaving the glove box open.

I looked to the left, eying the horny men. They were waving, smiling and looking so fucking childish. One of them had a camera phone, recording me.

He couldn't see anything. My pussy was shielded by the car door. I wanted a soundtrack so I turned on my CD player and pressed "play."

The mixed CD began to play. Amerie's "That's what I'm Talking About" boomed. I loved this song, plus she's a pretty bitch.

I inserted the tip of the nine inch cock inside me, grinding it the rest of the way in. Oooh, yeaaa, damn it.

That's what I was talking about, Amerie! My mouth ajar, my eyes were narrowed, as I prepared to take this plastic dick. Maybe I should talk dirty to it.

Give it to me, you *plastic* fucker! *Fuck me like you never fucked me before!* I'm your bitch; I loved plastic more than cash right now because your thickness was rocking my ass to sleep. Yes. Yes. Yes. Fuck me, Baby. Make Mama come all over this plastic cock! The heat from my pussy was so intense it was about to melt the dildo like it's a doll. Fuck me, Chucky! This pussy wants to play. I'll be your friend till the end! Hi-dee Ho, bitch! Ah, yes! Let Mama spread her legs wider. What? You want me to put a pump-clad foot on the dash board? Sure. I did what you said; now get in this pussy like a broke Niggah getting in a dime bag of weed.

Spread my pink walls apart like weed on some Swisher Sweet paper. Lick this cunt, bitch and roll your flame under my clit. Oh, yea! I was about to come! Oh, god! I love you, Your Plastic Majesty!

My pussy is clamping on your rod!

AHHHHH I'M COMINGGGGG GOD THIS FEELS SO GOOD! YES YES YES! HERBAL ESSENSE THIS PUSSY!

W hen my orgasm subsided, I smiled, sucking my come off the dildo. Tasted good.

It was thick, which told me I needed to drink more fluids and eat more fruits, like pineapples, oranges and grapes.

I was a freaky bitch, on her way to pick up a freaky niggah from the airport.

As far as the truck full of guys who watched me, they got a free show. But my exit was coming up, and from the looks of it we would be out of sight out of mind in about two minutes. Bye, boys!

It's been nice.

I braked, pulling over to the side of the road. Cars zooming by me, I buttoned my blouse and fixed my skirt. Replacing the dildo into the glove box, I closed and locked it. I felt rejuvenated. Interrupting me, my cell rang and I answered. It was Naygee. My titties tingled just thinking about his juicy steak.

"Are you coming?"

I put the car in "drive" and entered traffic. More and more cars were coming out of nowhere.

"Yes. Has the plane landed?"

"We're circling the airport now."

"Damn."

I mashed on the gas pedal, approaching the 836, which would take me past the airport to the exit I needed. I think it's called LeJune Road or some shit like that. I'll know it when I see it.

"I can't wait to see you."

I blushed. "And I can't wait to see you."

"I left my wife, Melissa."

See, now I was mad. Why couldn't we just meet up and leave the strings on the puppets?

Did I look like an episode of *Sesame Street*, Naygee?

The only thing he could do was stuff his Snufflelufugus in my Big Bird and call it a goddamn day. I wasn't trying to keep him.

There were still men I wanted to fuck and one dick never stopped a show. My pussy didn't start and stop with him.

If you read Page 3 of my Pussy Manual it clearly stated the following things:

My pussy came in

French
Creole
Spanish
German
Chinese
Afrikaans
English.

If you experience troubleshooting with my clit write the manufacture and fax a copy of the original warranty.

There was a mandatory three hundred dollar fee. If the warranty has expired, there was a re-certification fee of one hundred dollars, plus tips when you ate this pussy again.

I didn't care how good he was, I would never be tied down to a piece of cock.

"Did you hear me?"

"Yes, I heard you. Anyways, I'm almost there. I can't wait to see you."

"The plane is landing now."

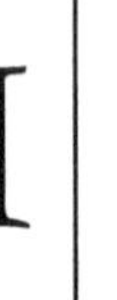

He entered the home, closing and locking the door. He turned on the light switch by the front door, smiling.

His eyes glittered as he moved about the living room. Lovely sofas, beautiful throw pillows and a light red carpet caught his attention.

It was an Asian meets African-American feel. He ran his hand over a 5x7 photo of a gorgeous woman. In it she wore an ankle-length dress and her hair was pinned atop her head.

He turned to put his bags on the floor. Entering the kitchen he opened the fridge, grabbing a Heineken. He used the back of a cigarette lighter to pop the difficult top.

Tossing the top in the trash, he took a hefty swig, wiping his thick lips. When he went back into the living room, he noticed it. A glittering China cabinet, with one thing in the center.

He smiled, shaking his head.

I was standing at the American Airlines corridor. The place bustled with activity. I just had to be cute, pulling my hair into a bun. You never knew who you were going to meet.

Someone tapped my shoulder and I looked at her. She was about five feet 8, cute little bitch, with nice titties.

"Hi."

"Hi," I said obtrusively, rolling eyes and popping my gum. "Can I help you?"

She touched my arm. "I just love your pumps."

Bitch, don't touch me! "Thank you."

"Where did you buy them, I would love to get a pair?"

Like I'm really gonna tell you! "Amazon.com." I lied smoothly. "Type in 'stilettos,' and viola, you can choose from the list."

She was appreciative. "Thank you. I'm Dana. I just flew in from Atlanta."

"And I'm Pauline." We shook hands. "I'm waiting for my lesbian lover."

She gave me the once over. "You're *gay*?"

"Gayer than the Flintstones."

She rushed off, mumbling "Ugh!" under her breath.

"Ugh you too, bitch!" I yelled after her. Several fellahs were chuckling, checking me out.

One walked behind me, looking at my ass. I farted so loud he averted his face, clearly turned off. Must have been the grilled cheese I bought when I got here. Shit, Mama always taught me it was better out than in.

I was just about to sit down when I saw him. Naygee. He turned the corner, throwing his arms up. Yes. He was still the same gorgeous specimen I sucked up on an airplane on the way to New York days ago. He still had the green bandana wrapped around his forehead and he looked gorgeous in black suede baggy jeans, fresh Jordan sneakers and a huge Plies T-shirt.

"Hi, Ma," he said, taking me into his arms.

"Hi, Naygee. I told you I'd be here."

He gave me some tongue. He moaned, grinding his hips on mine. We hunched standing up. I didn't care. I got off on people looking.

Taking his hand, I said, "Did you bring any bags?"

He looked deep into my eyes. "Nah. I just brought the bag I'm carrying."

"Well, let's go."

I had to squeeze my ass cheeks together because I had to fart.

hen I got home an hour later, I closed and locked the door when he dropped his bag, settling on the sofa. He kicked off his shoes.

"You have a nice pad." He was looking around, liking my set up. "Damn, that's a big ass plasma TV!"

I took off my blouse, my tits bare. I always lounged naked in my crib. "I know. It cost a pretty penny, too."

He pulled off his shirt, his killer abs well cut. He unbuckled his belt, pulling it off. I sat by him. We looked at each other, not saying another word.

I was glad that he came. I wasn't trying to keep him, but he was fine as wine and I wanted some Kool-Aid all of a sudden.

I looked past him at the China cabinet, my heart dropping. Oh my God!

I jumped up to my feet as if my couch was on fire. Where is it?

Naygee touched my arm. "What's wrong, Ma?"

"It's gone!"

"What's gone?" he asked, trying to figure out what the hell I was talking about.

Before I could say it a tall, stocky figure walked out of my kitchen, pausing in front of me. He was naked, his dick hanging like Tarzan.

He wore the Golden Mask.

aygee stood up, clearly disgusted at the sight of another man's dick. I was turned on. Who the hell was this man in my home standing in my living room like Santa Claus sent me an early gift? A big red bow was tied on his dick. He had the perfect body.

He was walking up to me.

"Melissa, why didn't you tell me your man was here?" Naygee asked, putting on his shirt. He looked like he was about to vomit. But the strangest thing happened. Naygee kept looking at the stranger's dick. What straight man looked at another man's package? Like he owned my house, the stranger swiftly walked past me, snatched the shirt and threw it across the room. Naygee steamed, taking a few steps back, like he was about to swing. I carefully watched him. He was looking at homeboy's package again, trying to keep up the disgusted attitude.

The stranger paused in front of me, sinking to his knees. He took my skirt and pulled it down, my booty cheeks free and jiggling, baby. He inhaled my womanly scent from the skirt, running his tongue over the leather. He then pulled my pussy to the slit in the mask and his tongue began ravaging me. This felt so good. He took his time, his fingers embedded in my skin.

The pain mixed with the pleasure and I welcomed it with open arms. I held his head for balance, Naygee's dick hard. Naygee tried to look away, but I saw his eyes watching, probing and studying. He began rubbing himself, sitting back on the sofa.

"Fuck it, I'll watch," he said, spreading his legs. "I surrender…but you better keep this shit quiet. What goes on in here stays in here…"

My Stranger Man told me to hump his tongue. Where had I heard that voice before? He talked like the rapper Bustah Rhymes. I grabbed his head and shivered when his tongue slid across my clit. He was lean and strong, my toes tingling with pleasure.

I was about to come already. I bit down on my tongue to stall it. I didn't want to come yet.

He picked me up and carried me to the couch like a lily. Laying me next to Naygee, he spread my legs and then spread my wet pussy lips. I looked at Naygee, reaching for his dick. He unzipped his pants, pulling it out. I gripped it, slightly jacking it. This had to be heaven because I hadn't known hell to be this virtuous.

The Stranger ate me out again, like my pussy was a plum. Naygee wanted in on the action so he got on his knees, and began tasting me also. He tongue kissed the stranger, making me shudder. This was hot. Two men (who were strangers to each other) were kissing my clit at the same time. Naygee finger fucked my asshole while the stranger fingered my cunt. I couldn't stand it.

The Stranger sat next to me and he raised a finger.

"I want you and Naygee to suck my dick," he said and I looked at Naygee. He struggled with himself.

"I don't know, dawg," he said. "Eating pussy with you was where I drew the line."

"Shut up and suck this dick, Niggah. Melissa, get on your motherfucking knees and suck this nut out. Make my dick spit."

"Yes!" I got on my knees and took his juicy dick into my mouth. My knees were tired, but that's ok. "Are you Freaky Deaky?" I asked him.

"Hell yes!"

I reached over and grabbed Naygee's dick. I sucked on it, rolling my tongue around like it was a juicy lollypop. I wanted to put them together so I asked the stranger to stand up and he did. I put both dicks in my mouth, handling it like the bitch I was. I was twirling my hips. My tits were shaking for dear life. I was so wet. I smelled my pussy in the air. I released the dicks and rubbed some juices on my hands. I then spread my pussy jizz on both dicks, massaging it in. It was time to suck them again.

Before I could, the stranger sat down, his legs cocked open. He was so sexy. I took him into my mouth and Naygee got on his knees next to me. The stranger reached up and pulled Naygee's lips down to the head of his pulsating dick.

Veins traveled like intersections all over the beautiful member.

Naygee and I tongue kissed the head of his dick, Naygee taking it into his mouth. He chocked a lot, and his teeth kept grazing the dick.

I was lost for words. Where did I know the stranger from? His body looked like familiar territory, so I paid close attention to it.

While Naygee necked his dick, I stood up and slapped Naygee's booty cheeks. He had a nice tush.

"Are you Freaky Deaky, Naygee?"

"Hell, yea!" he announced.

"I can't hear you!" I grabbed the paddle on my low-table and spanked his ass.

"HELL YEA!"

I got on my knees and spread his cheeks apart. I tasted the chocolate. His ass smelled so good and it was clean. I loved cleaned asses.

The stranger stood up and got behind Naygee, eating with me.

He used his big, hairy hands to hold Naygee's booty cheeks apart so we could both eat Thanksgiving dinner early.

He was nasty like me. Naygee grinded his hole on our tongues, lost for words. I looked at the stranger and he looked at me.

"Take the mask off my face."

I slowly took it off, my mouth falling open. My Bronx bred niggah has found me. The man I met in Manhattan. Melvin.

I was stunned into silence. He looked as gorgeous as ever. I must be one lucky girl. I had two fine ass men in my living room ready to fuck the brakes off my pussy and each other. Naygee stared at him, a small smile playing on his lips.

He stood up, looking into his eyes. We all hugged each other, rubbing each other's genitals. I kissed Melvin, the urgency in my body catapulting past Olympic heights.

I then kissed Naygee, while Melvin rubbed my pussy with his left hand and rubbed Naygee's ass with his right hand. We were both moaning when Melvin finger fucked us both.

He had his index finger deep inside Naygee and his other index finger in my pussy. We looked at each other with a pleasurable longing I had never experienced before.

Melvin wanted to run the show. He asked me to put on the Golden Mask and I did. He took Naygee's shirt and tied it around Naygee's eyes. He then pulled a condom from his bag on the side of the chair and put it on.

He took out a small container of lube, spread Naygee's cheeks and squirted it at the start of the crack of his ass, the liquid trailing over his hole. He massaged it in. He pushed Naygee on the chair, pushing his legs back. I helped him hold them in place. Melvin slowly inserted his dick, Naygee's mouth hanging open. Damn this was hot.

After he slowly inserted it, Melvin slow grinded, so Naygee's hole could get used to the beef. Didn't make sense to open Wendy's drive-thru if the menu wasn't established.

Once Naygee's walls slid against the thickness of Melvin's rod, Melvin went to town, fucking the shit outta him. I let Naygee's legs go, straddling his hips. Just because he was taking dick didn't mean he couldn't suck on my pussy. I held the couch, lowering my wet opening on those lips. He was moaning so loud I nearly went deaf.

"Damn, Son! Damn, shit, Niggah! Get it, Daddy! Goddamn, this shit feels good!"

Naygee blindly ate my pussy, Melvin kissing my back. Naygee's legs were behind his arms, and I reached back and grabbed both his feet for balance. My eyes rolling to the back of my head, I was starting to sweat. The mask was hot on my face.

Melvin sucked on the back of my neck, getting deeper inside Naygee. He grabbed me by the hair and snatched my head back, giving me some tongue.

"Are you Freaky Deaky?" Melvin asked me, stealing my line. This turned me off a tad. When I asked a man was he Freaky Deaky that was my catalyst because I was Queen bitch!

"Yes, I'm Freaky Deaky."

"ARE YOU FREAKY DEAKY?"

"YES!"

Melvin pulled out and turned me to face him. He took off the condom, and shoved his dick down my throat. I gagged, but being the pro that I was I recuperated lovingly. His dick was scratching my tonsils and I loved it.

He took the mask from my face and aligned the hole in the eye of the mask with my pussy. He put his dick through the eye, and into my warm center and I died. He told me to hold the mask and I did.

Naygee slipped on a condom and got behind Melvin.

"It's my turn."

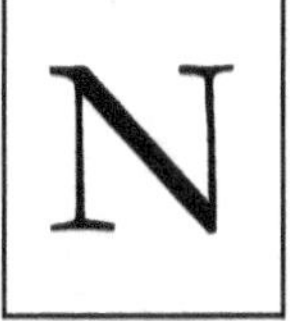

Naygee went up in Melvin without all the slow stuff and Melvin's body cringed from the pain. Naygee was more Gangsta with it, grabbing that ass and plowing him like he was planting watermelon seeds. We were tangled in our three way fuck, and I didn't want it to end.

Melvin and Naygee forgot about me and Melvin pulled out, while keeping Naygee deep inside him and they fucked all over my living room. Naygee had some skills. He made Melvin come without touching himself. I wiped up Melvin's come, lubing my fingers.

I then lay in front of Melvin's lips and coated my pussy like Pepto Bismol. Melvin munched the cooch, ordering a side Caesar salad from my clit. I couldn't stand it.

Naygee had to come. His sweaty body jerked, and he pulled out, snatching off the condom like a porn star. He stood on the couch and come dripped all over me and Melvin and we were wiping it up, sucking it off each other's fingers and faces. I loved the way Naygee made it rain and cleared this pussy out. I looked over the mountain for the rainbow and got nothing but Melvin's tongue, back inside me, searching for the lost gold and finding the Leprechaun and he was one mad motherfucker because he asked "Where's me Gold?" and I answered the instant my pussy locked up and exploded all over Melvin's thick fingers, falling into a deep sleep.

The Golden Mask on top of my titties.

I felt myself breathing, but my eyes were still closed. Inhaling, it was cold as hell in my room but the bed felt so comfortable I didn't dare move. I reached over and pat the bed but I didn't feel anyone.

I opened one eye, but the room was dark. The glow of my clock lit my face. It was 6 a.m. I reached over and fumbled for the lamp. I had to sit up, took great effort. I turned on the lamp and was surprised I was in a red night gown. Did I shower? Because I felt refreshed. Damn. I slept for hours on end.

I called Naygee's name. But he didn't answer.

I called Melvin's name, but he didn't answer. That's weird. Where were they? Hmm, they were probably fucking in the living room. Two hot and bothered black men on the DownLo were to be desired. Black love was a beautiful thing, in my opinion.

I stood up and walked around the house. I looked in the kitchen. Nothing. I looked in the bathroom, the back yard and the garage. Nothing. Melvin's stuff was gone. Naygee's stuff, too.

I picked up the house phone and called Naygee.

I heard the busy signal. "MSN Zero One. The mobile customer you are trying to reach does not answer."

I must have the wrong number. I called it again.

The same thing.

Damn it! His phone was off.

I called Melvin's number. I got the same thing. I called his home in New York. The prompt informed me that the number had been changed to an unlisted number.

I lowered myself on the couch, trying to understand this. Two men who didn't know each other came to my house and fucked me to sleep and when I woke up there was no place like home because Todo was nowhere to be seen and Dorothy was crying because the house fell on the Wicked Witch of the East and I was a lonely bitch.

"What the fuck is going on?" I lit a cigarette, blowing smoke in the air. I looked at the China Cabinet.

The Golden Mask was back inside, sitting gloriously in the center.

Sparkling.

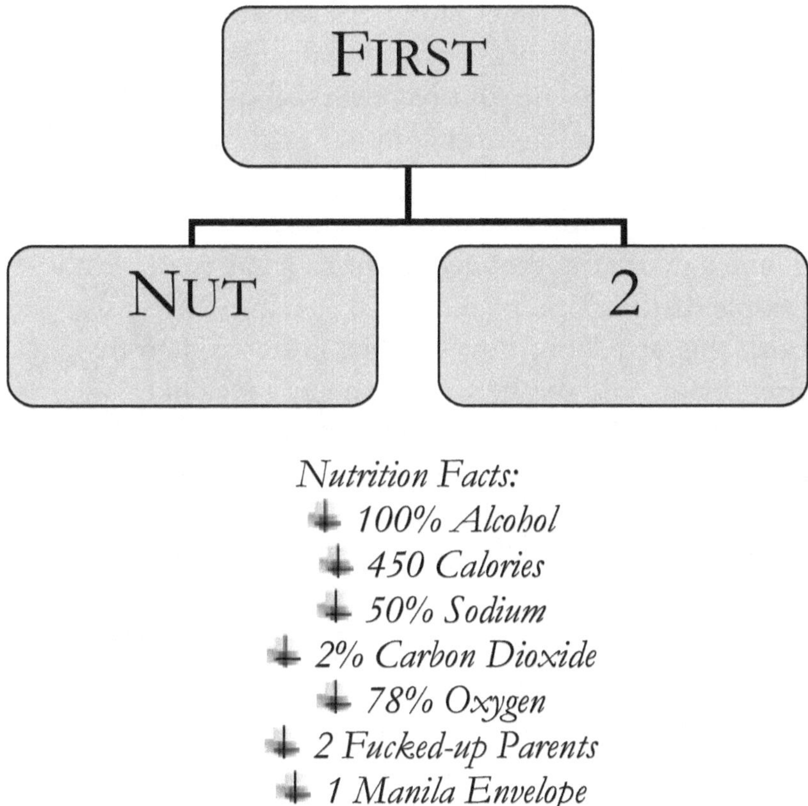

I have a story to tell. It's a story I have kept hidden for years. I lived in fear. I never exposed the fear or tried to understand it. Why should I? If I couldn't get rid of it why should I try to get rid of it? My sexuality was another matter. I felt like a monster. I felt like a weird fool because I had feelings for men. I love men. I couldn't help it. I've tried to dissect it. I tried looking at it under a microscope and in front of a telescope and I saw nothing but stars twinkling and atoms splitting. Was I born with it? Was it hereditary? Did it have something to do with genetics? I didn't think so.

I wasn't born a gay man. And people who say I was can kiss my ass. You couldn't tell me about me. If my father would have never emotionally and sexually fucked me up I wouldn't have turned out like this. In my heart I knew this and couldn't anybody tell me different.

In my opinion this gay lifestyle was a learned trait. There's no way someone was born a gay man. Some people justified their sexuality by saying, "Ah. I was born this way," but how do they know? When my gay friend Bob told me he was born gay I was like "Whatever." This was a touchy topic. Even when I debated it with friends it has resulted in fights. I never got my ass whipped, but I've seen people's faces get bashed in for not believing that people were born gay. This was equivalent to religion. Did you believe in Allah, Jehovah, Buddha, Gandhi or some angel? Sexuality and religion has become two of the most diverse, complicated topics in the world. People were passionate about what they believed in. Go to Iraq and say "Do it in the name of Allah," and people would be blowing themselves up by the thousands. Say "I am gay," and you might catch some bullets in your ass.

When babies were born what did they know? They didn't know what a penis looked like, they didn't know they had assholes and they didn't know how to spell their names. This was why they're taught to say their A-B-C's and 1-2-3's For understanding. For balance. That's a learned behavior. So what about sex, sexuality and fear? What about love, deception and liars? If I was born *knowing* I liked men then why wasn't I born knowing how to tie my shoe, ride a bike or drive a car?

Why were those things taught behaviors? Ding, ding, ding. You get my point.

But would mother? She has long suspected me of being gay. I never brought women around and she's seen me with more men than anything. No, I never brought the lifestyle around her house but come on. I didn't want kids and I didn't care to. I couldn't even take care of myself. I still lived in my parent's home. I still depended on them. And even though I worked at a retail department store (I got fucked tonight in the warehouse, and the dick was good), I still asked my parents for money and nine times out of ten they gave it to me. My mother was a business woman focused on her career and my father has been raping me for years. How did I tell her? I didn't know how and now she looked at me, as we sat in the living room, and she said, "Tell Mama about your first nut."

The request was a little over the top. Why would I discuss this with Mama? I felt weird even listening to it.

"Son, did you hear me?"

Why would she want to know about my first nut? It wasn't a pleasant memory and I didn't care to ever talk about it.

"So you're going to ignore me? I hate to be ignored. You know that's a pet peeve of mine."

Bad enough it engulfed me when I had dreams. Every time I looked at my father I remembered the pain he inflicted on me. Every time I heard his voice I figured it was my fault he did what he did. I had to pay the price. I was sacrificed. I didn't want to discuss this with her. How could I tell her that her husband, my father, raped me for years? How could I tell her that his abuse was a recycled entity he carried down from his own father and probably his father's father? I was ashamed enough. I didn't even like being a bisexual man. I hated the monster he turned me into. How could I explain to her he used to teach me how to kiss, how to caress and how to take him like a man?

Mama was determined to get me to talk to her.

"Baby...talk to me. I know something is there." She poured another drink. She tilted the glass towards me and I nodded. Maybe I did need a drink. And I needed one now!

I watched her pour some liquor into a small glass and then she put in three ice cubes. "Mama, drop it."

She handed me the drink. "You can talk to me," she said depressingly, like she was hinting at something.

"I can't, Ma. It hurts." I wolfed it down, the ice tinkling in the glass. I slammed the glass on the low-table. "Can I have more?"

She thought about it. "Sure."

"Fill it up."

"But you're not a heavy drinker."

"But I'm a heavy thinker and I have a lot on my mind."

She filled up the glass. "Talk to me, Son."

"Mom. No. It hurts too much."

She handed me the drink. "Why does it hurt? What hurts? Who caused the hurt?"

"Mama." I wolfed the drink down my throat. It burned, my watery eyes narrowing. I needed a blunt.

"Son. I know you're keeping secrets. I know you are. I've known for years"

"You are wrong." I jumped up to my feet. I was about to run. I had to run. Gradually my head was feeling light, like I was losing a grip on reality. If I uttered the product of my heart's discontentment it would destroy the fabric of the family. And I know she was one for image. She basked in the spot light. Being a political woman, she was into public perceptions, caring about what they thought. If I told Mama my secret it would crush her.

I started to leave the living room.

"Son. Please. Sit down and talk to me. Please. I am here to help you. Not hurt you."

I put my hands on the wall, next to Mama and Dad's wedding picture. In it Dad stood erect, like his penis once had. Ready to destroy me. Of course he brainwashed and groomed me. He made me think all fathers did this to their sons and I was so young and naïve I believed it. Why was I so dumb? Why? I was so powerless. I felt hopeless. I couldn't defend myself. And now every time I lay down with a man I thought about Dad. I recreated what he'd done. I didn't want kids of my own because I was scared. What if I harmed my child? I would kill myself.

"Mama I never wanted it to happen."

She was behind me. Handing me another drink. I took a moment to get it. Tears fell from my eyes. She was rubbing my back. I felt her breath on my face. "Drink it, Son. It'll help."

I slowly looked at her. I was losing it. I was about to click on a bitch. I didn't have to reveal the source of my pain. God had his reasons for allowing Satan to play hockey with my life. Satan was probably laughing at me.

Drop it! "Mama. No. I don't want to."

"Son. You can tell me about your first nut. I know all about it."

"Stop playing with my mind. Maybe I shouldn't have drunk that liquor so fast."

"Your first nut was with my husband. Your father…"

I closed my eyes.

She knows!

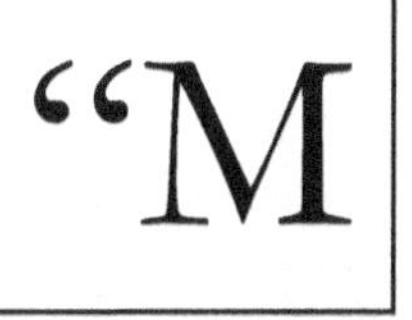

ama, you're off base. How could you…"

"Son. No sense in denying it. I knew for years."

"Nothing happened."

"Why do you think I poured myself into my work? Why do you think I hated and dreaded being home?"

I looked at her. I took the drink. I killed it. I threw the glass across the room. It slammed into Dad's picture.

"I know you're angry. I would be, too."

"How did you find out? Did he tell you? Did he say it was my fault?"

"No, son. No one told me. I saw it. I saw him kissing you one day. I dismissed it as father and son bonding. But then a week later I was standing in the door way. I saw him inside you. I saw it all. I was so shocked something snapped in my head. I died inside.

I lost it. I started working harder. I couldn't believe my husband would do this to you."

"So you chose to sweep it under the rug. You are my mother and you didn't protect me."

"Son, I had a career. I couldn't let this get out. Do you know what this would have done for my political career? I would have been dragged through the mud."

"DRAGGED?"

She wiped tears from her eyes, drinking from the bottle. I snatched it and threw it at her. It missed her face by inches. She grabbed me, trying to make me understand but there was no way I could. She just admitted to me that she saw my father deflower me. She saw it all. And all she cared about was what the public had to say. So what! I was her son!

"Son. Listen."

I pushed her off me. I hated putting my hands on a woman that gave me life. But I had to. I was tired of people touching me and I didn't want them to.

"Listen to what?" I stormed past her. I had to get some air. She grabbed my arm and I tried to punch her. I was scared. I felt trapped. I was suffocating.

She was a beast. "SON!"

I was a lion. "Let me go!"

"You don't understand. I couldn't tell anyone. I couldn't call the police. It would all come out."

What will come out? My rape? I'm getting the impression that there's more to this story! "Yes it would, Ma. And you were supposed to stand right by my side, look the media in the face and protect me. For my well being you were supposed to throw all that political bullshit out the window. I can't *believe* you. You're still worried about public opinion. This is worse than when I asked to meet my grandparents."

"You can't meet them. They are dead."

"Really?"

"Yes. They were bad people. They treated me like filth. I didn't want you to meet them."

"I want to. But of course I can't because you say they are dead and gone. But that's irrelevant. I can't get past the you-watched-your-husband-rape-me part. Are you sick?"

"Son, no. Just let it go. It's the past. You're a grown man."

Could you believe her? "And I'm supposed to forget it?"

"Yes. Let it go. Look how long you kept it a secret?"

"I gotta go. I can't be in this house. I will call the police myself. I can't go on like this. I'm trapped in a gay lifestyle and I can't break free because your husband, my Dad taught it to me."

"YOU CAN'T CALL THE POLICE! IT WILL ALL COME OUT!"

"What will come out? My rape?'

She studied me, wiping tears from her eyes. She wasn't the aristocratic bitch she normally was. Gone was her ruggedness. Gone was the toughness. What stood before me was a caricature. A woman I no longer respected. I was so angry I didn't think I loved her.

Mama said, "Wait right here. I have to tell you everything then maybe you'll understand."

"Tell me what?"

She vanished up the stairs. I sunk to my knees and stared at my lap. My own mother. Stood by and put her career before her own child. She gave me life and she watched that man snatch it away. All those years I thought I was keeping it from her because I didn't want her to feel she failed as a parent. And all this time SHE KNEW! BITCH!

She slowly came down the stairs holding an envelope. It was a manila one. She played around with it. Her heels clicked on the tile walking up to me. She refused to meet my eyes.

"It will all come out, Son."

She handed me the envelope.

"It's best if you heard it from me. It's time. You're old enough. You deserve to know the truth.

Before I could open it the front door opened.

Daddy walked inside.

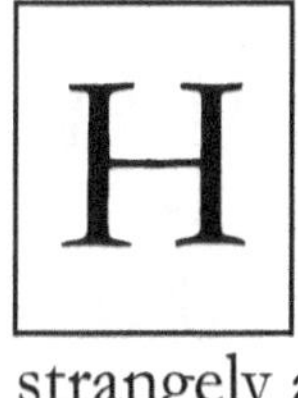 e smiled when he saw us. He walked over to Mom and kissed her cheek. It was like she got shocked. She jumped out of her skin, standing behind me. He looked strangely at us.

"Something is going on," he said, barely above a whisper. "What is it?"

Mama said, "Nothing."

I said, "She's lying. Something is going on."

He smiled at me, rubbing my head. "That's my boy."

I slapped his hand off me. "I hate you."

He grew quiet. Looking from me to her and back to me. Looking himself in the mirror, he was shaking his head. He saw the glass shattered by his shattered picture. The broken liquor bottle silenced him.

"You two got in a fight. Son, did you raise your hand to my wife?"

"No, but you raised your hand to me."

"Son, what are you talking about?"

Mama said, "I should have confronted you years ago. But I cared more about the image of family. My political career came before my family."

"Confronted me?" He shook his head again.

"For raping our son."

He turned and refused to face us.

"Look at me, Dad," I said, opening the manila envelope, suspense killed me. I had to know what was going on inside.

"Why did you lie to your mother?"

"Ha! I lied?" I asked, pulling out the papers. There were about five of them. I looked at the first one.

Mama said, "I'm sorry baby. Now you see. It'll all come out."

My face turned ashen. I couldn't breathe. I dropped them on the floor, looking at her.

"I'm adopted?"

Dad turned to face me.

Mom said, "Yes."

I couldn't believe my ears. She had to be lying. She told me she gave birth to me on June 5, 1977. It was all a lie? Was she serious? The official adoption forms and certificate was on the floor enshrining my feet. So she had to be telling the truth.

"Dad! You knew I was adopted. Is that why you abused me?"

"Son…"

"According to these papers we aren't related. I can't believe this. In one night I lost my family, but in all actuality I lost my family years ago. Both of you are sick individuals. Mom wanted a political career. So she shunned my feelings and emotions to have it. She saw you rape me, Mr. Dad. She saw you with her own eyes."

"She didn't."

"I did," she went on. There was a knock at the door.

Dad answered it. He was face to face with uniformed police men.

Mama said, "They are here for you, *husband.*"

"And for you, too," the shorter cop said, frowning. "Both of you are under arrest."

I didn't know what would become of my life. People called me gay yet no one understood what I have gone through. No one saw the vehicle my fake Daddy drove to get me to the destination. I didn't want this, I didn't ask for this. They say God didn't put on you no more than you could bear but who wanted to bear this? I was a monster. Or so I thought. I didn't love myself. Maybe I should start. I had a feeling this big ole house would be mine. And I would take it. All Mama's jewelry I would pawn it, but why? Diamonds and gold couldn't erase what was done to me. I picked up a phone book and called the first shrink's office I could find. Once I made an appointment I picked up the Bible and turned it to the book of Psalms.

God help me.

And I knew in my heart he would.

RAYNE

IN THE | **BEDROOM** | **3**

Nutrition Facts
+ *100% Protein*
+ *A few titties*
+ *100% Fruit Juice*
+ *A little freaky*

*M*y fantasy is ruined! How can it end like this? How dare a transsexual pose as a real woman in my home? How could the fledgling he/she pull out his penis in my face, just when I was about to eat her pussy? She didn't have a pussy at all. I can't believe the horror of a penis in my face! I hate dick! I haven't had a dick inside me since I was 19, and even when I did take said dick I poisoned him in the end because he told all his college friends. I am so grossed out. And to think Rayne was behind this. It wasn't my fault I tricked her into letting me suck her pussy. I love pussy more than men. Yes, I am a woman of impeccable standards. I slash the dots on the I's and I explode the crosses on the t's. I made my own rules and broke them. I was sexual by nature. I was one way in public, attending Catholic Church, hosting Bake sales, mingling with the common folk and doing what society expected of me. But inside my expensive home, I was another way. I was the lesbian Dr. Jekyll and Mr. Hyde. I *used toys to make myself come and rode dildos to my sheer delight. I hated real dicks but I loved the plastic ones. The difference between a real dick and a fake one were the batteries. I would masturbate with fruit and eat them to a polish. I would suck oranges and rub the stinging citrus all over my pussy. I would sleep while the citrus dried on my twat and awaken around 4 a.m. and fuck myself senseless on the Web cam. Women around the world have watched me work my pussy into the orgasm phase. I have watched them. Typing demands on the keyboard became their utter failure. If I told her to wipe piss on her tit and suck it off she would. Just to get a taste of Hollywood. But this wasn't the red carpet. This was sex. This was dominance. This was power. I never showed my face online. The internet could be a miserable vessel if you let it. I loved wearing fancy wigs and dressing like a boy. I got off on the trickery. I got off on tricking women into lesbian action for years. It was something I've been doing since I was a promising teenager. It was something I did after I got heartbroken by a man. I painfully remember when I first thought about it. I was dating a man named June. He had long, curly eyelashes and the creamiest black skin. He had an amazing body and the way he walked reminded one of poetry. He was a Ladies Man, but at the time I didn't care. He had the most heavenly eyes. The way he smiled parted my heart into beats never seen by my pulse. He came into my life a promising rose and left a dandelion. He tricked me into thinking he loved me, only to lay up with a male friend of his and make love to him the way a man made love to his woman. I remember standing in the forest watching them. I was taking a walk that night when my parents fell asleep. I was rubbing my arms, the breezy air blowing my hair into a frenzy. I'd spoken to June earlier that day and he told me he was going out of town to visit his grand mother. I didn't have any control over that so I didn't care. I told him to give her my best. He said he would. When I saw the forest I wanted to run. Because it was after ten p.m. and it was very dark. But something lured me to it. So I went. When I passed a huge oak tree I saw June's car. It was rocking. The lights were off. I slowly walked up to it, my heart thumping. I saw a male's face pressed against the driver side window. I walked closer. I heard the cursing and the moaning. This ass is good. Fuck this dick. I'm gonna come deep inside you. I was nailed to the grassy terrain. I cried for dear life. I was shaking my head, pounding on the windshield. The rocking stopped. The heavy breathing died. June was so shocked he couldn't move. His male lover ducked his head. But it was too late. I'd already seen his face. I started to scream and he got out of the car, his penis swinging. I didn't want it by me. It was suddenly a strange creature and I didn't care for it. I didn't want to feel it, touch it or taste it. My love had been cracked like swollen sea shells. Over by a huge root sticking from a tree I saw a brick. With all my might I picked it up and swung at his face and missed. I threw it at the windshield and it shattered. It hit his lover in the face and blood was everywhere. I covered my face, running off. "DON'T TELL ANYONE, CLEVER!" came the insightful call from behind me. But I didn't care. I didn't even want to tell myself. I was so in love I tried to commit suicide. I used to pray about it, begging the Good Lord to erase my blood line from the world and bury me a love sick fool. I would cry for weeks. My grades declined. My uptight, anal parents would whip my tail for bad grades but I welcomed the pain. Daddy noticed the change in me and wanted to know what was wrong but I closed up inside. I turned ugly and dark and gothic. I started wearing black nail polish and black lipstick. My hair once down to my ass I cut with sheers. It now hung just past my ears. I asked God to take my heart and get rid of it. But he gave me something else once I put on one of Daddy's suits. A split personality. Somewhere inside me I snapped. I* would begin to talk to myself in the mirror. Changing my voice like I was from Brazil. Or was it France? It was one of those overseas countries. I would do this day in and day out when I didn't have school. I would sit at the sowing machine and alter his smoke-colored suit so it fit me.

Thinking about June I wanted revenge. So this was how I got it. I befriended his mother behind his back. She was a timid little bitch, stuck on her divine looks. She used to stare at herself in the mirror for hours, asking the mirror who was the sexiest of 'em all. I remember I stole money from mother's expensive purse and caught the public bus to the local grocery store. I bought June's mother a chocolate cake and took it to her. When she saw me her lips parted in a very confusing way. She was clad in a floral dress with flowers all over it. I loved the way the satin at the bottom grazed her calves when she walked. She tossed her hair about her head, looking like an innocent bird.

After she accepted my cake she asked could she brush my hair. I said, "Yes."

"Who are you anyway? Are you here to see one of my sons?"

"No, ma'am. I don't even know your sons," I lied, anger surging all over my face.

"Then why are you here? Why did you bring me a chocolate cake?"

"Because I'm new in the neighborhood and I thought I'd extend a greeting, since the outside of your house is heaven."

She blushed. "Why thank you. I tend my gardens every day. It keeps me busy…would you like to come inside?"

"Sure," I said, nervous as hell. But I kept my cool. I was the enemy. You could never get too cozy with the enemy.

I had to remember my purpose and my mission. I had to get back at June for making me fall in love with his bisexual ass.

There was no way he could get away with it. Not on my life or his life. And right now his life was a bucket of peons.

Entering her home was awkward. Up until then I had never been inside anybody's home but my own. My parents forbade it. I could never tell them I was at June's home. Hell, they had never heard of or met June. My parents said I wasn't allowed to have boyfriends. So I never brought them around.

I took into account the Italian feel in the room. Italian chairs and beige Italian throw pillows. An old, yellowing black and white picture hung above the mantel.

"You have such long, long hair," she said, smiling at me. She sat on the sofa and I sat on the floor, between her legs. I could smell her pussy but I didn't say anything. I was a teen ager. She was an adult. I was into other men and women around my own age.

"Thank you."

She was brushing my hair lovingly, humming a famous tune I couldn't name. "I always wanted a daughter."

"Why didn't you try for one?"

She thought about it. "Because I have three sons. They run wild in the streets then come home when the sun goes down to rest. I guess I'm content with that."

"Are you really?"

She smiled again. She had a lovely smile. "Yes."

"Are you married?" I asked, looking around her living room with both awe and jubilancy.

"Yes. I'm married," she spat rather quickly. My pulse quickened thinking about it. Her fingers betrayed her words. There wasn't a ring on her finger. Even the faded marking wasn't there. I tried to understand why she fibbed. Was she embarrassed that she was a single mother trying to raise little rascals? Who knew? Some women thought their pussies started

and stopped life and all it did was give you pleasure or a kid or two. Nothing more. Nothing less.

The floor beneath my buttocks was uncomfortable. I shifted a little, wanting to go home. I just wanted to bring her a cake and analyze the inside of her home.

Retrospection interweaving her thoughts, Clever smiled, thinking back to that time. When she tricked her first lover into doing something he wasn't aware of. June paid dearly for cheating on her. Oh, yes. He did. And when she gave him the receipt for her endeavors he wouldn't know what hit him. But she knew what hit him. She wanted him to suffer. She wanted to play her tricks and make him squeal with misery. Oh, Yes. Thinking about it, she wanted a tonic but she decided against it. Now was not the time to drink and think. Rubbing her pussy, she inhaled deeply, the scent igniting in her heart vengeance and in her soul revenge…

June's mother was brushing my hair rather lovingly. I was uncomfortable now and I wanted to leave. I thought about Daddy's suit and wearing it. I wanted to be a man again. To talk like one and walk around my room like one. Practice made perfect.

Before I could say anything the front door opened and June walked inside. I lowered my head so he couldn't see my face. He slammed the door and the pictures on the walls shook. I was too afraid to look up. I didn't want to be found out. I wanted this all to be a trick, a game. The fantasy was to cunningly destroy his mental state and give him an image that wasn't there. I felt it pulsating through my veins.

He didn't even speak or find out who I was. He ran up to his room in tears. His mother didn't even seem interested in why he shed tears. She was more into brushing my hair. What was wrong with that picture? Why didn't the maternal instinct wash over her face? Why didn't she demand that her son tell her what's wrong? What kind of mother was she?

"Could you do me a favor?" I asked, testing the waters. How else would I find out if the lake was a damn or the sea?

"Yes?"

"Could you cut the cake? I have a taste for chocolate and I'm famished."

"Yes. I could do that. How about some supper?"

"Yes. I would like that."

"It isn't cooked yet. It would take a while."

I looked at her, my eyes sparkling like diamonds.

"Take all the time you need."

hen she left I stood up and explored the house. I wanted to know where her bedroom was. I walked down the hallway and saw an open door. It was the only room on the floor. Once I went inside I took into account a dim light coming from the closet. I walked to it. I pushed the door open, my heart terrorizing my chest. I shouldn't be in there but I had to get June.

I saw the clothing and I smiled.

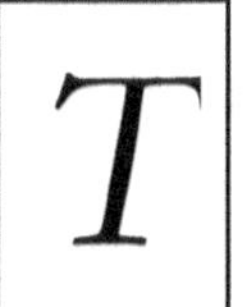

here was a knock on June's door. He answered it, his eyes red with sadness. He took one look at me and said, "Who are you?"

"I'm Tom. I'm a friend of your lover's."

"Did he send you here?"

I thought about it. "Yes."

"I don't know why. He left me. He blames me for Clever destroying his face."

"He blames Clever?"

"Yes. She threw the brick through my car windshield and it destroyed his dashing good looks."

"Oh…"

"Why are you here?"

"To help solve the problem. He asked me to."

June was confused. He looked me up and down, obviously liking what he saw.

"Well, the only way to help me…"

I caught the bait. "What way would that be?"

He pulled me in the room and closed the door. He was rubbing my buttocks, giving me some tongue. I fell into his charm. I died inside his heat.

"You like the boys, huh?" I asked him.

"Yes," he said breathlessly, unzipping his pants. "Get on your knees."

"Would that make you happy? Is that what you fantasize?"

"Yes…"

I got on my knees and took him into my mouth. My lips were clumsy and untrustworthy. I had never done this before and it was hot that I was trying. He loved it nonetheless, falling on the bed. I was on top of him, sucking him dry, putting my heart into it with a rookie spirit.

"I love it…"

"I do, too."

"Take off the hat…"

"Do you really want it off?"

"Yes."

I sat up and took off the hat. His eyes popped from his head. I then took my hair from the stocking cap and shook it *free. He sat up and I stood up, taking off his daddy's suit jacket and shirt. He was in denial.*

"Thought a boy was sucking on you, 'ey?"

"This has to be a game. How did you get in my house?"

"Easy. I bought your Mama a chocolate cake."

"What?"

"She was brushing my hair when you flew through the front door."

"Get out, Clever. You have caused my life enough hassle."

"I caused your life a hassle? You cheated on me and you blame me?"

He was apologetic then. But it was too little too late. "I am sorry, Clever. I really am. Please. I can't deal with this right now. It's bad enough I'm bisexual and I can never be free with it. I will have to live a fantasy for the rest of my life because I may lose my mother. If she found out I had wings and became a fairy she would disown me..."

I thought about his words. He would have to live a fantasy. Well, bozo! I will have to live a fantasy as well. Just like you tricked me into thinking you loved me and it was all a lie, all a game I will do the same thing to whoever I encounter in life. I will get off on their naivety. I will be a flesh blood hound and suck them dry. Just like you did to me.

"Have some chocolate cake, my dear," I said and he looked at me blankly.

"What cake?"

"The one I baked for your mother," I lied. "Have a piece. If you can have a piece with her and ask God to forgive you and to forgive yourself I will leave amicably and I will never bother you again."

"Are you serious? If I eat some cake then it's all over?" he asked, not believing me.

I glared into his eyes. "It will be all over. I promise. I will leave and never return. I will act like we don't know each other. I will never tell anyone you love men. I will take it to my grave."
We shook on it.

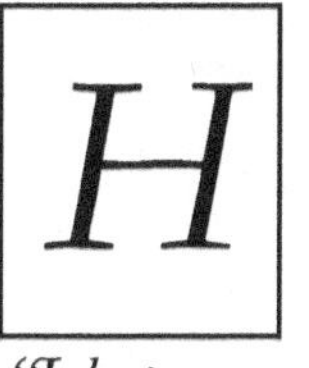 e left me standing in the room and I put back on his father's coat. Checking myself in the mirror, I looked down and noticed his mom's make-up. Piking up her lipstick, I coated my lips and said, "I hope you like the cake."

I looked at the clock and shook my head. I had to be getting home soon. I slowly grabbed my shoes and crept out the room. I had to see if he was holding up his end of the bargain.

When I got to the kitchen I stood there watching him clutch his throat. Falling to his knees he began to foam at the mouth.

When his eyes landed on me he tried to lash out and I laughed, my eyes locked on the ceiling.

"Die, gay boy. Die a horrible death. I told you if you ate the cake it would all be over. Didn't I promise you that?" I was slowly walking up to his twitching body, his legs thumping one of the dining room chairs amongst other things.

"Did you like the chocolate cake?" I asked, pausing by the stove. I picked up the rest of the cake and got on my knees.

I smashed the plate into his face. Blood spurted in my face. Licking my lips, I used my fingers to wipe up his blood and I taste it. Yummy. Blood was the best form of revenge.

Finally, when the house phone rang his body lay lifeless, his foot resting on top of his mother's face. She lay sprawled underneath the table, her legs carefully bent at the knees. She looked peaceful. I was laughing again, crawling over to her. I grabbed her legs and pulled her to me. Resting her head in my lap, I began to stroke her hair, the way she stroked mine.

"So your son gave you some cake. I'm glad you both liked it. What I didn't tell you was that it was laced with poison..."

I closed my eyes, sweeping my palms over her eyes.

Closing them.

Like my heart.

Depressingly, Clever unflinchingly sat on the long leather settee in her bedroom, her world in shambles. She stared at the flashing TV. On the floor was her wig. On the bed was the smoke-colored suit. Behind her was the glow of the computer screen.

Standing up, she stretched. It felt so good. Walking over to the closet she opened it. Looking around at the various clothes, she smiled, resting a finger on her temple.

Looking over her shoulder she stared at the rotary phone, next to her photo on the nightstand.

She picked up the phone and dialed a series of numbers. The dial of the phone snapped back to the "0" position with a snap. The phone started ringing and she sighed. She looked at her diamond watch and sat on the edge of the bed, debating…plotting.

When the person answered the phone she was elated.

Very.

A few months later, Rayne was sitting in her living room, watching her son talk on the phone with his girlfriend. Watching him with the phone, she reminded herself that she had to call her friend Diana because she said somebody she knew was found dead in a bushy terrain in Ft. Lauderdale and Rayne really didn't care because her family lived in her neighborhood and it wasn't one of them. And her kids were ok. So she wasn't interested at the moment. She remembered the voice mail. "Girl it happened about four months ago and we're just finding out about it now..." Rayne didn't care.

Smiling, she marveled at how her son matured. He was certainly turning into a fine young man. He looked just like his dumb ass father. In fact she couldn't get over the man because every time she looked in her son eyes she saw him. Looking back at her. Taunting her. Out of her mind was Clever and the nightmare of finding out she was really a woman dressed as a man. But she had gotten revenge by calling her transvestite friend and putting the joke on Clever. Part of her felt good about it, but the other part of her was disappointed that she would try to be a prostitute anyway. She just wanted the best for her kids and she would do anything for them. Most mothers would get two jobs but Rayne didn't want two jobs. Despite having kids she did have her own life and she had to love herself before she loved anyone else. Times were hard and men weren't fathers to their kids. Women had to pick up the slack, pick up the burden and pick up the tab. They had to pay for it all. They had to nurse their children's tears when they asked where Daddy was and she couldn't give them an accurate answer. That was her life. Cleaning up her Baby Daddy's mess, straightening his damn lies. She would never love again. She didn't need a man. She would focus on her kids and she would give it to God. She would buy a toy and give herself an orgasm a night and when she came down off her high she would feel great. She wouldn't need a man then.

Her son was laughing at something his girlfriend said and she stood up, looking at a Britney Spears video on TV. Pop tart. She liked her. Britney was her favorite entertainer.

"Son I am going to bed."

"Ok. But can I ask you something?" he asked, handsome in a Phat Farm shirt and black pants.

"Sure."

"Can I go out?"

"Yes, Son. Just be home by 12 midnight. You have school tomorrow."

"Bet that up, Ma," he said, standing up, clutching his cell phone. He hugged his mom, kissed her cheek and she retired for the evening…

"Lock the door behind you."

He did so.

Rayne lay in her bed and she closed her eyes. She had a long day. First she cleaned her house and cleaned out the dusty shed in the back. There was so much grime it sent her sinuses into a hissy fit. Then she took out the frozen pork chops so they could thaw. She then played with her pussy, had an orgasm and saw to her kids.

When they were squared away she went jogging around the neighborhood. But the funniest thing happened. When she was jogging home a black car kept following her. It had illegal tints and she feared her life. She ran up to her door, looking back and the window was lowered.

She looked at him and he looked at her.

It was her son's dad.

"What do you want?"

"I want to be a better father to my son…"

Rayne rolled her eyes, pulled her hair into a ponytail and she walked coolly up to his car.

"It's a little too late for that."

"It's never too late, Rayne."

"I don't even know why I'm wasting my time."

"Because you love me." He reached out of the window and touched her hand and she snatched it away.

"Every time we fuck you think we are supposed to get back together. It's just sex and nothing more and I haven't touched you in ions, man."

"I miss you," he said, clearly playing a game with her and she knew it. The man couldn't talk without lying. He always caused her trouble. Drama always seemed to find him and once a week a different thug shot at his ass, trying to take him out. He was a liar and a cheat.

"I'm going inside," she said, pivoting on her heel.

He parked the car in the drive way. When he opened the door, he rushed inside her home and locked the door.

God why won't he leave me alone? I don't want him. Don't he have other bitches?

He was knocking at the door and she peaked through the curtain. "WHAT?"

"Rayne, let's talk…"

She closed her eyes, sighing. She loved him so much and that was the problem. He knew she loved him and he played it to the tooth and nail and she was tired of it. It would be the same old shit, different day. Different problems. Different bullshit.

She closed the curtain and turned on the stereo, turning the volume as high as it would go.

He knocked louder but she didn't hear it.

She started to dance around the living room, putting him out of her mind. Her pussy wet, she thought about the tattoo he had on the small of his back. It said "Rayne." She shivered thinking about it. She used to love eating his ass and staring at her name. He was a freaky man. No he wasn't gay but he loved her tongue and finger deep in his asshole and she used to love giving it to him just the way he liked.

Those days are gone…

t was 2 a.m. when she opened her eyes and saw him standing in her room. The lamp was on and her son smiled down at her, standing next to his father.

"What is he doing in here?" she asked with an attitude. "GET OUT!"

"But Mom," her son said, his sad eyes weakening her. "He wants to talk to you. He doesn't mean any harm. Why do you hate him so much?"

"Because he cheated on me."

"But mom. You teach me to forgive and forget."

"It's different when your father is a sleaze bucket."

Snatching the covers from her body she pointed at him. "GET OUT!"

He looked sad. He rubbed his chin, looking at his son. "Leave us to talk," he whispered to his son, barely audible.

Her son smiled. "Sure, Dad…" and he closed the door.

Rayne was looking at her son's father. "Get out. I don't want to talk to you."

He walked up to her and touched her shoulder and she pushed him on the bed. He closed his eyes, holding in his anger.

Rayne said, "What do you want to talk about?"

He opened his eyes. She was falling for them. They seemed a little…different and distant. She sat next to him and said, "What do you want? Why are you here? There is a reason you show up on my doorstep unannounced. Is everything ok with you?"

He sat up and looked into her eyes. Their lips were getting closer.

Oh, God. I am about to fuck him!

When their lips touched she melted into his arms, feeling like a wounded bird, needing therapy so she could fly away, fly, fly away…

He lay her down and took off her panties. He inhaled her scent and kissed her pussy. Gave it some tongue.

"We are not getting…back…together," she promised, holding his head.

She loved the do-rag on his head, hiding his waves. She loved his chest and she wanted to see it but when she tried to take off his shirt he grabbed her hand and raised a finger.

He continued to eat, tasting the salt…running his lips over her passion…wanting her to come so he could taste it. He stuck his tongue so far in her pussy she jumped with jubilancy.

"Yes, Baby…yummy…eat my pussy, Daddy…"

He pushed her legs back and stuck his tongue inside her deeper, her skin starting to break out in sweats…he ate for dear life, like a starving lion without his cubs…like the clouds without air and rain, he needed to be fulfilled.

Her body tensed up and she said she had to come and he sucked on her clit, rubbing her wet pussy with her legs bent back even with her ears and she shrieked, her muscles contracting…pushing her…aiding her into silence.

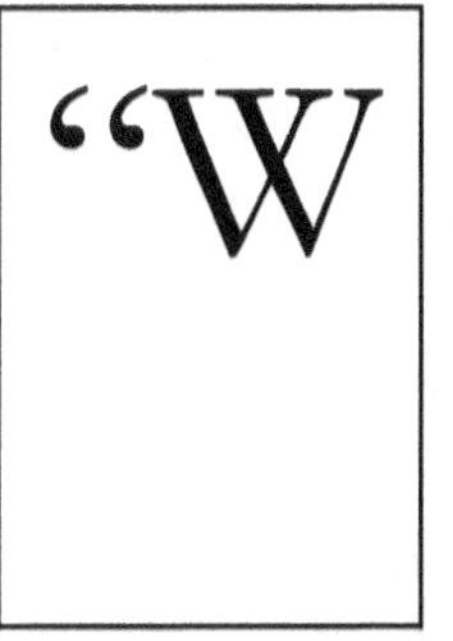

"Wow," she said, looking at him with love in his eyes. She hadn't seen the man in years and with him back in her life (momentarily) he seemed different. He was once a man with a lot of weight. He lost a lot of it, toning himself up. She wanted to get him out of his clothes, but if she did that he would think they were trying to make it work and she didn't want him back.

"I wanna taste you," Rayne said, patting the bed. "Lay on your stomach. I want to eat you….taste your skin…"

He lay on his stomach and she straddled his thigh. He rests his head on his hands and she raised the back of his shirt, kissing his back, loving the feel of his skin…softer than she remembered it.

He was twirling his ass, which was fuller than it used to be.

She loved how he toned up.

He must be working out.

She ran her tongue from the top of his back, down his spine…to the tattoo of her name…

The tattoo of her name always brought her joy. She closed her eyes and inhaled, sitting up. She couldn't open her eyes.

He is with the same old games. I can't be pulled back in. He has gotten over me. Because he took my name off the small of his back.

It's gone.

"T his isn't a good idea," Rayne said, getting back to her senses. She had to stand firm in her decisions. Once a man fucked up she didn't back step. She couldn't do it over. She wouldn't give him a second chance. Why should she? He would do the same deceitful things to her over and over and she didn't have time for it. He hurt her enough.

"Didn't you hear me?" Rayne asked him and he turned over, staring into her eyes with a smile.

"What kind of game are you playing?"

He shook his head in the negative and she said, "Yes you are! You're playing with me…

He stood up and picked up a piece of construction paper from her dresser and a black marker.

"Oh, God. You want to play charades?"

He shook his head yes with a smile.

"No, Man. Grow up! I can't believe I fell for your bullshit again. When will I learn?"

He drew a square…she was falling for it. She did like charades. She used to play that game with her mother.

"I don't know…it's a square…"

He drew a C.

"Umm, damn…A square…the letter C…"

He put a huge X over the box and the C.

"DAMN, MAN! GET OUT!"

He drew two stick figures holding hands…

"Man…when I guess this shit then get out!"

He drew an EKG machine, with a line zig-zagging across it.

"Love…live…"

"Yes!" he whispered. He wrote "Live" at the top of the paper.

He drew an eye ball…

Rayne was biting her lip. "Eyeball…I see. I see live…no, that doesn't make sense…I…"

"Yes…" he whispered again. "I…live…"

He drew a courtroom. It was a little rusty but she knew what it was.

"Courtroom…a place of just…"

He gave her the thumbs up. He wrote "just" on the paper…

He then drew a stick figure in a bed…

"Sleeping…"

He drew pictures over the stick figure's head…

"Dreams…"

"YES YES YES!" he screamed. "I JUST WANT TO LIVE OUT MY DREAMS!"

Rayne looked at him. "Huh? Why are you yelling at me?"

He pulled a small shiny gun from his crotch.

"Hi, Rayne!"

"Um…" Her heart pounding, she slowly stood up from the bed. She was shaking her head. "Why do you have a gun? Are you going to kill me? What did I do to you? You weren't a good father to your son! Is that my fault?"

"Yes," he said, but his voice didn't sound like a man. It sounded like a woman.

Rayne narrowed her eyes. "Why are you talking like a chick? You're scaring me…"

He said, "Look into my eyes Rayne…and tell me where you know me from…"

"You're my son's father! I know…"

He said, "I once paid you $500…I once ate your pussy…but I was dressed as a man…remember…you tricked me and sent that transvestite to my home and you tarnished my fantasy forever!"

Rayne began shaking, covering her face. "Oh my God! No, no, *noooooo* what are you saying to me…?"

"I am not you son's father. I am not the man you used to love. I am an illusion. I am an image. I am what you want to see…Isn't that what you did to me? Sent a man with tits to my home, knowing I was a lesbian and I hated dick of any kind. You sold me an image. An illusion…"

"But…you look just like my son's father, Clever! This can't be happening…"

"I will tell you how I did it! I killed your son's father months ago. We met at a bar and I lured him back to my home and we made out on the bed I ate your pussy on…When he came I stabbed him to death. Do you know how long it took me to pull him to my Buick? I drove to Ft. Lauderdale and I dumped him in the bushes…"

"Oh, God! Diana was trying to tell me someone I knew was murdered…but I didn't listen…Oh my God!"

"Before I had sex with him I took pictures of him. Of, yes. Pictures of everything. I gave them to my plastic surgeon. What a marvelous job he did. He then got rid of my breasts…He redid my nose and teeth…He did everything in his power to make me look like your son's father. This took three months total. I went through a lot of pain…but it was well worth it, bitch! I had to make you pay for what you did to me, you dirty WHORE!"

"But you sound like him…"

I have been taking hormones for months. So my voice is that of a man now. On top of that I studied your son's father, from the video I have of him. He has a very unique speaking pattern. I studied it. And now…"

Clever extended her arms. "I present to you a man who is about to kill you."

Clever closed her eyes and Rayne started screaming when the gun went off.

R ayne shook, pissing on herself. The wet spot beneath her was warm and stinky. She refused to open her eyes.

Oh God I'm losing a lot of blood!

She opened her eyes and saw her son holding the gun. He was screaming, falling to his knees. "Daddy! I didn't mean to shoot you! But you had a gun aimed at my mother…I'm so sorry Daddy! Wake up, please, DAD! Don't die please Daddy don't leave me! Why were you trying to shoot Mama?"

Rayne slowly stood up and walked over to her son. Taking the gun, she hugged him and he shook with fear in her arms. He just killed a man he thought was his father.

How do I tell him that the dead bitch on the floor isn't his father? How do I say it? Will he believe me if I told him? What if he thinks I was making it up? How do I let him know that his father died months ago, and his body was dumped as alligator food in Ft. Lauderdale?

I can never tell him. I have to give him an image, an illusion…like Clever gave me. What a sick bitch

I have to protect my son.

Rest in peace, Baby Daddy…

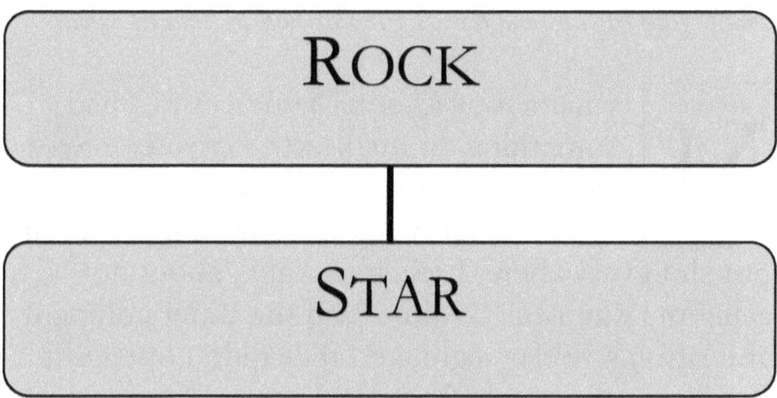

I guess I was about to find out how many licks it took to get to the center of my Tootsie Pop and all I wanted was a Blow Pop. I guess that's all good, because, dealing with Niggahs, I seem to get those little Dum Dum lollipops. You know…they hardly filled your mouth and were always overpowered by the movement of my…tongue. Standing up he purposely walked up to my desk, slowly undoing the buttons on his jacket with those cleaned-but-unshapely nails. Looking deeply into my eyes he flashed a shit-eating grin that turned me to poop. I shook like a hooker on a slow night with

her Pimp barking orders. I turned in my chair and cautiously spread my baby-smooth legs, rubbing my breasts. On his knees he went, pushing up my skirt, looking over my pussy and he realized I had on crotchless panties. The crotchless panties were the best way to go. The hell with those crack-riding thongs. Thongs gave my asshole rashes Preparation H couldn't heal...

My name was Quintet James. And I had something on my heart. *Party like a Rock star* blasted from the sufficient stereo system in my need-to-clean-it living room. I got shit everywhere, I tell you. Angry about not paying my water bill on time (and the water company cut it off, it's Friday night, and they didn't open until Monday morning, which meant I was without water for the entire weekend, so *not* cool) and forgetting to take out the turkey wings to thaw so I could make my Mama's favorite dish, complete with white steamy rice and well-seasoned squash, the Florida sunshine was starting to fade like my favorite pair of tight blue jeans, when I accidentally poured in bleach a few hours ago. I could have sworn I was washing white jeans. But I had forgotten I had earlier in the day washed and folded them. I didn't hang up my jeans. Why bother, when I was going to wear them anyways throughout the week. Which brought me to my closet? I needed to clean that also.

I headed up the hallway, towards my room, my sanctuary. Passing articulately-framed photos of Mama, daddy and my three sisters, Lisa, Stacey and Dash Gregory…I've since pushed my family away…I had my reasons…sometimes, when you were faced with life altering decisions, you tend to push loved ones away because you didn't want to hurt them, because you needed to deal with things on your own, because you didn't need a bunch of people yapping all up in your face, claiming they understood what you went through when they weren't even going through the source of your pain and suffering. And I loved my family, thrived for my family. But I changed my address and phone number months ago, moved from Philadelphia down to Florida without so much as a post card, a good bye or a see ya' later.

For a reason.

Fresh in my mind were blogs I read on Myspace. I was fond of Mercury Chyld, the Ogre poet and Legendary. I loved poetry; poetry got me through the day. I had about eight of Langston Hughes' collection of poems behind me on the ceiling-to-floor book shelf holding an array of books ranging from *Along Came a Spider* and *The Bluest Eye* to Hirohito and the Making of Modern Japan to A.H.M. Jones' *Sparta*.

I thought about Audrey Michelle's "ATM" poem while I looked around the semi darkness of a room I suddenly didn't want to be in.

My closet. I opened the door. From the fading Miami sunlight I could faintly see clothes, neatly folded, everywhere. Files were here and there and the three filing cabinets sat off in the corner of the closet. Awards I've won throughout my life hang on the wall, 189 pair of shoes carefully lined the top of my huge walk-in closet…I needed to go through all this shit and get rid of what I didn't need. And donate some of the clothes I outgrew or didn't wear anymore to the Goodwill so less fortunate people could rock what I used to look good in.

I turned on the bedroom lights by clapping my hands; yea I still got the played out The Clapper.

Lights come on. Voila. Dust city appears in places and on things I never knew existed. I needed to dust the TV, dust the dresser, my armoire, which holds my perfumes and big screen TV and lap top. I should have bought a Dell Laptop because this E Machines piece-of-shit I bought, after camping out in the Best Buy electronics store line all night long, broke down after two fucking weeks.

I tried to fight the sensation but I sneezed, my allergies kicking my hind part. I was a woman who lived by the mood. I smelled like Britney Spears, her perfume, *Curious*, had me pissed the hell off. When was I going to understand that buying perfume because Elizabeth Taylor or Celine Dion graced the bottles didn't merit good shit? Smelled like hot shit.

White Diamonds gave me a headache so I stopped wearing it years ago. And when I wore Celine I damn near broke out in hives trying to brush that stinky shit off me. My mother, Sue, loved Celine, her music, her Vegas show and her stank ass perfume. She always came over to my house, located in Homestead, not to far from the Super Wal-Mart, smelling like clouds of singer Celine's perfume.

I sighed, yawning. It was going on 7 p.m. I had a party to go to, but I really didn't feel up to it. Which was a stark contradiction because I loved parties, lived for them, breathed parties. This brings me to my story. Leaving to Inhale.

I read Terry McMillan's book *Waiting to Exhale*. Yes, I saw the movie. Yes, I loved it, the book better but she missed out on some parts. Sometimes women didn't give a good goddamn about men and their shit. Yea, the book was snappy and witty but they didn't have a bitch like me in there.

I met Benjamin last week. He came into the store, I worked at Scotts Unlimited, a retail store. Fortunately, I was the manager. He had a job application. Looking at him I told myself, damn, he's fine. I remembered seeing him somewhere before. He seemed confident, too goddamn confident. He had a swagger that told me, Yea I'ma get this marketing job because I was 6 feet 8 inches with a horse dick and big feet. Yea, baby!

I approached him, clad superbly and beautifully in a long skirt with slight split up the right leg. High heeled pumps that screamed make-over more than business. My hair piled atop my head with Janet Jackson ala 1993 That's the Way Love Goes Curls. I rocked this look longer than today's fucked-up breed partied like a rock star.

We shook hands. "How are you? And you are..."

"Benjamin," he told me, sizing me up like he worked for McDonalds and I was a Tony Romas chick with a side of Pollo Tropical. He then kissed my hand and I said, "I'm Quintet…Keep it business."

He challenged me. "I plan on it." His eyes fucked me from here to Kingdom Come but my eyes didn't fuck him past the front desk. Men like him I loved to diffuse. On second thought, maybe I should give him a dose of the funky stuff, wouldn't want him leaving out of here with a purple belly, meaning hungry…

I decided to play this man like a flute and I only played the clarinet. "You're punctual, fifteen minutes before the interview."

He looked dumb-founded. "Interview...I was, uh...just returning the job application."

Damn! Play along. Some things went over a man's head faster than my lips over their bulging mushroom heads when I'm sucking dick. Save all that shit for Maury Povich. I just wanna get in your briefs and see what kinda water hose you use to water the lawns of the woman's pussy.

Let the games begin! "I am the manager. Also the hiring manager. I wear many...hats. None of them say Magnum, but you..." I licked my lips. "...get my drift..."

He met my eyes eagerly. "Then I'm all yours."

"Nah, I think that's your mother's job." My voice dropped a couple notches. Nosey bitches worked here, always in my mouth, always in my goddamn business. I didn't really fuck men who worked here because every woman who worked here each fucked the men who worked here four times over. And there was nothing worse than bad dick than familiar dick.

I held up my hand, directing him to go to my office…and he proceeded to walk towards the corridor that took us to the back offices. I looked at Stacey, who was ringing up merchandise and giving me the thumbs up and an inconspicuous look. I nodded my head and watched his booty as we made our way to my office.

When we got there I closed the door and advised him to have a seat. He sat down, he did have good manners and he said, "Well thanks for your time. Thanks for the interview. I do need it."

"No problem." I took off my jacket and revealed a cream colored blouse that made my tits look huge. I sat down, released a large gush of air and said, "I had a long day." He eyed my tits like a little uncontrollable boy. "Very long day." I faked a yawn.

He looked concerned. "In what way?"

I looked at him. "Interviews. Lots and lots of…uh, interviews."

He was skeptical now. Wrinkles on his forehead, homeboy was doing some serious thinking. Don't think too hard, might burst a vein.

"Why did you give me one before reviewing my application?"

I said, "Looks like you could use a break."

"A break. I can handle myself."

Ok, girl. This one has a quick temper and hates when someone compromised his manhood. Ok, change gears, pump brakes…slow it down, girl bring it down a notch. Ok, ok. Challenge. He looked like the type of man who had it bad or rough, either way it was badly rough…

"I am sure you can. But a sister is trying to give you some help."

He frowned. "Some help."

"What are you, a goddamn parrot?"

"Nah, woman I am trying to…"

"Polly wants a cracker?" I asked with my little girl voice I used when I wanted to sucker someone.

Take the bait, Niggah. "Nah, I need a job. Don't play with me." Yes, he took it.

"I don't think I can play with you. How long have you been out of work?"

He snubbed my words with an audible, "Fuck you! I have a job!"

"Oh, yeah? Where do you work?"

"I work; um…I work for…I got my own business."

"*Where's* your resume?"

"You didn't ask for one."

"And you don't have a job, because if you did, any real business man or working man, neither applies to you, should already waltz in here with resume in hand, or in a portfolio and it don't even look like you can afford a portfolio let alone the Xerox paper to print your resume on."

"Look, you're pushing me." He had fire in his eyes.

Well, I had fire in *mine*. Fuck it; I got an inferno in my pupils. "Are you reliable?"

"More reliable than you are."

I played with files on my desk that I needed to shred. "Maybe this job isn't for you."

"Maybe that tired ass Janet weave isn't working for you." My mouth fell open. "Or is it a wig? I don't see it connecting to any follicles on your face, bitch!"

Ok, he was mad. Maybe I shouldn't have played this game. Brothah had it bad, made me feel kind of bad. Kind of. That meant I was having very little empathy.

"Can you handle the position if I gave it to you?"

He fell silent, swallowed the next word he was about to say. I wanted to slap the shit out of him for calling me a bitch. He looked like a homo and I wasn't talking about homosapien but I kept my mouth closed. If Tevin Campbell could turn out to be gay after making me wet with "Tell Me what you Want me to Do" and "Shh," and "I'm Ready," then I wouldn't put nothing past these men!

"I surely can, between having eight kids from eight different women and I'm only 23 I need a break. Child support and all." He looked proud. He looked down at his dick and played it off by brushing off imaginary dust. "I don't see my kids much." He looked up into my eyes and I shuddered. He was drop dead gorgeous. If a black Brad Pitt applied for a job it'd be Benjamin.

My pussy released tilted cups I didn't know it had and my panties got the tidal wave of its life. I felt my clitoris crying, that's how wet I was. His sternness and his cockiness turned me on full throttle.

I was shocked. "Eight kids...eight different women?"

He looked pleased at my reaction. That's funny. My pussy wasn't sending out party invites at this notable revelation. The once teeming-with-life Sahara Desert was starting to turn to rock and rubble. And that wasn't good at all.

"Yea, I was young."

This motherfucker talks like he's 60 years old. "You're *still* young."

He had piercing eyes. "I'ma man. I do what I have to do."

It sounded insulting. "I can tell." Time to teach him a lesson. A valuable lesson. I hated myself for even contemplating this mass deception.

I licked my lips. "What will you do for a job? We pay $19.50 an hour." His eyes enlarged with his dick, I could see it pulsating behind his slacks and it was huge. "If I hire you, how do I know you won't turn out to be a liability?"

I guess I was about to find out how many licks it took to get to the center of the Tootsie Pop and all I wanted was a Blow Pop.

Standing up he walked up to my desk, undoing the buttons on his jacket slowly. Looking deeply into my eyes he smiled a shit-eating grin that turned me to poop. I shook in the seat. I turned in my chair and spread my legs, rubbing my breasts. On his knees he went, pushing up my skirt, looking over my pussy and realized I had on crotchless panties. The crotch less panties were the best way to go, fuck thongs. Thongs gave my asshole rashes Preparation H couldn't heal.

Full of charm and grace, he massaged my thighs and I tilted my head back. I never thought of being a black woman abusing my authority, misusing my power but men have been doing this shit for years. If you could count the number of women and men who sucked a little dick or gave up a little ass for a job there wouldn't be enough rooms in the continental U.S that could hold them all. I should know, I sucked a little to get my position. I sucked my way into a hefty 401 (k), an off the chain pension, medical and dental. And I got to fire a bitch who looked at me the wrong way, dressed past company standards or showed up to work late.

He was fired up. Breathlessly, he looked up at me.

"You wanted this good dick the entire time, didn't you?"

Hell yes yes yes! "…Hell, no, Niggah!"

He laughed. "Sure you did. I got eleven inches, cut, three inches in diameter. I'm known to knock a woman's period on."

Damn! "You ain't gotta to lie, Craig you ain't gotta to lie!" We were laughing at my favorite line from Ice Cube's *Friday* movie.

"Do I get the job?" he asked, trying to seduce me.

Hell nah! "Rubbing me like teddy bears isn't going to convince me." I closed my eyes, taking his head and pulling those delicious lips up to my womanly embraced lips with the field of exotic hair, curly and moist. He slowly ran his tongue all over it, his head bobbing. I damn near screamed at the pleasure. He separated the pink curtains with his tongue and used his lips to tongue kiss my clit. God!

I looked down at him doing his thing. He used his fingers to separate, divide and conquer parts of my pussy I didn't know I had. He made it feel like I had three G-spots. Wow.

Abruptly, making me jump out of my skin, the telephone rang and I answered, urging him to eat quietly, no talking at the dinner table, ya' feel me? "Yes...hmmm mmmm, I'm doing just...peachy...yea, eat my *pussy*....yeah, girl this fine ass Niggah is chopping me up....yea, Benjamin suck right there....oh, yes girl sorry....can I call you back...? A girl gotta do what she gotta do...Ciao!"

I dropped the phone on the floor and before I could fall back into the groove the door opened but I didn't stop neither did Benjamin and when my higher up said, "What in the living hell are you doing? You are fired, clear your things..." I solemnly urged Ben to keep eating, and he did, unperturbed, and I said to my higher up, "First....damn, baby eat it, baby...you are going to keep your mouth shut..." I pushed back in the chair and it took everything in me to stand up. I was weak in the knees and even lighter in the ass.

Thinking lucidly, I crawled on top of my desk, my big booty on display, looking like a vixen, pussy all in Ben's face, and I knocked the lamp, books and my non-working company computer on the floor. Sparks were everywhere and I didn't care.

"Secondly, if you fire me your wife will find out I sucked you up for this job; third, close the door and fourth I expect a brand new computer by tomorrow or you will be on the 6 o'clock news for sexual harassment. Now have a good day..."

The door closed, he left in defeat. *Good ridden, beyotch!* Always good to hold something over the perpetrator's...head

It took a little minute for me to realize that Ben was ass naked. He had a huge dick. I took this time to survey all this land before my very eyes. Perky nipples, incredible chest. Tattoos everywhere. The tat "freak" on his neck. Thick lips, long, thick fingers. A nice ass. Homeboy had back for ribs and a few T-bone steaks.

I had to keep it together. I almost forgot what my real mission was here. I couldn't forget it. Mama always said good dick made you do good things you wouldn't care to do if it was bad dick.

Lord. My hands and knees were throbbing…He got on top of the desk, sliding his thick dick deep inside me. I gasped for dear life, looking back at him. I wanted to tell him to put on a rubber but I didn't feel like it. It didn't look like he had anything…and as for me, you know…uh, whatever.

He was full of fire, urgent and aggressive. Slapping my ass he started grinding inside me, slowly, controlling. I came instantly. All over him. He smiled then, grinning all in my face. He leaned forward and ran his tongue across my shoulders, sucked on the back of my neck as my ass and his dick played tennis.

Taking control of this ship, the way any real man should do, he pulled my curls; they fell all about my face, making me look more desperate than I intended to look. Never appear to be desperate for men. They would take that shit and run with it and nine times outta ten the dick wasn't even worth the inches God wasted on him. Some men had a nine inch brain and a small dick. Other men had a big ass dick and a six inch brain. Meaning men with a mind would fuck you to sleep with that little morsel-of-a-dick and men with a big dick would fuck you to a pack of Benson and Hedges menthol Lights because you need to smoke about six to figure out why a man with such a big dick can't fucking use it to its fullest potential. And if you really wanted to get technical roll a blunt and smoke it to the head before you let a big dick, can't-use-it man sex you up because weed + His Sexless ass = I'm high. So it didn't matter.

Men weren't designed to do shit but conquer the world and multiply the earth and the woman and her sweet tasting pussy was the catalyst, the start and the end and the goddamn captain of the ship. Eve was the start of destruction, not man. People get the game all fucked up.

And with this man in my face I couldn't breathe. I was being taken into pure ecstasy. Maybe this wasn't a good time to tell him I had genital herpes, which I was still bitter about it. Maybe I should tell him that I was going to infect every man that I possibly could. But not just any man, only the creeps, the bad fathers, the molesters and the rapists, the men who made eight kids with eight different women, men like him didn't deserve to be healthy. Men like him that played me back in the day. Men like him who broke my heart and sold it to their homeboys, allowing them to come into my life when I was vulnerable…opening doors for them to dig in my pussy like Timbuktu. Men who used and abused me, men who were savaged and cold-hearted. Men who took my money and spent it on other bitches. Men, who aided and abetted my own inner insecurity, took my beauty and handed me snowflakes when I was in Ice Land.

He pulled me up to him, hugging me from the back...he humped my woman hood like he never humped it before, his dick filling me up like O.J's hand in a glove...I was climbing the mountain as another earthquake started to send tremors up and down my spine...I was now in the river, it was taking me up the creek, past the damns and crevices, along the lakes and ponds, over the cliff of the Niagra and into the oceans, past Titanics and men overboard…God, past ski boats and floaters…I was about to fly, fly out of the water, drenched with sweat as my pussy told me, with an attitude, "Girl we about to cry again."

That male cockiness shining through. "You like it, baby?"

I could barely talk. "I love it!"

He pressed for more. Than I was willing to give. "I got the job?"

We were sweating profusely. I was in heaven; I didn't want it to end.

I was stuttering something terrible…"No, not yet...keep convincing me..." *I'm sorry, I wasn't gonna hire you. This was a game, and when you were in the game of deception you didn't follow the rules!*

And he did. Convince me, that was. By the time we both came together I sent him out of my office with his clothes barely on and let him know that I would call him with the date he could start working. I sat in my chair, breathing so hard I thought I was flushed.

I thought about my boss then. With his fat ass. A few years before, he was one of the finest men in town. But after a bad marriage, child support payments, getting drunk every night and excessive fucking and partying, he was reduced, well, he inflated past expectations.

I picked up the phone, and called him. He didn't answer. I called him again, getting annoyed. I knew he wasn't avoiding me. I knew his address, where he worked out at (as much as we fucked there) and I knew the wife's job number, cell phone and what route she drove to work.

Dusting my TV I smiled. That was three months ago. I put in a transfer. I left that job in Philly and was sent down here to Homestead. I know Benjamin was brooding with anger to find out I got a quick fuck at his expense. Maybe I was wrong, and I knew I was for having sex with an asshole when I had genital herpes.

But that should teach people. You didn't just fuck anybody, just because I had a fine body and a pretty face didn't mean I didn't have a disease. And on top of that I had H.I.V. Living that wild life back in the day led me to making hastily bad decisions. Mistakes were second to none, but bad decisions opened the door for reckless living.

My belief window was never met over time. I had sex to fit in. I wanted to teach people about my wrongs, but I kept meeting bad men. I didn't ask for H.I.V. *God*, no! But Mama warned me about going to the clubs. I didn't listen. A hard head made a soft ass! I thought I knew it all. And one day when I was 20, someone poked me on the arm with something sharp when I was maneuvering through the dancing, sweaty crowd at the club. I ignored it, thought it was a bug bite. Turned out it was a needle infected with H.I.V. blood. Someone had it out for me, and after I got checked out and the doctor told me I had H.I.V. I thought about that "bug bite" in the club. I was devastated. I couldn't function; I couldn't eat, drink or sleep. I cried for the next two weeks, going to work and cussing people, firing people for no reason and cussing the boss. I called his wife and told her we fucked and she filed for divorce. I pushed everyone away! It would turn out to be Cindy who poked me with the needle. She was a girl I met the year before who was married to a man I slept with behind her back. She wanted to get back at me, because her man infected her with a disease another bitch gave him, so she got back at me by passing on her death sentence. She's currently serving time for what she did. But before we even went to court I found that Ho and I beat her ass so bad with a stick she couldn't move by the time the paramedics got there. And I wouldn't have known it was her that infected me if it wasn't for my ex fuck buddy, her man, who came to me and told me she admitted to him what she did.

Now I tried to put this all out of my mind. I dusted the dressers and the mirrors, tears falling down my face. I still needed to do something, and I had no choice. I had to do what's right. When the doctor told me I had herpes he advised me to stop having sex immediately and to call any and everyone I fucked. Ha. Fat chance! But I told him I would, even though I knew in my heart I never would. I walked over to my purse and took out my cell. I contemplated calling him. I should, I should have a long time ago.

I was having a plethora of feelings. Mixed feelings finding their way out of the loop to become individual thoughts.

Empty inside.

I sat on the recliner by my bed and dialed the numbers. All ten numbers. It rung. My stomach dropped.

I closed my eyes when I heard his voice.
"He...Hello."
I was quiet, very silent.

"Anybody there?" he asked. His voice didn't sound the same. It was devoid of that fire I liked the day we met.

I forced myself to say it. My throat suddenly got dry.

"Hello Benjamin."

There was a long breath drawn. He was quiet. For a long time.

My heart sped up, maybe this was a mistake.

"I met a lot of women, half of them I will never remember. But I know this voice; a voice I met months ago, a woman who I thought would give me a job. And she did. She gave me a good job. And you know what that is?

The job of taking medications. The job of staying healthy. I've become a better man, I've become a leader. I teach my kids about the dangers of the world. I got a good job with the American Red Cross. I make more than that $19.50 you were supposedly going to pay me. I am healthy and strong.

I am alive and kicking. I am not even bitter, I'm not angry. Because your deception made me a warrior.

I teach kids all across the country about women like you. But I don't bad mouth you. I wish you well in life; I knew this phone call would come one day. If you ever need anything, just ask.

I won't stoop to your level. And when you go to bed tonight tell yourself one thing, you turned me from an irresponsible, sex-crazed fool into a real black man who finally took control of his life and kids and I married my high school Sweetheart. Good bye."

"Benjamin…I apologize, please forgive me."

He laughed playfully. And it was the weirdest thing. It was devoid of venom and betrayal. He sounded happy. That fire was back in his voice and it rendered me speechless.

He said, "I forgive you. And I forget you."

And the line disconnected.

I didn't know how long I have been crying. But I knew it has been days. I grabbed God's Bible and hugged it, flames licking through my soul. I cried and screamed, snot all in my nose to the point I couldn't breathe. I was wrong, dead wrong but I did my part. I thought I was hurting that man because I felt he wasn't worthy of a healthy life, and it turned out that I destroyed myself.

And days later, as the "Party like a Rock Star" song came back on, I turned over in my bed, my hair disheveled. I told myself that the reason dust was all over my room was because I was dreading picking up the telephone, for months, and calling Benjamin and telling him of my deception. It made me lazy, uncooperative and crazed.

I didn't take responsibility for my actions; I didn't want to accept it. I felt I didn't have to, that I was put here to punish bad men, even though I was a bad woman. I had to learn to forgive myself.

And now that I called him I had to call one other person. The Pastor's son, who was a part of a Golden Masks Orgy with me some months ago. We did it in the church.

I thought back to Roll Call.

From the King of Erotica 1 The Golden Masks.

ell goddamn! This bitch is what James Brown would call Super Bad. Watch it now! I might have to make this one mine.

"You look new," said the Inductor. The Pastor's Son.

His laptop open on the podium before him.

"I am." Elegance with long shaved legs shining from fluorescent lighting, nine inch stiletto heels gleaming. She licked her lips, tasting her lipstick. Her nipples erect, she stuck out her tits, beautiful in a Gucci dress and matching pumps.

"And you are?"

"Take It In the Ass Only."

He checked her profile on the lap top beside him. Model material. "You may enter."

She gave an attitude of model Naomi Campbell standards.

"Thank you. No one will touch my pussy, right?"

He looked around discreetly, coming around the podium. He got on his knees and kissed her pussy. Standing up, she smiled, pinching his cheek. "No one will touch it, but damn I just wanted to kiss it."

She wasn't impressed; in fact she shoulda pissed in his face.

"Can I go now?"

"Remember, follow the goddamn rules."

She smiled, silently farting as she went down the hallway.

Too much pasta last night.

Damn, I got to take a shit. Oh, well. Too late for that. They still can't touch my pussy. I mean business, too. Somebody's getting a…shitty dick today!

And I don't care.

Bad men had to pay. And oh, yeah. I had H.I.V. and genital herpes.

But I don't have to say all that now do I?

2 bonus stories for the

contest winners:

Whatever, Ho

"What can I do?"

"About?"

I was shaking my head, getting upset. "About seeing my son?"

"Right now it's best if you stay away from him."

I was fuming. I extracted a joint from the Backwood cigar container and put it between my lips. I needed this and badly.

"Why should I? He's my son, not just my baby Mama's."

"Well, according to our records you haven't been paying child support."

This white bitch was really pissing me off something terrible!

"I'm not giving her money to go spend on another man, let's be real, bitch."

"Calling me a bitch makes matters worse."

"Whatever, Ho. When it comes to my son I will fight you and the fucking state every step of the way."

"Just pay the three hundred a month."

"Who asked you for your input anyways? This is my child, I don't remember fucking you and getting you pregnant."

She said, "Thank God."

"You better thank God I don't know where you live."

"Is that a threat? These calls are monitored."

"Monitor these nuts in your mouth, Ho." I was so upset I forgot to light the joint. So I pulled out my lighter from my coat pocket and made that tip-of-the-blunt to flame connection, pulling on it.

"I wish I could help you but I don't help rude men."

"Help me get this nut," I said, clearly done with her. I didn't even wanna talk to her anymore. We were beating a dead horse and I couldn't afford horses, especially when the state was trying to take my hard earned money.

"You're gross."

"And you're not a virgin so go fuck yourself."

"Well I never…"

"And you never will."

"Administer your payment.

I was coughing, beating my chest, looking at the joint like I loved it. I pulled on it again. I wanted to take the blunt to the head, get that immediate contact high.

"…And what does she pay?" I asked, sitting on the chair in my room, in a goddamn suit. I felt crummy. I was itching all over because I wanted to suddenly break something.

"She cares for the child."

My eyes were fire balls. "The child has a name, bitch. Try using it. And if you take a trip to her apartment you will see that she is living in less than honorable conditions."

"This isn't an Army discharge, Sir and you have a few weeks to get her the child support or I will send a summons to have your pay garnished and your bank accounts seized."

"For your information, bitch, my bank accounts is in my Mama's name, how do you like me now?"

"You have your bases covered, huh?" Her voice lost that spunk. I was about to start laughing. I knew when to deflate these bitches. "Well there's nothing we can do if it's in your mother's name."

"Oh, and my house and car is in her name, too. Sorry to disappoint you."

"And your job?"

I was laughing. "Got you beat there, too. I'm on disability and I work. I go to dialysis three times a week because my kidneys don't work. If I truly wanna stop you from garnishing my check I'll just quit my fucking job. Ha, you lose. Tell the state to kiss my black ass, too."

"I can't believe this. You will quit your job so you won't have to support your son?"

I smiled victoriously. "Ding Ding Ding, Bob this woman is the next contestant on the Price Is Wrong, bitch!"

And I slammed the phone down on the receiver, angry with the world.

I finished the blunt, put three shots of Hennessy in my system and made another phone call.

"What do you want?" Nettie asked with an attitude. In fact she always had an attitude.

I wanted to make this simple. "I want my son."

"Pay for him and you'll get him."

I ignored her. "I'm coming to get him."

She spat, "And the police will be right here. Plus you can't come right now. I am about to go out with Buster."

I was getting revved up. "I don't want that Niggah around my child."

She guffawed. "Its funny how you tell your son that you don't want him saying the word Niggah yet you can say the word anytime you get ready. You are a grandiosity of bullshit"

I shook my head, needing another blunt. "Oh, shit, Nettie! She's using big words now. Spell grandiosity?"

She sucked her teeth. "G-R-A-N-D-I-O-S-I-T-Y! Grandiosity."

"Wrong. It's Y-O-U A-R-E A B-I-T-C-H"

"I am a bitch?"

"Damn, *that's* how you pronounce grandiosity."

"Go to hell."

All the pain I suffered with her came back with a vengeance. I could not keep it together. "Nah. Life with you was hell. Why go back."

"Whatever."

"And the word *Niggah* isn't the subject at hand. I will do whatever the hell I damn well choose. What I do with my son is my business. I feed him and buy him clothes and pay for his football shit and I am there for every birthday and every holiday. I take him to church every Sunday and I teach him God's Bible. You are so damn envious of that you try to stop my family from getting to know him…"

"Why is a hypocrite teaching my son the Bible? I don't understand you, never have. And my family deserves to get to know him. I take care of him. You throw your money around; I'm here for him where it counts. Tucking him in at night, doing things for him…"

"Your family is full of sluts, whores, faggots and crack heads and I don't want that around my son."

"Don't talk about my family. I draw the line there."

"Fuck them, and fuck you."

"DIE!" Her voice was a shriek. I loved pissing her off and making her feel like shit. I lived for it.

"And if you wanted more money why didn't you call and ask? You call the white people on me like you were going to get it faster."

"They tore a hole in your ass, huh?" she asked, pushing me to the limit. I poured another shot and took it to the head.

"You forgot something."

"What?"

"I'm on disability. Forgot?"

"Damn you! But you *have* a good job."

"And to stop you from getting my money guess what I'll do?"

She was almost afraid to ask. "What?"

"I'll quit, now try me. If I get one more phone call from the state, if I get a letter, anything, I will quit and your cash flow will be floored, you got me?"

"You make me sick!"

"Let me talk to my son!"

"He's in school."

"When can I come pick him up?"

"You get him on Sundays."

I was pacing the room, kicking off my shoes. I decided not to go in to the office today. I didn't feel up to all this bungling with this inept woman who couldn't put two quarters in the same dispenser.

"There are seven days in the week."

"I didn't know that."

"Giving me him one day a week tells me something."

"He doesn't miss you."

"Woman, please. Stop pulling rehearsed lines from your pussy. I don't fancy human waste. And my son does call me."

"Maybe I should put a stop to that. And we're going to Texas. I should be moving there in about four months."

I punched a hole in the wall, angry. My college graduation picture fell on the floor. My son was my universe. "You are not leaving with my son."

"Watch me. Jobs are scarce here. Can't find one. Cubans have come and taken over. My son deserves a chance."

"You . Are. Not. Taking. My. Son!"

"You. Can't. Stop. Me."

"I want him here."

"You should have thought about that when you left me shortly after I gave birth to him."

"I left you or you left me."

"Don't bring that up. Don't even try to throw that in my face."

I sat down and rubbed my temples. The alcohol was tearing me up, plus I was high so that didn't help my judgment right now.

"You were with me. I wanted to marry you. I was committed and everything. But you fucked my cousin behind my back and you wound up pregnant. I didn't know all this until me and my cousin got drunk one night and he spilled the beans and didn't even remember telling me. I kept my cool, I didn't even tell you. When my son was born I wanted a DNA test and you hit the roof. It came back that I was the father yet you didn't understand why I ordered one."

Nettie was crying through the phone. "But I loved you and…"

My head snapped up. I needed to get out of here. "You loved me by sleeping with my family and lying about it. You made a complete fool of me. Of course I didn't want to be with you and of course I didn't want to stay committed to you. Why should I?"

"But…"

I hung up. I grabbed my keys from the nightstand and I turned on my house alarm, closed and locked the door and wiped tears from my eyes as I walked to my car.

I couldn't lose my child.

I drove to the Florida's Turnpike and traveled North. I didn't get very far because when I passed the graveyard in Richmond Heights I ran right into traffic, which really bothered me. From the looks of it there was an accident so that mean we'd be sitting here for a while. Damn it. I turned on Tupac Shakur and rapped nearly the entire *All Eyez on Me* album before traffic moved again.

I couldn't take my mind off my son.

I was deeply upset. Maybe that was putting it mildly. I hated when my hard work was chopped up by dumb asses at the office. Motherfuckers who barely bust their asses or lifted a finger always had something foul to say. The very ones who continuously called out sick when they clearly weren't, raising my workload by eighty percent.

I was the type of man who only did what was in his job description. If it didn't say it in black and white then hey, sorry for ya' because I wasn't doing it. Fuck being a team player. How could you be a team player when the team hardly came to work? I was having better luck raising my son, even though his mother and I didn't get along so I hardly got to see him.

My co-workers were very ungrateful sonsofbitches and I'd had it up to here! Maybe I shouldn't have come to work today. That was the problem, if I could just be real with myself. I was intoxicated and high. When people did speak I walked right on by like I was an arrogant prick. I didn't care. All I could think about is my son.

I was already in a bad mood, my son was potentially going to Texas and the state was threatening to garnish my wages and I swear I'd quit this job if they even breathed towards my paycheck.

Then to make matters worse they viciously throw my work to the dogs by telling me it's not good enough when we all know it's the best. Haters breathe on someone's failure. Where did those kinds of hard-assed people come from?

I was a dedicated worker. Never late. I've been working as a telemarketer for six years plus and the instant I got the supervisor position people who were my friends suddenly turned on me because they felt they deserved it and all of these sissies started spreading rumors around the office that they sucked my dick or had sex with me just to ruin my reputation and my work performance took a nose dive because I started whipping their asses. Literally.

I stomped them under the desk, knocking the computer on the floor. I didn't pay to replace it, either. It has gotten to the point where I had to make a transition from an educated Negro to a brainless, gun-toting thug Niggah and show those fucks you didn't fuck with me. I hated using the word "Niggah" but when you're pushed to the brink of insanity you didn't give much thought to doing things rationally. At least I didn't.

The truth of the matter was I was bisexual, but I never been with a guy in my life. I hated feeling the way I did. Was I weird for having feelings for men when I could barely stand them? I could hardly stand myself and sometimes I hated even looking at my own dick.

I talked to a few Down Low brothers but it never led to anything. What did that Down Low shit mean anyway? Honestly, I thought the term was a bit overrated. Too overrated for my tastes, but I knew I had to live the double life because I didn't need the prejudice and the bigotry in my life.

I didn't want to hurt my son or my family or give my son the idea that fucking men was pleasing to God when we all know better.

Realizing my flesh was the weakest thing on my body; I secretly made accounts on gay sites and enjoyed the eye candy without uploading a picture of myself.

There were some very gorgeous men in the world, and sometimes my dick was so hard from "browsing" that I had to smoke a blunt and call over the fellahs and get drunk and talk about women just to push how I truly felt to the back of my mind.

But once they left and the high was gone and the intoxications left I was back online, "browsing." And if one of them requested a picture of me I hit the "BLOCK" feature. I did like and participated in a couple forum discussions:

WHO GOT THE BIGGEST DICK?
WHO GOT A PHAT ASS?
DOES GAY PORN DESTROY THE GAY
COMMUNITY?
ARE "BOTTOMS" HOES AND "TOPS" PIMPS?

I never got the "Bottom" and "Top" role playing thing. Was it really role playing? Who determined sexual orientations? The gay community or the individual? From what a friend tells me, "A bottom is the man who takes dick and the Top is the one who does the fucking." He seemed so sure of himself. So I asked, "What do you call a man who does both?" And he looked at me over an opened bottle of Heineken at the American Airlines Arena (during a Heat game) and said, "He's versatile. A flexible motherfucker."

But I never exchanged phone numbers with a guy. I never smelled a guy (outside of smelling musty bodies when I played basketball in high school and I had to share the showers) but I never *slept* with another man. Especially not at work. I didn't fuck where my 401 (k) came from. I didn't even play in my back yard. If I was to have sex with a guy he'd have to live in another state and I would give him a fake name and a pay phone number.

I didn't want to be here. So I grabbed my keys and I locked my office and clocked out.

Veronica stopped me just as I was walking out the front double doors.

"You're leaving mighty early," she said, a knock out in a pants suit that highlighted that bubble ass.

I smiled, shaking her hand. "Yea. I don't feel so well."

"Your eyes are red as hell. You must have had a rough night."

"And an even rougher morning."

"Are you free this evening?"

"Yea, why. What's up?"

She licked her lips and took my hand. "You know I just broke up with my boyfriend." She looked round, leaning to my ear. She sucked the earlobe, waking up my friend in my pants.

"Oh, yea…"

"And since he wanted to screw women behind my back I thought I'd have a little fun with you." She pulled me outside. I was looking at the booty, I couldn't lie.

"Where are we going?"

"Get in my car. Let me talk to you for a minute, before I clock in."

She unlocked her Mitsubishi with the police tinted windows and I got in the passenger seat. She got in, closed the door and put the key in the ignition. It was extremely hot in here. She turned on the AC, those huge earrings dangling with fierce abandon.

"So what do you wanna talk about?" I asked, wanting to go home. I had business to take care of.

"Us. You and me."

"I'm not looking for a relationship, Veronica."

She put her acrylic-clad hand on my upper thigh and looked deeply into my eyes. Damn she was fine. I was weakening.

"I just got out of a five year relationship. I loved that man with everything n me. He was my first and I wound up staying with my first because he showed me things I'd never seen before. I was his ride or die chick. But once that JaRule and Ashanti Murder Inc. fantasy died away and real life kicked in I realized that he had a lot of women. And I walked in on him last week having sex with three girls at the same time in my bed, I was crushed."

I thought about how I felt when I found out my baby Mama fucked my cousin. The pain of going through the DNA test. I dreaded every second. What if it would have turned out to be my cousin's son? It would have crushed me.

I wiped her tears away. "It's ok."

"So now I'm single again. I'm on the prowl."

"You're hurt. You just want to relinquish it for the moment."

"Fuck me. I want you to fuck me good. I had one dick for five years, one dick in my entire twenty one years on earth…" She was unbuckling my pants, the pain of his betrayal coloring her eyes and making them more majestic. I was putty in her hands, because I felt her vulnerability. I wanted to erase that evil picture she had of men in her mind.

I leaned over and gave her some tongue, holding her face. I didn't want to just pounce on her. She was actually a good girl. I sat back and watched how she used to treat her ex-Boo. He was her world. She gave him money, bought him a car and bent over backwards for him. She didn't question him a lot and there in the problem lied.

She was moaning, wrapping her arms around me. Her hardened nipples poked against my chest. I unbuttoned my shirt and she peeled it off cautiously.

"I need this. Please…"

"I do, too."

She tossed my shirt in the back seat and she turned on the car and drove to the back of the parking lot, by a slew of vehicles. I didn't worry about no one seeing us because she had police tints. Plus the people who parked back here got off work at about 5 p.m., so they wouldn't be over in this area until then. I looked at my watch. It was a quarter past two.

She cut the engine and she engulfed my left nipple, while playing with the right one. I was rubbing my dick, my eyes closed and my head tilted back. She felt so good. She knew just how to treat my body.

I reached over and started rubbing her pussy. I felt the wetness through her pants, which told me she was hot and heavy for me.

"That feels good," she said and I smiled.

She unbuckled my pants and pulled them down to my knees and took my dick into her mouth and I could have died. Her mouth was hotter than the sun and her throat deeper than the blue seas. My dick felt like an anchor in her mouth. She cupped my nuts just right, running her tongue across the head and sliding those lips along the shaft like she was licking up ice cream in the Miami heat.

I shudder, needing this. I hadn't had head on a little minute. I was brick city, little veins popping along my dick. I held her head and massaged her scalp while she brought me pleasure.

I was straining the muscles in my hips because she had to get to work and I had to see about my son. I spread my legs, sweat starting to drip down our bodies. It was then I realized she didn't turn on the AC.

I pushed her back and pulled off her pants. I told her to get on the back seat and she did. She spread her legs and I ran my tongue over her wet panties, sucking the lace, gripping her magnificent thighs.

"My man never ate my pussy before."

"Is this the first time?"

Her trembling legs told me "Yes."

I pulverized the cooch. I used my tongue to suck the juices; I pulled off her panties and put them in her mouth.

"To understand pussy you gotta taste your own," I told her, using my index and middle finger to spank the pussy like she's been bad.

Wide-eyed, she was grinding on the seat. Pussy in the air. I loved it.

I pushed the hood back and sucked the clit. In fact I punished it and she was about to die.

The panties fell from her mouth and I put them in mine, and continued to taste her velvet room. The lace slid across her clit with my lips and tongue.

"Goddamn! I can't believe it feels like this…"

I was proud to be her first. I put my all into it. When I started a job I liked to leave my signature, a job well done on the mind of the customer when they left a store. Her pussy was the store and my tongue would leave the signature.

I did the Hurricane Tongue, separating her pink walls and digging up in her twat deeper. She couldn't take it. She took off her blouse and her tits bounced for dear life. I reached up and squeezed them pleasurably while I continued to feast on good pussy.

Her cell phone rang and I told her to ignore it. She answered it with a curt, "This is how a real man takes care of pussy!"

She put the phone on speaker and she let go.

"You like how Daddy is eating this pussy?" I asked her, feeling competitive. I knew it was her ex, and since he treated her like dirt it was time to make him feel like shit.

"Ah, shit. Damn, oh my God! Why is my body tingling? Are my legs supposed to tremble?"

"Get that nut, Ma."

She looked confused. "Women can come?"

"Your man never made you come?"

"No, because after he came he quit…Damn, suck that pussy!"

"I'ma kill you Ho!" boomed into my ears and she laughed.

"I gotta go…" And she hung up, gripped my head and I ate her until she began to melt, like the ice cream in the Miami heat, like the scorned woman who wanted her revenge…

She wrapped her legs around my head and shouted, "Oh my God! What is this feeling…oh god OH GOD OH GOD!"

I felt her juices on my tongue. She was having her first orgasm. She shook so hard she was sliding in her own sweat, gripping her hair and telling me I was the most beautiful man.

When it was over I wasn't done.

"Oh my God! You are incredible…"

I spread those legs and I put on a condom. She looked at me, too tired to move.

"Baby, I'm drained. In about five minutes I gotta clock in."

I kissed her lips, letting her taste her pussy. I slowly slid up in the pussy and she gasped, receiving me.

"Damn, you're so big…Jesus, baby go slowly please don't hurt me."

I gave her some tongue. "I won't hurt you. And five minutes is all I need…"

I didn't keep my word. After a few minutes of grinding and slowly pushing myself deep inside of her, even pulling it out and rubbing the head of my dick on her clit, I fucked the shit out of her in that car, making it rock from here to Kingdom Come.

She would remember Ramses Senior.

She wouldn't want dick for weeks by the time I'm done.

Blow-Up Doll

I had a confession to make. And when I say it I know some of you will wince and be like "This Niggah is on some other shit." Guess what I do? It may be nasty, corny and despicable, but who gives a fuck. I was a grown man who hated religion, detested gay people and smoked weed every goddamn day of the calendar year. My secret was simple: I fucked a blow up doll. I didn't give a fuck. Niggahs hate lippy bitches so getting a blow up doll you get it all—pussy and silence. If you couldn't trust a bitch then trust your plastic pussy. I fucked the shit outta that doll. I had a bad day and I couldn't wait to get off work. I was a telemarketer and my phone didn't ring once. I was falling asleep because I was bored. I kept scratching my nuts, thinking about getting some new pussy but as my eyes scanned the huge room I yawned, covering my mouth. Fifty bitches worked in the room with me and I fucked thirty of them. The pussy was good, though. And the way they sucked dick made a niggah happy. But I got tired of the same tongue and lip game. And half of them sucked my dick expecting their phone bills to be paid.

When I first started working here I was elated. The women were FINE, YOU HEARD ME? But after being here for three years and fucking the same pussy…you get tired. My dick was set on autopilot and my nuts took a much needed hiatus. It has gotten to the point where I couldn't even come when I fucked those Hoes.

I kept looking at the clock. God damn when was four o'clock going to get here?

I yawned again and stood up, turning off my phone. One of my supervisors saw me and she walked over, with her huge ass. Her big ass feet were straining the hell outta those light blue pumps. Looking at her you'd swear she had it together, Miss Thing with a husband, six children who couldn't stand her ass and a Mama who nagged her left and right.

She paused before me, smiling. I stifled another yawn.

"Where are you going?"

I held my stomach. "I ate something that didn't agree with my stomach…"

She got the point.

"You didn't say that when you…" She looked around, leaning up to my ear. Her breath smelled like fried chicken and she was supposed to be on a diet. "…ate my pussy to get the job."

I snatched up my cell phone, wallet and keys. "That was three years ago."

She smiled. "And?"

"And you were a size 4 then. Now you are a hot air balloon."

"I beg your pardon…?"

"Bye. I got diarrhea."

When I got in the bathroom I went in the handicap stall and closed and locked the door. I set the alarm on my phone for 3:55 p.m. I leaned against the wall. I didn't even pull down my pants.

I went to sleep.

When four got here I rushed outside the door and I flew to my car like I had wings. Dick so hard I had blue balls by the time I got on the Turnpike.

When I got home I left the keys in the car, locked the door and rushed inside. I ran up the stairs and kicked down the door like batman.

Pow!

Bam!

Boom!

…I'm here, bitch!

She was on my bed, her mouth ajar. Her heavenly eyes wide, her pink rosey lips were begging to taste my stick. Her big plastic titties and plastic hairy pussy with a hummer vibrator on the pussy lips had me about to come just thinking about it.

I didn't have to put on a condom. I cleaned the Ho with Comet and Windex.

I slid up in her without a condom, the feeling washing over me like rip currents. I was so excited.

I told myself that she couldn't have HIV because Lord knows I had HIV and I infected all thirty bitches I worked with at my job. I felt crummy for doing so…but nobody warned me when my ex wife gave me herpes and HIV.

She was cheating on me with my brother Big Ham and I never knew. Big Ham had AIDS for ten years and he never told a soul. So when she let this man come in her a hundred different ways, and swallowing his come seven hundred more ways, she thought she was getting over on me when we made passionate love without protection and I was being infected. When I did find out I was HIV positive it was a fucked situation.

I had chest pains and I went to the hospital. They took my blood after taking my vitals and an hour later my doctor told me the disheartening news. I went home and beat my wife's ass so bad she was hospitalized for a few months and I was convicted of assault.

I did two years in prison and did three years on parole. I was a changed person. I no longer loved, cared or trusted no one.

Every time I took my pills I was angry all over again. That's why I got married. So I could be faithful to my wife and didn't have to worry about diseases. Biggest mistake of my life.

So now I cry tears of abandonment, betrayal and hurt while fucking this blow up doll. I knew she didn't have STDs. She was a blow up doll.

The blood swelling to the head of my dick, I grabbed the throat and squeezed as I fucked the doll. The bed started squeaking and this made me hornier.

"Yea take this dick!" my voice boomed throughout the room, bouncing off the furniture.

Her mouth was ajar, eyes wide with anticipation.

"Take it! Take this dick, Ho! You like this shit, don't you? Huh? Wanna taste your pussy off my dick? Yea, you do? Talk to me you plastic cunt!"

Her mouth was ajar, her eyes wide with anticipation.

I was started to sweat, slipping in plastic snatch. Damn this shit felt so good. I felt like I had to come already.

"Who's daddy?"

Nothing but silence. That's what I was talking about. Shut up, bitch, and take this dick. I'm daddy, take all ten inches.

"I wanna tap the bottom of your stomach and I don't want you to protest."

On her forehead was a name written with a red Sharpie, and I get angry every time I read it.

It was my ex wife's name.

Linda.

I talked shit to the plastic bitch. I mean, when I did catch my brother fucking Linda this was what he was telling her. Verbatim. Who's Daddy? I wanna tap the bottom of your stomach. He was bouncing in my wife's pussy without a care in the world and she was loving every second and every inch of his AIDS-infested cock. I knew she was in love with him. Standing there staring at them I knew this to be true. She couldn't stop looking in his eyes. He had dreamy eyes. I was always jealous of those eyes. Those eyes caused more havoc than anything. My Mama used to be a sucker for those eyes and Daddy used to give him what he wanted and I always got the shitty end of the stick.

So every time I fuck this doll I recreate what I saw in my brother's room. I fuck this doll the same way he hammered my wife. I crack open, tongue kissing plastic lips.

"Oh, you don't wanna kiss me you plastic fuck?"

She said nothing, eyes wide.

"Take it! This is some good pussy. I am about to pull out my wallet and I'll pay for it."

Her wig was moist from the humidity my cock and balls created.

"Take it, damn girl. You got some killer pussy. Goddamn yo, shit! Give me that pussy!"

Legs agape, leaning back on her plastic hands, the satin of the silk sheets tickling my balls because the covers were all over my legs, my sweaty booty cheeks jiggling, I was looking in the mirror.

Feeling adventurous, I took it out and put it in her plastic mouth. Voila, she didn't gag. She took it all, where was the tonsils? I watched my brother take it out and shove it in my wife's mouth as he was coming and she swallowed nut and dick like a pro. She just knew he didn't have diseases. He was tall, dark and fine as hell with a snake for a dick. He fooled her ass.

I put it back in the pussy. I wanted to cum, goddamn I wanna cum now, what was taking it so long. I was tongue kissing my dick from plastic lips…I was about to cum…

I felt it building in my toes, making me feel like air, where were the clouds?

I found them and got nothing but dirt. I was digging and planting seeds. Would I get a banana tree or a cherry bush?

I unplugged the doll, the air escaping with a resounding hiss…yes, I was about to cum, there it goes.

My dick pulsated in that plastic pussy, her face getting smaller and smaller, the hissing sounded like I was pissing.

I grunted, kissing her deflated lips.

I hopped up in bed in unlaced timbs and I kicked the deflated ho across the room.

Hell yea, I knocked the dust off that pussy.

Tired and drained, there was a knock on the door. I walked into the bathroom and grabbed my robe, putting it on.

Someone pounded on it. I rushed across the living room and answered it.

I smiled. It was Paula, one of my co-workers. She liked it in the ass more than the pussy.

"Hey."

She stared at me, tears falling from her eyes.

She clutched her purse.

"What's wrong?" I asked, taking her above the elbow.

"My hubby left me. He took the kids."

"Why?"

"You know why."

"No. I don't."

"He found out I was cheating on him."

"How?"

"He tested positive for HIV. I have HIV. The only man I fucked without a rubber was you. You gave it to me."

"No I…"

She pulled out a gun, aimed and all I remember was a loud bag.

And the explosion in my chest knocking me to the floor.

She was a blur…

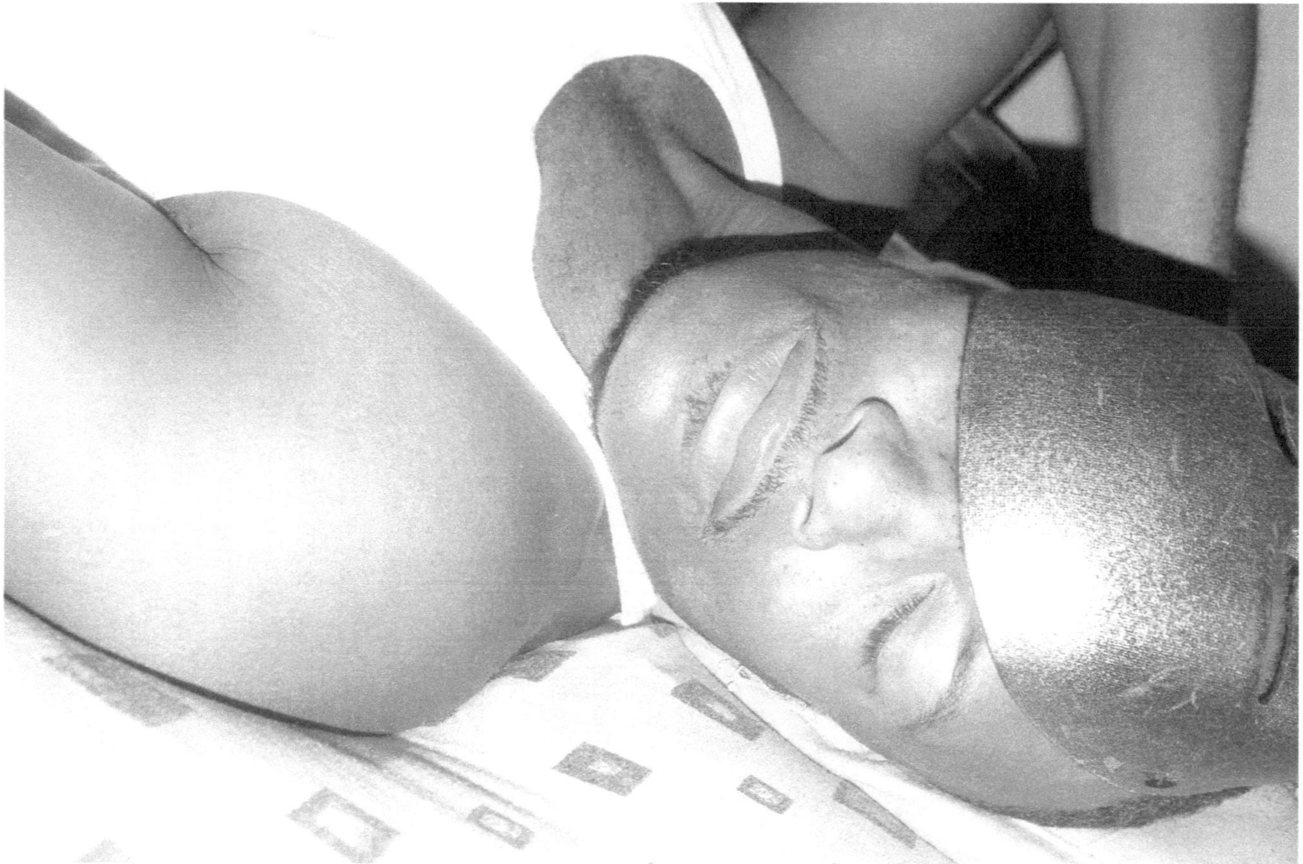

This is possibly the end of the road for The King of Erotica Series. It has been fun, gritty and bumpy. I accomplished what I wanted to accomplish with this series. It was written  for awareness, entertainment and education and stimulation. I wanted to prove that I was more than just an erotic author and I did just that. I love you all. I thank you all for your love and support. If I ever decide to do another King of Erotica book I will let you know. But as of right now, this is the last book, which I called the Dethronement. You live by the Sword…you will DIE by the Sword.

**The DeTHRONEment has
been initiated.
Rest in Peace Chad Render.
My best friend forever.**

Before you have sex
talk about it with your partner
I know you think you're cute
go **over the mishaps.**
Ask What if questions…
what if you get pregnant.
if you don't feel right don't do it.
Don't let dumb asses pressure you into sex.
And if you choose to have sex
Do one goddamn thing:
WEAR A FUCKING CONDOM!

Is it that hard?

Think about you.
But most importantly, think about your
partner's life also.

HIV and AIDS don't give a fuck about you or your family!

Pharoah.